RESUME HOSTILITIES

The Charlemagne Files Collection

Volume 3

Swallow
Quiet Move
Goat Rope

K.A. Bachus

Copyright © 2021, 2022, 2023, 2024 K.A. Bachus
All rights reserved

The characters and events portrayed in this book are fictitious. Any similarity to real persons, living or dead, is coincidental and not intended by the author.

No artificial intelligence or machine learning technology was used in the creation of this book or its cover. No part of this work may be used in the creation of machine learning or artificial intelligence technology without the author's express permission.

No part of this book may be reproduced in any form or by any electronic or mechanical means, including information storage and retrieval systems, without permission in writing from the publisher, except by reviewers, who may quote brief passages in a review.

Published in Bangor, Maine, United States of America
Contact the publisher at info@charlemagnefiles.com

Library of Congress Control Number: 2024921724
ISBN: 979-8-9916011-2-2

Visit: https://www.charlemagnefiles.com

Cover by Marigold Faith

CHARLEMAGNE FILE TIMELINES

Volume 1 - The Team
Trinity Icon, early 70s
Cetus Wedge, early 80s
Brevet Wedge, nine months later

Short Story Collection
A Lighter Shade of Night,
mid 60s to early 70s

Volume 2 - The Passion
Lion Tamer, five months later
State of Nature, early 90s
Vory, a year later

Volume 2 - Retirement
Swallow, five weeks later
Quiet Move, late 90s
Goat Rope, 1999

CONTENTS

SWALLOW — 10

PROLOGUE — 10
ONE — 12
TWO — 17
THREE — 21
FOUR — 24
FIVE — 27
SIX — 31
SEVEN — 36
EIGHT — 39
NINE — 43
TEN — 46
ELEVEN — 50
TWELVE — 54
THIRTEEN — 57
FOURTEEN — 61
FIFTEEN — 64
SIXTEEN — 67
SEVENTEEN — 71
EIGHTEEN — 75
NINETEEN — 79
TWENTY — 82
TWENTY-ONE — 85
TWENTY-TWO — 89
TWENTY-THREE — 93
TWENTY-FOUR — 98
TWENTY-FIVE — 103
TWENTY-SIX — 106

TWENTY-SEVEN	110
TWENTY-EIGHT	113
TWENTY-NINE	117
EPILOGUE	122
QUIET MOVE	**125**
PROLOGUE	125
ONE	127
TWO	133
THREE	137
FOUR	140
FIVE	144
SIX	149
SEVEN	153
EIGHT	155
NINE	158
TEN	162
ELEVEN	165
TWELVE	167
THIRTEEN	171
FOURTEEN	175
FIFTEEN	178
SIXTEEN	183
SEVENTEEN	186
EIGHTEEN	190
NINETEEN	192
TWENTY	197
TWENTY-ONE	199
TWENTY-TWO	202
TWENTY-THREE	205

TWENTY-FOUR	209
TWENTY-FIVE	211
TWENTY-SIX	215
TWENTY-SEVEN	219
TWENTY-EIGHT	222
TWENTY-NINE	225
THIRTY	228
THIRTY-ONE	232
THIRTY-TWO	236
THIRTY-THREE	238
THIRTY-FOUR	242
THIRTY-FIVE	244
THIRTY-SIX	246
THIRTY-SEVEN	250
THIRTY-EIGHT	252
THIRTY-NINE	257
FORTY	261
FORTY-ONE	266
EPILOGUE	271
GOAT ROPE	**274**
PROLOGUE	274
ONE	276
TWO	279
THREE	283
FOUR	286
FIVE	291
SIX	294
SEVEN	297
EIGHT	301

NINE	305
TEN	308
ELEVEN	311
TWELVE	315
THIRTEEN	319
FOURTEEN	323
FIFTEEN	327
SIXTEEN	330
SEVENTEEN	337
EIGHTEEN	340
NINETEEN	342
TWENTY	344
TWENTY-ONE	347
TWENTY-TWO	350
TWENTY-THREE	354
TWENTY-FOUR	358
TWENTY-FIVE	362
TWENTY-SIX	366
TWENTY-SEVEN	369
TWENTY-EIGHT	372
TWENTY-NINE	376
THIRTY	379
THIRTY-ONE	383
THIRTY-TWO	388
THIRTY-THREE	393
THIRTY-FOUR	398
THIRTY-FIVE	401
THIRTY-SIX	404
THIRTY-SEVEN	408
THIRTY-EIGHT	411

THIRTY-NINE	415
FORTY	419
FORTY-ONE	425
FORTY-TWO	430
FORTY-THREE	434
EPILOGUE	437
CHARLEMAGNE AND THE SECTION	440
GLOSSARY OF USEFUL TERMS (GUT)	442
GLOSSARY OF NAMES	445

SWALLOW
Six weeks later

Swallow—
An agent deployed to seduce a target

PROLOGUE

The man picked strange places to meet. Viktor suspected these choices allowed his boss to claim the expenses of his travels to the more pleasant places in America. Viktor could claim travel expenses also, but he never had time to stay and enjoy the sights. This ferry ride across Lake Champlain, from Vermont to the Adirondack Mountains, was no different. Novikov had reservations at a mountain resort. Viktor would take the next ferry back, find his car, and begin the long drive to Boston.

"Is he still with us?" asked Novikov. They leaned on the railing, watching the mountains grow larger against a blue sky.

"Yes."

"I hear hesitation in your voice."

"I do not know how long I can hold his interest. He is finding other ways to amuse himself. I must replace her as soon as possible."

"You should not have let them kill her in the first place. Have you found the boy?"

Viktor turned his head to hide the fury in his eyes—at his boss, at his enemies, at his circumstances. "No. I have not found the boy. I am sure they have him. By the time I return from Japan, I will have the place pinpointed. I have already determined the general area."

"We knew more than the general area a year ago when Pavlenko was still KGB. Then he betrayed us and we lost him and his work. He betrayed you as well, you know. Personally."

"I know. He will pay. They will pay."

"We must not lose this asset. Find the boy before he leads them to your prize. You cannot afford another failure. I doubt you would live to complete your sentence."

Novikov's smooth tone conveyed more threat than did his words, though they were plenty. Viktor had no trouble understanding it.

...

The pain had spread from his shoulder up his neck and down his ribcage by the time he found a parking spot at Logan International Airport. It was worse than usual but still nothing compared to what it would be if he found himself back in prison.

The asset, an unpleasant man who competed with Sally in stupidity, required constant placating. She was dead now, and Viktor faced more than pain if he did not find a suitable replacement soon. How hard could that be? She need only be pretty, a bit dim, and capable of satisfying a man with increasingly perverse tastes. In short, a perfect swallow.

As the wheels came up and the ground dropped away, Viktor assured himself he would resume his search through the brothels of New York City when he returned in a few days.

Then he would find and kill Sally's boy.

ONE

"May I help you, Miss?"

Captain Claire Nolan turned from her inspection of the baggage hold access panel. "It's locked. Do you have a key?"

They stood on the Kadena Air Base ramp under lights powered by aircraft ground equipment (AGE).[1] She looked at the older man, his sparse hair blowing wispy in the wind from the East China Sea. He wore a white shirt under a light jacket with embroidered wings on one side of his chest. One of the pilots, she decided. That explained the foreign accent evident in just those few words. She understood these were foreign visitors.

He did not answer, and she wondered if he had exhausted his available non-aviation related English. Very slowly, she said, "I need the key so my baggage detail can unload and take it to your quarters." She waved at the airmen on detail standing behind her, slumped and lounging in patient boredom.

"The team will unload," he said.

She decided the accent was German.

"Team? What team?" She had been told only that these were VIPs. They were being accommodated in the largest bungalow quarters for such guests. Were they a sports team?

---

[1] See Glossary of Useful Terms at the end of this volume for military terms.

"What's going on, Günther?"

It was an American voice. A bit southern. So he couldn't be one of them, but where else would this civilian out here on the ramp come from but the Challenger jet sitting before them? A breathtakingly beautiful American in a lightweight suit and wearing a tie. Lots of soft brown hair with just the right amount of curl and eyes to match. The eyes were gentle, but the look in them, granite. Probably around his mid-thirties. She was immediately captivated but managed to fashion a professional answer.

"I need the key so we can get the baggage to your quarters, Sir." She had decided he was not one of the pilots, therefore, he must be one of the visitors. Maybe not one of the pilots, but his eyes were fixed on her chest, and sadly, not for the reason she would like. It was one of the more insignificant parts of her anatomy, and his eyes were centered above the left breast where her wings glinted in the lights of the AGE.

"You fly?" He was almost dismissive about it.

"Yes." She wanted to say something biting and witty, but oh, those eyes.

"Charlie wants to know is there problem?" This one had a different accent. And a broken nose. He was joined by a beautiful blonde woman, a blond man who could have been her brother, and an older man leaning on a cane. An odd collection of people for a sports team. So far, the only thing they had in common with each other was their jet.

"Is this red hair your real color, or is it dyed?" the man with the broken nose asked.

The woman hit him in the shoulder. "Sergei, no! Never ask a lady if she dyes her hair."

"But I want to know."

"I apologize," the woman said to Claire.

"I assure you it's real," she said with a chuckle.

"There are no problems here besides the ones you're trying to cause, Sergei," said the American man. He turned those beautiful eyes on her, gesturing toward the baggage detail. "Get these people the fuck out of here, Captain. Then you can escort this gentleman—you should call him Mack—to that black car there. We'll do our own unloading. Where the fuck is Skosh?" He read her blank look, rolled his eyes, and said, "Nakamura. Where is he? He better not be off someplace chowing down on sushi."

"The General insisted on showing him your quarters. They should be here any moment. In fact, here they come."

"Fuck. A fucking General."

"Let me handle this, Steve," said Mack, the man with the cane. He had a heavy German accent and began walking slowly to meet the cars, one waiting for the important visitors, the other just then driving up with Nakamura and the General.

Claire watched as the General shook hands with the man, who with a gesture sent Nakamura running toward them. Two civilian drivers she did not know but recognized from their meeting in the office earlier that day brought both cars up onto the ramp, parking next to the airplane. She turned back to Steve. He was staring at her wings again.

"So what do you fly?" he asked.

"Tankers."

He nodded minimally but said nothing.

"I've applied for a fighter. The combat restriction's been lifted."

"I heard. What are you doing in Class B's playing toady to a general?"

The man was Air Force. Not now, obviously, but once. The haircut, or lack of one, said civilian, but his manner, his language, and his familiarity with the denizens of an airfield told her he was part of her tribe. He spoke her language. She was smitten.

"We were told you were foreigners."

"Yeah. I'm the token American. So answer my question."

"They did surgery on my knee for a torn ACL. I'm grounded until the flight surgeon clears me."

"So you're on this shit detail? I'm not saying this again: get those guys the fuck away from this airplane before they touch something and get hurt. Skosh should have told you not to bring them."

He had, but the General overruled him, as generals were wont to do on a regular basis. She was about to mention this but decided she needed to understand more about these visitors before she made candid observations about her boss. She liked General Hanahan, but he was sure he could navigate any airspace. These guys gave her the sense they might be outside even his experience. Certainly, they were outside hers.

She dismissed the baggage detail and approached Nakamura.

"Can we douse the lights?" he said as she walked up.

She gave the order.

"And get these other people out of here. Maybe give them a break or something." He indicated the transient ground crew waiting to move the aircraft to a parking spot. At least he didn't use fuck for every other word like the other American did.

She did as he requested. The team, as these VIPs had been dubbed, were busy carrying light luggage to one of the cars, a roomy sedan. The other car, an armored Mercedes, stood empty so far, its trunk lid raised. Now, two low footlockers went into it. Another one was wedged into the trunk of the sedan.

Claire was sure she did not gasp when the rifle cases came out, unmistakable in the moonlight, beginning with an exceptionally long one in the hands of the younger blond man. Ammo boxes, radio cases, and another, smaller locker painted with a first aid cross, all of it was stuffed into the Mercedes.

She steadied her voice before she said, "If I can speak to the pilots, I'll give them instructions on where they should park. Then I can call the ground crew back to guide them in."

"They won't be parking," said Nakamura. "The airplane is always kept off-site. They'll leave as soon as Mack gives the order. Or Charlie. Probably Charlie. Fuck."

So much for a lighter vocabulary. Claire had no idea what caused it, but he conveyed to her a sense of worry and dismay with each unconnected thought. He clipped his words and grimaced each time he said 'Charlie.'

"You'd better call for the General's car," he said. "There's no room for a general in either of those, and I have to go with them." He pointed to the sedan.

"I should go with you, too. I know where your quarters are and I have all the keys. The General can take the protocol truck back to his quarters."

"Good point. You may let your people back near the airplane so they can get it ready to go on its way. You'd better ride with us, not in the Mercedes. I'll put you between me and Goodwin. He'll be delighted."

Judging by the way Goodwin chatted and acted nonchalant about putting his arm around her until Skosh, as everybody called Nakamura, told him to knock it off, he was indeed delighted. It was too dark for Claire to see the two silent men who sat in front.

She unlocked the door to the largest VIP bungalow and stepped aside as this strange team shlepped footlockers, luggage, ammo boxes, and radio gear through it in a steady stream. She did her best to keep her eyes off the one they called Steve but knew she spent too much time watching him and could only hope nobody noticed.

They all, without exception, noticed. Even Goodwin.

TWO

Claire thought and rehearsed, debated, and despaired herself into a fitful sleep, springing out of bed at the first ding of her alarm clock. She had fallen asleep undecided but woke knowing she had to do it. She had never done anything like it before. There had never been a need. They always came after her, sometimes like pests. It was her turn to be the pest. Of course, she would not be a pest, she told herself. She would simply ask and accept the answer gracefully, whatever it was.

What if he's married? No matter, she decided. If he is, then he's on temporary duty here and qualifies as a Class B bachelor. Another portion of her moral code fell away at the thought.

She drove to the bungalow and waited for the guys from the chow hall who would be bringing breakfast. She would walk up to the door with them, as casually as possible, and sort of see if she could....

A solemn African American man with a liberal amount of grey in his hair met them at the door and acted as a block to the interior while Skosh and Goodwin and a bald man with round bulging eyes they called Frank took in each tray from the chow hall detail. She remembered them from the office the day before but did not know the names of two of them.

"Thank you," said the man at the door. "We'll give you the empty dishes when you come back with lunch." He was speaking to the detail, who said goodbye and climbed into their van.

The man regarded Claire calmly. "Is there something I can help you with, Captain?"

"Um..." She swallowed hard, pressed her eyes closed, and said the sentence she had rehearsed as quickly as she could get the words out, which was pretty quick. She tended to talk fast. "I was wondering if I might be able to sp... speak to the man they call Steve."

"Steve? Donovan?"

"Yes. Steve. I don't know his last name."

The man tilted his head to one side as he regarded her. "Why do you need to speak to him?"

"I just do."

"Captain, in about five minutes all the food will be gone and I shall be required to go without breakfast. My name is Jay Turner, FBI. Any message you wish for me to relay, say it now."

She felt the blush coming on, felt it rise up the skin of her throat, onto her face, and up to her hairline.

"Ah," he said and sighed. "What clearance do you have, may I ask?"

"Top secret, I had to do a bring-up to work for the general, I..."

He cut her off. "Skosh is going to have a fit. It delights me. Won't you come in?" With that, he opened the door behind him and ushered her directly into the large day room of the bungalow.

"Captain Nolan to see Mr. Donovan." He deliberately announced it like a butler in a nineteenth-century novel.

Claire wanted the ground to swallow her.

"What the fuck, Turner?" said Skosh. "She's not cleared."

"She's got a TS, just like Goodwin, Nakamura, and..."

"Enough," came a quiet voice that turned the room silent, as if by magic. Where there had been several voices talking amid the sounds of utensils on plates, all noise, all movement, ceased.

Claire wanted the ground to swallow her and erase the memory of this moment for all time. It was not just acutely embarrassing to be barging in on a 'team' of VIPs at breakfast in hope of asking one of them out to dinner, it was the failure of her effort to do it privately. And then, as her brain began to register what her eyes were seeing, she realized they were all without jackets or ties but very much with holsters and pistols. Even the young woman wore one.

To complete Claire's misery, the man who had said the word that caused this expectant silence, the older blond man with the cane, came to a stand with difficulty, and in response all the other men in the room did the same.

"Will you please join us, Captain Nolan?" he said with his German accent. "Have you eaten breakfast? Please sit here near me." He gestured to a chair next to him. The man with the broken nose and remarkably light eyes stepped away from it adroitly and then dislodged Goodwin from a similar chair before a small table on the other side of the room. Goodwin leaned against a wall, plate in hand.

Claire had no choice but to sit. She had read about manners like this. She just never expected them to be accompanied by so many guns. She sat, and so did the men.

"Hi, I'm Mara," said the blonde woman. She stood up from her seat on the other side of the man with the cane. "Can I get you something to eat?"

"No, thank you, I've eaten," Claire lied.

"Coffee then?"

"Yes, please."

With those words, it seemed, Claire released everybody to continue their breakfast. The noise resumed. Mara brought her a hot cup of coffee for which she was grateful, and she savored it first, before daring to glance at Steve where she had spotted him right away on entering the room.

It was the younger blond man who addressed her first, with the same quiet voice and still manner as the older one. She thought they might be related.

"So why have you come to see Steve?" He was doing his best to keep a straight face, but the corners of his mouth fought his efforts to keep them down.

She recognized that look. Her brothers had it whenever they were about to take the mickey out of someone. She had four brothers and could give as good as she got.

"That's my business." Then as an afterthought, she gave a belated and slightly saucy, "Sir."

She expected ribald, boisterous teasing among these men. Instead, there came another moment of silence. She sensed it was because these people were in the habit of being careful with this man and she had been unwisely flippant. She dropped her eyes and said, "I would like to speak with him privately if I may."

She swore she could hear nobody breathing. Then the older man said, "You may use the small office beside my room, Steve. No one will disturb you there."

And there he was standing before her, all arrogance, gesturing for her to precede him. He did not close the door behind him once they were in the room, standing in the few square feet unoccupied by desk and chair and fax machine. He said nothing and offered no encouragement.

The ground should swallow her, her memory be erased, and all the minerals of her body used by billions of other organisms scattered by a hurricane around the world.

" I... Will you have dinner with me this evening?" she squeaked.

She screwed up her courage to look at him after two beats of silence. He was watching her without expression, his head tilted. He gave a slight shake of his head, raised an eyebrow, and said simply, "No."

"Very well, thank you for your time," she rushed past him but turned, her brow furrowed by a new, rather belated realization. "You're a fighter pilot, aren't you? A fucking fighter pilot. I should have known better."

Claire managed to smile and thank Mara and the older man as she made her escape. She walked calmly to her car and did not start crying until she had driven halfway to the office.

How could she be so stupid, so desperate for one lousy man's touch, and that man a fucking arrogant prick of a fighter pilot? She was sure he was a fighter pilot now. It all fit. What was up with the gun? With all their guns? Did he need it to compensate for something else? Huh? That made her wonder about a certain part of his anatomy and... She shook herself, looked at the grim reality of painfully acute embarrassment, and wondered how she could fob off this VIP protocol detail on somebody else—in true military fashion.

Then, she sobbed.

THREE

"What did she ask you?" Mara said as soon as the door closed behind Claire.

"None of your business, Mara."

"Why is she upset then, Steve? She wants you, God knows why. Did you turn her down?"

Steve glared at her.

The room became quiet in an instant. The exchange between these two interested everybody and they wanted to listen. Charlie broke into the silence with his low voice. "Seriously? Tell me you did not turn down a delectable redhead. Why?"

Steve replied with some heat. "We're on an op for fuck's sake."

"Bullshit," said Frank, eyes more prominent than usual. "That never stopped any of you guys, ever. You, Steve, are the randiest of them all, in my experience, and that's saying something because I remember the Frenchman when he was your age."

Sergei pulled back the slide on his Makarov pistol to begin dismantling it for cleaning. "Someone should touch his forehead to see if he is ill."

Mara laid down a cleaning kit on the coffee table for Sergei and turned to Steve. "No more bullshit, Steve. What did she want?"

He sighed the sigh of the put-upon. "She asked me out to dinner. I said no. Okay? It's a fucking pain in the ass to arrange something like that right now. We leave for Okuma tonight."

"How did you say no?" Mara waited for an answer. Steve had none, only a petulant look. She said, "You bastard. You just said no, didn't you? You didn't even try to make up an excuse about how we operate, did you? Do you have any idea what it takes for a woman to tell a man she's interested? Do you?"

She was in full rant, all venom and fury. Sergei had a speculative eye on her, wondering how she came by such knowledge and uncomfortable with the idea that Mara ever could be interested in any other man.

She turned to Skosh. "Get the keys for the Mercedes. You are taking me and Steve to the Captain's office right now. I presume you know where it is. Sergei, we are going out to dinner tonight. You should shave."

Charlie and his father exchanged half smiles as Mara shoved Steve out the door.

...

Crying ruined her makeup and turned her eyes red, but Claire toned down the flame in her cheeks with a compact in the ladies' room. Flight suits did not require makeup. She stepped through the General's outer office on her way to the smaller side room where a mountain of correspondence waited in her in-basket. The cockpit had no space for in-baskets. She did her best to give a cheery good morning to the secretaries but knew she was no good at hiding her feelings. Luckily, they were busy with the agendas for two important meetings that day.

She sat behind her desk, staring at the in-basket, willing herself to pick up one, just one letter and get started. Her hands refused the order.

"May we speak to Captain Nolan, please?"

The woman outside sounded American and yet not, familiar, and yet not. There was a foreign music in those few words and Claire could not decide if she had heard the voice before. No matter, she thought, I can't face anybody right now. She prepared herself to tell Helen she was too busy and to ask the people to come back another time. She would wave in the direction of her in-basket as evidence.

Helen had no chance to ask anybody anything. Mara followed her through the door close on her heels, and Steve had no choice but to follow Mara to avoid looking churlish. Claire was sure he prided himself on being an accomplished churl, but maybe he thought there were too many witnesses today.

She stood. "Thank you, Helen." She indicated the two chairs before her desk. "Won't you have a seat, Mara, Steve?"

Helen closed the door behind her as she went back to her desk.

"Thank you, Captain," said Mara. "But we cannot sit with our backs to the door and this will not take long."

Indeed, Claire noticed now that Steve had moved to the side of her desk and turned toward the door. Why had Mara told her this?

"Steve told me how distraught he was that he had to turn down your kind invitation to dinner," said Mara.

It wasn't so much the accent, decided Claire, because there was none. It was the elegant courtesy in the woman's manner that made her sound a bit foreign to her ears. The same elegant courtesy the man with the cane had displayed. Come to think of it, there were other similarities, but she was cut off in mid-speculation as Mara continued.

"You see, we have many security concerns and Steve was reluctant to burden you with them."

The reluctant lump that was Steve stood watching the door while Mara spoke excuses for him.

"If you would not mind a double date for dinner, Sergei and I would be delighted if we could join you and Steve. It will solve our security problem if three of us are there."

On one hand, Claire longed to maintain her pride and say no, but on the other, she was suddenly dying to have dinner with people who could not sit with their backs to a door. How did that even work? And on the third hand, Steve seethed. She saw his jaw clenching and could not resist the chance to make him fume even more.

"That would be wonderful, Mara. I know a restaurant in Okinawa City that serves excellent teppanyaki. And please, call me Claire."

Skosh joined them in the outer office as she walked them to the door. The term he had used for his function, a strange synonym for minder, was apt. Minders and nervousness about doors and don't forget the guns, she told herself. How intriguing.

She never once thought they could be dangerous.

FOUR

Twelve people sat at their teppanyaki table, arranged in rows of four on three sides around a central well that contained the chef's domain. Their party had managed to sit lengthwise along a solid wall with the door across the room and to their right. It was a large room, with six of these tables, in three pairs. Each table had a chef wielding significant knives as he chopped vegetables and cubed beefsteak, sautéing all as the delicious steam rose into a giant hood over the well.

Steve sat to Claire's right and Mara on her left, with Sergei to Mara's left. Sergei seemed as jumpy as a flea, but Mara was all graciousness and charm. Steve spoke to nobody but himself. It mystified Claire at first.

"Is Skosh going to join us?" she asked him. The minder, or babysitter as they called him, had driven them here and disappeared before they walked through the door.

Steve impatiently shook his head at her question. "Well, where the fuck are you?" he said in a very low voice. Claire was about to mention to Mara that she was concerned about this when she noticed the device, almost invisible, in Mara's ear. They were talking to each other, not to her. Mara gave her a nervous smile.

"Just sit down and order some sushi, Skosh. We won't be much longer."

The chef filled each plate with vegetables. Claire was the only one of their party using chopsticks. At times, she was the only one eating.

"Fuck. Yeah, I see them," Steve said to nobody. Mara tensed beside her and became very still. Claire lost her taste for vegetables.

"Which one?"

A pause, presumably to listen for the answer coming into Steve's ear.

The chef added beef to their plates.

"Is that the one you saw in Fayetteville? Did he see you? Okay. We're finishing up. We'll be behind you."

Claire had managed to force herself to eat one bite of the beef on her plate when Steve threw down his napkin and a wad of Japanese yen and said, "Let's go." For the first time that evening, he looked at her. The hardness of his expression quelled the protest she wanted to make. It never made it out of her throat.

He took her arm as he led her around the tables to the door and muttered, "Smile, like you've had a wonderful time." Then, "No, not you, Skosh."

Claire managed a grimace that might have passed for a smile. She couldn't see Mara and Sergei. They were close behind her, with Sergei almost at her left elbow. They kept their pace leisurely but purposeful until they reached the street, when it became a fast walk toward the Mercedes they had arrived in. It felt like they were escaping. From what, she couldn't say.

"Shit," said Sergei.

"Let me handle this, Sergei," said Steve. "You take care of Claire. Now, everybody laugh and chatter. You too, Claire. Don't shut up on me now, for fuck's sake."

Claire felt the strain under her companions' studied nonchalance and joined them in asking inane questions and laughing at Mara's nonsense answers. As they neared a dark, narrow opening between two buildings, not even wide enough to qualify as an alley, she could hear grunting, a few cries of fury, the sound of blows. Steve pulled a step ahead of them and as soon as he was even with the opening shouted, "Hey what's going on in there?"

All Claire later remembered seeing at this point was the knife in the man's hand as he faced Steve, pointing it at his throat. Steve put up his hands and said, with a decided Texas drawl, "Now look here, I don't want no trouble. You're welcome to my wallet. Let me …"

Because she could not process the speed at which Steve had moved, the next thing Claire saw was the knife skidding and clattering along the pavement and into the gutter. Steve was holding the man's head, then let the man drop, his neck bent at an awkward angle. He was dead. It had happened in front of her, in the last moment before this, and it robbed her of thought, of emotion, of speech.

"You okay Skosh?" said Steve.

The labored answer came from the dark interior of the opening. "Yeah."

"Is your guy alive?"

"Yeah."

Claire watched Steve pick up the knife from the gutter, then grab the collar of the dead man and drag his body into the recess. Sergei took her arm and led—a more polite way of saying pulled—her to the Mercedes.

FIVE

"Thanks, Steve. I mean it. Thanks." Skosh was still breathless in the back seat next to Sergei in the middle.

Claire sat in the front passenger seat, silent for once, because she was still processing what she had seen and reconciling it with the beautiful eyes of the man at the wheel next to her.

"Come on Skosh, you were handling it just fine," he said.

"Yeah, but without you, they'd be talking to their bosses now and the op would be blown. Just drop me at the cop shop around the corner, and would you ask Frank to pick me up? I need to talk to him."

"What? Is he your father confessor now? You didn't make the decision. I did. You didn't kill them. I did. Your babysitter purity remains intact."

"In fifteen years with four different Asian teams, I was never anywhere close to it, Steve. In less than six weeks with you guys, I've been present three times."

Sergei weighed in. "Ixnay on the illingkay alktay."

Steve snorted with exasperation as he negotiated the turn. "Sergei, first of all, Claire was right there. She saw me break the first guy's neck. Second, she's an American and has been talking Pig Latin since she was at most five years old."

"Really?" said Mara. "Mama taught it to me. And as I remember, I was about five."

"It's an essential American skill." Steve pulled the car to the curb. "I'll tell Frank to come get you, Skosh."

The rest of the ride, which admittedly wasn't all that long, took place in silence. It was not exactly a strained atmosphere. Mara and Sergei were not aware that Claire was rarely quiet. She could not sense any tension coming from them, but she felt Steve's glances from time to time. At the front gate, she flashed her ID and assured the gate guard that these were her guests. As the guard examined the card, she felt the tension in spades, and it came from all three of her companions, in their stillness and the way Steve looked straight ahead, jaw clenched. She felt a flash of gratitude that they had not won the gate check lotto by being pulled over for a random search. Imagine it, she thought.

Okay, she told herself. This was a stupid idea to begin with. Why did I compound it? I am cured. Forever.

She glanced at him in the street lights. Oh, but he was gorgeous.

He walked her to the downstairs main door of the Q. "So I hope you get your fighter and have a great career and never, ever again proposition a man you don't know."

"I did not proposition you. I only asked you out to dinner. There is a difference."

"Not to me, there isn't."

Then he kissed her, more demandingly than she was used to, with his hands in places he had no right to touch, and ... and it was over all too soon. She forgot that crooked-necked corpse on the pavement. Momentarily.

...

Jay Turner forced himself to relax so as not to be perceived as standing at attention. He felt like a second lieutenant. Scratch that, like a cadet. Still not accurate. He felt like a doolie, a first-year cadet, though he had never heard of a doolie standing in the presence of a general officer wearing a faded bathrobe and slippers unless they were related.

"I presume," said General Hanahan, "that you have some purpose in disturbing me at this hour, Mr. Turner."

He sounded like every other general Jay had ever met, comfortable bathrobe notwithstanding.

"Yes, Sir, I do. I would like to ask you some questions about Captain Nolan and then make a request."

The General nodded and he continued.

"First, to satisfy one of my concerns, I see you have upgraded her security clearance, and I want to know if you are satisfied with that decision, and you do not consider her a risk in any way, especially with classified information."

"Of course not. Next." The General was testy. He had not asked Jay to sit down, though two plush armchairs faced the desk in his study. They stood on a Chinese carpet in intricate shades of blue illuminated by a desk lamp with a green shade.

"Can you tell me something about her personality? Is she outgoing, for example, or secretive, quiet, or garrulous?" He had been ordered to gather intelligence like this.

"Outgoing and completely garrulous. Sometimes I have to tell her to shut up. It's all meaningful stuff, not mindless prattle, mostly questions, mind you, but after a while, I need time to catch up to the last few sentences."

"Would you say she's a good officer?"

"She's a great officer. Competent at whatever you tell her to do."

"And her career?"

"Brilliant. She will go far. Made regular right away."

"She's not a Zoomie…"

"No. But I'd say she can expect to reach at least O-6. And I'd also say you are a Zoomie. What class?"

The man could give Mack a run for his money in the mind-reading department. Maybe Jay made it obvious by not relaxing enough. "Seventy-six, Sir. Finally, can you tell me her record as a pilot?"

"Again, first rate. She made aircraft commander in minimal time and we're going to get her into a fighter. As one of the first women to fly a combat aircraft, she'll have a shot at flag rank, even without the academy. Now, what's your ask? I'd like to get back to my evening."

Jay took a deep breath. "We'd like Captain Nolan to be our liaison at Okuma." He did not say, by order of Mack, but he was sorely tempted.

Now, after a significant pause, the General indicated one of the chairs and sat down in the other. "And if I say no?"

Jay sat down and measured each word before letting it out. "My superiors do not have the connections necessary to force the issue in a timely manner, Sir, but Mr. Nakamura's do. Even so, with the time required for communications at several levels, across the date line and so many time zones, it could delay and possibly endanger the operation and.…"

"And my ass would be grass, is what you're saying. Who is pushing my buttons here? Is it the man I met on the flightline, the one with the cane?"

"Yes, Sir."

General Hanahan and Mack had become two of a kind in Jay's book.

"And this assignment you want Captain Nolan for, is it dangerous?"

Again, Jay spoke carefully. "The people on both sides are particularly dangerous."

The General digested this before speaking. "If I tried to keep her from a dangerous assignment just because she's a pretty girl, she'd be furious. She has skill and brains and anything else necessary to do the job." He narrowed his eyes at Jay. "Has she caught the eye of one of those guys with all the weapons?"

Jay's eyebrows rose. So much for expensive, well-cut suits. "Sir, I honestly do not know all the plans and motivations involved. I do know that I would prefer not to have yet another person set eyes on this team. Therefore, my motivation is a security concern. She has already seen them and she is competent."

"This team, you say. They're the killing kind of spooks, aren't they?"

Jay could not and did not need to answer.

The General stood, picked up the phone on his desk, and dialed. "Hello, Captain. This is General Hanahan. I'm sending a Mr. Turner to you right now. You are to obey his orders as though they were mine. He'll be there in a few minutes. And my dear, good luck and be careful."

SIX

"What the fuck are you doing here?" Steve was cleaning a rifle at the conference room table when Claire came in from the small anteroom to the outside.

As conference rooms went, it was a pretty typical space, aside from the rifle in pieces on the large table that dominated it. Navigating around that table was complicated by two computer stations with printers, radios, footlockers, chairs, and now the important supplies Claire had brought with her.

She arrived at the Okuma event center at midnight and bumbled through the doorway of the conference room with a crate of food in the form of MREs—meals, ready to eat. Steve watched her struggle but did nothing to help. Goodwin did though, rushing to take the box from her with a wide grin.

"Here, let me help you with that," he said "I understand you'll be our liaison. I'll be happy to show you around when we get settled in."

Claire did not tell him she knew both the military resort and the entire chain of command of the people who ran it. He was so eager to please, like a golden retriever, she could not bring herself to crush that eagerness.

Steve could, though. "Go set up your fucking computer, Goodwin."

The younger blond man she had seen at Kadena came in with Jay Turner at that moment, carrying a sniper rifle. He stopped and took in all of her, she was sure, as he moved his eyes from her feet to her red hair. He raised an eyebrow, seeming to register even the momentary surge of caution she felt.

"Did you bring a bathing suit for Mara?" he asked.

She did not know his name, but she knew by instinct how to address him. "Yes, Sir. I did." Jay had told her to bring two suits.

"Bathing suit?" Mara entered the room, a computer keyboard and mouse in her hands. She placed them before one of the computers on a table against the wall. "What are you talking about, Charlie?"

"I told you to bring a bathing suit, but you did not. Why?"

"Because I am not here to be looked at."

"When there is an operational necessity, you will do as I say, including being looked at, Mara. Behold your legend." He gestured toward Claire. "You can't go alone and going with a man will defeat the purpose. I have found you an accomplice in attracting Borodinov."

"What the fuck, Charlie? You can't put this woman in that kind of danger." Steve stared at Charlie until the room temperature dropped to the point that it made him look away. "Sorry. You're right. It's perfect. I wasn't thinking."

"She is a line officer, Donovan," said Jay. He received the full force of Steve's glare until he remembered something really important he needed to do in another room.

None of this made Claire comfortable. She wanted to fly the F-15. She wanted to fly in air-to-air combat. Suddenly, she found herself wanting to live long enough just to get into the training for it. She slipped away from the company of the mutual glare society and out the door to fetch the next box from her car. Steve followed and took the box from her as she lifted it.

"So how'd you finagle this assignment?" he demanded. They stood in a small parking area within the sound of the East China Sea washing the sand a few yards away.

"Finagle? I was ordered. I didn't *finagle* anything. You think I'm pursuing you, don't you? Huh? You arrogant son of a bitch. You think you're God's gift to women, totally irresistible. Well, you can think what you want, but you're not. I made a mistake, that's all. You think I want you, well let me tell you ..."

He put the box down and kissed her, and by doing so discovered the best way to shut her up.

In an insight that only a decent kiss by no matter how wrong a man can reveal, she discovered whatever he thought about what she wanted, he was right.

Steve took the box inside for her without a word and she turned to her car for the next one. On her way back past the beach, she heard the sounds of a fight. It had been only a few hours since she was introduced to that sound in a narrow alley in Okinawa City and here it was again. She froze and turned toward the all too familiar sound of violence. It came from near the waterline where she saw Charlie, highlighted by starlight reflected off the water, kick sideways into Steve's gut, sending him sprawling across the sand.

"Fuck, Michael, it was a momentary lapse," said Steve as he struggled for breath.

"Don't ever defy me like that again, Steve. I need you solid in front of the others. And I need you sane. I thought you didn't like her. Tell me your cock won't fuck up this op. We'll all be dead then. Tell me you're solid, Steve."

Steve stood up. "You know I am. There will be no mistakes."

She stood mesmerized by the vehemence of both their language and actions and was still holding the crate, frozen in place, when the two walked up to her. The blond man took the box from her and lifted his chin to indicate she should go inside. She stood confused. "What should I call you?" she said.

"Sir will do nicely. But you should use Charlie for now."

She saw Steve roll his eyes and smirk at her as they went through the door and remembered how her brothers always refused to take the winner of a recent match seriously, no matter how soundly they had been defeated.

Claire met Charlie again in the kitchen cubicle off the conference room a few minutes later. He drained the last of a pot of coffee into his mug and put the empty pot down in the sink. She was about to leave, having no desire to be in a small space with this man, when he grabbed the back of her tee shirt and pulled her back in.

"Coffee needs making."

"So make it." She made another effort to leave.

He held her arm this time, tightly, and turned her to face him. After taking a sip of his coffee, he said quietly, "Do you understand who I am?"

"You're Charlie or Michael and you appear perfectly capable of making coffee."

"Turner!"

Jay appeared at the cubicle entrance almost immediately.

"What did that general order this captain to do?" asked Charlie. He did not release her arm.

"To obey my orders like she would obey his."

"You will want to transfer that instruction to me."

Jay sighed. She could see in the way he dipped his chin that he sensed the tension and resolved to do what he could, though he knew it would not be much help and might backfire.

"Captain," he said. "You will obey this man's orders as you would your general's. He is in charge. Do not defy him." That said, he went in search of Steve.

"General Hanahan would never order me to make coffee," she said to Charlie. "It is demeaning."

He became very still, moving only to take a sip from the mug in his hand. "If you want me to give you an example of how thoroughly I am capable of demeaning you, Captain. I will oblige. Then, you will consider coffee making to be a high honor."

"Hey, is there coffee?" asked Steve, filling the entrance and looking past her to Charlie.

"There is not," he said. "And Claire, as I understand she wishes to be called, refuses to make any. Would you like to see to it?"

"Sure."

"To be clear, I mean see to it that she follows my orders in general."

"Of course."

"And remind her of that word, 'sir.'"

"I will."

"I leave it to you then."

Claire felt herself shaking and did her best to hide it from Charlie. He squeezed her shoulder as he moved her aside. The gesture did not reassure; it warned. She dropped her gaze, still seething.

Steve took hold of both shoulders and turned her to face him and the coffee maker. "Look, Claire, you can thank Jay for this little rescue. He came to get me and I said I'd do it once. But that's all. There is nothing between us."

"I never wanted anything between us, as you put it, Steve. I just wanted the use of your body for one night." The brief shock in his eyes gratified her. "What? Did you think women don't think the way you do?"

She looked into a new fury that matched her own.

"This is not a deployment exercise, Claire. It's the real deal. I don't know what Charlie has in mind for you to do, but I guarantee it's both necessary and fucking dangerous. If you disobey him and screw it up you can cost us all our lives and it will certainly cost you yours. Now, you will make the fucking coffee and call him Sir."

The voice was so low and the anger so barely contained, it made the words burst into her consciousness with no ambiguity. "Yes, Sir." She said it reflexively at the very moment Charlie called from the other room for Steve to get dressed.

"Now."

They were going out.

SEVEN

Steve, Sergei, and Charlie came in from outside through the vestibule and into the conference room less than an hour later. They removed Kevlar balaclavas from their heads and plopped into chairs at the table. Skosh and the frog-eyed man named Frank brought them mugs of the coffee Claire had made. Charlie sat to the left of the man they were calling Mack, the one with the cane.

She figured now would be a good time to make her escape. They intended to hold a meeting. She knew the signs. Even in peaceful circumstances, meetings tried her patience. These were not peaceful people. She did not want to know what they had to say. Whatever they said was not likely to be healthy for her to hear. Charlie would brief her on her role soon enough and she would do as she was told. Within reason. Never mind that. Whatever she was told. She inwardly practiced that resolution.

In the meantime, she had work to do before she could leave. The room was noisy. She used her command voice.

"Listen up, people!" She waited for a brief moment. The noise level dipped just a bit. She had Goodwin's attention—a bit too rapt for her taste. "There are three big boxes here of MREs. The one on your left as you look at the door, is filled with possible breakfast choices. That's probably what you'll want now. It's almost dawn. Next are cold lunch meals, and finally, the box on the right contains dinner menu items. I will be in my room if you need anything else from Kadena. Good night."

She was about to skirt around Mack to reach the back hallway to her room when she realized he was staring at her. His eyes were very blue and he did not move. She was contemplating going around the other end of the table when he spoke, making such a low, even sound she had the impression of a big cat purring.

"You amuse me, Captain. I see no one has ventured to sit here on my right." He pointed to the empty chair and said no more.

Claire thought up several excuses, discarding each in turn primarily because she could not bring herself to make a sound. She tore her eyes away from him long enough to see everyone at the table watching for her reaction. If Charlie was the colonel in command here, Mack was their general. She sat down in the seat indicated with as much grace as she could muster and was rewarded with a suggestion of a smile from this civilian flag officer.

Skosh spoke first, on a prompting glance from Mack. "How many?" he asked Charlie.

"One."

"Blood? Guns? Whose?" These questions and their answers came in rapid succession like individual rounds from a semi-auto.

"No. No. Steve's. We used a perimeter watcher to call the inside man and lure him outside so Sergei could slip in. Inside guy searched for a while and went back in after having no joy."

"Where is the body?"

"In a grove near the entrance to the resort," said Steve.

Skosh nodded.

Mack looked at Sergei, who spoke next.

"I placed eight taps in the room, two behind pictures in the hallway, and one in the toilet."

"Why the toilet?" asked Jay.

Sergei shrugged. "People talk. Also, the hallway is not long and toilets have good acoustics."

Mara nodded to confirm. "I tested one very briefly and will continue to test randomly until the conference."

"I have spoken to Alex," said Mack. "She has made some progress with Danny, but first, let me not be rude to Captain Nolan by speaking of people she does not know.

Claire had a momentary burst of hope that this was a prelude to dismissal. It was not. He looked at her with those blue, blue eyes, even bluer than Charlie's, whose eyes were more the color of ice. He leaned back in his chair and tilted his head to one side as he regarded her.

"Alex is my wife, Captain, and Danny is Steve's son. He is eleven years old. Our target wants very much to kill Danny and is looking for him. We must determine why before we kill our target. If he finds Danny, he will find us. Have you been told the purpose of this operation before now?" He gestured around the room at large.

"No, Sir." She could not help swallowing hard.

"Only repeatedly threatened, I should think."

"Yes, Sir."

"You will do well to heed every warning you have been given. Mr. Nakamura will give you a form to sign from your government that says if you ever say anything to anyone about us or this operation, the best thing that can happen to you is your government will quickly put you in prison. We cannot reach you there. Are my words clear to you?"

"Yes, Sir," she croaked.

Mack shifted, pushing his left leg out straight. He did not wince, but a minimal grimace suggested discomfort.

"Very good," he said. "Sometimes, I am accused of ambiguity. You have an important part to play in this operation and there must be nothing unclear in your mind." He leaned forward over the corner of the table and addressed her almost intimately in a one-on-one discussion, except that she remained mute and knew she was expected to do so.

"I understand you have a great facility for asking questions. Normally, this is not a good trait in our business, but in this instance, it will be very helpful. I want you to exercise it. Ask and ask and ask, about every detail of what you are to do and what those around you will be doing, until you know your duty here as well as you know the emergency procedures in your airplane." He looked across the table at Steve. "Mr. Donovan has explained such things to me and it is a perfect example of what I require. If you successfully recite this procedure it does not mean you will be permitted to fly. It means you may remain alive."

She had to hand it to this scariest of all generals. His succinct little briefing held no trace of ambiguity.

EIGHT

"I'm not sure where to put you in the schedule, Captain," said Frank. He held a pen and looked down at a small notebook.

"Schedule?"

"Yes. You have noticed that we sleep in shifts, haven't you?"

"I've noticed that nobody seems to have slept. You're all exhausted and I'm not exactly rested myself."

Frank did not know what to make of this woman. She came in a dainty package. Her cap of curly red hair and green eyes gave her an elfin look, but she spoke with more assurance than she had a right to, especially here. He sighed.

"You'll be sleeping in the same room as Mara."

"I have my own room."

"No, you don't." We have five rooms with beds. One of those is the room you think you have the key to. That has been assigned to Donovan and Pavlenko. You and Mara will use the one at the end of the hall, furthest from the main door, across from the largest room, which is used by Mack and Charlie. There is an attached bath in their room and I'm assured you and she can use it. You'll probably want to. The fire door has been secured. Now …"

"Look, Mr …"

"Cardova. Call me Frank."

"Look, Frank, I'm a liaison. Whatever task Charlie or Mack—that is his name isn't it?"

"That's what you should call him, yes."

"Whatever task he has for me will be minor. In the meantime, I have a job to do and part of that job is to stay out of your way. I will stay in my room."

"Not when Mara's in there, you won't?"

"I don't understand."

"I repeat, we sleep in shifts. There is no space for anybody to have their own room. And it's not safe to be in the same room as a sleeping specialist. Mara's not nutso, like the others—yet—but she has the reflexes and it's not good to startle them when they're wired, which they rapidly are becoming. Close your mouth. You are too intelligent not to understand me."

He looked at his notebook again, saw no guidance there, and continued with a sigh. "I have no idea what your task is, and I'm not used to outsiders staying with us. You're not a babysitter, or minder as you have referred to us—very accurate, by the way—but you're also not a specialist. We had a couple of people, related to but not members of the team with us during the last op and that was difficult at best, but once everybody, especially Goodwin, knew they were off limits, it worked out. I'm hoping you will decisively put Goodwin in his place before he gets himself beat up again."

The man had more steel in him than the round eyes and bald pate suggested. He was no lightweight, Claire decided. She put a hold on everything she had wanted to say about the noise, the crowded conditions, and her constant state of confusion.

She had much to process and almost no time to do so. The conversation with Frank illustrated how every time she tried to understand something said or done or just hinted at, another thing would be said, done, and hinted at and it would be her turn to make coffee. She and the babysitters—though Jay and Justin were at pains to explain they were FBI, not babysitters—seemed to be the sole coffee makers. Steve and Sergei contributed occasionally, Mara a little more frequently, but Charlie and Mack, never.

She felt more comfortable once she had placed everybody in a category, by AFSC, or in other words by career field, and by rank. First, like the essential difference between flying and not flying, there were specialists and non-specialists. She belonged to the latter group here, in what capacity, not yet determined. In this group were the FBI special agents, one of whom was a near-criminal hacker with an aggressive eye, and then the 'proper' babysitters who came from so shadowy a part of the government they never mentioned who, exactly, they worked for. She decided here, at least, the babysitters were the foundation of this, whatever this was, like essential noncommissioned officers, though they were both rather senior civil servants.

The specialists specialized. Thus, the name. Their specialty was the nastier side of HUMINT, which was in itself predicated on sleight of hand, clandestine behavior, manipulation, and frankly, lying. In addition, these particular people added killing to their resumes. She got that. She had seen it happen in front of her after dinner, after one bite of Kobe-style teppanyaki beef. What she didn't get was how she could be of any use to them. She instinctively understood their peculiar chain of command. If Mack appointed a task and Charlie directed her in it, she would have to trust that the order would be lawful.

"You think so?" said Steve when she brought up this point.

"General Hanahan would not order me to take part in an illegal operation." She sorted the remaining breakfast MREs into related piles and lined them up neatly in their box.

Steve snorted as he pushed a rod with a solvent-soaked patch through the barrel of a submachine gun. "Just so you understand, if it's not lawful, he's not the one they'll hang out to dry. And anyway, can he delegate his authority to a civilian?"

Claire opened her eyes wide. She didn't know.

"I know my profs tried to teach me all that," he said, "but I never listened well to anything they said. I just wanted to fly. It doesn't matter anyway. If the worst happens, don't say you were following an order. Just say you were threatened with death if you didn't obey. It's true enough. The UCMJ doesn't require martyrdom. If you choose to go ahead and die, you'll maybe get a medal on your casket, but it's not required." He forced dry patches through the barrel, one after the other, until they came out clean.

"Your profs? You're an Academy grad?"

"Yeah. So? So's Turner. He was cadet wing commander during my doolie year. It gives me great pleasure to see him make coffee. What's your point?"

She had no point. She was busy having questions instead. He was cleaning the firing pin with solvent and a brush.

"Did Jay fly?"

"I don't think so."

"But you did."

He put the weapon back together, pushed in a magazine, and chambered a round.

"Claire, listen. I got nothing for you. I fight. I kill. I don't even make love; I fuck. That's all there is to me. Fuck, fight, kill. Look elsewhere, little girl. We've got nothing in common."

Of all that speech, the only thing that minimally put her off were the words 'little girl.'

"We both fly. You fly the Challenger you came in on."

"When my real job allows it. I'm checked out in it, but only right seat." He paused. "I was told you're an AC."

She nodded and wondered, was he jealous? She knew she would be, especially if leaving the cockpit was not her choice. The knee injury had proven to be more of a trial than she thought possible, and it was only temporary. She drew two conclusions as she studied his sullen expression. He did not leave voluntarily, and he was more complicated than he let on.

Reluctantly, she acknowledged a third conclusion. She wanted more than his body. She wanted him. All of him. Every complicated molecule. Maybe not forever, but certainly for now. The only remaining question was, did she want him more than the cockpit, any cockpit, not just a fighter?

The cockpit won the contest hands down. For now.

NINE

As he returned to their conference room from another intense interview with the authorities, Skosh worried about pretty much everything, but especially about the Captain. He could probably pass off any damage to her as the unfortunate result of some sort of military exigency, but he wasn't exactly sure what the exigency was, let alone the military angle.

He knew the target and the difficulties surrounding the commission. They hadn't even been able to touch the target's conference room until his sweepers went through it and declared it free of bugs. This meant Charlemagne had to wait until the sweep was done and a guard set, requiring the guard to be dealt with. Donovan had dealt with that as only he could, but shit, for Skosh it meant another stony-faced discussion with local authorities over tea. He had assured them there were no signs of intrusion (by Pavlenko) nor any indication of unnatural death (by Donovan) in the perimeter guard, but shit. They were not fools.

And now there was this strange woman. Not strange as in Steve's ex-wife's delusional strange, but strange in the way she straddled every demographic in the safehouse. She was federal, a military officer, an aviator, and very much a frighteningly modern woman, all at the same time. No wonder she terrified Steve. He didn't know what he would do if she propositioned him. No, not true. He did know. He would say yes. What the fuck was Donovan's problem?

He called loudly down the hallway as Frank and Jay made their weary ways toward their rooms. He depended on them to eject Goodwin immediately and was not disappointed.

"Justin," he said pointing to the conference room, "get in there and get started. We need flight arrival times for the gangsters coming in tonight and check the manifests for those we don't know about."

"Can I pee first?"

"Don't make a fucking mess." Skosh was anything if not gracious. The bathroom was not. Nonetheless, it was the only one they had at the moment and a line had developed. There was another toilet in the larger suite occupied by Charlie and Mack, but they were in conference. He had no intention of disturbing that.

Claire came out of the bathroom, faced the line of men, none of them patient, and said to Skosh, "You know it's disgusting in there, don't you?"

"What do you want me to do about it? We're lucky we have coffee. Get in the conference room. The bathroom's about to get worse."

He saw Pavlenko slip into Mara's room. He had tried to keep them on separate watches but had been overruled by Mack himself. The man was up to something.

...

"I am mystified about two things," said Michael as he savored a sip of some very old single malt whiskey. "I mean, Papa, I do not understand either Steve's rejection of the Captain nor her desire for him, but especially why you told her to ask questions. It is not like you."

Misha sipped his wee dram as he stretched his left leg onto a conference chair that he had pressed into service as an ottoman.

"It is a mystery why any person feels attracted to another. The more questions she asks, the more we will know about her and how her mind works. She fell into our laps by fate and seems to satisfy all criteria. We need more information to be sure."

"It occurs to me," Michael said carefully, "that she resembles Alex in some ways, but is also very different. She is also much younger. But he rejects her. Could he be that infatuated with Alex?"

"No. He is not infatuated. Nor is he in love. He desires Alex, nothing more. And he will take her if I am gone and you will have a mess on your hands. Do make an effort to not let this captain be sacrificed as a dangle. We may not find a better candidate for Steve. She appears to be perfect for him in every way. She will not let him destroy her." He did not say aloud what they both were thinking. Steve would destroy Alex.

Michael wondered how realistic any of it might be. They were not matchmakers. He knew Steve had it bad for Alex, despite his largely successful efforts to disguise it. And how, exactly, was he supposed to ensure Claire's survival? His father had pegged the problem, however, in his usual prescient way. If the last fight over Alex nine years before was anything to judge by, a young enough widow would be a problem. Add an unattached male to the mix and the team would be at each other's throats again. Let him have Steve's reputation and skill and it could tear them apart. Given their occupation and its propensity for creating widows, Claire's advent on the scene was serendipity. They must not screw this up.

"Papa, we have less than two days. What if they do not…?"

"Günther has told me he wishes to retire. Uwe will move up and we will have an opening. I will offer it to her. Uwe will manage very well until Steve marries her. Then we can hire someone else."

Michael shook his head. "She is an aircraft commander, Papa, with more flying hours than Steve. General Hanahan predicts a successful military career. She will not be content to fly right seat under Uwe and then quit upon marriage. Why should she? Theresa is still practicing medicine."

"Not after you have a child, surely?" Misha's eyebrows rose in astonishment.

"We have discussed it. We have plenty of servants. There is no reason for Theresa to give up her career."

"You are so very modern. I am not sure it is a good thing."

Michael was sure it was a good thing that the subject had come up in this context. He thanked Fate and Steve for opening the topic. In a few days, if they lived, he would inform his father about the impending child.

"I suppose I must offer her more money to take the position," said Misha.

"More money and left seat in the Challenger." Michael swallowed the last of his scotch.

"More money and they alternate duties as aircraft commander. If she wants him badly enough, she will agree to it. And if not, then she would never succeed with him anyway."

"I agree, Papa. She will need all the desire she can muster to tame him. Let us hope she will have the chance—if we live."

Misha swallowed the last of his whiskey and agreed. "If we live."

TEN

She had been allowed three and a half hours of sleep. This was not especially different from what she was used to on deployment, though as aircrew, she had enjoyed a guaranteed eight hours. The biggest difference was the lack of beer.

There were jokes, most of which she did not get, often spoken in languages she did not understand. Justin Goodwin continued trying to get close to her. Occasionally, he saw Mack watching him, became suddenly businesslike, and went back to his computer. It was only when Claire spoke briefly to Steve about the lunch MREs that she realized Mack was watching neither Justin nor Steve; his eyes were on her. It made her curious and a little nervous.

Her normal dinner time approached and Claire felt hungry but noticed nobody on her shift dipping into the box of dinner MREs. Instinct, born after almost ten years of living in groups under pressure, told her it might be best to stay hungry. She watched for signs of the ruling routines in this group. So far, most of these centered on the usual: telex messages, maps and charts, cleaning things—in this case, weapons—a sleep rota, and coffee.

The team also spent time exercising, mostly in the hallway because there was no room anywhere else. Equipment dominated the space in the conference room. Nobody went outside after dawn. Like vampires.

Claire occupied her time alternating between boredom and frantic activity, mostly in the form of sorting caveated messages she had no business seeing in the first place. Occasionally, she fell asleep sitting at the table. She had entered dreamland, forehead nestled on her arms when a hand grasped the back of her neck. She would have jumped out of her skin, but another hand held her shoulder in such a way that she knew she should not try to move.

A voice said quietly into her ear, "Come in the kitchen. I'll help you make coffee."

The hands released her. As she stood to precede Steve into the kitchen, she noticed Mack watching them.

No coffee was made.

Steve had been working out in the hallway for about an hour.

"You smell really bad," she told him when he let her breathe.

"You smell really good."

Somebody at the door cleared his throat. Steve broke off the kiss but did not relinquish his hold. "What Skosh?"

"Shift change, Steve."

"Fuck shift change."

Next came a silence. It was not accurate to say simply there was silence or the room was silent or even silence reigned. This was *a* silence. Steve had pinned Claire against the refrigerator at the end of the galley. She could see the entrance over his shoulder. He had been nuzzling her neck. He became still.

"It's Misha, isn't it?" he murmured in her ear.

"If you mean Mack, yes, it is."

He let go and turned.

"I am happy to see you are yourself again, Steve," said Mack. "But we are all hungry. It is time for dinner."

Nobody made coffee until Jay directed Justin to make it. Both shifts found space at the table. They broke bread, or rather, MREs, together and began the briefings.

At Charlie's direction, Skosh led the discussion.

"Borodinov will land in Naha in about an hour. He is still using the name John Earnest but has dropped his association with Brighton Associates. That company has been dissolved. I recruited and found room in the budget for one of my old teams. They flew in from Hokkaido this afternoon. They will track him to the civilian resort and let us know in real time when he arrives."

Charlie raised a quizzical eyebrow at Mara.

"Skosh," she said, "does your intelligence contain any information on Borodinov's COMSEC procedures? I searched but could not find it. Does he do an additional sweep upon arrival? If so, how soon?"

Skosh opened a packet of artificially flavored sugar and starch purporting to be apple pie, according to its label. "Our information is that he depends on his advance party to sweep three times and then get out of his way before he arrives."

Mara looked skeptical. "Nonetheless, I think I prefer to use short activations of just one device for the first fifteen minutes, despite what may be lost."

Charlie nodded approval as he tore the wrapping on the crackers that came with his beef stew. "Will your Hokkaido team be available for other assignments if we need them, Skosh?"

"Only surveillance, but yes, and for the duration."

"And the manifests?"

Skosh looked at Jay who signaled to Justin.

"Um. Um." Justin cleared his throat and wiped spaghetti sauce from his lips with a filthy kitchen towel. "It appears, from the manifests of inbound flights over the next twelve hours, that there will be representatives of all the major criminal organizations. Clarification. All the major white organizations around the world, the Yamaguchigumi, and one other Asian gang. Latin, African, and African American drug gangs are conspicuously absent. There are people from both the Sicilians and the Camorra."

Claire raised her hand.

"Yes?" said Mack.

"I thought they were the same."

"No," said Justin, with just a hint of condescension. "The Camorra are Neapolitans. From Naples." He continued on a gesture from Mack. "The Glaswegians, some Scandinavians, several out of the Balkans, and all the main Russian groups are arriving. There is even a man loosely associated with Mogilevich himself. He is due in at eight o'clock tomorrow morning."

"Drug cartels?" asked Mack.

"Not Latin ones, no."

"Which Asians again?" asked Skosh.

"Yamaguchigumi and a lesser-known group out of Malaysia."

"Is that all of them?" asked Charlie.

Justin shook his head. "Also, The Commission from the United States and several small gangs out of Brighton Beach, including the organizer of the summit, Borodinov, going by the name Earnest."

"Numbers?"

"Around thirty. Only about half will sit at the table. Borodinov has guaranteed security, but many will bring their own, notably the Yamaguchigumi and the Camorra."

Charlie turned his ice blue eyes on the babysitter. "Now is your opportunity, Skosh, to tell me why I cannot have Sergei set a simple charge on that conference room and rid the world of half its most despicable felons." He waited in his customary still manner.

Skosh cleared his throat. "Um. The Japanese are sensitive to what they see as a Western propensity to just blow up our problems. They especially object to such events taking place on Japanese soil. Historically touchy about it, shall we say. We have been asked to minimize death in this operation, most especially by firearms. I infer that explosives would be included in that prohibition. Explosions are not popular here, and the resort that would suffer the damage is Japanese-owned. The authorities are less troubled by non-firearms induced death, for example, knives and whatever it is Donovan specializes in."

He and Donovan exchanged filthy looks.

"If I may make a point here," said Frank. "I don't know what guidelines Skosh has been given by our government, but if we were to rid ourselves of so much criminal leadership, their organizations would continue to operate, but it may take us years to know who the new leadership would be."

"I was about to make the same point," said Jay.

Charlie nodded slightly. "I smell coffee. Five minutes should be enough time for everyone to be back in their seats. I will want a succinct list of the goals of each organization represented in this table. We will plan how to accomplish them without the use of firearms."

He sounded like a CEO at a board meeting.

Pandemonium. A long line at the bathroom, again, into which the specialists cut shamelessly. Claire had to make more coffee. She was late returning and could feel Charlie's displeasure. Why did she have a mental impression of a knife edge?

ELEVEN

Charlie began this session with the FBI. Justin Goodwin led the discussion with his efforts to trace the interference in the FBI computer system that had shielded Borodinov's company, Brighton Associates, the previous month.

"I want to know who hacked into our system to put that protection on the company. I did some preliminary work before we came out here, but only had a couple of weeks to use the mainframes that can help me trace it. I suspect the protection order did not come from within the United States."

"Indeed," said Jay. "I checked with the guys in the investigation division. They never heard of Brighton and did not place the protection."

"And is this also your goal, Jay?" asked Charlie.

"It is. But of course, I want all the intelligence I can gather to take back to the guys in that office, especially as it relates to this latest movement to collaborate among criminal organizations. There seems to be a different quality to it. Perhaps I am sensing a more subtle mind behind it. On the counterintelligence side, I would like to know what kind of operation Borodinov is running, how many Americans are targeted, and how many have turned. Names are imperative. Finally, I need the threat Borodinov poses to be eliminated so that my family may return home in safety."

"Of course. Skosh?"

Skosh looked up from an unsuccessful effort to squeeze peanut butter onto a cracker. Most of it landed on the table. "I need an up-to-date organizational chart of the FSB, SVR, and GRU," he said, scooping as much of the mess as he could onto the cracker. "Key players and responsibilities would be nice. Why, for example, did the GRU man have orders to preserve Sally but not Nick who, though SVR, was Sally's handler? Borodinov is also SVR and there was no such order for him. Even though we didn't know he existed at the time, it makes no sense."

"It makes perfect sense," said Sergei.

"How so?"

"There is chaos in Russia now, but there is always a way for a smart man to succeed. This was the case with the black market, and it is happening now, all over the country, in every business. I think at last a man who knows how to run intelligence has taken a position where there is scope for his talents."

"I want his name. Do you think he's GRU or FSB?"

"FSB, I think. GRU can be…" he spoke a word softly to Mara.

"Plodders?" she said. "Those who walk steady, but slow."

"Plodders," he repeated. "Not all and not always, especially not the technical people, but the leadership is not…" he squinted one eye, "imaginative. And they do not think very far into the future. FSB, like KGB, always thinks ahead. They will spend twenty years to develop a single asset. This new mind is old KGB. But what is new is that he has friends in GRU too. He has been working somewhere else for a few years,"

"Mind?" said Frank. "Not man?"

Sergei thought for a moment. "It could be a woman. Soviet intelligence had many excellent women. But it is difficult for a woman to reach a position where she can exercise this kind of talent. So, probably a man. A ruthless man."

Charlie pointed at Frank. "You are next."

"I want to know everything Sally told Borodinov, where his files are, and who has copies."

The two men stared at each other across the table. Another meeting of the mutual glare society. Claire noticed the other babysitters avoided being included in this contest by looking down at their hands. The specialists also looked away, but Mack's gaze was riveted on her.

"You have questions, Captain?"

Remembering his admonition to ask all her questions, Claire hesitated briefly, pushed away the empty food wrappers in front of her, and then ventured a caveat before standing to launch into the list that might slake her thirst for an understanding of these strange people and their alien vocabulary.

"I'm afraid my questions are not relevant to the task Charlie has for me. Not that I have any idea what that task is."

"Nonetheless, ask. What is it you wish to know?"

She took a deep breath. "Why does Charlie look like you and Mara look like Charlie? Why does Sergei act like he's about to lose Mara at any moment when she's obviously devoted to him? Why is she devoted to him? He seems more unhinged every hour. Who the hell are Borodinov, Earnest, and Brighton? Why do you and Charlie never, ever make coffee? You drink enough of it. Why can't we go outside in daylight? What's in all the footlockers? Why is everybody wearing a gun? Why am I not wearing a gun? What's with the animosity between Frank and Charlie? Why is Steve not himself when calm and arrogant, but back to himself when violent and demanding? For what reason did I have to bring two bathing suits? Why does Jay Turner talk like a character out of a Jane Austen novel? Why do men always make a pigsty out of any bathroom they enter? That one was disgusting within half an hour." She pointed down the hall.

"Is that all of your questions?"

She bit her lip. "Why does everything have to be so public?"

"Ask it."

"Is it possible to have some private ... some private time with somebody? I mean, if what I'm here to do is that dangerous, I don't want to die without ... um ... having some private time."

"Steve's blushing," said Frank.

He was blushing and angry, while Sergei and Charlie grinned wide, playful, boyish, and slightly malicious smiles at him. She knew she shouldn't have done it, but hell, it was true enough. If these were her last days, she wanted what she wanted in them. Death lasts a long time.

Mack rested his forehead on his hand, ruffling his greying blond hair, and blew his breath through pursed lips. He looked up at her.

"Charlie looks like me, Captain, because he is my son, as I am sure you have surmised. I will not answer your questions about Mara because it concerns me that you tend to make statements that, though they do not contain government secrets, do have the potential to cause damage in the wrong ears. Charlie and I do not make coffee for the same reason your boss, General Hanahan, does not make coffee. We cannot go outside in daylight because there is a direct line of sight and only a few hundred yards between this facility and the private resort where our target is staying. The footlockers contain what we need to operate. We wear guns because we live by them. The babysitters wear them so that they may be able to defend themselves against the target should we fail. I assume the military has taught you how to handle a gun. Do you think you can wear one without inadvertently threatening one of us and thus causing us to shoot you?"

She shook her head. He nodded back and continued. "I leave it to you to fathom Steve's personality as well as you can. Mr. Turner has a doctorate in English Literature and specializes in the Napoleonic period, thus his speech patterns are archaic at times. The lack of privacy and the state of the toilet are the result of our inability to secure a suitable safe place nearby in which to put the babysitters. Believe me, they tried. Regarding the toilet, I must ask why women do not clean the bathroom rather than complain about it. I see the flash in those green eyes, Captain. Did I insult you? Which is more insulting: to be told to clean or to be called disgusting? As for the bathing suits and Borodinov, have patience. Charlie will instruct you soon."

He sighed and sat back in his chair, pausing just long enough to register her shiver with a half-smile.

"I have no doubt Steve will oblige you, Captain, but do not expect privacy. Your open declaration has foreclosed that already slim possibility. It also has caused every man here, including me, to think about what it would be like to be Steve."

The ground should swallow her, her memory be erased, and all the minerals of her body used by billions of other organisms scattered by a hurricane around the world and then dispersed through the universe as subatomic particles.

TWELVE

The way they engineered it was like this. They, of course, were everybody, even Mara, even Goodwin. Frank was asleep with his arms folded on the table, but had he been awake, he would have concurred. Charlie casually joined Mack in the conference room during his watch, began a quiet conversation, and moved only his eyes toward the backroom in a signal to Steve. Steve shook his head. Charlie glared an imperative.

Mara scooted into the main toilet just before Claire, apologizing, and came out appalled at the condition it was in, advising Claire to use the other one.

"But Charlie ..."

"He's not there right now. It's safe."

Steve turned as she came into the room intent on making a beeline for the toilet.

"Do you have any idea how fucking embarrassing this is?" he railed.

She jumped once or twice, but then simply dashed into the bathroom, not closing the door because he was in it. Thus, their first intimacy was her peeing while he shouted at her.

"You don't look like you'd have trouble getting proper offers from men, so why the fuck would you demean yourself going after a man you don't know? And what do you think it does to me to be treated like some cheap trick, some male bimbo, huh? Tell me. What the fuck possessed you to say that to Misha, and in front of everybody? And quit washing your hands like you're too clean to touch the likes of me. You're going to, you know, because you asked for it, publicly, and my boss wants your wish granted. Well, I have news for you, princess, I'll still be a frog when I'm done fucking you."

"You're jealous because I'm still flying." That shut him up, briefly, so she pressed on. "And I'm going to fly the F-15."

The frightening stillness, the taught jaw, the fury in his eyes backed by a painful snarl, made her stare back at him as her mind worked. She knew now that he had flown the F-15. Of course, he did. But there was more. His name was not Steve Donovan. There had been three fighter pilots in her flight at Squadron Officer's School. One of them, a guy who made a point of looking down on the other two because he flew air-to-air missions while they were air-to-mud, did his Air Force briefing about an incident. He told the class what he'd tell them, then told them, and then told them what he had told them about the court-martial, around ten years ago now, of an F-15 pilot who had followed an order to pickle off a missile aimed at a bogey that turned out to be a civilian airliner.

She knew he could read it on her face anyway and so confirmed it for him. "Your son's name is Danny," she said.

It took a moment before he spoke, still standing in that most romantic of spots, the bathroom doorway. "I knew it wasn't a Bear or a MIG, so don't go fantasizing that I'm somehow innocent."

"And you told them that—in real time."

"It's in the record and is both why I was court-martialed and why I was acquitted. And if you so much as breathe that name to another living soul, my vengeance will be nothing compared to what Misha will do to you." He stepped away at last from the bathroom doorway to let her through, indicating with a sweep of his arm that she should precede him out of the room.

"What? No," she said. "We can't disappoint them. And your boss wants my wish granted."

"You're fucking nuts. Have it your way. Take off your clothes, lay down, and spread your legs." He unbuckled his holster and laid it on a nightstand. "And don't think about touching this. I'll get to it first."

She stood without moving, until he gave her a pointed, imperious look of command, glancing at the bed.

"Half the fun," she said, "is in the undressing. Treat me like a woman, not a whore."

"So now you're giving me orders?" He pulled her to him and covered her mouth with his own, exploring with his tongue as he unsnapped the shorts she was wearing, unhooked her bra, and efficiently had her naked before she could finish unbuttoning his shirt.

Why do men have so many tiny buttons on their shirts?

It was her last coherent thought before they were both naked and he laid her on the bed. He lost no time in plunging into her until she thought she could feel him from the other side of her tonsils.

He collapsed, spent, heart still pounding, and lay on top of her, crushing her gloriously, and biting her neck.

"Well, princess, are you satisfied?"

"Oh, sweet mystery of life at last I found you."

He raised his head and looked at her, puzzled.

"It's a quote. From a movie. Probably the kind of movie you wouldn't watch."

He grunted, rolled off, and found his trousers, then his shirt, then his holster. As he buckled it on last, he said, "I'm still a frog. Don't forget that."

THIRTEEN

"Sergei says you are very modern like me," said Mara. "He also says he does not think about you like Misha said all the men would do, but I don't believe him. Still, a woman should be able to ask for what she wants. I think the younger men agree, even Steve. Misha is just old-fashioned."

They stood side by side at the bathroom mirror, each wearing one of Claire's bathing suits, a single makeup case between them. Luckily, both had very fair complexions and green eyes. Mara had brought no makeup. They were using Claire's.

"Mara, out of curiosity, why didn't you bring a bathing suit or makeup to a beach resort?"

Mara became solemn, maybe a little sad. "Last year, I learned that when people are important to each other, they must not be foolhardy and take unnecessary risks. It is a responsibility for the loved to remain alive for those who love them. Do you see?"

Using a clean brush, Mara spread a minuscule dab of foundation on each cheek, chin, nose, and forehead. "I have been dutiful in that way, but the team, all of them, but especially my family, do not allow me to use my talents. Talents *they* have given me. They will, however, allow me to wear a bikini to attract a target. I should have gone with Steve to put those touches on that conference room in the other resort, not Sergei. It is my job, my expertise. He did it well, but I would have done better."

"So you didn't bring a bikini. I'm sorry, I didn't know or I would not have brought one for you."

"You could not have known, Claire. And you would have had no choice if you did. Do not participate in my little rebellion, I advise you. It is not safe for you to cross Charlie."

"Yeah. I get that impression."

"Still, for all their old notions," Mara said, "Charlie and Misha stayed out of their room for you and Steve. Was it as you had hoped?"

It was every bit better than she had hoped. He had been direct and demanding, she, raucous and joyful. She had escaped, ever so briefly, from the tedious realities of the conference room and the corrosive self-doubts about her infatuation with a killer.

"It was the best orgasm I've ever had," she admitted.

Mara stopped brushing mascara on an eyelash and regarded her gravely. "He kissed me once, you know, last year before I married Sergei. He terrified me."

Claire raised her eyebrows at this. Mara had confirmed a moment before that she was a specialist like the rest of them, none of whom seemed particularly safe to be around. In her view, Sergei had an especially wicked way about him, and he was this woman's beloved.

The uncomfortable self-doubts surged. "Am I a fool to want Steve?"

Mara brushed the other eyelash. "What do you mean by wanting him? Are you wanting more orgasms or just more of him?"

"I begin to think both." Claire's quick responses contrasted with the younger woman's more deliberate pauses. After what seemed an eternity, Mara snapped shut the eyeshadow case and looked at her with the still consideration Claire had seen in Charlie and Mack.

"I think perhaps you see something in Steve others do not."

"Is it a delusion?"

"If it is, but you can make it real for him, we will cooperate to help you. He has become Sergei's best friend." She paused as her eyes focused on the side of Claire's neck near the start of her shoulder. "What is this?"

Claire blushed, "Oh ... you know."

"Does Charlie know?"

"Why should he?"

Mara grabbed her wrist and pulled her down the short hallway and into the conference room. Charlie stood at one of the printers reading a telex message. Claire found herself forced to stand square before him, Mara's hands gripping her upper arms like vises from behind. He registered no surprise at that moment, but his eyes immediately locked onto the mark on her neck.

"What the fuck were you thinking, Steve?"

"You don't want to know, Charlie." Steve polished the barrel of his Beretta.

"It looks too new. Goodwin! Get over here."

Goodwin stared at it in dismay. "I'll have to work that into the legend. A party at Kadena, maybe. Last night."

Claire noticed a smirk on Steve's face. She narrowed her eyes at him.

"Can I put on a tee shirt?" she asked Charlie.

"Yes. Do. You, too, Mara, before Sergei gouges out somebody's eyes. I want both legends fully ready to be briefed in two minutes, Goodwin."

…

Goodwin had his briefing ready in a minute and a half. Skosh gave credit to the young FBI special agent. He had a real gift for weaving a plausible story around a fictitious person. Maybe it had something to do with all those computer games he played.

There was the usual critical nitpicking, bickering, and complaining over every element of Claire's, and then Mara's, legends. Mara hated the name Kristin. Tough, said Charlie.

"You're treating us like slabs of beef at a meat market," said Claire.

"Get used to it." Charlie looked down at the page that contained her legend.

"That's not an answer." Claire stamped her cute little foot.

Skosh caught himself thinking that last thought, suspected Claire would hate being called cute, wiped it from his mind, and glanced surreptitiously at Steve, knowing that any such ideas would not be popular in that quarter. Despite Donovan's efforts to appear uninterested in her, he didn't fool Skosh.

Charlie adopted the still, quiet purr that signaled danger to everybody, even Justin, but not Claire. "There can be no defiance from a slab of meat once it is dead, Captain," he said.

She opened her mouth to ignore this warning when Mack weighed in. "Claire, you have the misfortune to be considered a commodity by many in this business. Indeed, we are using you ruthlessly, not for your knowledge or talent, which are no doubt considerable, but for your appearance. We hope to attract the attention of a man who will submit you to even more unpleasant scrutiny. Once you have gained entry into his arena, we will need your courage and good sense to find the information we need. Until then, I am afraid, we must console ourselves with the joy of looking at you and give our target the same privilege."

Steve looked up at Mack, slammed home a magazine, and pulled back the slide to chamber a round.

Mack smiled.

FOURTEEN

"Emily, tell me about Hanover," said Charlie. Claire stood like a schoolgirl with her hands folded before her. "Stop clowning," said Charlie.

"Hanover is booooring. I couldn't wait to get out of there. And I hate Dartmouth boys. They think they're all that. Really, they're just a bunch of arrogant pr …."

"Stop ad-libbing. You're ordinary, not white trash." This was from Justin. He was rewarded by a particularly dark look from Steve.

She cleared her throat and stood at ease, hands behind her, feet shoulder-width apart. Her normal business voice kicked in. "It was a good place to grow up, but there just wasn't any opportunity for me. After my mom died, well, I figured I could start a career or something. Anything's better than waiting tables."

"What are some of your favorite places?" asked Charlie.

"South Street used to be. I love all the coffee shops and boutiques there and on Main, but even if I was there now, I wouldn't be able to afford anything."

"Even if you *were* there now," said Sergei. "It is conditional."

"No, Sergei," said Justin. "*Was* is perfect for the legend."

Skosh was glad to see a sense of self-preservation kick in as Justin quickly amended his reply when Sergei's brow lowered. "But you have highlighted a very important point. You see, Claire, you want to sound educated, but not to a very high level. Despite her degree, Steve's late ex-wife had some pretty low standards."

Predictably, there came a reaction. Steve launched himself at Justin, reaching him despite Skosh's effort to pull the agent out of the way in time. Charlie prevented murder, but only just, hauling Steve off his victim and throwing him back across the table. Three coffee mugs broke and several shirts were spattered. Charlie murmured in German, to no one in particular, something to the effect that women should never be allowed anywhere near an operation. They were nothing but trouble.

Skosh had been studying the language hard since he was promoted to this team, but while he understood what Charlie said, could not reply without sounding like a third-grader. So he said it in English.

"To be fair, Charlie, it's not the women who are losing their shit every ten minutes." For which remark, the response was automatic and painful.

Jay pulled Goodwin into the bathroom for first aid and some good old-fashioned supervisory truth-telling. Skosh figured he chose the bathroom hoping the fan would mask some of his more choice observations. It didn't. Everybody heard a great deal of language from Jay that was not recorded as being prevalent during Napoleonic times.

Claire stood stupefied next to the computer and watched Steve calmly check his Beretta for damage as though there had been no sudden burst of violence.

"Late? Ex? Wife?" she said, staccato, almost in a whisper.

Steve's look, as he holstered the gun, held more than an element of belligerence.

Ever the peacemaker—it was, after all, part of his job—Skosh quietly filled her in, for her sake, not Steve's. "They were divorced long ago, almost nine years. She died recently and was working for Borodinov at the time. And no, Steve did not kill her."

"Thank you, Skosh," she said sincerely.

She likes him, thought Skosh. *Poor girl*.

The session continued smoothly after the dust settled, with the kind of muted exhaustion that comes after a lightning storm. Mara knew her legend backward, answering every question flawlessly, to Charlie's evident annoyance as he narrowed his eyes at her. When he turned his back, she stuck out her tongue at him but instantly blanched when Mack shook his head in disapproval.

An earlier decision was revisited and reaffirmed to wire only Mara and with just a microphone. She wore her wedding ring in accordance with her legend as the wife of an Air Force sergeant. Charlie thought the ring would be enough to deter unwanted attention. Skosh wondered if he was blind.

"Act like an old married lady," he whispered to her. "And a little bitchy." He held up the tiny microphone at the end of a gossamer wire that led to a more substantial transmitter pack. She shrugged off the terry cloth beach coat she had been wearing. Skosh could feel all the eyes on him, of her brother, her biological father, and more especially the colorless clear eyes of the Russian with the badly set nose. Sergei was at his shoulder. He could feel him breathe.

Frank stepped into that awkward moment, to Skosh's relief. "As an old married man," he said, "I think it's best I do this."

He placed the microphone between Mara's breasts, securing it to the bridge of the bikini top, then ran the wire only a short way to her side. He tucked the transmitter into the side panel under her arm, secured the clip, and advised her to keep the wrap on as much as possible.

She was an operational specialist going out without her team and without a weapon. They would be able to hear if she were in trouble, but disaster moves faster than radio waves. The man she called father, Vasily Sobieski, had been the last member of Charlemagne to go out naked, so to speak, and he had not survived the experiment.

Skosh studied each face briefly and saw plenty of concern, but more strikingly, he saw respect. Mara's steady courage provided a better rebuke to Charlie's earlier comment about trouble caused by women than Skosh ever could have uttered. Even the always-clueless Justin dropped his eyes and stepped back as she walked past him to join Claire at the door.

And then they were through the door, two pretty young women enjoying a beach vacation. The door closed behind them, and for once, Skosh could see the weight of it all in Charlie's ice blue eyes.

FIFTEEN

"I am having difficulty with discipline," said Michael. He stood before the window as if the curtains were not drawn and as if the sunlight behind them were welcome. His father sat on the bed, propped by two pillows, with his left leg eased horizontally for the first time in hours. Michael knew he was in pain, but he needed something, anything—fast. Then he would let his father rest.

"What worries you?"

Everything would make a truthful reply, but the question forced Michael to find the priority.

"Steve. He worries me. I kicked him last night. He challenged me in front of the others."

"I hit him many times when he first joined us," said Misha. "He has difficulty with authority."

"He has become moody. The disaster in the conference room...."

"Was not a failure of your leadership. It was a failure of Jay's. That young man has no business creating a contest with someone like Steve. You may wish to speak to Jay."

"I will. But Steve is my responsibility. How do I make him less volatile?"

"Should he be? He is like Louis in his volatility. Excellent to have with you in a firefight, not so excellent when his temper sparks the firefight."

Michael could not help a brief chuckle. "But I sense he is more unpredictable than usual and I think it is the result of some internal upset. It concerns me because he is my first real friend, but more because he carries the most weight on the team."

"You carry the most weight on the team. You are not leading the team because you are my son. I asked you to take responsibility because you have the temperament."

Michael could have argued that he had the temperament because he was his cold, calculating father's son, a real chip off the old block as the English saying went, and so an inheritor of all the relationship problems that came with that legacy. He sighed and turned to face his father.

"How do I help my friend while I impose discipline as his boss?" He did not try to hide the pleading in his voice.

"Michael," said his father, "Steve recently met his son for the first time in nine years. That son is in great danger and the attraction of our enemies to young Danny as a target puts us equally in peril. Steve was already in turmoil when we came to Japan, and now he has met a young woman, a suitable, professional woman, with whom he may have much in common, and she has publicly seduced him. He cannot tell himself that she does not know better, because he killed a man in her presence the very first evening. He knows what he is and she likes him despite it. Such would confuse me."

"Did it confuse you with Alex?"

His father did not answer immediately. "She did not like me for a long time. Nothing was confusing in that."

"You would have killed her when you met her, Papa."

"No. I would not. I would have allowed the tangos to do so. Vasily intervened."

Charlie tilted his head, considering. "Louis's wife Millie was excellent for him, and so for the team, and I would have killed her when they met. I told her so."

"Ah. So you are afraid of making a mistake."

"Yes." Michael leaned over the back of a chair but did not sit down. "Missing a chord or mistakes in timing during a piano concerto worry me, Papa. An unnecessary death terrifies me. An unnecessary death among my own because I did not take steps in time to prevent it horrifies me."

"You will be worried, terrified, and horrified often, Michael. It is the nature of this business. Do not be paralyzed by error. Sometimes a mistake will work for you."

"And Steve?"

"Do you need him?"

"You know I do. Mara and Sergei are excellent but inexperienced in comparison."

"Tell him so, from time to time. No, of course, you cannot say it as a bald statement. He would not accept it. But you can find ways to assure him that you are still his friend as well as leader of the team. You might ask his advice occasionally. Only remember Steve's advice and your decision are different things. But perhaps there may be a time when his advice will keep you from making a mistake."

"And Claire?"

His father's face was white with pain, showing his desperate need for rest, but Michael's need of advice was equally imperative.

Misha opened his eyes. "Consulting with Steve will tell you if her survival is important to us."

SIXTEEN

Claire had difficulty pretending to be Emily and engaging in conversation with Kristin. This was the perfect opportunity to talk about, well everything, but especially about the men, and frankly, Steve. Before she could begin, Mara shut the conversation down by explaining a thing called a directional parabolic listening device and that it meant they were going to have to stick with their legends as they walked along the sparsely populated beach.

A typhoon was brewing in the Pacific and most people on the island had responsibilities that depended on its final track. Aircraft could evacuate, or the base might receive evacuated airplanes from other places in the region. Vacations were postponed. In the meantime, the water became turbulent. Wind forces far away sent it slapping to the Okuma shore in choppy intervals.

People who never attended high school don't have old high school chums to laugh and talk with about old times. Mara smiled her calm smile and tried a few innocuous comments instead of the irreverent and even bawdy conversations Claire wanted and was used to. In a too-quiet moment, as they approached the wet sand and looked out on banks of clouds off-shore, she devised a way to save at least the appearance of their legends and pry some information out of Mara at the same time.

"Kristin, do you remember that boy I went out with one time in junior year? The one with the dreamy brown eyes?"

Mara's look gave a priceless study in 'What in hell are you talking about?'

"You know who I'm talking about. Remember? I had such a crush on him and everybody in school knew it. I couldn't hide a thing."

Mara caught on. "Oh. Yeah. Him. I remember now. What was his name?"

"Scott. I couldn't get him out of my head. I wonder what he's doing now."

"Probably working at something or other."

"Do you think he's married?" Claire paused to dip her feet in the foaming water. A wavelet soaked her to the knees.

"No. Do you?" Mara dipped her toes, briefly, and they walked on, finally looking like their legends as they chatted.

"No. Somebody told me he's not married. He was, but not anymore."

"Ah, yes. I've heard that, too."

"Do you think if I go back there sometime and see him again—I don't know—do you think we'd hit it off?"

Mara took a moment to think about the question and put her answer in the context of their legends. "Do you mean you would like to marry him? But you hardly know him."

"I don't know what I want, Kristin. And anyway, these are hypothetical questions. I would not presume he'd even ask. You knew him much better back then. You could tell me all about him."

Mara stopped and laughed out loud, a musical belly laugh that inspired Claire to join in and would convince any would-be listener that they were exactly who they seemed to be.

"First, Emily, remember when I told you Scott kissed me that time? Please do me a favor and never mention it to my Robbie. He's insanely jealous and I don't want him getting any ideas. As I told you, I never felt anything for Scott, but it would be awkward if Robbie knew about that incident."

At this point, Claire remembered the wire. "Um, you have something ..." she pointed at Mara's chest. "Some insect ..."

Mara opened her eyes in alarm, thought a moment, shrugged, and said, "I'm sure no one will pay any attention for at least half an hour."

She was wrong.

...

Sergei heard everything except Mara's last statement about her lack of attraction to Steve because he was already on his way to the room where Steve slept.

After Skosh helped Charlie pull them apart, Charlie pounded a fist into Sergei, careful to avoid an area that had been badly damaged the year before, but painfully enough.

"What the fuck Sergei?" Steve held a pillowcase to his bleeding lip.

"You kissed her. You kissed Mara!"

"What? No, I never …" The memory showed on his face and he closed his eyes, then rolled them upward. "That was fucking last year, you idiot. Before you married her. I would never touch her now."

Sergei gave him a skeptical look. "But if I die?"

"No! What do you want from me? Some kind of pledge? A vow of chastity? She's all yours. Even in death. I won't touch her. Ever."

Charlie could see Sergei didn't believe it any more than he did, but he gave in with good grace and a mumbled apology and went back to the conference room.

"Go back to sleep," Charlie told Steve.

Papa is right, he thought. It's not about what Steve will or will not do; it's about what we all think he will do. Either Claire or castration could solve it. Now, how to get Steve to see it that way and choose one.

…

"So tell me about him," said Claire. "I remember he was pretty arrogant and didn't talk much, but that could be because he was such a jock."

"Jock?" Mara struggled to understand American high school English.

"Yeah, you know, he was an athlete, wasn't he?"

"Oh yes. So is Robbie and he is the same way. Very full of himself and does not always want to talk. I think they are all like that, such men."

"I suppose you're right. What about girls? Did he have a lot of girlfriends?"

"I know that Scott is—was—respectful and a little bit distant around his team captain's girlfriend because he knew the captain would beat the shit out of him if he were not. I am sure he behaved the same way with the girlfriends of all his teammates."

"But what about other girls?"

Mara rolled her eyes. "He never misses—missed—a chance even when it was a pain in the ass for everybody else. That is why we were all astonished one time when he pretended he was not interested in a pretty girl who liked him."

"Pretended?"

"Yes. He was not a thinker, in my opinion, except about his sport. But around that girl, he was always watching her and thinking. But I am wondering, Emily, why you thought so much of him. He reminded me of a primitive barbarian."

Claire stared at her briefly. "And Robbie is not?"

"Ah. You have me there," admitted Mara. "But tell me why you were so attracted to Scott?"

"I don't know why. He was certainly handsome and seemed powerful. Maybe these physical things called up some deep and primitive instinct in me, but I think there was more to my attraction. I wanted to know him better and to share so much with him. I think I told you once that I felt foolish about the whole thing."

Mara nodded and turned her still, slow smile on Claire, who wanted more of this interesting conversation—but they had arrived.

"What a pretty place!" said Claire. "Do you think this is the civilian beach we are supposed to avoid? Should we turn back?"

"Not yet. Let's see if we can get somebody to buy us a cold drink. I am so warm and did not bring any money. Look, there is a beach bar just up there and two men who look Western. Maybe ..."

"Him?" Claire murmured as they slogged through dry sand.

"Yes."

"Tall and skinny or short and fat?"

"Tall and skinny."

SEVENTEEN

"He wasn't fat, actually, not short and fat. More like, short and wide, but it wasn't fat, and he wasn't all that short." Claire stood at one end of the conference table facing Mack at the other end. Her briefing was for everyone this time. Both shifts had been kept awake for it while they ate their recommended lunchtime MREs, which after only one day already tasted like salted cardboard.

"What, precisely, did Borodinov say to you?" said Mack.

She could tell he was a bit testy. He sat at an angle, with his left leg held up by an extra chair pressed into service for the purpose. He must be in pain, she thought and quashed the smart-aleck reply on her lips.

"He said I was like a little bird, a swallow, and would I come back this evening. He asked if I had a job right now and I said no, so he hinted he might know of a good job for me. I told him I was interested."

"Sergei?" Mack said when Sergei raised a hand.

The Russian was holding his gut and Charlie worried he had ruptured something, while Mara wondered why her husband seemed subdued.

"Swallow is old KGB term for honey trap," said Sergei.

Sage nods all around.

"What does that mean?" demanded Claire.

Mack gestured for Skosh to answer, and the babysitter hid behind his professional training to deliver the news in as businesslike a tone as possible.

"A honey trap is a sexual encounter that can be used to compromise a target so as to gain information or cooperation or turn an agent. The Soviets personalized the term to indicate the woman, or sometimes man, who acted as bait."

"Do you mean I'm going to have to have sex with that stick figure?" Her tone of voice indicated Claire did not seem pleased with the idea.

"May I explain it?" Frank looked to Mack before proceeding and when he nodded, continued. "It appears that Borodinov used a guy named Nick Beridze to groom Sally, Danny's mom, for the job. He became her lover and prepared her for Borodinov to use with particular targets. She was already deeply enmeshed in the game by a friend named Linda Bertram, and was not aware … she was not sufficiently…"

"She was fucking stupid," said Steve.

After an awkward pause, Frank said, "At least one of Borodinov's prospects must have paid off. The man thus trapped is successful, and perhaps political. He employs a car and driver and never came into the house. Danny, Steve's son, is certain of that. The target sent the car to pick her up while Linda and Nick stayed in the house ostensibly babysitting the boy."

"But she went off in the car to have sex with some guy?" asked Claire. "That's the job he has for me? He's some kind of pimp?"

"Essentially, yes," said Frank. "Everything they did will have been recorded and then used as leverage against the target to gain his cooperation. He must be an extremely valuable asset to make Borodinov target the child. Word in our circles is that they are searching very hard for Danny. Borodinov must think the boy can identify the man, which would render him useless as an asset. They are beside themselves with worry. The more they worry, the more certain we are that the asset is a big one, and the more danger Danny is in."

"But then, what does he want with me?"

It was Charlie who answered. "Sally has been dead for several weeks now. Borodinov will need to replace her soon, to keep his target happy and working."

"So about this Nick person? Am I going to have to, um, deal with him? And what about Linda? How should I act around her?"

"They will not be a problem."

"Not a problem. Does that mean they're dead, too?" She was catching on to the way they used language.

Claire took the lack of answer for the answer that it was but could not leave it alone.

"Who killed all these people?"

Mack broke the awkward silence. "Are you worried that Borodinov is a deranged killer who shoots his allies?"

"Something like that, yes."

"He is not. He is technically not a killer at all, but he has killed and remains capable despite his injured arm."

"So who …?"

Mack sighed in probable regret for his admonition that she ask all her questions. "Charlemagne killed them, at my direction, and it was I, personally, who executed Sally."

She had begun to consider him to be a kindly older gentleman, a kind of uncle, what with the limp and the cane and the obvious pain he was in, the greying temples, the extreme courtesy, and the deference paid him by everybody else. She decided she didn't need to know who the hell Charlemagne was.

Mack dropped his chin, exasperated. He swept his hand across the table, pointing to each specialist in turn. "We are Charlemagne."

Claire was certain she had not spoken the question.

Skosh cleared his throat. "Can we go back to short and wide? Was he Asian?"

"Maybe part Asian," she said. "He had dark hair, a wide face, and dark eyes, maybe a suggestion of the fold."

"Any tattoos? Especially on the hands."

"I did not see any. He has only four fingers on one hand, or rather, three and a thumb…"

"Which hand?"

"Um. The left. Yes, I'm sure it was the left."

"Little finger?"

Claire nodded.

"Yakuza," said Skosh. "Did he say anything to you?"

"No. But he couldn't take his eyes off Mara."

"Did you hear a name at all?"

Claire thought for a moment. "Key something."

"Did the something end in *San* or *Sama*?"

"Two syllables. *Sama*."

"*Kyaku-sama*. Who said it, short and wide or Borodinov?"

"Borodinov."

Skosh sat back, all eyes riveted on him.

"We're waiting," said Charlie.

"It is not his name. It's a term of respect for someone who may be a customer or who has favors at his disposal, but you do not know his name. Borodinov does not know the name and has been told to use this. The yakuza, perhaps the Yamaguchigumi but it could be others, want something from him, probably in return for allowing his conference to take place here. They will expect him to provide it."

After a significant pause, Mack said, "I see there is more. Tell us all of it."

Skosh looked up at them all, sweeping the table, only momentarily resting on Mara. "This is largely conjecture."

"Based on your experience in intelligence?"

"That, and my acquaintance with a few Asian criminals. The heaviest money maker here, besides drugs to the West and real estate, is women. Specifically, captive women, usually young girls from the PI, the Philippines." He looked down and had difficulty looking up again, and so brought his hands to the table and stared at them. "Mara would be a prize beyond price."

EIGHTEEN

It was Skosh who put up a fight, a verbal one which, in that setting, was a refreshing change. "She cannot go unarmed! They won't be in bathing suits. She needs to wear the Glock. I'd give her a machine gun if there were someplace to hide it!"

The sheer vehemence with which he said it, screamed it into the face of one of the most ice-cold killers anybody in the room had ever encountered, took everybody by surprise. Skosh's face turned red with rage and he was spitting by the time he reached the last few syllables.

"They are young women on a beach holiday," said Charlie. His stillness contrasted starkly with Skosh's near hysteria. "They must not wear anything bulky or meant to conceal. She cannot wear the Glock."

"I have a shrug she can wear," said Claire. "It may help to conceal something." When she brought it out, she conceded that it was too light and gauzy to conceal much.

It was Mack who remembered a small .25 backup pistol in one of the footlockers. He directed them to it, then went to his room to lie down.

They all agreed the little firearm was just this side of useless but better than nothing. After much debate on where it should be hidden so that a casual touch or a friendly arm around her would not reveal it, Sergei fashioned a holster out of surgical tape and attached it with staples from the Footlocker of Useful Things (FUT) inside the front left side of the waistband of a pair of black palazzo trousers. The shrug and the way she carried a small clutch purse in her left hand helped conceal the bulge, made more inconspicuous by the dark color of her outfit.

"All of Borodinov's guests have arrived," said Frank as he arranged the wire in her bra the way he had done earlier with the bikini. You will be his guests in the main dining room. The noise may make it difficult for us to hear you at times. If there is a problem, be loud about it."

"Someone should be there," said Sergei. "I can stay at the bar."

"Borodinov went to prison for killing a man who should have been you, Sergei. Not a good idea." Steve slouched even further in his chair, pretending not to notice Claire's sea-green semitransparent tank top.

Justin spoke up, hesitation in his voice. "I can go. If Skosh will help with the language, I'll get myself a room number on the hotel's computer and I'll look like one of the western hoodlums. They'll be too jet-lagged to notice that I'm alone. I'll look aloof and tough and I'll go armed."

"Not with that coat, you won't," said Steve. "It screams FBI. Here, try this one." He tossed over the coat that had been on the back of his chair.

It was a bit loose in the shoulders, but it fit overall and concealed Justin's sidearm nicely. Sergei narrowed his eyes at Steve, who returned the glare and pointed to his still swollen lip.

Skosh stepped in, again, and again with heat. "For God's sake Pavlenko, when are you going to start trusting your wife?"

"I trust her. I do not trust any other man."

"She can lick just about any other man. One kick from her would put Goodwin in the hospital for a week. She's not exactly a delicate flower, for fuck's sake. But if it helps, I'll go, too. I can blend even better than Justin and I'll report to you if he so much as leers at her. How's that?"

Sergei took a deep breath, winced, and hid the wince when he noticed Mara's puzzled look. "It will be good. You are both useless in a fight, but with two, maybe ..."

"Do not show any recognition of each other," said Jay. "And I will take your credential now, Goodwin." When Justin hesitated, Jay said, "The last thing you need is an ID on you. Also, this way when we find your body, I can throw it down nearby so your next of kin will know you died in the line of duty."

"Always the compassionate leader, Turner," said Steve.

As Frank fitted wires to Justin and Skosh, Charlie briefed everybody going out.

"This should be just dinner. Borodinov will continue to lure you into working for him, Claire. He will make it sound grandiose, perhaps patriotic. We know he has pretended to be with the FBI in the past. He has a small team of heavies with him, four of them, but he will make sure they are not visible. If he talks about the man he wants you to meet—that is how he will put it—try to get him to tell you about him. Don't act too interested but ask a few unrelated questions. Do not, under any circumstance, give him your usual hundred-question interrogation."

He looked at Mara. "Continue using Skosh's excellent advice and be very married and more than a little bitchy." He repeated the last sentence in German so that he could add just the right nuance. "Kyaku-sama may or may not be at dinner, but he will be in the room, perhaps shopping you to his superiors. Stay aware."

Charlie closed his eyes, opened slowly, and tightened his jaw. "Goodwin, don't say anything to anybody. Nod, act tipsy, smile like you don't understand but want to be polite. There will be multiple languages spoken in that room. Above all, do not respond to anything said in English. Act stupid.

"Skosh, we need a word that will bring us running with explosives and automatic rifles. It should be clear over the wire even with background noise. Something other than fuck. You are as bad as Steve sometimes."

"How about jolly? If I can't shout it into the mike, I'll work it into a sentence, like, 'What a jolly big knife you're sticking in me.'"

"That will work." Charlie turned away and went to wake his exhausted father, as Mara and Claire left the room.

The women carried strappy sandals in their hands as they made their way down to the wet sand at the waterline. Busy with their own thoughts, they walked at a solemn pace as though the freshening surf from off-shore had dampened their holiday.

"You're awfully quiet, Kristin," said Claire.

"I am worried about Robbie." Mara took a moment to form a legend-friendly way to explain it. "He was badly injured last year and I know he is not feeling well."

"I am sorry. It is hard to see somebody you love in pain."

"I feel it that way, of course, but there is more. His job is important. If he cannot perform it …" She left the thought hanging, counting on Claire's ability to comprehend. Had she been with them long enough now to understand the stakes?

To Claire, the cockpit seemed suddenly so much safer in comparison. Any cockpit, even a fighter, even in battle. She whispered, "I see."

NINETEEN

"I have come to tell you that Jay asked the General to send a doctor to check Sergei." Michael pushed back the hair that had fallen across his forehead. He did not sit down but elected to pace slowly across the limited floor space at the foot of the bed.

"Surely, he is only bruised."

"Still, I must be certain."

Misha did not answer and kept his eyes closed, willing his son to leave the room.

"Papa, as long as the doctor is here, he can look at your hip, also."

"My hip is fine."

"Nonetheless, it is good to make use of the doctor while he is here."

When there was no answer, Michael said, "I promised Alex …"

"I am on the other side of the world and still that woman interferes with me."

Michael turned his head to hide that he was fighting a smile. "You could have stayed home and given it more time."

"Do you wish I had?"

"No. I am glad you are here. I worry; that's all."

"If I were at home I would go mad with all the women trying to coddle me. The way you are coddling Sergei."

"I am not coddling him. I am the one who hit him. He has serious damage from last year. I cannot afford for him to drop at a critical moment. I must know he will not fail."

"Did you come here for my help in absolving yourself of being too soft?"

"I begin to understand why Frank thinks you are a wizard, Papa. How did you know? I did not know my real purpose until this minute."

Misha elected to change the subject. "When will the women arrive there?"

"In ten minutes."

"I will join you in the conference room in five. Is there coffee?"

"Of course. I will make sure it is fresh."

...

"You will be handling a very special agent, Emily. You will like him. The pay and benefits are excellent when you are working for the government." Borodinov, who was using the name John Earnest, took a minimal sip of his wine while asking the waiter to again fill Claire's.

"Agent? What, like a spy? For Uncle Sam? How exciting! Don't you think so, Kristin?"

"Working for the federal government isn't all it's cracked up to be, Emily. The recruiters told Robbie all kinds of shit. We're still broke."

Claire marveled at Mara's ability to nail the role she had been saddled with. Everything about her was perfect. The example challenged her to improve her own game. "Tell me about him, John. Is he gorgeous? Like, lantern jaw and all that?"

"He is. Very handsome." This time Borodinov did drink some of his wine. It helped him stomach his lies.

"What about his eyes? I love a man with beautiful eyes. Yours aren't bad either. Are his eyes as interesting? Let me see, what color are yours? Nice. Hazel with flecks of green. Perfect. Mine are green. Yours are great, but frankly, I like brown eyes. Does he have brown eyes? Deep brown eyes?"

Borodinov could not help himself. The woman's chatter bounced through his brain, a constant game of pinball against his heart. Anoushka liked his eyes. Once. He wondered if his asset would put up with this woman's way of talking. And talking.

"No," he said. "They're blue."

No doubt the asset would beat her into silence. He hoped that would happen before he lost patience and put a bullet in her the way he had Anoushka and the man he thought was her lover. He needed Emily alive, but some things just cannot be borne.

"Oh. Well, that's okay," said Claire. "I'm sure they're pretty anyway. A lot of women are into blue eyes. I've always thought them a bit cold. I mean, I know this guy with blue eyes who could freeze an ice cube in a lit furnace with one look, but I bet your guy is a real sweetie. When can I meet him?"

She noticed he was swilling his wine now, in gulps, and wincing whenever the bad arm inadvertently moved.

"Hello, Earnest-san, may I join you?" Short and Wide, aka Kyaku-sama, pulled out the chair next to Mara, across from Claire. Borodinov gestured for him to sit.

Claire stood quickly but without being too abrupt. She smiled at Kyaku-sama. "While you two are catching up, pardon us girls while we visit the little girls' room. Kristin?"

Mara wasted no time moving away from the man. As they walked through the crowded room and down the narrow hall to the toilets, Claire murmured. "Don't sit next to him. We'll trade. Let me suggest it."

"Why?"

"I thought I saw something."

TWENTY

The first thing the flight surgeon, Captain Saul Kramer, saw when he entered the conference room was the excessive number of guns. Everybody wore one, and at least three larger weapons lay on the table in pieces. There was a conversation going on, in two languages, between a voice coming over a radio on a table by the wall and various people in the room. He was told to sit. He complied.

The voice on the radio spoke halting German with an American accent. A balding man with big eyes translated what was said back into the radio in English.

"I'm translating for Skosh, Justin. He's speaking to you in German because he doesn't want to be seen speaking English and you should not. He says he does not like the look of the room or the people in it. He figures Short and Wide is up to something. He is talking to you *auf Deutsch* so as not to look like he's talking to himself. Skosh says it's all jolly in about two minutes. Do you agree?"

This made no sense at all to Saul.

Another non-native German speaker said yes over the radio. Saul winced a little. How hard could it be to speak one syllable correctly?

"You better not be lying, Skosh," said Baldy. "Right. Where?" He looked up at the blond man standing on the other side of the table rapidly reassembling one of the guns. "Skosh recommends the parking lot, Justin. Here's his plan. You're a friend of Robbie. You and he just drove up to see the girls. Somebody's watching the kids. Ad-lib and get them the hell out of there. Skosh will be behind you. The Mercedes will be there…wait."

The blond man was looking at Saul, who had the sense to find his stare uncomfortable.

"Did you bring a car, your car?" the man said in English.

Saul nodded and was told to describe his car on the radio. He was to drive alone, only a couple hundred yards, they said, and he should leave his bag here. Then he and the bald man were pushed out the door by four others who followed them. One used a cane and was favoring his left leg. The other three carried the newly reassembled rifles.

Baldy briefed him on the way to his car. "Your name is Robbie. A blonde woman will greet you as her husband and kiss you. She'll get in front with you and another couple with her will climb in the back." He stuck an earpiece in Saul's ear, shoved a small box in his pocket, and said, "Go."

…

Emily's bright smile as she and Kristin returned from the ladies' room deepened Borodinov's scowl.

"John, we're trading places so I can see you without getting a crick in my neck. I want to see your beautiful hazel eyes. I'm sure Mr. Kyaku-sama won't mind looking at Kristin for a while, and I promise I won't tell Robbie, Kristin. He's terribly jealous, John. I had a hell of a time getting him to let her come and have a holiday with me, and he's only just down Highway 58."

Borodinov fumed as he downed more wine. He had his own plans and it seemed so did everybody else. Kyaku-sama had something in his pocket. He kept his hand there and Borodinov could only guess. Probably a syringe. He had told the man to have patience. If he rushed this it could blow up in their faces and they would lose both women. Damn him.

"Kristin! Hey! Robbie said you might be here." A young man wearing an expensive sports coat strode up to the table. "Hi, Emily. We drove up and somebody at the desk on the other side said he thought he saw you walking this way. I've been standing over there seeing if I could spot you."

He looked at Borodinov. "Hi, I'm Brad." He held out his hand, forcing Borodinov to stand and shake it, his shoulder screaming at the movement, his face as bland as he could make it despite the pain and fury coursing through him. He wanted to shoot the lot of them, starting with this loud, gauche, obnoxious American.

Kyaku-sama also stood to shake hands while Emily made the introductions.

"Jill's watching the kids," said Brad. "Robbie brought a cooler with snacks and beer. I hope you didn't eat already."

"No, we haven't even ordered yet," said Emily. "You don't mind, do you, John? Maybe we can meet up again tomorrow after your conference."

Borodinov forced himself to nod, mutely at first, then shook himself into a more cheerful countenance. "That will be great. Five o'clock? At the beach bar? I hope to see you both then." He emphasized 'both' as a sop to Kyaku-sama, but he wanted to kill him as well as everybody else.

Emily and Kristin rewarded him with dazzling smiles.

Kyaku-sama scowled like a thundercloud as they waved farewell, turned away, and proceeded with calm purpose to the parking lot. Both men followed casually a few yards behind and signaled to their associates in the room.

The car waited, its driver standing on the passenger side, door open, engine running.

"Hey, Robbie!" shouted Justin, every bit the annoying American. "I found them. Let's get us some brewskies."

Saul could feel the shadowy figures around them as his passengers climbed into the car. He dutifully kissed his purported wife Kristin, a breathtaking blonde, ran to the driver's side, and put the car in gear almost before the other couple had closed their doors.

They passed a Mercedes before the gate. It followed them back into the military resort, into safety he hoped, but then he remembered the rifles.

TWENTY-ONE

Saul blinked in the pandemonium. "You'll have to excuse them, Doctor," said Baldy. "The adrenaline is up. It'll take a little while to subside. Then they'll be almost normal. My name is Frank Cardova, by the way."

Saul gave him a weak smile.

"You kissed her!"

The statement came from a broken-nosed man with light eyes. Probably Russian, Saul decided from the accent. He knew the type. The tone was unfriendly.

"He saved her ass, Sergei," said a brown-haired man with rather remarkable eyes. "So did Goodwin and Skosh."

"So did Claire," said his make-believe wife Kristin. "She knew something was wrong."

"Coffee is ready," announced an African-American man, also wearing a sidearm in a shoulder holster.

More pandemonium as everybody grabbed mugs. One was pressed into Saul's hand, full of hot black coffee. A tall Asian man walked in the door. Frank pressed a freshly poured mug into his hand and patted him on the back. Saul guessed this was Skosh.

Two people in the room, though they smiled slightly, were not as boisterous. They remained quite still. One was the man with the cane, the other a younger version of him, who had pressed Saul and his car into service. The older one spoke. His accent explained the German he was hearing.

"We are grateful to you, Skosh, to Justin, and to the Doctor. It was well done. They are safe for the moment." He turned toward the red-haired woman. "Claire, I must ask what you saw that gave you concern."

She had been warming her hands, steadying them more likely, around her mug as she sat to his right. "I saw somebody give Short-And-Wide a thing. He quickly put it in his pocket and then kept his hand in that pocket. It wasn't a gun. But it wasn't something good. He acted furtive about it. Then he came to our table and kept holding onto whatever it was in his pocket." She looked at Justin. "Thank you. You have a gift for making things up."

"I had help." He indicated Skosh and the others.

"Enough babysitter congratulations," said the younger blond man. "Doctor, I am afraid you must stay with us tonight. It will not be safe for you to return to the base. I apologize for the situation. We are short of space. I hope you will not mind."

Saul understood the subtext as being 'tough shit if you mind'. He nodded graciously and said, "I am expected on duty tomorrow morning."

The African American picked up the wall phone and called the General. Not the base, not the Flight Surgeon's Office, the General.

Saul thought the redheaded woman seemed familiar. After studying her for a few minutes he remembered—the tanker pilot with a bad knee. He had diagnosed a torn ACL. A Navy surgeon at the hospital on Camp Lester took over from there to fix it. He wrenched his eyes away in time to see a filthy look from him with the pretty eyes and another look of impatience from the blond guy—son of. The filthy looks especially were wearing on him.

"Doctor," said Blondy, "we would like you to examine one of the team. Sergei ...," he jerked his head toward the hallway.

"I am fine," said the recipient of Blondy's less than solicitous concern.

"Do you prefer to be examined here, on this table? We can clear it." He again indicated the hallway. It was as obligatory as any military order.

Both Blondy and Kristin followed Saul and the patient to a pigsty of a bedroom in total disarray and unpleasantly aromatic. Saul took a deep breath before going in. It didn't help. He still had to breathe once inside. The Russian with the broken nose pulled his shirt out of his belt and lifted it.

"Take off your holster, Sergei," said Blondy.

The young woman held the holster as Saul examined the bruised torso and a couple of relatively recent bullet wounds. Blondy gave the history.

"Wait. You shot him?"

"No," said Blondy. "His friends shot him. We were his enemies. We broke his nose. You can see that can't you?"

How does one answer this?

"And this large bruise is from …?"

"I punched him in the gut to stop his attack on Steve."

"Who is?"

"My best friend," said the patient. "He kissed my wife."

Saul swallowed. Hard.

"You heard that? Why were you listening?" said the woman.

"You were in danger. Of course, I listened."

"Oh, Sergei." She leaned over and kissed him.

Blondy looked disgusted at the sentiment. "Do you think it could be more than just a bruise, Doctor?"

Saul was tempted to argue that a hematoma four inches across on a torso peppered with the scars of old bullet wounds could hardly be termed 'just a bruise,' but he elected to answer the underlying question rather than the words it came in.

"He will be okay. I don't think anything vital is affected." It occurred to him as he said this that the man who hit the Russian, the man standing in front of him, must have known what he was doing.

Blondy then took Saul by the arm and pulled him to the door. "I have another for you, Doctor." His English was American, but he pronounced 'Doctor,' as a German would. "This may be delicate. He is convinced nothing is wrong."

"Sounds like a pilot," said Saul. "If they complain, it's serious, because it means they can't fly."

"Just so."

Again, he sounded German. In the hallway, Saul asked, "What should I call you?"

"Charlie."

"And this new patient?"

"Mack."

The man lay along the full length of the bed, fully clothed, even to the tie, though the shirt was not precisely clean. The holster and its occupying semiautomatic gleamed, however. His head lay raised on an arrangement of pillows. He opened his eyes and closed them again in annoyance.

"I told you, Michael…" he said in German with an obscure Austrian accent.

"I have been told you are experiencing more pain lately," interrupted Saul, also in German. "Let me see that there is no danger. I may be able to help with the pain."

"Charlie will explain to you that we do not take narcotics during an operation."

"There are non-narcotic pain remedies these days that are very effective. They cannot be used long, but they can get you through until you are in a position to get the rest you need, Sir." Saul didn't know why he added the sir at the end. The man was a civilian, even wearing his hair a trifle long by modern standards, but there was something in the blue eyes that demanded it. "Please let me examine the site of your pain, Sir, and then I can prescribe."

Charlie interrupted. "Doctor, we have no way to fill a prescription, but we do have antibiotics with us. Please, just check for infection."

Mack sighed. "Michael, it is my hip that is affected, not my mind, I will answer for myself." He heaved himself to a stand and bared his left hip for Saul's inspection.

It had been a fearful wound, devastating in its breadth, and must have destroyed the joint itself. The scars were red and angry, but not hot.

"When and how did this happen?" he asked.

"It has been five weeks."

Saul looked up. "And how?"

Both men stood looking at him. He could almost see 'guess' written on their faces. He had become so used to the presence of their guns that he initially failed to make the connection. He cleared his throat.

"Whoever did the surgery did an impressive job of restoration. I assume there was enough bone left to allow a joint replacement?"

"Yes, by my daughter-in-law."

An Austrian Adams Family on a Japanese island in the Pacific doing God-knew what but most assuredly nothing good, Saul concluded. He prescribed rest, knowing it was unavailable to any of these people, but the diagnosis pleased Charlie whose sigh could be translated as 'Is that all?'

Saul determined he would sneak out before the shooting started.

TWENTY-TWO

Claire trudged into the silent conference room on her way to the coffee machine. She heard the sound of running water from the bathroom behind her. All shifts were awake now. Technically. Reality would depend on coffee. Three of the four people at the table were still asleep in their chairs, heads nestled in their arms. Two snored. Jay was awake, reading messages.

She pointed to the blond head snoring at the end of the table and raised her eyebrows. Jay nodded as if to say it surprised him as well but indicated his watch and the room at the end of the hall. It was all the language Claire needed to understand that Charlie had let Mack sleep a double shift. Probably because the doctor had said something.

The doctor snored also. Skosh never snored and was adept at sleeping this way. She continued her trudge into the kitchen. There was no coffee. She made a pot and stood before the machine, willing its designer to enter a time warp and make it brew faster. She could hear voices at the table beginning to murmur. A pair of arms in a white shirt with filthy cuffs encircled her waist from behind and Steve began nibbling her ear.

"I want you again," he whispered, then "Fuck. What is it Doc?"

"The blond guy, Charlie, wants to know if there is coffee. He sent me to ask."

"Of course he did." Then loudly, "Fuck you, Charlie!"

Loud laughter from the room made Claire turn around in surprise. "Is that Charlie laughing?"

"It happens," said Steve. "Not like it used to, but every once in a while still. I don't know why he's less tightly wound now, but he is."

"What do I tell him?" said Saul.

Claire poured a mug from the first finished pot and handed it to him. "Give him this." It bought them less than a second.

"Is there coffee?" said Sergei.

"I thought you were with Mara," Steve said through clenched teeth.

"She kicked me out. Said she wants to sleep." He was all indignation. "Also, Misha is in the conference room now."

Claire poured another two mugs and took one to Mack before sitting down in her usual place. It took a few minutes for the group to decide where the doctor should sit. It had been less than forty-eight hours, but their positions at the table had become set in stone by force of habit and no one was shifting. The extra chair supported Mack's bad leg.

Charlie solved the problem by fiat, pointing the doctor to the chair in front of Mara's computer. "I will allow her to sleep a while longer. Sergei will tell her what she needs to know."

Claire was pretty sure Mara would not appreciate the concession.

While Saul was grateful for the hot coffee in his hand, he liked cream and sugar, was told there was none, mentioned leaving now that it was morning, was told to stay for the briefing, and continued to receive narrow looks from the Russian.

The noise level grew as voices became louder and two telex printers added their clatter, producing streams of paper and ink.

He was glad to see Mack looking much better thanks to Charlie spending the night at the table to allow his father more time to sleep. It was always gratifying, though rare, when patients and their families took his advice. Saul had spent the night the same way at the table because though he had been assigned to a room, it contained only a single bed and there was no way he would deny either Jay or Frank their turn in it. Not when he would be home in a couple of hours anyway.

And then he learned he would not be home anytime soon.

They did say the word 'soon,' but he heard an indefinite quality in the tone in which it was said.

"I don't even have a toothbrush with me," he said.

Sergei produced one from something called a FUT. Donovan, the guy with the long eyelashes, translated it as the Footlocker of Useful Things.

"Look, Doc," said Skosh, waving a sheaf of printed paper. "Sit down and shut up and all will be revealed when we get to it."

Saul didn't think Charlie could get more still, but he sat like a statue as he stared at Skosh, who waved the paper back at him and said, "Over to you, Boss Man."

Charlie's cold, slow blink did not make him seem more human. He nodded minimally at Jay Turner, the FBI guy, who began the meeting.

"Claire's intelligence that Borodinov's mark has blue eyes has allowed us to narrow the list from fifteen possibles to six. Three are local politicians. One is a U.S. congressman; another a prominent businessman; and the last one is the scion of a wealthy North Carolina family with political leanings."

"What is number five's business?" asked Mack.

"He trades pork belly futures."

"He is not the one. So five. Can you handle five?"

"Two would be optimal."

Mack was good at the statue thing, too. Jay dropped his eyes.

"Okay. Three," said Jay. "With difficulty, we can keep three iced while we find out which one it is."

It was all pretty standard staff meeting fare, except that Saul understood none of it. He revised the last thought, realizing he rarely understood staff meetings, what with unspoken subtexts and private animosities, so this was just as standard as any he'd ever attended, but without medical jargon.

Charlie nodded to Skosh next.

"So I heard from my old team. They've been tailing Borodinov continually. Pretty soft duty considering he hasn't budged from the resort since he got there, but they've had eyeballs on him almost the entire time, and consequently, on those around him, including Kyaku-sama, or as Claire calls him, Short and Wide.

"They saw the whole thing in the parking lot—including me—which is unfortunate because I had led them to believe I was in DC. They are pissed at me for the deceit, which I think is rich coming from them, and they are telling me they don't like the guy who took over from me even though I appointed him specifically with them in mind...."

"Get on with it," interrupted Charlie with a sigh.

Skosh paused. "Kyaku-sama has an entire surveillance team watching the doctor's car, twenty-four-seven. He cannot leave Okuma without being taken."

TWENTY-THREE

"Taken?" said Saul. "Taken where?"

"Taken to where they can extract from you who we are and where we are," said Charlie.

"Well, obviously I wouldn't tell them anything." Saul became a bit apprehensive about the stillness in the room and in Charlie and Mack particularly.

"Do you think so?" said Mack. "Do you understand how they will ask?"

"You're saying I've landed in some macabre scenario of spy versus spy? I don't know anything."

"You know enough to make you dangerous to us."

"Now hold on," said Skosh. "The Doc is not a danger to you. He's a danger to himself, but not to you. He'll just stay here till it's all over. Right, Doc?"

"Oh. Right, absolutely. I'll stay. I even have a toothbrush now. I'm perfectly content. And I know how to make coffee."

Maybe that was the magic incantation, Saul didn't know, but the matter seemed to be dropped when the blonde woman, Kristin, walked into the room. She wore shorts, a tee shirt, and a Glock in a shoulder holster. And everybody called her Mara, which confused him. Saul stood to let her have her spot at the computer, but she waved him back into it and began rummaging in one of the large boxes along the wall next to the door to the vestibule.

"Sit down, Mara," said Charlie, ignoring the fact there was no place for her to sit. "It is not time yet for breakfast."

"I did not eat last night. You pulled me out of there before I could have dinner. The same thing happened the first night here. It appears to be a pattern on this op."

"I pulled you out because Kyaku-sama had a syringe in his pocket, ready to take you." Charlie's jaw tightened as he spoke through his teeth.

"Yes, I know. I am grateful. But I am also hungry."

"Sit down!"

Saul jumped up and held out his chair to her. She sat, but she kept the MRE in her hand. Sergei gave her his coffee.

She opened the MRE.

"Do not begin a contest with me, Mara," said Charlie. "Especially over a piece of cardboard disguised as food. You will lose and you know it."

"I want to go with Claire this afternoon," she said, softly but with steel.

"No."

"If I do not go, you will be required to rescue her."

"If you do, I will be required to rescue you both. I said no."

"Kyaku-sama will want me there. If I am not, he will hurt her."

"This is not open for discussion, Mara. I will maintain discipline and you will be silent or you will pay for every word, every saucy glance, in bruises."

She looked at each stone-faced team member in turn. Perhaps it was her husband's scowl that made her put down the MRE and drink her coffee.

The discussion turned to the details of the anticipated meeting between Claire and Borodinov at the beach pavilion. Frank volunteered to position himself in a drainage ditch between the two resorts and monitor the rendezvous with a parabolic microphone. Justin would link the device's transmitter to the radio system in the conference room.

Saul watched Mack ease the position of his leg with difficulty in the crowded room. "You know," he said during a lull in the proceedings, "I remember I have some samples of that pain med in my old B-4 deployment bag. It's in the trunk of my car. If we can reach it, it will get you through the day, Mack."

Mack shook his head in a negative, but Charlie took up the idea. "Skosh. How many watchers did your team see?"

"Anywhere from one to three. I would imagine it would depend on shift changes."

"Are the watchers wearing wires?"
"Yes."
"Goodwin, can you set up interference with their signal?"
"Of course."
"Start now. Short, random bursts, to make it seem like normal atmospherics. Skosh, are they fighters or just watchers?"
"My guys say they can fight. They have seen them before."
"Doctor, where is your car?"
"By the administration building, away from the gate."
"It is still early, but the sun is up, so it may be possible," said Charlie. "You will need protection."
"It will be quite natural for his wife to accompany him," said Mara with a look of studied innocence.
Charlie glowered at her. "You are spoiling for a fight."
"But not with you, brother. Let me accompany the doctor. I tire of being so protected." She smiled. "This is a Mara-sized fight, made to order, and it will leave fewer tangos available to come after me."
"You will wear a wire."
"Of course."
"Goodwin, can you keep a channel open for her?"
Justin nodded.
"Mara, attach a suppressor before you go. Perhaps wear one of Sergei's tee shirts to cover that holster. Do not leave them alive. We have no time."
"Understood."
Saul thought this moment was the most shocking of his life until he felt rather than saw Mara become very still as she stood next to him at the car. He had been rummaging in the bag in his trunk, found the medication, and turned to her as he held it up in triumph.
A man stood behind her right shoulder and was reaching to put his arm around her neck. Before he got any further than the thought, Mara's left hand flew up to guard her face while her right elbow connected with the man's eye. As the man dealt with the blow, Saul was not sure how she did it, but she seemed to first slide forward and then fly back at him. Her foot hit his groin squarely, powerfully, and he crumpled.
He was still falling, clutching his crotch when Mara coolly put a bullet between his eyes with an oddly elongated handgun. There

was a sound but it was not a boom. It resembled a pop-buzz, decided Saul. The entire episode took no more than a few seconds.

"Wait here," Mara ordered.

She checked possible hiding places at the side of the administration building and in an overgrown area across from it for any other watchers before being satisfied the man had been alone. They dragged the body well behind the building and disguised it with the contents of an overturned trash can. Saul slammed his trunk lid and walked back with her to the conference room, pausing to vomit outside the door. They had been gone about ninety seconds.

Mara ate a hearty, if tasteless, breakfast. Saul had no appetite.

After their meal, the room became strangely quiet. Everyone remained awake and seated at the table. An extra chair had been found in one of the back rooms. The coffee maker in the kitchen was quietly replenished periodically by different people as if on a rota.

The reels of a tape machine turned, and Justin flipped a switch. They were listening to a meeting, a conference. With that flip of a switch, they had doubled the attendees to a meeting in a different conference room a few hundred yards away.

Jay Turner took notes, reams of them, scribbling names as they were introduced, listening and copying as one of the specialists or Skosh translated various languages. It dawned on Saul that these armed polyglots, whom he had heard termed specialists, were rather more than linguists. They were more than intelligence operatives. They were Mara, and he had seen her in action.

He suddenly understood why Skosh was so concerned that he not be considered a danger to them. He wondered how many times we can know how close we are to real danger. The thought made him shiver.

As with any conference, they heard speakers who ran the gamut of rambling nonsense, profound wisdom (from a criminal perspective), and brilliant wit. Most of the discussion consisted of polemics against governments, against laws, against prosecutors and investigators, against ex-wives and taxes, and for freedom from all of these things. They were popular topics.

Each time a participant at the table sniped at another over a past theft or murder or just an insult, a man named Earnest brought the discussion around to one of these issues with a phrase or sometimes a mere word. Once launched on a complaint, the adversaries became united in their common cause. The man was a brilliant manipulator.

As the main conference took a break, so did the shadow group, rushing to the coffee machine and one of the two toilets, whichever had the shortest line, then back to their seats. Jay sat before his stack of notes looking solemn and ignoring the hot coffee Justin placed in front of him.

By the end of the one-day conference, in the late afternoon, the surreptitious shadow conferees had heard enough but sat in silence as they listened to Earnest sum up for his guests.

"I know you are all diligent about getting and keeping your friendly authorities, both appointed and elected, happy and productive guardians of your interests. I applaud that. But think of the profits we could reap if we were to support not just the politicians who fix things for us, but the ones who will fix these issues for everybody. And as these guys make their way into the power structures of our real enemies, the state itself, we should use our usual methods to keep them in line, certainly, but do what we can to make them succeed. That is my project in the United States. I hope you can do the same wherever you operate."

"My God," said Skosh. "He is forming a political party of criminals."

"A transnational one," said Jay.

The other conference broke up with noise and bonhomie. Their shadow listeners sat in silent gloom.

"I told you," Sergei said to no one in particular and thus to all of them, "the Cold War will resume when a man who knows how to exploit what we built comes to power."

"But that's not Borodinov," said Skosh.

"No, it is someone probably much higher than even his boss," Sergei agreed. "But Borodinov is desperate to stay out of prison and you can see he is intelligent enough to be very effective. He is the danger to us today. The threat of the vory belongs to tomorrow."

Jay grimaced. "So this is just a holding action?"

"Every operation is no more than that," said Mack. "For us, it is enough to know why protecting Borodinov's asset is so vital it requires the death of Steve's child."

TWENTY-FOUR

Mack continued. "Now we have why. When we know who, we can destroy the project that endangers Danny after we have eliminated Borodinov himself."

With that quiet, sinister call to order, their conference began, ably led by Charlie.

He began by asking Jay why a field of five was not small enough for investigation.

Jay cleared his throat. "We need at least a reasonable suspicion to open an investigation. Looking into five or six people becomes a fishing expedition. No court will countenance it."

"We need only the name. He will never see a court."

Jay swallowed. "But then four or five people whose lives were examined and found blameless will sue for civil rights violations, and they will rightly win."

Charlie took a slow considering sip from his coffee mug. "We would find that acceptable but do not wish to lose you, Jay. I assume any such a suit would affect your career?"

Jay nodded.

"For that reason, then, Captain Nolan must keep her appointment with Borodinov," said Charlie.

Claire raised her head from a minute contemplation of a fingernail. She had been musing on the theory that another reason flying was superior to all other occupations was the lack of space in the cockpit for fucking meetings.

"I will go as well," said Mara.

"You will not," said Charlie.

"You have no faith in my ability."

"I have no faith in anyone's ability to prevail against a much heavier opponent."

"Yet I did prevail against the watcher at the doctor's car, and only last month you fought and won against a man thirty kilos heavier than you."

"That is different."

"The only difference is that I am female."

"The difference is that you are my sister, Mara! You will not accompany Claire and that is the end of it."

Claire held her breath and suspected everyone else was doing the same.

"Or what, Michael Joachim? Or what? I am publicly challenging your authority. What did you do to Steve when he mildly disagreed with you yesterday? What did you do to Sergei when he attacked Steve? When has Papa ever pulled his punches with you?"

"Are you saying you want me to hit you?" The voice had dropped back down to a soft, still purr as everybody wished themselves elsewhere.

"I am saying I am either a member of this team or I am not."

"Fine."

There was no discernible time between the word and his subsequent action. Despite the obstacles of people, furniture, equipment, and lockers, Charlie crossed the room without haste but with speed and sent Mara sliding back across the table with one solid fist to the gut. The resulting damage to shirt fronts was mitigated by the memory of Steve's having traveled the same ground the day before. Everybody picked up their mugs in time to save the coffee.

"You will go armed."

"Yes, of course," she gasped.

"You will wear a wire, both ways. Cover the earpiece with your hair."

"Yes, Charlie." Her breathing had improved.

"You will pull her out of there the moment either Claire obtains the information or Kyaku-sama shows up."

Mara pulled herself to a stand. "Whichever is first, yes."

"Claire, you will wear a wire as well, just the mic. And you will do exactly as Mara directs."

"Yes, Sir." This time she meant the sir. She had no desire to slide across the table.

...

"Not that I care what Skosh thinks or wants," said Charlie, as he poured a small amount of single malt scotch from a flask into three rinsed-out coffee mugs and handed two to Steve and Sergei, "but he wants a minimum of violence inflicted on or witnessed by the local populace. It shouldn't be that hard. Borodinov's little knot of goons is hardly a match for us, and the tourist season is almost over."

"True," said Steve. "But he does have that tall guy we just heard about from Skosh's old team, who may or may not have any skills. I'd rather not wait to find out which it is at the moment I face him."

Sergei raised his eyebrows. "He is vor. He has skills. Skosh says he has the tattoos."

"The other three are not vory, just small-time mobsters and so should be easier targets," said Charlie. He savored a sip from the mug he held. "Kyaku-sama is an unforeseen complication and will be more dangerous. I think both he and Borodinov will move very quickly this evening. Skosh is busy dealing with the Americans to keep the body Mara created this morning from being known until we are done here. Jay will man the radios. Frank volunteered to handle the directional in a concealment area near the beach bar. You never know what conversations he may pick up in the vicinity."

He looked at Steve. "What do you think about using the doctor and Goodwin again?"

"You mean to help get the women out? How?" Steve grimaced. "They can't pull the same gambit twice, can they? It was brilliant, but I think Borodinov will catch on. He's pretty smart."

Charlie looked into his empty mug. "There are too many moving parts," he said, suppressing a sigh. "We are stationary, but they are not. Their allies, the international gangs, are leaving the island as we speak, but we face still too many wild cards, and they're all on the other side. I don't like it."

"I agree," said Sergei. "The big guy working with Borodinov makes me worry. He is too calm. I am sure he is a specialist."

"When were you going to tell me?"

"I just now told you?"

Sergei's puzzled look required patience—a commodity Charlie was fast running short on. He steeled himself to carry on with his original thought rather than launch into everybody's faults and reminded himself that his performance this trip had been less than stellar.

"I'd like Saul and Justin to become extra unknowns on our side that require Borodinov to think again, that throw Kyaku-sama's calculations off just enough to make him less of a factor for us. The two wouldn't have to do anything. Mara's right: she can handle it, but their appearance may create a distraction she can exploit if she needs to."

Steve swallowed the last of his whiskey. "You know, Charlie, they're innocents. Saul and Claire, certainly, but also Justin. I know I've done my share of putting some bruises on him, but he's too junior. Despite flashes of brilliance, he's in way over his head. Skosh won't be able to protect him from Borodinov and Co. as he shields him from us."

"I agree," said Sergei. "Frank also is not regular. He has retired, but at least he knows what he is doing. Justin does not."

Charlie looked up from his contemplation of the mug. "Jay says Claire is a combatant, Steve, and fully aware of that fact, even though she's not armed. Are you saying it won't work?"

"I didn't say that," said Steve. "I'm saying that the cost may be unbearable."

Charlie knew then, as thoroughly and organically as he had ever known anything else, what his father meant about Steve's advice and his own decision. He knew how much all the decisions his father had made over the years must still weigh. And he already felt the weight of the next few hours down to the smallest milligram.

He also realized Steve had a stake in the outcome beyond survival.

Charlie became all business, delivering directives. Discussion ended. "We will have them park Saul's car in front of the hotel and saunter down to the beach bar. Nothing more. I want to see everyone wired for two-way communication, except Claire. She will not have an earpiece. Her hair is too short. But I want to hear everything anyone says to her. We three will dress tactically, but only in Kevlar vests. It's too damn hot for full armor. I am not worried about Claire or Mara stopping a bullet. Borodinov and Kyaku-sama want them alive.

"Pack up both cars, the sedan and the Mercedes, and make sure they are ready to go before the women step foot on the beach. Then we wait, we intercept, we kill the target, and we roll back to Kadena immediately. I will ask Jay to call in the airplane now since Skosh is busy." He unrolled a chart of the area and indicated each ambush point and its fallbacks.

He had assigned no role to his father on the assumption that Papa would do what he thought fit to do; it would be exactly the right thing at the right time, and its overarching purpose would be to keep Claire Nolan alive.

TWENTY-FIVE

Frank took his position in the vegetation surrounding the lowest part of a drainage ditch marking the beach-side boundary between the two resorts. He trained the disc antenna of his directional microphone on the bar seventy feet away. He had been instructed by the iceberg that was his son-in-law to not transmit the noise of ice in cocktail glasses until he picked up some human conversations.

Mack was handing over at least some of the reins. This trip was Charlie's debut in the starring role of scariest killer Frank ever had the misfortune to meet. So much depended on this thirty-something child's judgment, not least his own daughter's life and happiness. He had acceded to the reality of her choice, but good intentions don't translate right away into fond feelings. He still could not bring himself to like the kid. It did not help that the kid seemed to hate his guts in return, never forgiving him his role way back when… Frank winced at the memory. Kid was a misnomer. Charlie was as ancient as danger itself and more lethal than old age, something his targets never had the luxury to reach.

Something slithered across Frank's lower leg as he knelt in the ditch. He tried not to think about it as he watched Mara and Claire walk up to the pavilion. Borodinov and another taller man were there, the only patrons in the place. With the conferees gone, the resort had become largely deserted. It was the end of the tourist season and well into typhoon season.

Frank listened to the introductions and the small talk. He heard Claire's clever chatter, Mara's bitchy English rejoinders to the tall man's attempts to engage her in conversation in Russian as Borodinov interpreted for him, calling him Anatoly. He listened as Claire's efforts began to pay off. Borodinov gave a few more descriptive clues about his prize asset. Jay would now have approximate height, weight, and body build. Good job Claire.

Then he heard something else. Frank increased the gain on the antenna. He searched the area around where he was concealed to try to pinpoint the voices, the Japanese voices his microphone was picking up. There were no other people visible besides the bartender and the group at the pavilion, and there were not many places to hide. It followed then, that these voices were hiding. They spoke in low tones and occasional whispers. He rotated the antenna. People going about their legitimate business do not hide in overgrown vegetation between buildings. Frank was himself a case in point.

They had positioned themselves twenty feet from the corner of the bar. He could not see them and hoped with everything in him that Skosh had finished his business and was listening. Frank was about to say the word himself when he heard three voices in quick succession. Borodinov said, "He has a stutter." Jay ordered, "That's it, get out," and Skosh screamed, "Jolly, Mara."

Frank tore off his headphones and threw down the equipment. He drew his Walther PPK as he ran toward the fight. Mara leapt into the air a good three feet swinging the outside of one foot in an arc and slamming it into Kyaku-sama's shoulder. The syringe he had been holding flew out of the pavilion and into the sand. He fell sideways onto a table and then to the floor where he wasted no time in trying to get up and instead, produced a pistol bringing it to bear on Mara as she kicked and punched two more assailants.

As a career establishment functionary, Frank had always condemned colleagues who had the misfortune of doing what he did next. To hell with condemnation, he thought as he shot and killed Kyaku-sama. Hit him between the eyes, he was pleased to see. He could see because everything they said about what happens in a fight like this was true. Time slowed and his vision narrowed, but what it lost in breadth it gained in clarity. Thus, he saw Mara kick a third man across the bar and into the glasses on shelves behind it, showering bloody splinters as he fell. Then he watched her shoot one man, fire a second round into the man who lay in the glass shards behind the bar, and then hit Borodinov in the lower back as he pushed Claire up the path to the street, his henchman Anatoly dragging her by one arm.

They changed course toward the right as Saul and Justin came around the corner of the building on the left. Justin had drawn his weapon but wisely kept it at his side and held back. Anatoly and Borodinov held Claire in a way that made a clean shot impossible. Frank was not sure what ambush points the team had chosen, but they were not likely to be set up within a public resort, no matter how deserted.

Mara took off at a run, with Frank close behind, when the henchman turned and fired. The round ricocheted off a metal awning support and into the body of Justin Goodwin.

"Your keys!" said Frank as he ran up to Saul panting.

Saul crouched beside Justin. He brought the keys out of his pocket. "He's alive."

In their ears, they heard Jay, "Where?" Then, "Doctor get back here. Now! I'll take care of Goodwin."

There was more, but Frank was not listening. He was starting Saul's car with Mara as his passenger, shaking the cockroaches[2] off his ankle, and pulling out of its parking spot a few yards behind Borodinov as he sped by. Whether or not it was the detour forced by the appearance of the doctor and Goodwin, or the fourth member of Borodinov's team running out to try to intercept his boss, only to be shot by Sergei from a point beside the road, Frank did not know. Whether it was one or both, the delay proved enough to ensure he and Mara could keep them in view on the twisting road through the forests of Yonabaru Park.

---

[2] See Glossary of Useful Terms, p. 422

TWENTY-SIX

Skosh was already wired to the network when he met the sergeant in charge of the Okuma military police. After two hours of negotiations, he bought the team six hours' grace and a better hiding place for the body. As he walked back to the military conference center, he heard Kyaku-sama's voice, transmitting through Frank's parabolic microphone to the general network they were all on (excellent radio discipline by the way, he thought, no chatter). The voice came into his ear with instructions on the subduing and snatching of the blonde treasure.

It was imminent.

"Jolly, Mara!" he shouted into his mic.

He crossed a driveway and was almost hit by a speeding Mercedes, making him jump back. The brakes squealed and Steve got out, held the driver's door, and said, "Drive."

The team had been in the process of setting up two ambush points when Kyaku-sama's voice came over the network. Charlie aborted the plan and turned around. After another sliding stop to pick up Sergei from the first ambush point, Skosh found himself stuck in a car with three specialists high on adrenaline and spouting threats as he negotiated the twists and turns of the park road, barreling at full speed through an increasingly dark forest of bamboo and tree ferns.

"I need you, Skosh," Jay said into his ear. "Goodwin is bad, but still alive. Kyaku-sama and two of his men are shot dead, and one of Borodinov's. The police are here and are not friendly. I need to be in the ambulance to the Camp Lester Hospital with Goodwin. If it helps, all of Kyaku-sama's people were carrying, and I presume, illegally."

"Give the cop you're dealing with your earbud," said Skosh as he negotiated another sharp curve. He spouted every name he knew on the island, every official, every date of every meeting, and every provisional approval. He apologized repeatedly in the best language, with utmost respect and humility. He waited, well Jay waited, he was busy marveling at how the Mercedes handled these turns, while the officer phoned his headquarters to consult with at least two of the officials cited.

Between these conversations, if they could be called that, were updates from Frank, and then from Mara. Skosh also made an emergency call to General Hanahan because, for some inexplicable reason, Mack had robbed the Okuma first aid station at sword point. Of course, that cane of his would have a sharp implement in it. Why not? It was Mack after all. He was long gone, having taken the sedan, but Skosh thought it best to solve the uproar before chaos and panic took hold of the military resort.

Concentrating on his own tasks, Skosh didn't notice when Frank's voice dropped off and Mara's took over, but soon after he brought the Mercedes around an almost 180-degree bend, he came upon two cars in the brush on the left. The first car had developed a flat that shredded the tire. The second car was the doctor's. Both were empty.

Mara's voice came into their ears. "Not good. Frank is hit. He is thirty meters in along the trail to the left of our car. He will direct you. I follow them."

Not good meant really bad with this team. They traveled light. The heaviest thing anyone carried was Charlie's sniper rifle. The delinquents carried Škorpion machine pistols slung loosely over their shoulders. The evening light darkened the gloom in bamboo thickets lining a single-file path. The ground grew steeper, throwing occasional flat boulders, a foot or two tall, in their way. They had flashlights but dared not use them, pausing every few yards to listen in the murk.

It was only a minute or so before they heard a quiet gasp beyond a tree on their right during one of these pauses. Steve approached the sound as they waited. "Here," he said quietly.

Frank sat against a tree, his shirt front seeping red and a narrow dribble of the same color leaking from the corner of his mouth. He pointed to the right of a slight separation in the path. "She's headed north-northeast," he whispered. "Careful. One is lagging behind to ambush."

"How many altogether, besides Borodinov?" asked Charlie.

It took Frank a moment to gather breath to say, "Three."

Charlie squatted before him. "Listen old man. You've got another grandchild coming in about seven months. You're the first I've told. You have to stick around."

Frank smiled.

Sergei checked his pulse. "Jay is sending an ambulance. It will be in time."

As they struck the path Frank had indicated, Sergei whispered, "I hope it will be in time."

It was more than radio discipline that kept the line clear for several minutes. Mara checked in briefly at intervals, giving compass directions and describing landmarks she could discern along the way. Occasionally they heard low murmurs, always to their left and ahead. Charlie began using hand signals.

The path skirted a rocky obstruction to their right that reached up to about fifteen meters at a steep angle. Charlie signaled a halt, telling Steve and Sergei to stay below while he and Skosh scrambled upward. They came to a jutting promontory with a carpet of treetops dropping off beneath them in the dwindling daylight. Charlie handed Skosh a pair of binoculars while he took up his rifle, training its night scope on the terrain below.

"Look for signs of the path," he said.

The jungle evening was anything but still, as foragers scurried through the brush and birds called, but they saw no signs of any larger animals until Skosh spied a flick of white cloth snaking through the blackening green below them. Charlie's night scope tracked three warm bodies below. One wore sandals. He could see her feet on low bare patches of the trail. He moved Skosh in front of him roughly, told him to stop breathing, steadied the rifle's barrel on his left shoulder, and sighted on the top of the tallest figure moving at the end of the little group.

Skosh had never been this still in his life. He helped to support the position of the barrel with his left hand. The suppressor extended well beyond his chest at a downward angle, and the scope ended just past his cheek. Charlie pointed it into what Skosh considered impenetrable murk. He felt the recoil and the boom and saw the shell case blow by his nose.

Charlie kept the scope trained on that little section of pathway. The body at the rear had stopped and slunk to the ground. Its infrared signature began to cool. Further up, a great raucous thrashing in the vegetation suggested the other two bodies he caught on the scope were running but not well or efficiently. He did not dare try another shot.

Mara called in her position again. She was on the same path, but several hundred yards behind the target.

"Not good," came a quiet voice in their ears. Sergei's voice.

Skosh and Charlie wheeled to the descent, letting gravity speed their way. "Tell me," Charlie said quietly into his mic. No words came back to them, only grunts. Halfway down they heard the fight in progress. As they neared the final few yards of steep descent, Skosh could see Sergei close in to grapple with a man whose knife glinted in the remains of sunlight. He had raised it above Sergei's chest and appeared to lower it like a hammer onto the back of his neck, but he jerked up and back suddenly, falling off Sergei's upthrust knife, spilling intestines down to his knees.

A few feet away, Steve rolled in a clench with a man, each of them scrambling for purchase among the rocks and debris at the point where the ground rose on this side of the escarpment. They could see the man's blade in the waning sunlight, his arm straining toward Steve's neck, Steve's hand circling the wrist and the veins in his neck bulging as he struggled to hold that arm. Charlie searched for an angle for his Glock to make the difference in this contest when Steve's other hand drove his knife up and under the man's ribs. There came a pause, a gush of blood, and a mighty heave as Steve came out from underneath his dead opponent.

They picked up their Škorpions and followed Charlie along the path in Mara's wake.

TWENTY-SEVEN

It was Anatoly who saw the wire and ripped it out of her bra. Claire sat squashed between him and Borodinov in the back seat. The discovery sparked a vehement conversation in Russian. She did her best to appear mystified by the wire, but that can be difficult when the tall man next to you can see the microphone in your cleavage.

She had seen Justin fall to one of Anatoly's bullets, though she was sure he was shooting at Mara. An especially dangerous man, but a lousy shot. Hell, everybody she had met in the past two days was especially dangerous. She wanted to believe the champions on her side were better marksmen. And that they would get to her in time. Anatoly shared a few choice words with Borodinov. She did not understand them, but then again, she had enough military experience to know that special vocabulary most useful under stress. So, essentially, she did understand.

Borodinov occupied himself with breathing, mostly, and with bleeding slowly onto the left side of her white blouse. "Whoever the fuck you are, little girl, you better hope I live long enough to keep Anatoly off you. You can start talking right now. He does not speak English. Does he, boys?"

One of the men in front said, "That's right, boss. Anatoly don't speak no English. Make it good girlie. Now's your chance."

"I don't know what you mean, John."

"Yes, you do. You can stop the pretense. The name is Viktor. You are our ticket out of here, but I can't convince Anatoly you are worth preserving unless you start talking. Start with the name of the team who will want you back badly enough to let us out of here."

"I don't know what you're talking about."

Anatoly placed a mighty paw on her right thigh, fairly high up, and squeezed.

Viktor said something in Russian and the hand was removed.

"You know exactly what I'm talking about. The name starts with C and ends with e. Say it out loud. That will help me convince him I'm getting you to talk and it's a good idea to keep you alive a while longer. Say the name. I already know it. You won't betray anything or anybody."

She was about to say Charlie but remembered Mack introducing the team a lifetime ago in the conference room.

"I don't know if you've noticed, girlie," said Viktor through his teeth, "but we're the ones in trouble here, not your friends. Saying the name out loud will not affect them. It only helps me keep the gorilla next to you from tearing you to pieces."

"You're so weak you need me to help you control your own goon?"

She had little doubt this was a trick, except that the bleeding and occasional gasps tended to confirm his position as a possible underdog here. But if he was the underdog, she surmised, then she was close to becoming the dead dog in this equation.

He pointed to the front seat. "They're my guys, aren't you, fellas?"

"Sure thing, Boss."

"The man next to you—I will not say his name or he will know I'm talking about him—was sent by Moscow to 'assist' me. We have a few common objectives, but I do not control him. Say the name."

The paw returned to her thigh. Another sharp exchange in Russian removed it.

"Say it," said Viktor.

"Charlemagne?"

Viktor nodded and spoke to Anatoly in the tone of a demand. The big man scowled and handed him the microphone and transmitter he had seized from her in two unconnected pieces.

"He has pulled the fucking wire out of the box. I have no way to contact them to arrange a trade," said Viktor.

"Maybe I can hook it up again, Boss," said the man in the front passenger seat.

But it was no good.

"It was soldered in, Boss. I can't fix it here."

Viktor let loose a series of choice Russian words for Anatoly, whose jaw tightened and hand squeezed her thigh again, even higher up.

"What's that noise?" The driver downshifted around a bend in the road as the car began to shake. "I think it's a flat."

"Just keep going," said Viktor.

"I can't. I think we're on the rim. I can't keep it straight." He pulled over on the left.

"We're fucking sitting ducks," said the front passenger.

Viktor grunted. "Get out. I see a trail. Let's go."

Anatoly tried to pull Claire out with him, but Viktor resisted and made her follow him out the door on the left side. She felt a tincture of gratitude for that.

They had walked, or stumbled, in Viktor's case, less than a hundred or so feet, when they heard a car door closing behind them. The sound came from the road and preceded the first steps of someone entering the path. Anatoly held back after a quiet conference with Viktor, while the rest of them continued in silence.

Claire heard the shot though Anatoly used a suppressor. When he caught up to them, they moved more quickly. Viktor struggled to keep up and argued for Anatoly to stay in the rear. At a rocky outcrop with a steep upward incline, he made them pause while he struggled to stay upright and breathe at the same time. He pulled the two American hoodlums aside and spoke to them quietly in English. Not long after, they disappeared.

"Where are they?" asked Claire.

"Setting up an ambush," said Viktor. "I hope none of Charlemagne's guys mean anything to you, little girl. My guys are nasty fighters. They'll catch up with us as soon as they're done."

She shivered.

Anatoly must have asked the same question, but for some reason, the answer took longer to explain in Russian. Maybe because of the argument it caused. They trudged on, with the path looping through an increasingly narrow and dark forest, sometimes forcing them to squeeze between bamboo stalks. Viktor paused to breathe again when they reached a space, still narrow, but relatively open beneath some trees. Claire saw it when she looked up in search of the sky just to remind herself there was such a thing as light. She saw it and tried to step aside, but it was too late. The snake landed on her thigh and struck the calf just below the end of the scar from her recent surgery.

"Fuck," said Viktor.

Anatoly practiced the new English word several times.

TWENTY-EIGHT

Saul flashed his ID at the gate guard and ran smack dab into Mack, who grabbed his shirt sleeve and said, "Come."

Together they burst through the door of the first aid station in the closest admin building. A medic enjoying the choicest of assignments at a beach resort sat behind a short counter reading a magazine.

"You have a snake on this island," Mack said.

The airman nodded. "The habu. Yes."

"There is antivenom. Is it here?"

"Yes, but I'm not authorized …"

"This doctor is authorized. We will need perhaps three doses."

Saul hauled out his ID in preparation for the argument.

"I can't …" said the airman.

Mack pulled a sword out of his cane. He had a better argument. The room was small and Mack's reach sufficiently long when added to the sword so that he could and did force the end of the airman's protest simply by using the point to move his chin up to close his mouth.

"You can. Keys." Then, as the airman pointed to the key cabinet, "Doctor?"

Saul took enough for three initial average adult doses, with needles, tubing, saline, and other supplies for mixing.

"Also, Doctor, take whatever else you think might be useful. Where is your bag?"

"In my car. Frank took it, but there is a pretty good first aid kit in this other cabinet. I'll grab that."

They took the sedan. Saul drove in silence somewhere behind the Mercedes as he and Mack turned off their transmitters but continued to listen to the sporadic comments of the others they were trying to trace. Mara's information seemed the most helpful. During a lull in the radio traffic, Mack spoke briefly in German. "Why do you speak such excellent German, Doctor?"

"My grandmother was a holocaust survivor. She raised us while our parents were working."

At least a minute went by before Mack spoke again. "Which camp?"

"Dachau."

"Have you seen it?"

Saul caught his breath. "No. I don't think I could handle it."

"Your family understands what it is to be hunted by implacable enemies who wish to annihilate them. You have no need to see it. Those who do not understand, they should see a place like Dachau."

Saul was sure Mack was not Jewish but wondered which of the many peoples hunted by the genocidal he might belong to.

It was shortly after this that they heard Sergei's whisper about Frank's critical condition. Mack became a stone statue, a primitive angry god, his jaw set at an angle of vengeance. He opened a map that had been stuffed in the door pocket and studied it. Mara checked in again, in a quietly stealthy voice. She was close to her quarry and gave exact details of her position. They reached the two cars on the side of the road. Mack gestured for Saul to drive past them and then after a couple of minutes, take a left turn.

"Stop here," he said, indicating a wide shoulder on the left. "You must mix the anti-venom."

"How much? I mean, for what weight?"

"Both women weigh, perhaps, fifty-six kilos. Frank is about eighty."

Saul did a quick calculation. "The women and Frank Cardova? You think they could be bitten? We have not heard…"

"Claire has lost her microphone. We are ignorant of her state, but we should be ready. She and Mara are lightly clad and with only sandals on their feet. Frank is badly wounded, sitting against a tree, and cannot move. The others are well enough prepared. Three doses for those weights should be enough for initial needs in any eventuality."

"The habu is known to drop from trees also, you know."

"Thank you. My mind had insufficient things to worry about." Mack pointed across the road. "There is the trail we will take. Bring supplies."

They crossed the road, plunged into the forest gloom, and began tramping steadily upward.

…

Claire said nothing. She was surprised by the speed and intensity of the pain within minutes. Anatoly tried to support her, but the last thing she wanted was his hands on her. She shoved him off and limped on after Viktor, who was in the lead. Dizzy and nauseous, she fought to keep up as burning pain spread upward and downward from the site of the bite. She alternated between feeling severe heat and chattering cold in a hot, humid semi-tropical forest.

A tree root made her stumble and Anatoly had to put her back on her feet. He then pushed her on and she felt rather than heard an impact behind her that sent a gritty spray against the back of her head. She glanced back and watched, as if in slow motion, Anatoly sink to his knees and then to the ground. A large portion of his head had disappeared.

Claire tried to stop to vomit, but Viktor grabbed her arm and viciously hauled her after him. They ran, both in equal agony, up a steep incline and onto a rocky ledge next to a waterfall. They had no appreciation for the beauty of the spot where the cascade fell into a pool thirty feet below, but it looked clean and inviting. Claire was in a sweating phase and contemplated falling into its cool relief.

Viktor slid to a seat against the rock face, his legs straight before him. Claire slumped a few feet earlier, still thinking how nice it would be to drown when a shadow across the ledge made her aware they were not alone.

She recognized the cane immediately, then the blue eyes, but they had only a glance for her before Mack moved past her.

"I heard you were badly injured in North Carolina," Viktor said to him.

"Not so badly that I will fail to destroy your asset as well as you."

"You know I had no choice."

"And you know my knowledge of your plight will not help you."

Viktor closed his eyes when he saw the knife.

Saul knelt next to Claire, stuck a needle in her vein, and held up a bag as they both watched Mack grab Viktor's shirt collar and hold it to keep the fountain his knife had opened in the man's carotid from spraying over them. Instead, it soaked the other side of the ledge and from there poured into the waterfall and down into the pool.

Claire vomited.

TWENTY-NINE

The snakebite delayed but did not stop Claire's return to the cockpit. Jay Turner visited her once in the naval hospital at Camp Lester, and she looked in on Justin Goodwin as he lay comatose in ICU before being medevacked from the island, but she saw no one else in the months after Skosh made her sign that form just before they slammed the door on her ambulance.

There was no word. At first, she pined and fantasized about a happily ever after, but she was not one given to myth-making. Daily pressures edged aside the more acute pain. It was at night that she missed him most, wondered about him, wondered if he thought about her. Again, she told herself, stop the fantasies. He is exactly what he said he is, a frog.

Even worse was her realization that she missed them all. She missed the confusion, the fear, the sense of purpose, and the coffee. It just did not taste as good without being surrounded by disagreeing and disagreeable people in tedious meetings.

The only viable approximation, she decided, would be to fly in combat. She made it her mission to be selected for a fighter. The effort helped take her mind off things.

Every landing had to be perfect, because every day brought her closer to the news she wanted, to the summons to fighter lead-in training. Today, she greased it on and her co-pilot Russ gave her a congratulatory grin. It had to be soon and it had to be a yes. She climbed down from the airplane and her heart leapt. Her squadron commander stood there ready to greet her. But why was he not smiling?

He gestured toward the 909th ops truck. "Take the truck. General Hanahan wants to see you now. I take that back. He wants to see you an hour ago."

"But I need to …"

"I'll do all that. Russ and I will. Go. Now."

It was not yet two o'clock, but for Claire, it had been a long flight with an o-dark-thirty show for flight planning and briefing. She did not look her best, but the general would understand that. It had to be *the news*. Claire was sure of it as she greeted Helen.

"Go right in," said Helen. "I already told him you're here."

She strode toward the desk, between two of the red-leather wing-backed chairs that stood at a slant before it and saluted. "Sir," she said. She could feel the chairs were inhabited, but they were behind her now and she was still at attention. The general returned the salute and gestured toward another chair placed at the side so that the desk and three chairs made a malformed circle.

"Sit down, Captain," he said. "These men have come to speak with you and have asked me to be present. I hope you don't object."

She was dying to look at them but was in the presence of, and still being addressed by, a general. "No sir, I don't object."

As she turned, the brown eyes nearly made her miss the seat and sit on the arm of the chair she had been offered. Looking at him brought back all the emotions of that time and the time after when she had heard nothing, not a word, not a thank you, not a how the fuck are you. Bupkis.

Once over the surprise, new emotions seized her including fury at having been ignored for so many months and an incredible yearning for him right this minute. She hardly noticed Mack, though her last experience of him was nothing if not memorable.

"I'm sure you remember Mack," said the General, "and this man is a Mr. Steve Donovan. I believe you have met."

"Yes, Sir."

"Mack has told me, and your squadron commander has confirmed it—though why I should be given this news through such channels is a mystery,—that you have been selected for fighter lead-in. Congratulations, Captain."

"Thank you, Sir." She knew her face was flushed with the pleasure of such news and could feel she was being watched closely, not by Steve, who was studying the carpet, between glances at the door behind him, but by Mack.

After a brief rearrangement of chairs at Mack's request, so that everybody could see the door, the General indicated that he should proceed. Despite the new chair position, Steve stood and leaned against the wall facing the door with a relaxed posture that fooled no one. She and Steve were in the presence of their generals. There was no such thing as relaxing.

Mack began. "I have come to ask you, Captain Nolan, to work for me. The position is in support of both my family and the team. Günther is retiring and we have need of a skilled senior pilot. With this news that you are selected for a fighter, are you sufficiently interested in my offer to listen to details or have you decided to stay in your current career?"

The only detail she was interested in at the moment was busy studying the carpet at the bottom of the door.

"Yes," she said in a half whisper. "I will listen."

Steve looked up, saw that she saw, and looked away.

"Uwe will become chief pilot, but your pay and benefits will be the same as his." Mack detailed these. "I ask you to not discuss this with him should you take the position. When you fly together, you will share left seat time, fifty-fifty. He has agreed to this. When you fly with one of the more junior pilots, you will be in command. Would this arrangement suit you?"

"Um. Ye-es. Are we talking about the Challenger?"

"That, yes. Also, we have a Lear 45 and a Cessna Citation. The team does not fly in the Citation. We use it mostly for logistics, but I am told it is fun to fly. You would be required to become proficient with a pistol and be armed at all times. Also, we will require that you learn German and Russian. Do you have any questions for me so far?"

She was intrigued. The being armed part was alarming, though. She knew she could pickle off a missile at a MIG, but … "You're not suggesting I become a specialist?"

"No. You will fly but must be capable of defending yourself and the airplane."

"I saw a Lear on the ramp as we came in. Is that yours?"

Mack nodded.

"I would have type ratings in three airplanes?"

"Yes. And be required to maintain proficiency in all of them. You will fly very often and for many hours."

"And the places that you fly to, are they..." she searched for a word, "challenging?"

Was that a hint of a smile? On Mack? "They are often dangerous. Yes."

On the one hand, a fighter and all it meant. On the other, peacetime tedium and an eventual desk job. Only a fiend would wish for war. She was no such fiend, but the progression of these thoughts made her realize she was a bit of an adrenaline junkie. The desk job especially made her pause. This little bit of self-knowledge and the fact that Charlemagne lived in a permanent state of emergency made her way clear.

"Sign me up. I'll take it."

The blue eyes widened; the General said, "Claire!" and the lump facing the door narrowed his eyes at her. "Just so we're clear, Claire, I'm not part of some package deal."

"Who said you were?"

"You're way too quick to throw up a fighter for a fucking business jet. What else are you after?"

"What business is that of yours? You just said you have nothing to do with it. I imagine you're here as just some kind of brute muscle."

"That's right. I'm a brute. Not at all suitable for the likes of you."

"I ..."

She got no further when Mack suggested dinner and asked the General to join them.

"I wouldn't miss it," he said. "May I suggest the Skoshi KOOM? It's right here on base and may solve some of your security issues. They have a private teppanyaki room."

...

Claire's second dinner date with Steve went somewhat better than the first. Everybody behaved. Nobody fought. Nobody died. Mack and the General mapped out her professional future. She and Steve exchanged a few commonplace words, not all of them polite.

He was angry with her for giving up the fighter because he flattered himself that she did it for him. He resented being under obligation, and she found it tough to convince him he was only the icing on a layer cake of three airplanes, thousands of hours, and a life very different from anything she had ever imagined. Not all romance requires a man, she told him.

As the dinner party broke up, she was reminded of just how different that life would be. General Hanahan shook Mack's hand and said, "I have to ask you. Why not just shoot him?"

Of course, he knows what happened, thought Claire. Maybe Saul told him. Maybe, like Mack, he just knows.

Mack took an extra beat to answer with a direct blue stare into the General's eyes. "It is my mark. He threatened us directly. It is important for others to know how he paid for it."

There was no ambiguity in that.

EPILOGUE

Archibald Goodwin opened the front door of his small suburban Indiana house, scowled, and said, "Oh, it's you."

"Good afternoon Mr. Goodwin," said Jay Turner. "Is Justin at home?"

"No. He's in the park playing football." Archibald turned and led the way to the back of the house. "Of course, he's fucking at home. Where the fuck else would he be?"

As they entered the room, Justin looked up from a large computer screen with a cracked corner sitting on a ragged table. Keyboards, disc drives, circuit boards, and wires littered the surface. He held a joystick and employed the button at its top continually, his eyes tracking the path of his missiles as they exploded enemies on the screen.

"Justin, it's Mr. Turner."

"What the fuck does he want?"

"I came by to see how you are doing."

"I'm doing fine."

"He's doing fuck all," said his father.

"I heard you turned down the civilian job they offered you at the Bureau," said Jay.

"Writing code for office file clerks? No, thank you." He hit high score, lost the game on the next shot, threw down the joystick, and turned his wheelchair to face his old boss.

"What do you want, Jay?"

"I want you to take a ride with me."

"Getting in and out of a car is a pain in the ass."

"Nonetheless, it will give us a chance to talk."

"Do it," said his father. "I had the good fortune to work for a smart man for thirty years. Spending time with this one can only do you good, Justin."

Justin spent half an hour complaining about the medics, the therapists, the width of doorways, and the lack of meaningful employment when you have useless appendages in place of legs. Then he complained about the biggest beef of them all: the lack of information. How was everybody? Did they get the bad guys? Did they live or die? Did they know he lived and wished he hadn't?

"It's the nature of the black world, Justin. Even everyday personal information is compartmentalized."

"Like whether Claire got her man?"

"Like that. She did, by the way."

"So she's alive. Good, though I don't think much of her taste. What about Frank?"

"I understand he has recovered but it has been slow."

"I'm glad to hear he made it. Which one was Borodinov's asset and did they get him?"

"It was the son of a wealthy family with political ambitions. He died in a tragic accident when he fell down a staircase."

"So Steve. I guess that's justice of a sort." Justin paused as they entered a highway on-ramp.

"You know the worst thing about it, Jay? I never fired at anybody and the asshole who hit me wasn't even shooting at me. How can something so random cost so much? Why are we northbound on the Dan Ryan?"

"There is someone I would like you to meet."

Jay did not budge when pressed for clues, so they talked about other things during the drive, like how happy Jay was to have his family back with him, and that Justin's work had laid the foundation for them to trace the hack of the criminal investigation unit to St. Petersburg, and not the one in Florida, just as he had predicted. They discussed the procedures needed to stop future hacks, the money pit that was his collection of second-hand computers, and the money pit that was his dad's boat.

For the first time since he woke from the coma almost a year ago, Justin felt human as the elevator door opened into the vestibule of a penthouse apartment on the lake.

Jay pressed an intercom button, the double doors opened, and Alex smiled and said hello.

Justin felt himself crying. He tried to stop, but that made it worse. He sobbed and did not realize Jay had excused himself and gone into another room, leaving him alone with Alex, who rubbed his back and handed him a lace-edged handkerchief.

When she was sure he had stopped, she led him toward a door at the other end of the living room they were in. He appreciated that she did not push him but instead led the way, allowing him to make his way under his own power. He tucked the handkerchief into a pocket because the polite thing to do was to launder and return it. He had no intention of ever returning it.

Mack and Jay were already seated in armchairs in this other, smaller sitting room. Alex excused herself, closing the door behind her and the negotiations began.

When Jay dropped him off at home several hours later, he figured he must look different. He knew he felt different, and his dad's face set itself into an expectant question mark the moment he opened the door.

"I have a job," said Justin. "We're moving to Chicago. I'll have better access to equipment and communications infrastructure. I still need you, so please come with me. My employer will pay the marina fees on Lake Michigan for the boat."

He did not say out loud that his dad still needed him as well, though Mack was the one who had brought this up.

It took Archibald a few seconds to close his mouth and open it again with a proper question. "What will you be doing?"

Justin repeated Mack's explanation. "My boss says the next century will bring us new wars, battles, skirmishes, and weapons. I am one of the new weapons."

The End

QUIET MOVE
Late 1990s

PROLOGUE

"Why not, Skosh? We were made for each other. I know you enjoyed it as much as I did." Candace had chosen a small table for two by the window. Skosh found it uncomfortably public.

"Of course I enjoyed it," he said. "I've never not enjoyed sex. That doesn't mean we're even compatible, let alone made for each other. Believe me, I would never make you happy."

He was being careful. What he meant was that she could never make him happy. She could make him horny in a manufactured scenario, but that did not equate to happiness.

A waitress appeared. Candace ordered a chef's salad and white wine. Skosh asked for coffee, black, and kept his face turned away from the window.

"This lunch is on me, Skosh. Surely you don't maintain that beautiful body of yours with just coffee?"

She blinked slowly, accentuating her large grey eyes, her finest feature. Her only fine feature thought Skosh.

She continued, "It's too early in our relationship to assume we're incompatible."

"There is no relationship, Candace."

Coffee and wine arrived. Candace sipped with a show of daintiness. Skosh gulped.

"But we should get to know each other," insisted his reptilian lunch companion. "All I know about you is that I enjoyed the other night. It made me want to know every part of you. For example, I see the contracts you work on, because that's my job, but the language is so specialized, the words don't even tell me what you do. I want to know more. Tell me."

She may as well have described an excruciating torture. As a natural spook of the old school, Skosh had so compartmentalized his life that any personal disclosure felt like a threat. But she was much more highly placed in their organization, albeit in an administrative role, and could conceivably damage him badly. He chose his next words with utmost caution.

"Candace, this is not a good idea for either of us but especially for you. Gossip can be vicious. You have a brilliant career and should not spoil it on the likes of me."

"With all due respect, Skosh, as the senior person in this relationship, that is for me to decide."

"Again. There. Is. No. Relationship."

He could not stop the vehemence with which he punctuated each word.

"But I promise you, Skosh, there will be."

Her words were sweet and smooth, like the wine she sipped, but Skosh had seen the flash of anger in those grey eyes and became as alert to danger as the hot, acidic bean brew he was drinking could make him.

ONE

Sekmet stretched a tawny foreleg, claws extended, and pulled the blanket from Penny's bare shoulder, but neither cold air nor loud purring woke her. The cat, offended by the sudden blare of the telephone, jumped away before trying again. Penny groped for the handset, knocked it off the receiver, felt around the floor by the nightstand, and picked it up by its cord.

"Hello," she croaked into the earpiece. She turned over the handset and heard a voice.

"Is this Penelope Prendergast?"

Penny squinted one eye at the alarm clock. Seven minutes past midnight.

"Who is this?" she demanded.

She recognized the name he gave as belonging to one of the muckety-mucks in Personnel.

"Ms. Prendergast," he said, "would you be willing to assist an ops guy? Your role will be strictly administrative, no danger involved."

Penny said yes, hoping secretly for at least a little bit of danger.

She fielded the usual questions. When was her last bring-up investigation? Her last polygraph? Evidently, her answers satisfied him. She hoped asking a question of her own would not irritate.

"When?"

"Now. Pack a bag. Leave all identification at home. He'll pick you up in front of your apartment in fifteen minutes."

Only after the call ended did she think it might have been nice to know who was picking her up and kicked herself for missing the opportunity to ask. Ready in five minutes, including makeup and the unsnarling of a nest of dark hair, she made her way downstairs and outside in seven, then stood waiting, freezing, for twenty. It dawned on her as she shivered that she had packed only winter clothes. What if the op was in a warm climate? Maybe someplace tropical? Another question she forgot to ask—where?

She debated running upstairs for lighter clothes until a black government sedan pulled up at the main entrance. The driver climbed out, took her bag, and opened a back door for her. He put her suitcase in the trunk as she sat on the back seat. There were no interior lights. The man next to her could have been anybody. Well, he is in black ops, she told herself. What do you expect? Of course, they take this shit seriously.

"I've cleared you for WEDGE material," he said. He had a smooth baritone voice, but she could not see his face or gauge his size in the dark car, though she felt his bulk.

"There is no file by that name in my document vault," she said.

"There fucking better not be."

This was a marked departure from other polished executives she met in this job, solemn visitors in business suits who signed into the large inner vault where the most sensitive documents in her library sheltered behind thick concrete and steel.

This man reminded her more of people she had knew in the Army, both men and women, accustomed to the talented use of the language of stress. She found it refreshingly real and disturbingly aggressive in this civilian context.

Occasional streetlights revealed no more about her companion aside from a head of dark hair. Unrelenting dark shadowed his face. After a long, silent interval, he said, "I'll brief you on the airplane."

She screwed up her courage. "This is not the way to either airport."

"Correct. They've sent one of theirs."

She had no idea who 'they' were nor what of theirs they might send. Nobody could send a third airport, could they? So far, the dots in this sparse conversation did not connect. They didn't even suggest a pattern. Just a random spattering, like paint flung off a brush.

They drove through a wooded area and onto the taxiway of a dark airfield she never knew existed. The car stopped next to a black Lear 45. In the headlights, a red-haired woman opened the cargo compartment. Jade's shadowy new boss did not introduce them as he grabbed their bags from the trunk and threw them into the cargo compartment. Jade stood cold and awkward to one side.

"How's it going, Claire?" he asked the woman.

"Good. I'm still loving the job."

"Are you in command this trip?"

"I am."

"I feel safer just knowing that."

He took Penny's arm and guided her to the stairs, steadying her from behind as she climbed into the gloomy cabin. Small, dim floor lights kept her from walking into black shapes of low tables and large seats. The window shades were fastened down; she could see no hint of the lighter shade of starlight outside. The man helped her into an overstuffed armchair of a seat, found one end of her seat belt, and dug under her hip for the other, oblivious to her gasp. She still could not see his face but caught a whiff of expensive aftershave.

As the wheels came up after takeoff, the cabin lights came on and she saw her traveling companion for the first time. He faced her across a small table. The first thing she noticed was the way his shirt stretched across wide shoulders supporting a holster bearing a semi-auto. He was tall—she estimated six feet and a little—and Asian, with black hair, black eyes, and a well-formed jaw. She thought he might be approaching forty.

He did not wear a wedding ring, something she checked as a habit, especially when she met a man as appealing as this. It heartened her until she remembered that as a black ops operative, he was not likely to wear a ring. She probably wouldn't even be told his real name.

"Call me John Nakamura," he said. "It's my game name. Everybody calls me Skosh. Penelope Prendergast? Really?"

"My mother is a hopeless romantic. Please call me Penny."

"No. Normally an admin-type shouldn't need a game name, but with these guys, it's not advisable to use your real name. Especially not one as distinctive as yours. It won't take them long to find you either way, but it's not good policy to make it too easy."

He pulled a sealed envelope out of the coat draped over the back of his seat and handed it to her.

"Your name for this op is Jade Wilmerton. Personnel made up your shoes. I did not ask them to generate a legend for you because there was no time. If you are unlucky enough to come into contact with the team, you can give the unclassified part of your job description, nothing more. Stay away from personal details. I will do my best to keep you out of that situation, but shit happens. Be prepared."

He might as well have been speaking a foreign language for all she understood of it and as if to read her mind, he brought that up.

"You speak any languages?"

"French. I attended the Sorbonne for a couple of years." She did not mention her computer languages, because they were not spoken, except to a machine.

"German? Russian?"

She shook her head. He sighed. It seemed she was already a disappointment to this beautiful man.

She opened the envelope containing her operational shoes and found a passport, driver's license, and credit card in the name of Jade Wilmerton. Both passport and license included recent pictures, neither of them flattering. You can take realism too far, she thought. The passport had a few French, British, and Canadian entry stamps. They knew where she had been, though the dates were slightly off.

"Officially, you're coming along to manage the landlord, the food, and the cars and make sure everybody gets paid." He paused to drink from a water bottle. "You should drink water. Flying is dehydrating. There's a refrigerator in the back. Help yourself."

When she returned with a bottle of water, he resumed his briefing in a low voice.

"You'll do those admin-type things, of course, but there is another reason I'm bringing you with me and we will get to that when we land and find a secure place to talk. For now, understand that I intend to keep you as far as possible from the team. Please cooperate with me on that."

This was a second reference to a team. She raised her eyebrows and tilted her head forward.

"Don't ask," he said.

That made her even more curious.

He spoke again before she could get the question out. "And don't go around trying to find out. I will tell you what you need to know, like the fact that they are dangerous. There, I just told you everything you need. Don't be curious. Don't think about what I'm doing. Just do the job I ask you to do."

"Yes, Sir."

"And cut the military shit. I hear enough of it from Claire up front. Even though she's the boss when we fly, she sirs me all the time. Incidentally, be careful when you talk to her. She works for them, not us."

Penny drew up some courage and asked, "Where are we going?"

She hoped for a smidgeon of information that at least would tell her if the bag she brought would turn out to be useless for the climate.

"Lithuania, on the Baltic coast. I hope you packed warm clothes. It's more than a bit of a hike to get there, so I recommend you get as much sleep as you can now."

This was welcome news. So was his assistance with her seat. It had to be the most comfortable airplane seat ever made. Once he configured hers for sleep, he adjusted his own and doused the overhead lights. He did not snore. Penny hoped with all her heart that she did not. She woke twice, once when they touched down in Goose Bay and then in Reykjavik, but she didn't try to raise the shade next to her seat. Too tired to wonder about these places for long, she fell asleep again.

She woke fully the third time the airplane touched down and rehearsed her new name internally to make it her own. She sensed a different quality in the activity around her. Skosh stood and donned his coat in the dark cabin. Penny had considerable difficulty getting out of her seat because she didn't know which button did what. He simply took her hand and pulled her up, then handed over her coat.

The airplane taxied along the ramp in a place she never heard of called Palanga. Skosh was about to say more when Claire stepped into the cabin.

"I think it's only fair to tell you the Challenger is here."

"Fuck! They're two days early." Skosh paused, then said through his teeth, "You told them I brought someone, didn't you?"

"I know who I work for, Skosh. Don't tell me you're surprised."

"She's just an administrative assistant."

"I'm not the one you'll need to convince."

Penny could feel Skosh fuming beside her. He took quick, hissing breaths and loosened the fists his hands had been making. She tried to lighten the tension by using her friendliest voice, pretending the man next to her, her new boss, was not about to explode for reasons beyond her understanding.

"Hi," she said to the pilot, "I'm Jade Wilmerton."

"Call me Claire." Turning to Skosh, Claire continued, "You and Jade are requested to board the Challenger the minute you deplane. It will be in the next parking spot. Please try to remember your manners, Skosh, and use something other than your usual string of f-words when you introduce Jade to Charlemagne."

TWO

"Don't say anything. Let me do the talking," Skosh murmured as they crossed the tarmac.

Jade was smiling too much. He doubted anything he said had gotten through to her. Her palpable excitement made her step bouncy, swinging her glossy, deep auburn hair around her shoulders. It increased his sense of doom. This fiasco might kill him.

The roomy main cabin of the Challenger had been updated since the last time he was inside, several years before. They stepped into what could be mistaken for a stylish living room, with eight overstuffed chairs arranged in two shallow semi-circles. Clear space in the center would accommodate a conference table, probably something that dropped from the ceiling or rose from the floor, Bond-style, but presently absent. The team occupied five seats as comfortable as those in the Lear.

Charlie, son of the team's leader, Mack, nodded to Jade and pointed at the seat between him and his father. With a minimal lift of his chin, he banished Skosh to the other side of the cabin, isolating Jade between the two blue-eyed men who ran the team.

"What languages do you speak?" asked Mack, when Jade had settled into the seat next to him.

Skosh answered for her. "She speaks French."

There came a long silence as Mack stared at him. He stared back, doing his best to scrub out any hint of belligerence.

"Good," said Mack, "we will use French."

"Except that I don't have any French," protested Skosh.

"I expect you will remedy that deficiency soon."

Skosh nodded slightly.

The cabin harbored the usual suspicious undercurrents, now augmented by the presence of a non-operational woman who was too attractive for her own good. And Skosh was the guilty party who had introduced her. Let's see, he thought, how many complications have I created? As if we needed more. He probed the air around him and the breath within. Tension certainly, perhaps a touch more than usual, followed by way more suspicion, and... there it was—he could almost taste it in the air around him—latent violence.

He felt it in every word, every glance, every subtle effort to loosen tensed muscles. It was their default reaction to mistakes like this. He had introduced an unknown element on an operation already nudging the outer limits of possibility. The team known as Charlemagne didn't become the best in the business—they didn't stay alive, in other words—by making allowances.

He could see Mack was not happy as he turned again to Jade, subjecting her to his most quelling glare. Her brown eyes became saucers. Skosh knew the innocence in that expression would not protect her. It might even do the opposite. It would deepen suspicion.

"Skosh calls me Mack and the game name of the man to your left is Charlie," he said. "The others will introduce themselves in time. What may we call you?"

"Jade," said Skosh, again rushing to answer. "Jade Wilmerton."

Another long silence, then a feminine voice across the cabin to Skosh's right said, "It is nice to meet you, Jade. Please, call me Mara."

More strikingly beautiful than ever, thought Skosh, cutting his admiration short before Mara's husband, Sergei, should notice it. Sergei had the lethal skills to back up his jealous nature.

Jade opened her mouth to respond, probably with something polite, but the less said the better, so Skosh interrupted and changed the subject, addressing Charlie.

"You're early. I haven't set up your safehouse yet."

"But you brought help with you," Charlie said smoothly. "It should not be difficult to move up the date." He gave Jade a pointed look. "Many people here speak German. Klaipeda, the port city nearby, was once Prussian, I understand. There is a minority who speak Polish, and most people understand Russian from the more recent Soviet times." His gaze returned to Skosh. "You have been working on that language at least, haven't you?"

Quiet Move

"You know damn well I speak Russian now."

"I find it intriguing that you brought an administrative assistant at all. You have, before now, been sufficiently competent on your own, especially in your choice of caterers."

The others nodded their agreement.

"Turner is better at coffee," said Steve Donovan. He sat next to Sergei, his fellow delinquent, as Skosh liked to call them.

"Did you bring Jade to make coffee?" Charlie asked.

Skosh glowered in reply.

"Perhaps," said Sergei, enjoying an attempt at mischief, "she is his lover." His light grey eyes examined her more thoroughly than was strictly polite. Mara frowned at him.

"I see from Jade's reaction that this also is not the case," said Mack. "Keep your temper, Skosh. Now tell me, Miss Wilmerton, what are you allowed to reveal about your occupation? We know you did not come to make coffee, though you will do that also. What are your usual duties?"

Skosh could give her no help and instead made his face a blank study in unconcern, hoping she would remember his earlier advice.

"I'm a librarian."

"Ah, then your business is information. Skosh has brought a librarian who speaks none of the most prevalent languages of this country to help him with his already more than competent catering, and he wonders why we question this." Mack turned to Skosh. "You must see your plan to shield her from us has failed. I have canceled Miss Wilmerton's hotel reservation. She must stay with you in your safehouse. You know you cannot protect her from us. It remains to be seen whether we can protect her from our enemies or whether we will want to."

"You canceled it? How did you even know about it?" Forcing his words through clenched teeth strangled them.

Mack's answer came in the form of a gaze with slow blinks and a minimal head tilt, the kind of telepathic communication Skosh had learned to interpret. Danger is not imminent, it said but can escalate quickly, depending on your behavior. I will know why you did this in a short while and you will know my decision the moment I make it.

The blue stare helped Skosh find the inner resources needed to control his temper. He relaxed his jaw, looked away, and said, "I see. My assistant will have you in the safehouse in four hours. Come along, Jade."

"I think she should stay with us while you make arrangements," said Charlie.

"Stop winding up the babysitter, Charlie," said Steve in a slow drawl. "He has finally found us two safehouses so we don't have to look at his ugly mug all the time."

"But I want very much to look at his assistant," replied Charlie, still using that soft, smooth voice. "As much as possible."

He looked her in the eye as he said this, but only briefly because Skosh was hauling her through the door, catching her as she fell down the first three steps.

"That man is scary," she said when she regained her feet.

He let her go when he was sure she was steady and looked at her again through a different lens. Could she be his type? Who was he fooling? Any reasonably attractive woman with a pulse was his type. That wasn't why he looked again. Her reaction to Charlie suggested there might be more to her than wearing a Burberry coat to a black op might suggest.

She smiled up at him under a waxing moon, full of trust and questions.

If she is no more than fluff, he thought, what I have done to her is inexcusable. If she is more than that, it's also intolerable. Great. Now I have sunk so low as to measure her damage by its effect on me. He set his jaw and looked away before responding.

"Yeah. Stay clear of Charlie. We have a shit-ton of things to do. The answer to Mack's question about how you were going to cope without the language is named Rimantas. We need to find him, and you'll have to glue yourself to him when you talk to the landlord. He'll translate. I think he's trustworthy. Well, maybe."

THREE

With several hours of forced inactivity ahead of them, Mara, Sergei, and Steve hoarded sleep, knowing operational needs would soon eliminate the possibility. Sergei's badly set broken nose made him snore. The Challenger jet sat reasonably secure on the ramp, with little winter traffic at the airfield and good visibility all around. Michael and his father Misha took the first watch,

Michael handed his father a mug of black coffee from the galley and sat in the seat facing him.

"You've been elevating that leg often lately, Papa. Is it worse?"

Misha winced as he shifted his left leg to ease a cramp.

"No worse than usual."

"Has Alex …?" Michael stopped at a glare from his father.

"Has your stepmother nagged me to listen to the doctors?" said Misha. "Yes. Has she suggested I quit? No."

"I remember the argument you two had after Vasily died." Michael's mind could still hear the screaming and door slamming between his father and Vasily's widow Alex, despite the passage of a dozen years. She was now his stepmother.

Misha closed his eyes as he drank his coffee.

"I accused her of causing Vasily to go to that meeting unarmed," he said. "She swore she never spoke to him about such things, and I did not believe her. Now, I do. She avoids any mention of my work."

"Then it is not Alex who convinced you to leave more of the responsibility to me?"

"No, my leg is persuasive enough."

"But your judgment is more vital to us than the ability to run twenty kilometers, Papa. I am amazed the Americans agreed to your demand to access their information. How did you get them to accept that clause in the contract?"

Misha shrugged, a rare enough gesture. He was seldom unsure about anything. "I requested it. I am as surprised as you are that they agreed."

"I would wager Skosh did not agree." Michael gulped the last of his coffee. "He brought this woman with him to help evade the clause. I have no idea how he plans to use her."

Misha nodded. "Very true. I cannot think of a more unlikely ploy. Does he mean to distract us with her? No. He could not have agreed with that clause. It is probable he did not know about it until it was too late to make a change. The woman's presence is the result of a hasty, maybe desperate, plan to circumvent the contract. It will fail."

Michael smiled. No matter how much his father argued with Alex and assured him he would continue with the team, he sensed his drifting thoughts of retirement. How would he cope without Misha's pinpoint understanding of others? Michael was at the height of his physical powers and had much of his father's intuitive mind, but would it ever be enough?

He took a deep breath. He would have to broach the subject.

"Papa, Steve's son Danny told me he means to join the team. But it will be several years before he is ready. My brother...."

"Max should not," interrupted Misha. "If you would produce an heir there would be no problem, but as it is, given your occupation, Max may be required to inherit."

Michael suppressed a wave of resentment at this perpetual undeserved criticism and repeated his usual answer.

"Theresa and I will keep trying for a son, Papa, but Max is determined to fight, and I see no way to prevent him once he is of age, no matter how many daughters I produce. But that is a side issue. My point is that I need you to stay active at least until Danny is ready."

Misha interrupted again.

"No, you need an older version of Danny, and you need him now. I am no replacement for a young, fit fighter. Your sister is formidable for her weight, but her power is chiefly useful only when you need finesse. You, Sergei, and Steve are in your prime. So were Louis and I when you joined us. It surprised us how much faster and more nimble you were. That is what you need. Strength and speed. You have plenty of judgment."

Michael allowed himself a brief inner jubilation at this rare compliment from his father before letting his heart sink. Misha was certainly considering retirement. For the last four years, Michael had uncomfortably borne more of the burden of responsibility. But his father's presence on each operation had not only taught him how to think and decide; it acted as a buffer, a shield around his conscience.

For Michael, his father's retirement would shift the full weight of responsibility to him. He was old enough, skilled enough, physically and mentally strong enough.

But he didn't want it.

FOUR

Skosh told Jade not to worry about the cost of moving up their tenancy of the safehouses by two days, but haggling had always been a way of life for her. She got a very good price, considering the inconvenience to the landlord, not to mention the late-evening request.

She had to admit the carte blanche Skosh gave her came as a shock. Although the contents of her vault were all related to black ops, Jade's library was considered simple overhead, not part of the secret budget of the organization. As library director, she was required to account for every line item by name. Skosh had figuratively written her a blank check to get his team off the tarmac two days early and then looked at her as if she had three heads when she did so at a reasonable price.

The two safehouses comprised a kind of duplex. More like a small two-story house that had grown a cottage on one side, like a wart, thought Jade. Skosh's side consisted of a tiny single-story one-bedroom cabin sharing a long wall with the team's larger house. Their side of the duplex had two bedrooms upstairs under a steeply pitched roof. In the cabin, a small sitting area just inside the front door contained a bench seat against the outside wall, a table, and two kitchen chairs. Both houses were heated by wood-burning stoves which, Jade suspected, she would be required to tend. Making coffee seemed like light duty in comparison.

Skosh had brought a small 240-volt coffee maker and set it up on top of an unplugged two-burner electric stove near the table.

They needed the plug for the coffee maker. Jade fully concurred. The Army taught her that fresh coffee always trumps hot food.

The team had a larger, industrial-sized coffee machine tended by everybody except Mack and Charlie. Water heaters in both houses were electric, thank heaven. Skosh's had been squashed into a corner next to a tiny refrigerator. There was no heat in what was being inaccurately called 'Jade's bedroom', but the room was snug and the down duvet did its job. She just never had time to fully enjoy it.

They stood in the kitchen of their safehouse that night discussing sleeping arrangements. Skosh insisted she use the lone bedroom and directed her to buy a good lock for it. "Not that it'll do any fucking good," he muttered.

He covered catering procedures next.

"You'll take delivery of the food in here, then I will bring it next door. I'm sure Mara will help me coordinate that. As long as she's around, Sergei won't bother you. Maybe now that he's married Steve might be safe … -ish."

"I should help you bring the food," Jade suggested, "or we should have it delivered over there." She pointed at the wall they shared with the team's safehouse.

"The caterers were vetted by my Lithuanian contact," he said, "but nobody should see any of the team, and that house is not a lot bigger than this, so there are bound to be strays in and out of whatever room we try to take delivery in. It's safer for me to bring it over there."

"Then I should help you with that, Skosh. Why are you so worried?"

Jade did not allude to the as-yet unknown additional task he wanted her to do. Watching him check under and behind every picture and stick of furniture for signs of listening devices reminded her it was better not to bring up things he could not discuss openly. She had to admit she was becoming impatient to find a secure place to talk, but this certainly was not it, as noises on the other side of the wall grew louder.

He opened his mouth to answer and might have said a word, but she could not hear it because of the low explosion that sent a ribbon of plaster hurtling toward them, covering their clothes in white powder. She watched a roughly rectangular line of missing plaster appear on the wall to her left. As the air cleared, a light from the other side shone through that thin line.

"What the fuck?" Skosh shouted.

He had to shout it. Someone was noisily kicking the rectangle and it had begun to fall. A second cloud of dust settled slowly and revealed two men standing in their kitchen.

Skosh turned purple with rage.

"What the fuck do you think you're doing, Pavlenko? We have to pay for that. You are not going to have free access to this house. That was the whole point of having a second house."

The man they called Steve, the one with the southern accent, held up a hand. "Hold on there, Skosh. Sergei, tell him."

"It occurs to me you cannot carry food between the two houses without being seen and causing remarks," said Sergei. Jade recognized a Russian accent. "I have solved problem. It is not a load-bearing wall."

"And besides, Skosh," added Steve, "with the addition of your assistant here, we're thinking the real purpose of the second house is a need for privacy. You should thank me for not letting him put a hole in the bedroom wall."

The man had begun to frankly inspect her, in detail, in an assessing manner. She would have been angry, certainly, frightened, if it did not make her tingle just a little in certain places. He had that effect, she suspected, on many women. He saw her eyes widen and gave her a knowledgeable half-smile. Skosh scowled and took a step forward.

Holding up a hand, Steve said, "Down, Fido. I won't encroach."

Her boss took a deep breath and loosened the fists he had formed.

Steve turned away and said over his shoulder, "Yet."

Jade wondered what Skosh would have done if Sergei had not stopped him before he could reach the man. The stopping was not exactly gentle, and it took the scary guy, Charlie, to put an end to it.

"The last thing I need is a babysitter unhinged by a woman, Skosh. She's yours, all yours. I will enforce it. Satisfied? Can we get on with it? You had better clean up this mess and find something to cover that hole before the caterers get here with breakfast."

Skosh took a colorful woven rug from under the woodpile beneath the kitchen table and tried to stuff it artistically into the hole. Sergei gave him a hammer and a few nails from something called the Footlocker of Useful Things and the result turned out to be quite decorative, once Jade had brushed away a few spiders displaced from their snug woodpile.

She swept debris into a dustpan as Skosh knelt, holding it in place. He looked up at her.

"After breakfast," he whispered through his teeth, "buy a very, very stout lock."

FIVE

Jade ate breakfast alone in the tiny kitchen, while Skosh sat with the team and stayed in their main room for meetings. He had handed her a penciled note on a scrap of printer paper with a list of things she should look for with Rimantas in Klaipeda. He included an unnecessary instruction to thoroughly destroy the paper.

Her interpreter arrived before she finished eating, but she was glad he interrupted what had become an empty, unwanted chewing exercise accompanied by vacant speculation.

"Call me Rimas," he said as he put an old Škoda sedan into gear. "Where do you wish to go?"

Jade had spent several hours with him the evening before, haggling with the landlord. On this bright, cold morning she noticed how young he was, and at the same time, how old. His boyish face turned toward her, looking through blue eyes that seemed older, though he couldn't be more than thirty. He carried his tall, lanky frame with a loose-limbed, athletic gait and wore his dark-brown hair a bit on the long side. The smile arrested her immediately, mischievous but eager to please. She could not help liking him.

Knowing Skosh's ambivalence about trusting the young man, Jade spoke carefully, but she desperately wanted a friend just now and hoped Rimas would not disappoint her.

The safehouses were in a village named Juodkrantė, set back from the long primary road that served the entire length of the Curonian Spit. To the south was the Russian border at Kaliningrad. Rimas headed east and drove onto a ferry that took them across the Curonian Lagoon and into the Lithuanian port city of Klaipeda.

He led Jade down a narrow street no wider than an alley that ended near the harbor. Despite the barrier presented by forests and shifting dunes on the spit across the lagoon, wind coming off the Baltic whistled through the street as if in a tunnel. It shook the wooden signs over shop doors and pierced her prized winter coat, a genuine Burberry she had found in a thrift shop back home. Her teeth chattered with cold as they entered a wondrous establishment dedicated to everything iron, from hinges and nails to doorknobs and locks.

The proprietor proudly set out five stout iron methods of securing a door. He and Rimas engaged in a lively, cheerful conversation. Rimas translated, holding a particularly heavy iron deadbolt.

"He says this one has been known to delay the KGB long enough to allow their quarry to escape through a window."

The man continued in Lithuanian watching her face. Rimas laughed and again translated. "Unfortunately, the window was quite high, and the man fell heavily, but neighbors dragged him away and hid him until he caught his breath and could row a boat. The KGB made sure to watch even high windows after that."

What struck her, besides the joy with which they talked about the past as being past, was the communal sense of shared truth, of common enemies and common defense.

She bought the stout lock.

They passed another cubby-hole of a shop which she could not resist browsing through. Piled high with boxes of new and husks of old computers and their parts, the shop provided a physical tour of recent cyber history. Though she was not sure how she would use it, she recognized and bought an intriguing old encryption modem card and a necessary new notebook computer. It came at an irresistible price in litas, the Lithuanian currency.

As she climbed into the car, Jade felt an attraction to her younger companion that surprised her, though it was nowhere near as compelling as what she felt when near Skosh.

"I have an older brother," Rimas said as if he read her thoughts about his age.

She smiled. "Is he as good-looking as you?"

"Better. But he is what you call in English, gay. He has invited us to lunch. Would you like to meet him?" There was a cautious quality to the question as if he expected her to say no.

"Yes, of course. How kind of him to invite me."

Antanas lived on the third floor of an ancient stone building with an elaborately tiled entrance. They climbed a broad staircase graced by carved wooden railings on either side. The aroma of good food reached Jade as their host opened the door. He was as elegant as his apartment, tall and graceful with long hair and a handsome face made more interesting by a nose with just a suggestion of beakiness. A magnificent set of drums dominated his high-ceilinged living room.

"Do your neighbors like your drums?" she asked.

He laughed and shook his head.

Antanas understood simple English but kept Rimas busy acting as a translator on more complex ideas. The three were soon laughing over a glass of pretty decent wine and Jade enjoyed the delicious soup. The dense black bread that went with it made a substantial meal all by itself.

"Do you know the musician, Tommy Taurus?" asked Rimas.

"Yes. I love his music. Why?"

"They were lovers."

"Really?" She looked at Antanas, allowing her amazement to show. Then her face fell and registered the alarm she felt for him with her next thought.

"Wait. Didn't Tommy die of AIDS?"

"Yes, but he contracted the disease after he went back to America," said Antanas. "It took him very quickly. I am unaffected, except by his loss." He became somber and refilled her glass. "I miss him badly. He gave me this flat, you know." He said something else in Lithuanian and Rimas took up the explanation.

"While I can live at home with our parents," he said, "our father does not ... he will not allow ..." Rimas sighed as Antanas watched for her reaction. "If Tommy had not been so generous, my brother would have no place to live. Apartments can be difficult to find."

"Tommy saved my life when he was here," said Antanas.

"He was here?"

Antanas nodded. "We met during one of his visits to his mother. She was Lithuanian. His father is American. Now that he is gone, I have only this apartment to remind me how happy we were. He told me never to let it go and he promised it would keep me safe. I will never sell it."

Safe. She had only recently been introduced to her lack of safety and here was a man acutely aware of how precarious life could be.

…

Skosh's house in Juodkrantė seemed deserted when they pulled up. Rimas helped her gather her packages and stood outside the car gazing at the house. The drawn curtains gave it an uncommonly forlorn air.

"I will wait here to be sure you have no trouble getting in," he said. "Wave to me if all is well when you open the door."

She had spent the better part of the last ten hours in the presence of armed men and watched them blow a hole in the kitchen wall for the purpose of catering, but it was her interpreter's concern for her that made her shiver.

Skosh let her in, and she waved to Rimas.

"Where the fuck have you been?"

Despite this stark contrast to a pleasant morning, Skosh managed to make her heart flutter with an almost schoolgirl crush. She kicked herself for it, but he looked tired, harried, and magnificent.

"You said to buy a lock."

"All fucking morning?"

She eyed him carefully. Coffee stained his white shirt. He had rolled up his sleeves and taken off his coat but not his weapon. His hair stuck out at wild angles, in straight, black tufts. In short, he was adorable.

After rummaging through the packages, Jade produced the prime example of ironmongery she had scored.

"See? Guaranteed to stop the KGB." She gave him her best smile.

"Did you get anything to install it with?"

Her smile fell. "I didn't think of that. Maybe in Sergei's footlocker…."

"They are the people the lock is supposed to keep out."

"But if they just lend us the tools?"

She could see he wanted to make her understand. She saw him leaf through the pages of his brain searching for the perfect explanation and waited, curiously.

"What else did you buy?" he asked with a defeated sigh.

She brought out linen tea towels with sheep printed on them for the kitchen, two hand-thrown coffee mugs, an assortment of kitchen utensils, especially large wooden spoons since the food would be catered and there were never enough of those in her experience, a healthy supply of blank diskettes and finally her greatest find, the encryption card dangling on its ribbon connector.

She answered his puzzled look. "It's a compu …."

He pushed her against the wall and clapped his hand over her mouth.

SIX

Skosh stared into her eyes, bug-eyed with the physical imposition of silence by his hand. He spoke aloud, a bit too loud, to make sure the spooks on the other side of the rug could hear him.

"Why don't we go for a walk, Jade? I could use some fresh air. How about you?" He nodded at her and slowly released his hand.

"Um. Yes, that sounds lovely. Why don't we do that?"

She matched his volume. He liked women who could catch on quickly and girls with long dark hair and … He caught himself and squashed the thought.

Grabbing his coat from a hook on the back of the door, he threw it on and pushed her out in front of him.

"Smile," he muttered. He grabbed her hand and led her down the front path to the street and across to a paved walkway along the shore.

Her hand served to warm his while he brought her half a mile away to a small deserted dry dock area with a view of Klaipeda across the lagoon. They had both left the house without gloves and her warm hand was welcome in the biting wind.

He caught himself thinking again and returned to business, taking out of his pocket the encryption modem he had grabbed from her.

"Now, tell me about this."

"It's just an interesting, somewhat old-fashioned modem for encrypting data transferring between computers. It's old, but still very effective and not easy to come by, so I bought it."

He stared at her. "You found a computer store?"

"Yes. You told me this morning you wanted me to be in a hotel with access to a computer and you gave me a note saying I should buy one. Where else would I look for one? Are you going to explain anything to me? Because as much as I think all this secret squirrel stuff is kind of sexy, not knowing what's going on does get old."

He looked in dismay at her carefully arranged hair, her designer coat, and boots and sighed. She did not belong in his world, but he wanted to belong in hers. Impossibilities sap your strength, he told himself. You're in enough fucking trouble without adding fantasies and wishes. Back to the business at hand, he made his voice gruffer than he felt.

"I told you I have another reason for bringing you. As I said this morning, I meant to put you in a hotel in Klaipeda where I could get to you, but the team couldn't. It was a forlorn hope, I know now, and you heard Mack quash it when we met on the Challenger. Even if Claire hadn't betrayed me, Mack would have known. He always knows. He reads minds."

"I have the impression Mack is not his real name."

"It's not. The others on the team call him Misha, but that name is reserved for people close to him. I don't know why; he's not Russian. My old boss named him Mack because he's famous for using a knife."

She wrinkled her brow.

He took her hand again because he needed the warmth, though he knew it was not good for him, and led her strolling along the shore, slowly.

"We're going to need reams of research and some of it will have to come from your vault. I need you to find a way to get the information I am contracted to give them. They are cleared for whatever pertains to this operation."

Skosh could see she did not understand but had the good sense to wait for him to tell her more. He wondered how much he would have to explain, and how much he could explain.

"It must be done within our established procedures, but without Mack's people knowing how you're doing it. Have you seen the new information security directive?"

Jade nodded. "Any breach, no matter how minor is guaranteed instant dismissal and maybe criminal charges." She let go of his hand and stopped. "Why not just call my office?"

He turned, took her hand again, and led her back toward the dry dock. How could he explain the professional trap that had been laid for him without whining, and more importantly, without naming names that once spoken would surely get back to Mack?

"The closest secure phone is three hours away. So I asked the personnel office for somebody who understood the system and had computer knowledge. They gave me your name. I figured only an old woman could have a name like that, so I made last-minute arrangements to bring you. I thought you'd have gray hair and sensible shoes and like I said, would stay in a hotel. Those are not sensible shoes."

He pointed at her designer half-boots with kitten heels. They went with the rest of her. Of course, she would wear kitten heels. He imagined what it would be like to work in the same office. They worked in the same building, but he wondered why he had never noticed her. Probably because she worked regular hours, with other people who also worked regular hours. He never noticed them, either.

"I got them for a very good price at a resale shop. I think they're cute. I always wanted …"

"My point is …" he interrupted, not wanting to think about kitten heels anymore. "The point is that I never intended to bring anybody, let alone a young, attractive woman, within shouting distance of those guys and here you are. I am also under a few other pressures that it's best they do not know about. They're acting like they think I'm having a fling with you, and I figure I'll run with that and give them what they want by taking walks and holding hands. Maybe some kind of fucking assassin's code will stop them from finding you too interesting. So, I'm afraid you'll have to put up with that for your own safety. I assure you, I have no designs on you."

She did not hide the way her face fell at these words.

Great, he thought, I expanded the problem by trying to solve it. How could she go for me?

He continued. "Mack, of course, knows a lot and will figure out the rest, but I hope not before you have devised a way to do what I need."

"Which is?"

"He's hired an ex-FBI computer cracker, trained at MIT. The guy's in Chicago with a state-of-the-art setup. Mara, Mack's daughter—you met her on the Challenger—is also savvy with the machines. The two of them are like magicians. I don't think any communication between Lithuania and Virginia will go unnoticed by them unless you can devise a way. That's your mission here. Protect the vault from Charlemagne while giving them all the information they need to kill their target."

Jade tilted her head in shock. "Kill?"

He nodded. "They're assassins, Jade. That's what they do. The target is a bad guy, don't worry, but also don't think nice guys do this work successfully, and this team is unbeaten. Stay away from them."

"But you ...?"

"No. I've never killed. But I'm not one of those purists who swear he never will. If it means saving the op or the team or an innocent, hell yeah, I will. And, unlike a lot of babysitters, I have the skills."

"Babysitters?"

He raised his eyebrows in surprise. "You don't know what The Section does?"

She shook her head.

He marveled. She ran a library devoted to The Section. Had she never read any of it? But then, a lot of things were never written down.

"We provide intelligence and logistics support to the teams or individuals the government hires to take care of, shall we say, special problems," he explained. "We keep the government sanitized from such solutions. You and I are here in unacknowledged support of a wet operation. If it goes wrong, it's not only our careers at stake. It can get us killed. It's not just the target who's a nasty piece of work. Like I said, the team is just as dangerous and we're closer to them. As time goes on, they will become more volatile, more unstable, and they are very, very skilled."

SEVEN

"A woman? He has brought an American woman? Why?" Rimas had no answer and no breath with which to speak. Kestutis had set a fast pace for this warmup run. At the end of it, the questions intensified while he took in much needed air.

"What does she look like? What is her name? Do you think she is his lover? I thought the Americans were more professional than this. The ministry has vetted him, but who is this woman?"

Rimas caught his breath, explained what he could, and stopped himself thinking about any lovers she might have.

"You took her shopping? For what?" asked Kestutis.

"Kitchen things, a good lock, and a computer. Also something for the computer that I did not recognize."

"And she has no languages?"

"She has English, of course, and also French. She attended the Sorbonne."

"The Sorbonne? And he brought her to Lithuania?"

Rimas took advantage of the time they spent stretching to ask his questions. He knew there would be no opportunity once they began sparring.

"This other American you met, the older man, what was his name?"

"Prion," said Kestutis.

"Did the ministry vet him as well? Are the two Americans working together?"

Kestutis stretched one hamstring, then the other before answering. "No, his late wife was a Lithuanian. She came home to live here after they divorced. He is very rich and wants to do something good for the country."

"By hiring fighters?"

"I suspect he wants to fight the Russians. He surveys the border with Kaliningrad. And he has brought a few American fighters as well. That is why I have been watching his compound. I thought this man Nakamura's presence might be a sign the Americans are involved, but the young woman makes me question it. Who brings a woman to such a battle?"

"American women fight, Kestutis. They are no longer restricted from combat."

"Decadent. They will soon have an army wearing high heels. Even the men."

Rimas wanted to let this go, but Kestutis would not leave it alone.

"Imagine your brother fighting the Russians," he laughed, flopping his hands on limp wrists.

Kestutis had taught him everything, how to think, how to fight, how to survive. Though he loved the man like an uncle, Rimas could not allow this to pass.

"He is my brother, Kestutis."

"He is an abomination, young man. The product of a father too weak and a mother too strong. It is well known."

"Nothing of the sort is known. Antanas and I have the same parents."

"Then you have a stronger character. That is all."

Rimas put his heart and all his strength into their sparring session and, for the first time, beat his mentor.

When Kestutis caught his breath, he said, "I want you to get close to this woman. It should not be unpleasant if she is as pretty as you say. I must know what role she is here to play."

Initially, Rimas wondered if Kestutis wanted to know if he had the same tastes as his brother, but then he remembered all information was like currency to the man. He never had enough of it.

Besides, she was certainly pretty enough to make it a pleasant task.

EIGHT

"Misha wants to know where you've been," Steve told Skosh. "You'd better go explain yourself. I'll stay and entertain Jade for you."

He gave her a suggestive smile. Everything about this guy sizzled. It reminded her of the boys she had grown up with. Only one thing on their minds, ever.

"Like hell you will, Steve," said Skosh. "Tell him I'll be right there. Let me get my coat off, for fuck's sake."

He hung his coat on the hook behind the door and pointed toward Jade, then the bedroom. He made a gesture like turning a key. She translated it as 'Go lock yourself in the bedroom.' The lock was not yet installed, but she made as if to comply and walked back to where, lo and behold, the lock was on the door. She tested it and found it fully functional. The keys, two of them, lay on the dresser. She hadn't installed it, and Skosh couldn't have, but it made her feel a little safer.

She grabbed her ditty bag from her suitcase and headed for the bathroom. It sported a small but deep freestanding tub and Jade could think of no better way to get her brain working on the puzzle Skosh had given her than by soaking her body in hot water.

Carefully locking the bathroom door, she thought it seemed a bit flimsy but figured it would at least warn her that someone was trying to come in and so give her time to throw on a towel. She soaked and luxuriated for a few minutes calling up and then rejecting one refinement after another to the problem of keeping Charlemagne out of her vault's computer. The shopping trip had given her not only an idea but also the hardware necessary to execute it.

When the water had cooled a bit, she used a toe to turn on the hot tap, supporting herself with her arms on the sides of the tub so as not to slide underwater.

The bathroom door opened. So much for that lock.

"What the fuck are you doing?" said her boss.

She saw no purpose in answering. After all, he was reasonably intelligent.

"We're on an op for chrissake. Get out of there. Now. Before somebody comes in here."

The water was deep, but it did not quite cover her breasts and there were no concealing bubbles. Maybe he heard his own voice and processed the absurdity of his words, or perhaps he finally realized what he was seeing. Either way, he turned, red-faced, and slammed the door behind him.

She did as ordered and was dry and wrapped in a towel preparing to leave when the door opened again. Sergei and Steve stood in the doorway grinning.

"A bath? On an op? Really?" This from Steve.

"If Mara did this, I would have to kill anyone who went near the door," said Sergei. "It is not good to do on an operation. Do you like the lock on your bedroom?"

"Yes, thank you, but I thought I remembered three keys."

"Correct. Misha has the third."

The conversation stalled at this point, with both men raking the towel with their eyes and Jade feeling the cold through her bare feet on a stone floor.

"Right, you two," came a voice from outside, "out of there before the babysitter has a coronary."

They scattered like magic, and she faced the scary one, Charlie. Worse, he came into the small space and closed the door behind him. He did not move, but stood there, using his eyes to x-ray behind the towel, noting every fold of it, watching her shiver, first with cold and then because of his gaze. Finally, he spoke.

"I presume Skosh has told you who we are, but did he also explain what we are?"

She nodded. He waited for more of an answer, her nod being insufficient.

"He said you are assassins." She squeaked this.

"And do you think, given our occupation, that we are what you might refer to as nice people?"

She had no way of answering this, it seemed, without increasing both her discomfort and her danger, so she did not.

"If Skosh has given you instructions and warnings regarding us, it would be wise to heed them. We are none of us incapable of forcing our attentions upon you. Your presence here, and your behavior especially, threatens to destabilize my team. I will not permit it."

He turned and opened the door. Skosh stood there tight-jawed and fists clenched.

"What did you say to her?" he said through his teeth.

Charlie's answer came slow and smooth. "Ask her. By all means, ask her."

Jade locked the bedroom door before getting dressed, while Skosh stood outside telling her to hurry up. She chose her best designer jeans, despite their having become creased in the suitcase, and a Ralph Lauren sweater that she dearly loved. She needed the mirror and lighting in the bathroom to attempt makeup, but Skosh was pretty agitated, so she simply brushed her hair and piled it on top of her head, holding it in place with a tortoiseshell comb.

She opened the door, feeling undressed without makeup.

"What did he say?" He whispered the question, so she replied in kind, repeating Charlie's words exactly. He closed his eyes and opened them slowly. "It was a threat. I'm sending you home. I'll just give them the fucking passwords to the vault."

"Hell no, you won't. I have a plan."

He did not seem to hear her but was staring at the lock on the door. "Tell me you installed this."

"No, I didn't. Sergei did."

She took the keys from the dresser, gave him one, and put the other in her pocket.

"He said somebody called Misha has the third one. Have I met him?"

"Mack. I told you, they call him Misha."

As if summoned by the reference, the man stood in spectral silence behind Skosh, who turned around when he saw her reaction.

"The caterers will soon be here, Skosh. We will be honored if you and Miss Wilmerton will join us at all mealtimes. Please bring chairs with you."

In the space of half an hour, Jade had heard a finely worded threat and a polite direct order, both of them mandatory and unambiguous.

NINE

They offered Jade a seat as far as possible away from Skosh. The courtesy with which the offer was made created a pretense that she had the option to decline, but she knew it for the fairy tale it was.

She sat next to Mack, who peppered her from time to time with slow questions, often doubling back to previous answers and pinning down all minor inconsistencies. He did not appreciate incomplete answers either, attacking every sketchy explanation she gave with terrifyingly polite tenacity.

"Where do you live?"

"I have an apartment near my library."

"Your library? What sort of library?"

"Oh, you know, just a library."

"With books?"

"Yes."

"And documents?"

The mental gymnastics required to avoid answering took too long. He smiled slightly and changed the subject.

She would have liked to listen to the general conversation in the room, but Mack was the only person speaking English. There must have been some funny jokes told, especially by Steve and Sergei. They kept up a steady banter. Even Charlie chuckled from time to time. Judging by the overall hilarity and the stony, patient look on Skosh's face, much of it was at his expense.

Twice, Jade caught herself nearly blurting out a detail about her apartment, her friends, or the job. Mack registered all near misses with that same slow smile.

Mara brought her a mug of black coffee. "Tell me, Jade," she said, "have you and Skosh been seeing each other long?"

How was she supposed to answer that? She looked at him on the other side of the small room, but Skosh didn't seem to notice her alarm. She sipped hot coffee to gain time to think of an answer, and it caught in her throat, sparking the most welcome coughing fit of her life. Mara patted her on the back to calm the cough, smiling the same slow, almost secret smile Jade had seen on Mack.

She did not eat much, but the team decimated the catered meal. There were several unpronounceable potato casserole dishes with bacon, baked chicken in a cream sauce, Brussels sprouts, sausage, sauerkraut, and fried strips of bread that looked like French fries and came with a tasty cheese dip. It all looked delicious, but Jade got precious little of it. The only thing the team consumed more of than food was coffee. She noticed Skosh was no slouch in either department.

After following the others as they placed their plates in an empty tub next to Mara's computer, she turned from there to the rug over the hole in the wall to make her escape. Charlie headed her off, taking her arm none too gently and sending her to a chair that had opened up next to Skosh.

"We will need you to attend all meetings," he said. "And I expect you to brief us about the real reason you are here, preferably without the need for torture." He smiled when he said this as if he were joking, but his eyes told her he was not.

"I don't think my assistant needs to be here," Skosh said as Jade sat next to him.

Charlie answered him with a smirk. "I think differently. We know you're up to something, Skosh, and that you think it's in support of the operation. It follows that she should hear the details directly, not as whispered pillow talk between you."

Mack opened proceedings.

"Miss Wilmerton, the target's name is Earl Prion."

"Please, call me Jade," she said, hoping he would be less likely to kill her if they were on a first-name basis. It was becoming uncomfortably clear that these people were not playing. What had Skosh said about a knife?

"Very well, Jade," said Mack. "Prion is an American who recently came into great wealth through unknown means. He has begun to spend his money in ways that disturb your government. We have been asked to discover why he is building a small private army before we eliminate him and neutralize his force. Today, he arrived in Lithuania."

He nodded minimally at Skosh, who took up the briefing.

"My contact in Lithuanian counterintelligence, Kestutis Girdauskas, tells me Prion is recruiting locals with fighting skills, sons and grandsons of former anti-Soviet partisans, a few criminals, that sort of thing, promising money and appealing to patriotism. Americans are popular now, but not Russians. Prion has hinted that Russia is his target."

Skosh consulted a small notebook before he continued.

"Our Resident in Vilnius briefed me on the local situation. It has been just over six years since fourteen protesters were killed by Soviet troops at the TV tower in Vilnius. Russian propaganda and provocations are ongoing and are broadcast widely, along with a great many popular Russian-language cultural programs. Most Lithuanians speak at least some Russian and all educated citizens are fluent.

"The propaganda has perversely stirred peoples' memories of lionized anti-Soviet fighters, even though a few of these may have had fascist histories. Loyalties can be formed based more on emotion than reality, though there's plenty of fact to warrant it. Given Lithuanian losses under Stalin, it is perhaps understandable but does not bode well for a liberal democracy, which the people want, but their neighbor, the Bear, does not want them to have."

He put the notebook away as Mack nodded to Charlie, who turned an unwanted stare toward Jade.

"You say you are a librarian. May we assume your library is part of Skosh's organization? Don't look to him for guidance. Just answer the question."

She decided it would be unwise to lie. The man's eyes seemed to have access to every secret she had ever tried to keep.

"Yes."

"Then at least part of your reason for being here is to support our need for information?"

"Yes."

Sergei was making the rounds with a coffee pot, and Charlie paused as he held out his mug.

"Mara," said Charlie, "give Jade a notebook and pen from the FUT so she can jot down my questions." He saw the puzzled look on Jade's face and gave the definition. "Footlocker of Useful Things."

Taking a long sip of coffee, he subjected her to a malign stare, or was she suspecting more malevolence than was real?

"Your list stays in this room, however," he continued in a kind of soft purr, "but you are welcome to come and refresh your memory at any time."

No, she decided, she had been *under*estimating his malice.

"I see you are catching on," he said. His lips turned up in a half smile.

Okay, this guy is beyond scary. When his smile widened even further, she promised herself she would stop thinking thoughts he could read so readily.

Charlie dictated his list as she wrote. "First, we need a place to start, a hint as to the source of Prion's funding. Your authorities must have some idea, or they would not have given us this commission. At least they should know where he banks. I want that information as soon as possible."

He swiftly piled on more questions she knew would test her system.

"Feel free to use Mara's computer to consult your database." Charlie pointed to the excellent, state-of-the-art hardware sitting on a decrepit table against one wall.

Mara turned and smiled at her. Had she not been there, Jade would have had a look at the setup, not to send out the questions of course, but rather to get a feel for how Mara operated.

"Thank you, Mara," she said, "but I will muddle along with my notebook computer. I'm sure it will do the job."

The ambient noise of shuffling feet and sipping coffee, of occasional murmured asides in a neighbor's ear and countless audible clues to the presence of too many people gathered in a small space ceased abruptly. Only the computer behind Mara did not know any better and continued its now deafening hum in the hush. Even Skosh threw eye daggers at Jade. She beamed at them all, feigning innocence, but nobody was buying it.

Sergei broke the breathless quiet. "There was no notebook in your luggage."

This time he was the one receiving a warning frown from Charlie. He had searched her things when he installed the lock.

The lock that Mack had a key to.

TEN

"When the fuck did you acquire a notebook computer, Jade?"
"Do you ever create a sentence without using the f-word?"

Skosh snorted. Or maybe it was more of a snarl, as he squeezed her hand.

"Ow. Can't we find some other way to communicate that doesn't require us to freeze?" She peered down at the ice under the dock they were standing on.

"No, we can't, unless you want to take Charlie's suggestion and go whisper pillow talk."

She had already decided such a necessity would make her very happy indeed but sighed when he continued without pause.

"It would be completely unsecure anyway. No doubt Pavlenko has half a dozen devices planted around your mattress. It's hard enough trying to keep an eye out for a directional microphone out here; we'll never find all the touches he has set. I hope you've been inspecting your pockets. Also, check the lining of your coat before we go out on our oh-so-romantic walks. Fuck, it's freezing out here. Now tell me your plan and how you got this computer."

He pointed to the bag slung over her shoulder. He had made her bring it with them. She objected at first, but the memory of Charlie's smile came to mind, and she stopped mid-protest. The new suggestion that Sergei may have hidden bugs around her pillow convinced her further, at least until she could come up with a system that would alert her to tampering.

"I bought it at that computer shop," she said. "It's a Pentium and I got it for an excellent price. I'll use it to get the answers they need."

Skosh's glare seemed a tad belligerent.

"How?"

She returned the belligerence with an extra frown as interest.

"By using a system and a decoy. Do you still have that encryption modem you took from me this afternoon? You put it in your pocket."

He handed it back to her. "Explain."

"Rimas and I had lunch at his brother's apartment. I borrowed the phone—and paid him for it, of course—and called my assistant, Dennis. He has a key to my apartment."

"He?"

"Yes. He."

"Why does he have a key to your place?"

She refrained from telling him it was none of his business and chose instead to serve him the silence the question deserved.

But he was not satisfied.

"You're sleeping with your assistant? You know that's wrong, right?"

She stopped and tilted her head at this preposterous statement. "Why would it be wrong?"

"Because of the power difference."

"He hasn't forced himself on me." She turned away from him, unwilling to let him see her blush.

He held her upper arm to keep her facing him. "Not him. You. You have too much power over him to make it a truly consensual relationship."

"All couples share power in different ways. If he and I were in such a relationship—and mind you, I'm not saying we are—I couldn't possibly be more powerful. He's almost as tall as you." Though nowhere near as fit, she thought.

"Can you fire him?"

Her argument crashed to the ground.

"It never occurred to me," she whispered.

Jade was new to the concept of having power. In the Army, her biggest job had been as an assistant to a colonel. He had the power. No one ever reported to her. Now in the vault, she held the livelihoods of five people in her hands. Skosh watched her face as thought followed thought. She looked up at him, mortified.

"Dennis is gay," she said finally. "He takes care of my cat when I travel. I made arrangements with him to use email to check up on the cat and told him to use my old notebook. It has the same encryption device. I will use it to get Charlie's answers."

Jade could have sworn Skosh was fighting a smile until he glanced over her shoulder and rolled his eyes. She was about to turn to look behind her when he took her chin, tilted it up, and kissed her. Seriously. Surprise opened her eyes. The cold made them tear. His eyes were open, too, but were looking past her. How very disappointing, but she closed her eyes and enjoyed what it could have been.

"So is this the power difference you guys were discussing? Feeling guilty are we, Skosh?"

He broke off the kiss. "Fuck off, Donovan."

"This is a shit detail, Skosh, having to follow you around the frozen North with a directional. How about you just go tell Misha what you're really up to, so I don't have to freeze my ass off every time you want to brief your assistant."

"A little privacy goes a long way, Steve."

"So does a little information. It's time you provided it." Steve took Jade's arm and turned her toward him. "What's this in your hand?"

"Hands off her," said Skosh.

"Make me."

"Gladly."

During this rather electric exchange, Jade put the modem in her pocket, acting secretive and making sure Steve noticed. The pause gave Skosh a chance to hit him and send the parabolic microphone he had been carrying sliding along the peer. Skosh soon followed it onto the concrete, courtesy of Steve's fist, but he came up whirling a long-legged kick through the air before Steve could close the distance enough to punch again. Steve took the blow from Skosh's foot to his midsection like it never happened and would have replied in kind, but all three of them became aware of an audience at the same moment.

They turned to face Mack, standing hatless in the cold wind under a path light in the dusk. No one had seen or heard him approach. He invited them to precede him to the house with a minimal sweep of one hand.

ELEVEN

At first, Skosh was more concerned Mack had allowed Steve to enter the smaller safehouse, unsupervised, with Jade. He knew Donovan too well to trust him alone with a pretty woman. Presumably, Mack also knew Donovan's habits better than anybody else. Skosh was surprised, then, as he pulled him to the back of the house.

"Really, Mack? Literally hauling me behind the fucking woodshed? Isn't that a bit old fash…."

Mack's fist pounded into his gut, arresting the word mid-larynx. Skosh struggled for breath as Mack shoved him up against the shed wall with a twisting grip on his coat collar.

"How dare you strike a member of my team."

The tone was low and almost conversational, but punctuated by increased pain as Mack tightened his grip on Skosh's throat. He continued.

"Touch one of them again and I promise you a slow and painful death. Now, you will explain to me why you are not yourself."

He loosened the twist sufficiently for Skosh to catch enough air to speak. Unfortunately, the labyrinth of his problems disoriented him, making the response too slow for Mack's purposes.

Mack twisted the collar again.

"Tell me!"

"I… I can't. It has nothing to do with the operation. It is my problem alone. I…."

"Who has set you up?"

Skosh had known since childhood that the inscrutable Asian thing was a myth because he had never managed to pull it off.

This time was no exception. Not only did Mack read his surprise accurately, but he then leapt to the heart of the problem with Mack-like accuracy and hissed a demand.

"There is a woman involved. But it is not this woman, Jade. I want her name."

"I can't. Ethical...."

"Ethics? You put us all at risk and plead ethics as your reason? You work in the most unethical section of a largely unethical organization within the government of an historically unethical nation and you pretend to be behaving ethically?"

Skosh had never before been the recipient of this kind of slow, concentrated anger. Because it came from a famously efficient killer, it helped him find his own steel core. He would not die sniveling. It gave him the strength to look into those blue eyes, though he was careful to filter out any suggestion of insolence.

"I cannot divulge details of my organization, Mack, and my conscience will not allow me to put an innocent, no matter how ignorant, in danger."

Mack's eyebrows rose in surprise. He released his hold and pointed toward the house.

"Instead, you brought that innocent into the heart of danger. A librarian, no less. An attractive one."

"That was not the plan, as you well know."

"Do you know what will happen to you if you fail?"

Skosh wondered briefly which of several failures Mack was referring to, but he knew all the outcomes and relished none of them. He answered simply, "Yes."

"Does she know what will happen to her?" Mack gestured again toward the house.

Skosh had no answer.

With a hard shove, Mack sent him sprawling over the stacked firewood.

"I will know who and why and where, Skosh, with or without your cooperation, and I will take action to protect my interests. It is time for you to adopt my interests as your own. There is a large difference between damaging your career and losing your life."

TWELVE

Jade was not present for the great chewing out of her boss. Fairness would dictate that Steve also should get a tongue lashing, but she noticed a bruise on Skosh's cheek when he came back and never saw one on Steve. There were more bruises on Skosh's abdomen. She noticed them when he changed into a set of black cold-weather clothing in the kitchen.

She did her best not to enjoy the view, but some things are impossible.

"We are all headed out to recce the target," he told her as he inserted an earbud and ran the wire to a small radio attached to his belt. "Both safehouses will be locked and the sensors around the perimeter are working. Lock yourself in the bedroom and don't move. You should be safe enough this early in the op."

"I have to get answers to Charlie's questions," she reminded him.

He stared at her. She pointed to the notebook on the kitchen table. He mouthed 'be careful' without sound and said aloud, "Do it quick and then lock yourself in. We won't be long."

It took her no more than half an hour, and that included the phone call to Dennis's cellular phone. She shut down the computer, hid the modem in her pillow, and locked the bedroom door behind her as she crept to the hole in the wall and nudged the carpet aside.

A dim light glowed in one corner of the main downstairs room. Jade was grateful for it as she focused on her objective. She would have barked her shin on a footlocker had the room been totally dark. As she reached her right hand behind the CPU of Mara's computer and felt for the power switch, she became aware of a feeling. A presence. It reminded her of a ghost movie when the heroine gets all goose-pimply just before a hideous ghoul jumps out at her.

This was much worse.

She stood straight, turned slowly, and faced Mack. Again, the minimal gesture to precede him. He pointed to a chair until she sat down in it, then sat in the one facing her. So far, despite no words being spoken and no weapons brandished, she felt the presence of danger. He stayed close to her in a way she knew he meant as a threat. He seemed ready at any moment to escalate the situation.

"I see you have an interest in computers, Jade."

"Yes, Sir." Now, what would be the use in denying it? She ventured to look at him, doing her best not to show her fear. In the low light from the table lamp next to her, his face was partially shaded and what she knew to be grey hair at the temples appeared blond. His skin showed some years, she supposed, but it also gave her a good idea of what he looked like when he was her age. He had rolled up the sleeves of his white shirt and removed his tie. He wore a gun in a shoulder holster. She swallowed hard and he spoke again.

"I am amazed that so small a machine has become important to our survival."

This was not her idea of conversation. Instinct told her not to pry and self-preservation counseled silence.

After almost a minute, during which time she steeled herself to meet his gaze, he said, "I see that my words perplex you. Are you unaware that Skosh's mistake has imperiled your survival?"

She wondered if he could see her wide eyes in the dim light, or if he could hear the pounding of her heart. She could.

"Perhaps you harbor the illusion that you are safe with us?" he added in a low voice.

She sucked in her breath audibly.

"Good. You are no longer deceived. Now, I will explain my position. I know that Skosh has made a mistake."

She wondered how he would explain this conclusion and remembered Skosh's comment that somebody named Penelope should be old and wearing sensible shoes.

Mack resumed. "Every man on the team is now married, but except for Sergei, none of us is incapable of taking advantage of a propitious situation."

What a way with language this guy had.

"Sergei would be more likely than most to avail himself of such an opportunity. He had a deplorable reputation in the KGB, but he knows Mara would kill him. Skosh understands us. He is experienced with other teams and has been trained in his present position by a man who has known us for thirty years. He would not bring a young, attractive woman into our proximity. At least not for purposes other than …"

He let the thought drop without naming it. She was grateful. His long pause made her think he might expect a comment from her, but when he began again, she realized he had been carefully arranging his words.

"Perhaps your real name is ambiguous. It may appear to be male. From the list of possible candidates we have assembled, however, I think it more likely that he thought you to be considerably older. Either way, Skosh now realizes his mistake, and it has deranged him. He hit Steve this evening, a reckless act very unlike him. Luckily, Steve saw me before he could kill him outright."

In all this time, the man barely moved, yet Jade was never unaware that he'd be pretty speedy in any direction, and she was directly in front of him. She didn't know if he noticed how firm a grasp she had on the arms of her chair. Foolishly, she hoped everybody would return immediately and the noise and bustle would take his mind off his intentions, whatever they were.

What had caused her mere serious concern was well on its way to becoming terror and he was not finished producing more of it. He continued.

"Skosh is a very good babysitter, and we need him on this operation. It is too late and too difficult to replace him with someone as competent. Your presence, then, threatens the success of the operation and therefore our lives. My normal response would be to shoot you immediately, but I fear this would worsen Skosh's derangement and make him a liability as well. I hope you understand how tenuous your fate remains."

He tilted his head, expecting a response for the first time.

She managed a hoarse whisper. "I do."

"I will not ask you to tell me your real purpose here. You are the subordinate, and such a revelation would be a betrayal of your superior. We will give you and Skosh sufficient privacy for you to repeat to him what I have said. I will leave it to him to discuss the topic with me."

The team returned at this point, noisy, muddy, and sweating despite the cold, and Jade felt a tidal wave of joy and relief until Mack said, "Whatever system you have devised to obtain the answers to Charlie's questions should have borne fruit by now. If it has not, your method is unacceptable."

With that dismissal, she lost no time in slipping through the rug under cover of the chaos filling the room.

THIRTEEN

Skosh turned, the kitchen phone in his hand. "Where the fuck did you come from?"

He had to ask though the answer was pretty obvious. The rug behind Jade still swayed.

"I need that phone line to download the answers," she said as she headed for the bedroom to fetch the modem. He followed her.

"I thought I was pretty clear. What were you doing over there? Mack was there. He stayed behind. Don't tell me you went over there for some incredibly dumb reason. He didn't come over here, did he? He didn't …"

They were interrupted by Steve, disheveled and panting, his face still blackened by camo paint. The brown eyes were unmistakable or Skosh would have thought he was Sergei. He leaned against the door jamb, smirking.

"Lover's tiff?"

"Get the fuck out of here, Donovan."

"You going to hit me again if I don't, Skosh?"

He did not answer because he was counting to ten.

Steve spoke again. "Misha told me to assure you that the devices in this house are turned off. He gives you his word. Ask him directly, if you don't believe me." He tilted his head. "What's that?"

"I believe you. I don't have time to deal with your devices right now. My Lithuanian counterpart will be here any minute because of what you left behind out there."

"Not my work, Skosh."

"One of your methods, though."

"It's not like I have a patent on it."

"Get out of here before Kestutis sees you."

Skosh slipped outside the front door and made a show of locking it with his key, pretending no one else was inside. *I'm good at my job. I'm experienced. Why am I unraveling?*

Kestutis stood waiting on the sidewalk.

They took the Lithuanian agent's government car because this was an official meeting, and because Skosh did not want the man anywhere near a vehicle that might be used by the team. The two did not speak as they drove toward Nida at the southern end of the Lithuanian portion of the Spit.

Skosh used the time to examine the peril he was in and how uncommonly off his game he had become in the past few days. The past week. He should have read that commission much earlier and not waited until the night before he was to leave. Why didn't he? He knew why. He had been busy fending off Candace.

Kestutis pulled onto a narrow forest track as Skosh pointed to it. It ended abruptly a few hundred yards in, and they got out to walk, still without speaking. Skosh led the way.

As he pushed aside tree branches, he remembered he didn't get the damned commission until late that evening. That was unusual. Timing was not as critical for this op, but administrative delays were always frowned upon. He briefly wondered if she had anything to do with processing that commission. She was high enough in the hierarchy. Surely, a woman wouldn't use her position for revenge, would she?

Skosh tripped on the tree root that told him they were close, but he kept his balance, turned sixty degrees right, and saw the opening in a shaft of moonlight.

"The man is dead," said Kestustis.

Biting back a sarcastic reply, Skosh said nothing. He liked his Lithuanian counterpart but did not trust him enough to venture too much friendliness.

"You just came across the body?" There was the tiniest bit of irony in Kestutis's tone.

Skosh nodded, wondering if it was friendly sarcasm, or otherwise.

A muscular man in middle age, Kestutis moved quietly through the brush on the forest floor. He nudged the body with the toe of one boot, then grabbed a shoulder and heaved the corpse onto its back.

The dead man stared unseeing at the moon. The neck bulged unnaturally to one side, betraying the cause of death, but spots of blood glistened on the jacket, and the forest floor all around had been trampled. Kestutis searched the jacket pockets and handed Skosh an American passport.

"One of yours?"

Skosh examined the document while Kestutis opened the jacket and shirt, revealing an abdominal stab wound and a great many tattoos. A flashlight confirmed that most of these were gang tattoos, probably done in prison.

The Lithuanian official waited for a reply.

"Not one of our best, shall we say," said Skosh. "He must have met with an accident."

Surely, Kestutis would be astute enough to know the rules of this game.

"I see. I will take you back to your house, Skosh. I can find this place again in the morning. Thank you for alerting me."

When he returned to the safehouse, Skosh lay beside Jade on the bed for the purportedly private briefing Mack had both promised and demanded of them earlier. He noticed with regret that she seemed indifferent to his proximity. He felt anything but indifferent to hers.

They lay on top of the duvet, fully clothed and filthy. Well, he was filthy. Also cold, disheveled and dispirited. At least she didn't have mud in her hair. He knew she would have liked a bath but hoped she finally understood that was a thing of the past. He would have told her how attractive she remained despite the snarls in that magnificent hair, but it would have been inappropriate and unprofessional, and he refused to make yet another mistake this trip.

"Charlie was pleased with the answers," she said before he could ask.

"Did they get into the vault?"

"No, there is no connection to the vault."

"But the information comes from there, doesn't it?"

"Yes, but by way of a clean floppy each time. Dennis is using my old portable computer and the reception desk phone line, not the T-1 at the vault."

He turned his head toward her and whispered. "Why the encryption?"

"To keep their hacker busy for a while and protect the classified."

"With an old modem?"

"It's good enough up to Secret, and so far that's as high as the information has been, though there have been some sensitive sources. Because my old laptop has the same modem, the data is encrypted end to end. Even when—not if—the former FBI guy...." she turned her head to look at him, eyebrows up in a question mark.

"Justin."

"Justin, then. Even when he breaks it, it won't matter because they'll only see what they're already getting from me."

He found her hand and squeezed it.

"Thank you."

He took a few deep breaths and asked about her conversation with Mack.

"I'm sorry," he said when she finished.

She didn't answer. He realized nothing she could say would make him feel better, and pretty much anything it was possible to say would be more likely to make him feel worse. She simply squeezed his hand back.

He smiled, relieved, and fell asleep within two breaths.

When he jumped off the bed shortly before dawn, Skosh did his best not to wake her but failed. She sat up, blinking in the overhead light. Sergei stood in the doorway.

"What, Sergei?" he said, annoyed.

"Misha said to tell you devices are back on, and he expects you to speak to him now."

Jade was busy trying to free her hair from a decorative comb that had been overwhelmed by her new reality. She met Skosh's look and gave a slight nod that he understood meant it was safe to tell Mack the real reason he had brought her.

The man would take it out of his hide again, Skosh knew, but it would be a mistake not to tell him. And he was done making mistakes. At any cost.

FOURTEEN

Jade poured a fresh mug of coffee and handed it to Skosh when he returned from his meeting with Mack. He winked at her, put the mug on the kitchen table, and hugged her, whispering an operational sweet nothing into her ear.

"Mack is pissed. Well done."

On the one hand, her boss was happy. On the other, the man who had threatened her was not.

Skosh pulled a blood-smeared American passport out of a pocket and handed it to her.

"I need to know everything we have on this guy."

She accepted it with her fingertips and dropped it on the table immediately. Acutely conscious of the inadequate bathroom lock, she had managed to wash her face and hands and had run a toothbrush briefly over her teeth. Blood was not on the list of substances she found acceptable to dabble in that morning. The passport sat next to their coffee, so she moved the mugs lest they be contaminated.

"Well, come on," said Skosh. "Get going. Put it in with the list Charlie gave you this morning."

Jade tried to remember a list. She did remember Charlie. He was difficult to forget, entering the bathroom as he did when the toothbrush had only just begun to dispel the fuzz of a luxurious three hours of sleep. She had spat at the mirror in panic.

At Skosh's mention of a list, Jade dashed into the bedroom and dug into her suitcase, locating yesterday's crumpled pair of jeans, the ones she had slept in—the ones she had put on despite a crease, a mere crease, from the suitcase. There was indeed a slip of paper in one back pocket. Tiny, cramped writing filled a torn section of Sergei's unmistakable lined paper from the FUT. She was going to need a magnifying glass. After retrieving her notebook computer and the encryption modem, she headed back to the kitchen table.

The coffee in her mug had gone cold.

At breakfast, Mack gave her a few of the slow gazes that seemed to be his specialty. He was letting her know he noticed her, that he was displeased with her, and that he was still tempted to kill her. She accepted the danger with a tinge of pride because she had beaten him in such a small way using old technology. Perhaps he would come to respect her. Then again, maybe water flows naturally uphill, emptying the sea.

Mara sat down next to Jade, grinning. She spoke softly, out of the side of her mouth while nibbling a piece of toast. "You have bested Misha. That is excellent but do be careful. He can be dangerous."

Can be? Jade wished she could shout this question with full sarcasm.

"I think I know your method," Mara continued. "It appears to be insurmountable. Even the telephone call to your assistant gives us nothing. Tell me, should I care about the encryption?"

Jade was tempted to thank her for her kindness by telling her not to bother, but she had decided she would give no quarter. She could not know what or when something would create more danger for herself or Skosh. Responding with a quiet shrug, she did her best to look enigmatic. Mara widened her grin.

The grin fell as Charlie stood before them.

"What is it, Charlie?" Mara asked.

He tilted his chin; she sighed, took her plate, and moved away with an apologetic smile. As he sat beside her, Jade felt cold tension run up her spine.

"You should lock the bathroom door when you're in there," he said.

"I did."

She refrained from pointing out that it was the bathroom in Skosh's safehouse, not in his, and that he knew she was in there because he had been looking for her. She was pretty sure a properly working lock would not have stopped him.

"It is faulty then," he said as if that had been in question. "I will ask Sergei to look at it." He turned his head and smiled at her. Not a full, genuine smile, but a seductive one, full of suggestion. "Then you can resume your baths in safety."

If she had any illusion that the word safety meant the same thing to Charlie as it did to her, it was dispelled by the look of wide-eyed alarm on Skosh's face across the room. He swallowed quickly, took his half-full plate to the container on the table, and tossed his head toward the hole in the wall. It was an order to follow him ASAP.

"Excuse me," she told Charlie, trying to stand.

He held her by the arm. "Skosh will wait. He cannot afford to confront me. I'll tell Sergei to fix the lock."

He let go with the same meaningful smile, and she skedaddled through the hole in the wall. Grabbing the modem from the kitchen table, she slipped it into her pocket as Skosh pulled her out the door.

FIFTEEN

"He terrifies me, Skosh."

"That's probably his intention."

"Why? He must know I get it. I don't need those icy eyes reminding me he's dangerous."

They had walked for some time before Skosh asked her about her conversation with Charlie. She recounted it, word for word, doing her best not to let her voice shake. When they reached the center of a small parking lot with a clear view all around them, Skosh stopped to face her, stamping his feet against the cold. His breath made little clouds as he spoke.

"He could be just scratching an itch. Such things are possible. You are an attractive woman, and your hair is almost the same shade of deep auburn as his wife's, but when he's on an operation, Charlie is more like one of your computers. Everything is programmed; all actions have purpose. He has a reason for scaring you that way. That's not to say he won't follow through and try to seduce you, so beware, but if he does, he will have some other more primary agenda, even if enjoyment is a side benefit."

"What agenda?" *And whose enjoyment?* She was pretty sure it would not be hers.

"My guess is he wants to break your system for keeping them out of the vault. It's been a while since they helped themselves to our information."

"They had access?"

"Several times over the years. So have many others, especially once the bulk of our files were computerized. It used to be everybody had to recruit and pay traitors and spies. Now they just hire the Justins of this world."

"The answer to the Justins of the world," she said, "is the Dennises of the world. Good old-fashioned legwork, but with an electronic vector."

"You're sure they can't find a way in?"

"Not with the information we provide, no. There is no communication between the files we receive from Dennis and the computer itself. If they find a back door, it won't be because they asked where Prion banks."

"You found that?"

She nodded. "Turns out it's a German bank called Felixsee. I was surprised. I think Mack was, too. Tell me about your, um, interview with him. What did he ask you?"

Skosh took a deep breath. It was a simple, inadvertent indication of the strain he was under and reminded her that for him, Mack was more than a threat. He was a reality. She caught a glimpse of her own situation in that inverted sigh and shivered.

He took her arm and led her down the street instead of out to the pier. His cloud of words condensed in the air.

"Mack repeated the theory of my 'mistake' that he explained to you. I did my best not to let on that he was right, but he's such an arrogant son of a bitch, I'm sure he took it for granted."

"Then I am a mistake?"

She was not sure how she felt about this, but it made her uncomfortable.

"That is the fiction Mack is maintaining. It is at least half true. He is also dead-on correct that I should send you home, but I can't."

She looked up at him, puzzled. He stopped and frowned.

"I guess I owe you the truth."

Jade wondered which portion of whose truth she was about to hear.

Skosh released another sigh and began walking again. She noticed he did not check the vicinity for lurkers with listening devices. They must have been granted another period of privacy, she decided, and Steve had the luxury of staying warm inside.

Starting with a few ums and ahs, Skosh tried to find the words he needed to convey his version of the past two days. Jade waited, ready to sift it through the many bullshit filters these people had been teaching her during the last day and a half.

"I didn't get the full copy of the commission until late in the evening we flew out," he began. "I read it before turning in. The team was due in-country in two days' time, and I expected to fly out in the morning. I don't think Mack thought I would read it, but I always do, and it's almost always standard. This time it wasn't."

"What was wrong with it?" Jade wondered how, exactly such things were done, who signed them, and where the documents were stored. They were not in her vault.

Skosh turned back toward the house.

"I don't want to stray too far," he said. "Last night's corpse displayed a few unsavory tattoos. There are likely to be more of those guys not far enough away.

"When I read the commission, I noticed a stipulation that I was to provide access to any necessary information kept in The Section's database."

"Did it define necessary?"

"No. That would be covered in a general provision that says the team leader has the final say in all such questions."

"I see."

What Jade could see was that Mack knew how to play chess.

Skosh continued. "I called Brent in personnel and got a list of people who could act as an in-country liaison with the vault. I needed someone who could connect with the vault's computer without letting Justin piggyback into the system."

"And you picked an old woman with sensible shoes named Penelope."

It took him a moment to answer. She decided the hesitation came from embarrassment, a possible sign of truth.

"Ye-es," he said. "I made a few quiet arrangements, booking us on separate airlines. Then Claire called while I was packing and told me she was about to land, and did I understand I was to ride with her? I think Mack must have launched her earlier in the day. He knew what I was doing before I had thought of it."

"Now you're saying he knows you always read the commissions? You just said he didn't know that."

"He reads minds, like I told you yesterday. But I had to stick to my plan to bring Penelope out here. I didn't have any backup strategy. I had just closed my suitcase when the airline called. Penelope's reservation had been canceled. Okay, I thought, I'll take her with me. He won't think anything of me bringing an old secretary to arrange catering, so I proceeded with the plan knowing full well Claire would radio ahead.

"When the lights came on in the cabin, I saw you and knew I was sunk. He wasn't going to buy it, and on top of that, I had brought a desirable young woman into the midst of what I know is a gang of amoral reprobates. Last night, Mack reminded me about all of this in the choicest language you can imagine. As Steve would say, he tore me a new one."

"Do you mean he was concerned about my safety?" It did not seem to fit with Jade's overall impression of the man.

"Oh, no. He repeated what he said on the Challenger. He is still not sure he will risk anything to protect you. You see, if something happens to you, I will have to give him access to the vault's computer in order to abide by the agreement. There is no other choice. It would be limited access, but that's all Justin needs."

"But if you refuse?"

"That would be an act of seppuku."

"Suicide? How?"

"Without the information, the team will pull out, making the operation fail. An unexplained pull-out would damage their reputation, giving them no choice but to make sure the world knows whose fault it was. They will publish the agreement and kill the babysitter. They'll be sorry about it, no doubt, but I'll be too dead to enjoy their regret."

She gasped and stopped to look at him, stunned. Grabbing his sleeve with one pink mitten, she turned him toward her, wishing with everything she had that the moment was filled with romantic magic in a sunny location and not deadly reality in the frozen North.

"He made a quiet move," she said, "then when you tried a similar move, he interfered by canceling the hotel. Now he has pinned me with a direct threat to you. I protect the vault, your king. It is a fork as well."

He wrinkled his brow.

"He's playing chess, Skosh."

Jade was dismayed by the familiar look on Skosh's face, the dawning realization that she had a brain. She felt flattered that he had found her appealing enough to be blinded by attraction, but usually when she betrayed her intellect, it spelled the end of any interest. It wasn't like she could turn it off and keep only the feminine appearance part of her whole self.

He hesitated with more apparent confusion than concern, visibly masking it with a return to business.

"There is one more thing I should tell you, Jade. Mack complained that your answers to their questions are too slow and too heavily redacted. He is turning up the heat. But then, so is Prion. Were you able to get the information Charlie asked for? And what about that passport I gave you?"

One of the best things about having had military training was that it taught her to simply shut up when her boss pressed her for a result that he was, himself, at that very moment preventing her from attaining.

"It will be there when we go inside," she said.

She fervently hoped so as they reached the door.

SIXTEEN

At first, Misha winced as he and Michael walked toward the pier but with every step the pain became easier. I was a fool to let them goad me into that fight, he thought. Each injury takes longer to heal. How long this time? Three weeks. Unacceptable.

He glanced to the side. Michael had not seen the wince. Good. He did not need nagging from his son. Alex was perfectly capable of annoying him all on her own.

"Has Justin found a way into their system yet?" he asked.

"No."

Michael's jaw was set. The sight of it reminded Misha that he was grinding his own teeth. He consciously relaxed but could not help stewing over being thwarted by a young American woman without sense enough to dress appropriately.

"But I think I know how she does it," said Michael, "and have taken steps."

Misha nodded, wondering what it was he considered appropriate dress. Was he so old he could criticize a tight sweater on a pretty woman? Mara did not wear such things in these conditions. She had better sense. No, she didn't, he realized. She had a husband who would kill a man for looking at her too long. Misha was glad of it. It meant he did not have to.

"She is completely unqualified to be here," said Michael. "Skosh has lost his mind."

"But she found a way to block Justin."

Misha stared out over the lagoon toward Klaipeda and watched the thoughts his mind had conjured. Why, exactly, was he bothered? The woman had no protection. Well, she had Skosh. Could he? According to his information, he could. Would he? He allowed his mind to explore the question.

Michael cleared his throat. "Justin broke into the computer at Prion's German bank."

Misha stopped his calculations and waited for more.

"Prion sent a letter to a bank officer thanking him for meeting with him in Manhattan. According to the letter, they had enjoyed a long conversation over whiskey and cigars that planted the seeds of an idea, and would he like to hear it?"

"Did the officer reply?"

"There is no reply in the file. But not long afterward, the bank approved a loan for several million dollars."

"Is Justin looking elsewhere?"

"He found quite a few internet forums where Prion is active. He uses various aliases to rally men to one cause or another."

"Men?"

"Yes. All of them are men, or pretend to be, though I cannot imagine a woman would want to discuss such topics. Justin sent me samples. Mostly frank discussions about women, weapons, street fighting, that kind of thing. Prion gave a contact email to several men he met on these forums."

"And the loan? How much has he spent? Where?"

"He has drawn only about half of it so far, mostly in cash. There is the compound at the southern end of the spit near Nida. He paid cash for the land after possibly paying bribes to be allowed to build there— primarily wooden huts. He brings in shipments of packaged foods, much like field rations, by truck from Germany. He is loose with this kind of information, but careful where it counts."

"How so?" Misha shifted his gaze back to Klaipeda as he listened.

"Large sums of cash are unaccounted for. Justin could find nothing, but I read again through every internet discussion that ended with contact information and one of the conversations about weaponry dealt specifically with small arms, tactical explosives, and equipment for light infantry. Prion gave his email at the end of it. Justin is working on getting into it."

"So, an arms dealer."

Michael nodded. "One more thing about that conversation, Papa. Prion began it by saying his banker had recommended the forum they were on."

Misha studied the white sky, the cranes at the port, the steel-grey lagoon.

"Increase the pressure, Michael. Who is this banker? And what weapons dealer did he recommend? It will tell us who is behind this. The Americans know or they would not have offered the commission. Damn them."

"The verification …"

"Was partial," interrupted Misha. "It contained only Prion's recruitment efforts. The information clause was meant to complete it. The bastards are jeopardizing this op to keep us from information we will need now and for the future."

"Skosh is already unhinged."

"Dismantle him completely then. Use the woman. There is no one to protect her and he knows it."

SEVENTEEN

Dennis had failed her. Lucky for Jade, another meeting started just then, and she used the chaos that begins most meetings, even ones chaired by scary people like Charlie, to call her assistant.

"What the hell, Dennis?"

She put plenty of urgency in her voice even before she felt Charlie's looming presence way too close behind her. She turned and looked up at his smug half-smile as she heard Dennis tell her all about the hell.

"Okay," she said into the phone. "Do what you can, please."

Urgency was replaced by defeat. She hung up the phone and turned back to Charlie.

"That's dirty," she said, closing her eyes immediately and wishing she could take back the complaint, regretting that she gave him the satisfaction of acknowledging his victory.

Charlie held the rug aside for her and pointed to the chair next to Mack.

Meetings were not new to Jade. If it's true an Army marches on its stomach, then the menu is planned in a meeting. Make that a series of meetings. When she had worked for the colonel, she was required to attend all staff meetings. She never had a speaking part but took copious notes because she was the invisible one, responsible for researching solutions and drafting instructions after the brass were done complaining. Here, she was sure the same concepts applied. The attendees had changed into suits and ties—the uniform of civilians with serious business.

Jade sat down next to Mack wishing she had paper and pen because she expected to be required to remember a long series of ramblings disguised as reports. The meeting opened in silence. Busy noticing a regrettable shiny spot on her right suede half-boot, she did not register the lack of reports and complaints that should have been droning on in the background noise of her attention. But she felt the uncomfortable gaze of the man next to her. Jade hoped she was imagining it and threw a sideways glance in that direction to confirm she was as invisible in this as well as in every other meeting she ever had the misfortune to attend.

He caught the glance and held it. Those eyes were very blue. Alien, she would say, because none of the usual reactions to her were contained in them. They showed no indications of repulsion or attraction, compassion or disdain, curiosity or indifference. She could call that look hostile, but even that would be less than accurate because hostility is an emotion. Jade stared into the eyes of a big cat who was not particularly hungry at the moment but would either walk away or attack based on an algorithm she had no hope of discerning.

Skosh cleared his throat to break the silence. "Did you bring the information, Jade?"

He knew damn well she hadn't. She had walked in empty-handed. She welcomed the question nonetheless because it broke the spell and told her what they were waiting for.

As she launched an explanation, doing her best not to whine, she laid the blame squarely on Charlie by looking at him as she gave her excuses.

"Dennis had to find four tires and that at midnight, no less, but he has done so, and I expect to receive his report momentarily. I should probably check on that now. I think the malicious damage to Dennis's car was unconscionable as well as unforeseeable."

She did not expect a reply and did not want one. Jade was playing a tactical game of defiance and thought she was holding her own. Her belligerent glare made her point for her, but Charlie answered her words in a purr.

"Surely not as unconscionable as malicious damage to Dennis himself would be."

Jade realized suddenly that while she moved plastic checkers around a paper board, Charlie played three-dimensional chess with live bodies in an alien world. This was a skewer, with Dennis directly threatened while she was the true target behind the attack. Charlie sat as still and emotionless as a computer, giving nothing away. The purr, his words, and his stillness left her breathless until Mara tried to rescue her.

"You should bring your new notebook in here," said the equally alien young woman. "You can connect it on our telephone line and watch for Dennis's email with the information. Why don't you go get it now?"

Jade stared at her, blinking.

"It will be just the same as consulting your computer on your line, Jade. We have been watching everything on that line anyway. It makes no difference to your excellent system."

Jade wanted an excuse to leave the room. She needed to stand alone in that tiny kitchen beyond the hanging rug and let her body shake for a little while. But her legs refused the order to stand, and her feet did not move. Sergei got up, went through the rug, and came back with the notebook. He handed it to her along with the encryption modem. She had hidden the device carefully in what she thought was a secret place behind the locked door of her bedroom.

Consciousness relies on breath. She had neglected this fact for too long and promptly passed out.

The shouted f-words in various voices helped bring her around immediately when her body's autonomic system sucked in the required air as she slid off her chair and onto the floor, still sitting up. Skosh loomed over her.

"What the fuck, Skosh?" came a voice. "Not only did you bring a librarian, but one that fucking faints."

She recognized the soft southern accent of Steve.

"What the hell did you say to her, Pavlenko?" This came from Skosh.

"I said nothing. I give her computer. That's all."

"You must realize this is not going to work, Skosh." The purr was unmistakable.

"Not if you're going to fucking terrify her every five minutes, Charlie, and then you add her assistant to your scary-as-shit threat list."

"Jade! Jade! Look at me." It was a woman's voice.

She managed to focus on the person in front of her. Mara held her hand and patted her wrist in the time-honored tradition of bringing around a swooning female. Jade gave her an embarrassed smile.

Skosh pulled her to a stand and turned to Mack, who had not moved from the chair next to her.

"I need fifteen minutes."

Mack nodded almost imperceptibly toward Sergei, presumably signaling that he should turn off the listening devices.

Skosh pushed her through the crowd, through the rug, and toward her room, where he had to unlock the door. Sergei had thoughtfully locked it again after raiding it for her modem. Nothing seemed out of place. Except the modem. That was now in Mara's hands.

They stood beside the dresser. Jade hung her head and could not look up at Skosh. She knew he wanted to send her back and that such an act would cost him everything. Fighting tears, she was determined not to add yet another weak-looking reaction to the repertoire of Jade-The-Unsuitable.

Skosh lifted her chin as she manufactured a pretend strength, dry-eyed and, she hoped, dignified. Total honesty presented itself as the only reasonable solution. Well, almost total. She wouldn't confess how much she still wanted him.

"I'm so out of my depth, Skosh. Please, give me time."

EIGHTEEN

"Your assistant has sent you the information," Mara told her as Jade took the seat next to Mack ten minutes later. "But I cannot decipher it because I do not have the key."

Jade counted carefully and winced. The next key contained a word, but there was no way to avoid giving it.

"A-B-A-R-E-O."

Mara typed it in and the printer next to her computer went into action.

Mack looked at the printout first, then handed it to Jade, indicating that she should read it aloud.

"Prion's wealth appears to be based on debt," she read, as steadily as she could. "It is a secured debt, but Felixsee Bank refuses to allow US authorities access to the loan documents."

"Mara," said Mack, giving her a pointed glance. She turned to her keyboard.

Jade continued with the answer to the morning's second question. "The dead man went by the alias Bert Badass. His real name was Bernard Pasker. He served a complete ten-year sentence for armed robbery at Attica in New York. Though he was a model prisoner with no disciplinary record, he was repeatedly denied parole because of his membership in the Skinhead Nation."

Having reached the end of the printout, Jade sat down.

She opened her mouth to ask why everyone was still looking at her when the low growling murmur of Mack's voice came to her ear.

"And what is the Skinhead Nation?"

She had no answer beyond the word 'gang' and perhaps a few adjectives like 'violent,' none of which would be particularly descriptive here. She knew nothing else about Skinheads. Dennis had sent minimal information, because, she suspected, he was pissed-off about his tires. She knew she would have to cover his costs. For a fleeting moment, she thought she might ask Charlie to cover it since he was the responsible party, but he was sitting very still and staring at her, waiting for her answer to Mack's question.

She cleared her throat and forced out a few words. "I'll get right on that."

"I have it here," said Mara. She had been busy at the keyboard, and her printer spewed a full-page summary. "It is from American open sources, not your library, but it may be enough."

She tore the paper off the printer and handed it to her with a smile.

Jade stood again and read the entire thing aloud, doing her best to keep her shaking knees out of her voice. The article covered the cultural aspects, the origins in Britain, and the gang's prevalence in American prisons.

"While some youths who like the music and shave their heads are not white supremacists," she read in summary, "in the US, at least, they have become increasingly associated with neo-nazism. They often have white supremacist tattoos and are known to employ extreme violence."

Having delivered her short lecture to a roomful of the extremely violent—though, one would hope, not neo-Nazis—she considered her duty done and sat down again.

Skosh spoke up.

"Kestutis told me more Americans have arrived in the country with similar tattoos to those on Pasker, especially the 88 that stands for Heil Hitler. They are not popular with the sixteen or seventeen Lithuanians—that count has been fluctuating—who have joined them. There are twenty-four Americans bivouacked at Prion's compound near Nida. Make that twenty-three without Pasker. Speaking of that incident, I need more information about what happened there."

The information would not be forthcoming anytime soon. At that moment, the row of sensor lights next to Mara's computer became multi-colored strobes. Frantic pounding and shouting at the front door of the smaller safehouse brought Jade to her feet, and everybody around her, Skosh included, drew their weapons.

NINETEEN

The man outside shouted, "Jade, Jade, please!"
She recognized Rimas's voice as he repeated, "You must help us."

Pound, bang, pound.

"It's an emergency."

Pound, pound.

"You have to be in there. It's too cold to be anywhere else."

Rattle, pound.

"Are you asleep? Wake up!"

Skosh moved toward the rug. Mack whispered, "No," before putting his gun away and taking Jade's arm. He gave a series of hand signals she did not understand to Charlie, who raised his chin in assent. Another signal was directed at Skosh and he holstered his weapon. The others in the room remained poised to fire at the intruder.

Mack led her through the rug. The racket at the door increased. Rimas sounded frantic. Backing against the wall next to the hinges, Mack signaled for Jade to open it. She wanted to argue, desperate to make him let her handle it for Rimas's sake, but she remembered Skosh's uncertainty about the interpreter and contented herself with being glad Mack did not have a weapon in his hand at the moment.

She opened the door. "Rimas, what ...?"

That was as far as she got before he burst in shoving something in her face. Not a gun or knife, but a piece of paper, capable of a paper cut, she supposed, but no more than that.

"Jade, Antanas ...."

That was as far as he got before he found himself face first against the back of the door, which had been slammed shut by Mack as he drove the full weight of Rimas's body into it.

The paper fluttered to the floor. Jade picked it up and a name caught her eye. She could not help saying it aloud. "Prion?"

It was exactly the wrong thing to say. Sergei and Steve appeared on her side of the rug but were ordered back with a jerk of Mack's head. Fortunately, they made no more noise than a zephyr, and Rimas was still kissing the door, so he could not see them or their guns. With a significant glance and a lift of his chin, Mack ordered Jade to read the paper.

"It's from a court in Michigan, an order telling Antanas Dockus, that's Rimas's brother, that he must vacate his flat by tomorrow. This is in a probate case concerning the estate of Thomas Prion. It has been endorsed and forwarded through a Lithuanian court. I can't read that part. There is a certified translation of the order into Lithuanian."

She paused as it hit her. "Rimas, was Tommy Taurus's real name Prion?"

His voice muffled by the door, Rimas said, "Yes."

Skosh tried to come in. He retreated under Mack's glare.

Mack held Rimas fast while roughly but thoroughly checking him for weapons. When he stepped back, he reminded her again of a big cat watching possible prey, ready to move in any direction.

Rimas turned cautiously, instinctively keeping his hands up, palms out.

"Tell us," said Mack.

Jade caught Rimas's glance. She could see he was full of questions but could not help him with any answers. She asked a question of her own to get him started.

"Did Tommy tell Antanas he was giving him the flat?"

"Yes. We told you…."

Mack interrupted. "Did he give a deed?"

"No," Rimas whispered, defeated. "He just made him promise never to leave it."

"You speak German?"

"No, I…"

Mack looked at Jade as if he were talking to her, giving her a string of instructions, none of which she could decipher, because they were all in German for the benefit of the listeners beyond the rug. She nodded as though she understood. He took her fleece jacket off the door hook and threw it to her, grabbed the paper from her hand, and pushed Rimas through the door as he opened it. She was still trying to put on her jacket when she reached the back seat of Rimas's Škoda. Mack held the door open and climbed in next to her.

As he put the car in gear and pulled out onto the road to the ferry, Rimas said, "Jade, I am thinking this man could either help Antanas or hurt him badly. Am I right?"

She had no answer to give him.

...

Rimas wore a worried scowl. With sideways glances, he studied the man as they climbed three long, straight flights up the elegant staircase in Antanas's building. Jade trailed behind them, puffing a bit. There was no sign of stress or fatigue in the older man who never slowed, never hurried. Not surprising considering the skill with which he handled me at the door, thought Rimas.

"Tell me about Thomas," said the man after telling both brothers to call him Mack.

They stood just inside the door of the apartment. There had been no other introductions, no invitation to sit. Antanas fought tears as he recounted the most important romance of his life. Rimas watched Mack for his reaction. His face betrayed nothing of his thoughts.

"His father is Earl Prion? And he disapproved?" asked Mack.

It occurred to Rimas that Mack might also be the sort of father to disapprove of most things—this above all.

"Yes," said Antanas. "He was vicious to Tommy. Hateful. He even threatened his ex-wife and accused her of making Tommy gay just to spite him."

He shifted from one foot to another, evidently having had the same thought about Mack's attitude. "My father also disapproved. Our fathers' disapproval was one of the things that bonded us. Tommy left shortly after his mother's funeral and said he would be back, but then he became ill and …"

"He contracted AIDS in the United States?"

Was Mack's minimally raised eyebrow a comment or just part of the question?

"Yes. It took him quickly." Antanas hurried to explain. "We were neither of us exclusive; we just loved each other. He said he would be back and would explain about the flat and other things."

"Other things? What things?"

Antanas shrugged.

Mack's blue eyes scanned the graceful tall windows to the polished parquet floor and the magnificent drum set near the wall across from where they stood.

"Tell me what he said when he said goodbye—the exact words."

This startled Antanas enough to arrest his tears for the moment.

"He… He told me not to leave the flat."

"The words. I want the words."

It was an unmistakable command. Antanas took a deep breath and closed his eyes.

"Our future is here, Antanas. Do not leave the flat. I will explain everything when I come back."

The tears began again.

"Where were his eyes when he said this?" Mack's peremptory tone held no sign of contempt but was equally devoid of compassion.

Antanas tilted his head and wrinkled his brow. He did not understand.

"What was he seeing?" Mack was losing patience, his voice becoming ever sharper.

Shrugging with a slight shake of his head at this madman, Antanas swept a gracile hand toward the drums. "There!"

Rimas exchanged bewildered glances with Jade and his brother as Mack inspected the drum set and the floor around it. He lifted a stand that held a cymbal and shifted two other pieces, including the large bass drum. Rimas shook his head, warning Antanas to quell a growing protest.

Mack drew a knife that was too large to be carried as a mere useful tool. He knelt on the floor and pried three strips of the intricate parquet wood out of their places side by side, then reached into the subsequent hole and pulled out a plastic folder tied with string. It contained a thick stack of folded documents.

The sight of the gun under his coat, as Mack slid this find into an inner pocket, added more confirmation of what Rimas had suspected when he stood immobilized with his nose against the door of Jade's little house. She gave him an unnecessary look of wide-eyed warning. He knew exactly what he was dealing with.

Mack took Jade's arm and led her toward the door, where he turned to Rimas

"Do you fight?"

Rimas nodded. It would be of no use to deny it.

"Your brother will need protection," said Mack. "Hide him somewhere. Not here. Lock this door, close the curtains, and leave. Now."

"If there is danger," said Rimas, "let me take Jade to safety with us."

Mack gazed at him for several seconds before nodding in assent without consulting Jade. Rimas realized the man had been making a calculated decision about his character.

He and his brother followed them through the downstairs door and out into a cold blast from the Baltic.

"If he values his life," Mack said quietly, though loud enough for Rimas to hear, "Skosh has followed my directions and is waiting outside."

Rimas spotted the car a few meters down the street, recognizing in the driver's seat the American who had been working with Kestutis. Next to him sat a brown-haired man he had not seen before, but he was familiar with the air of strictly business with which the man scanned the street, front, back, and side to side.

He took Jade's arm from Mack and led her and Antanas to the Škoda to drive them into hiding. From what or whom, he was not sure, but avoiding the proximity of this Mack character would be a healthy start. If it could be done.

TWENTY

Skosh drove to the ferry in an uncomfortable silence. It bothered him that Jade was not with them. He had to ask the question but knew no answer would be satisfactory.

"Why is Jade not coming with us?"

Mack answered from the back seat with a question.

"The young man she calls Rimas, why did he come to her for help?"

"Maybe he remembered how she handled the landlord when you needed the safehouse two days early, and so he figured she might be able to help with his problem."

Skosh did not disguise the touch of resentment in his words.

"Why did he know how she handled the landlord?"

"He was her interpreter that night."

"Interpreter," Mack said in a flat tone. "Because she does not speak Lithuanian. Nor Russian. Nor German."

These were statements, not questions, with Mack's voice becoming smoother as he delivered each phrase. "Where did you get this 'interpreter?'"

Skosh distinctly heard the quotation marks. He took a breath.

"Kestutis provided him. You approved Kestutis."

The car boarded the ferry with its occupants in perfect silence, a silence broken by Mack when the boat set off for the other shore.

"I have other information about Kestutis and for one purpose, only for that purpose, is his involvement acceptable. I approved him to help you coordinate with the local authorities. Not to know where my safehouse is. Not to introduce an unknown interpreter into the operation. Not to further complicate your egregious mistake of trying to salvage something that may be without remedy."

The man did not shout, but each 'not' contained a special emphasis that made Skosh cringe inwardly with every iteration. The only saving grace about this dressing down was that the car made it inconvenient for Mack to punctuate his anger with fists.

Skosh said nothing. Mack continued.

"Your authorities signed an agreement to give me access to information I need. You know very well that I do not care which of your political groups is out of favor or which politicians are compromised. I know these things already. What little is left of such things that I do not know, I can find in The New York Times. What I need is information on the killers, madmen, criminals, assassins, and double agents that you pay me to fight for you. I need that information to stay alive. Instead of abiding by the contract agreed to by your organization, you chose to protect your precious vault and by doing so, you put Kestutis's man, a man I know nothing about, at my safehouse, and now that man has seen me."

Skosh laid his forehead on his knuckles at the top of the steering wheel as the ferry chugged along. "Kestutis vouched ..."

"Kestutis is the son and grandson of anti-Soviet partisans who fought in the forests after the war. He is a fighter. Not all of the original fighters were sound. Some began their careers aiding the Nazis. War creates ambiguity in the characters of men. This man also is a fighter. I do not know his origins, and he has seen me and my safehouse."

At this, Steve turned around and made eye contact with Mack, watching for a signal.

Skosh sat up. "You can't know that." Both belligerence and defeat inflected his voice at the same time.

"I do know it. I handled him. He recognized what I am and made a decision, a conscious decision not to react. We knew each other. Charlemagne is vastly outnumbered, and you have made it infinitely worse by bringing with you a woman whose presence has no purpose but to keep me ignorant of the enemies we must face within the next thirty hours or sooner."

As the ferry docked, Skosh put the car in gear. They drove in palpable tension down an empty road with a thick evergreen forest arching overhead like a tunnel. The tension heightened as they pulled up behind the team's safehouse, where the blackness of thick forest formed a wall and where Skosh expected to be more vulnerable than ever to Mack's fists.

But as Mack shoved him through the back door of the team's house, he said, "I remind you, Skosh, you worry about your secrets and your career when it is your life that is at stake."

TWENTY-ONE

"Rimas, where are we going?"

He glanced at his passenger. She was indeed pretty. And he loved her accent. He had learned British English and enjoyed cataloging the differences every time she spoke. She was so very American, supremely exotic.

Antanas answered her from the back seat.

"We are going to Užupis. It is a special place. Have you been to Paris?"

"Yes. I attended the Sorbonne. Do you speak French?"

Rimas heard a hopeful note in her voice.

"No," said Antanas. "Do you know a place called Montmartre, where there are artists?"

"Yes. I lived not far from there."

"Užupis is the Montmartre of Lithuania. You will like it. I have a friend who paints. It is very Bohemian and original in Užupis. There is no plumbing even, and some houses have no roof or windows, but it is full of interesting people. I know one who has the perfect motto. 'Never fight. Never win. Never surrender.'"

"Is it far?"

"About three hours," said Rimas as he accelerated the car. "But we will make rather better time than that. I know someone who has done it in two hours, nine minutes."

"What? No! I can't be gone that long. Stop. Take me back, please, Rimas. It's important. I must go back."

She was searching for her door handle. He took hold of her arm, his left hand remaining on the wheel, his foot pressed onto the accelerator. The odometer needle read 160 kilometers per hour. She squirmed under his grasp, trying and failing to pry his fingers open.

Antanas spoke from the back with a voice full of surprise.

"Your friend agreed that you should come as well, for your safety. Don't worry. I will find space for both of us."

"My friend! He is not a friend. He ..." She interrupted herself with a note of despair.

"If he is not a friend," said Rimas, "what is he? An enemy?"

"No."

Her voice had become small, her manner calm. She stopped reaching for the door handle, and Rimas let go.

"Not a friend and not an enemy," he said quietly. "What was his name again?"

He could tell she knew his purpose in asking. She thought before answering.

"Not 'again', Rimas. I have no doubt you remember very well that he told you other people call him Mack. If fishing for information I don't have is your reason for taking me away, then you can turn around now. I know nothing else. This is a game of grandmaster chess, and I am nothing more than a beginner, at best a pawn. Please. Take me back."

"You will like my friends, Jade," Antanas said in a pleading voice. "Vilnius is a beautiful old city. You must see it."

...

How she would have loved to go there as a tourist, to revel in history and culture and art, to meet exciting new people. She corrected the thought. Interesting people. Exciting had become overrated. Jade longed to sip wine and listen to music. She wanted lively conversation on inconsequential topics. She badly needed a bath.

She glanced at Rimas at the wheel next to her and noticed for the first time, the hard set of his jaw. There was more to him than she had realized. He did not fit the motto of Užupis. He would fight, she decided, and he would win.

"I don't have any clothes with me," she said. "Not even a toothbrush, or a hairbrush."

It was the missing hairbrush that threatened to bring tears. She knew how to stop them, would normally stop them. Jade was adept at controlling her emotions, but maybe this time she could weaponize them. Rimas had turned out to be tougher than she originally thought. This newly discovered hard edge suggested he did not find Mack as alien to him as she did. But he was a young man and had never mentioned a sister who would have hardened him to feminine manipulation. He might be susceptible.

She released the flood.

...

Rimas pulled over at Antanas's insistence. Luckily, his brother had a clean handkerchief and soothing words. The handkerchief was soon soaked, and the sweet words initially sparked only a pitiable wailing, but eventually, Antanas was able to elicit a few intelligible sentences.

"I can't... I don't have any makeup with me. I look a fright. These are old clothes, rags. I can't... I just can't meet new people like this. Please don't make me. Please, Rimas, please take me back!"

Rimas told himself his decision did not amount to capitulation. It was more of a reevaluation. Yes, that was it, he decided. It had nothing to do with his sudden inability to deal with the hysterical female sitting next to him. There would be other ways to get the information out of her if she had any. This display made him think that was unlikely.

"Listen!" he shouted over the din.

Jade subsided into shudders.

"We are almost at Užupis. We will see Antanas settled safely. After that—no more than half an hour, I promise—I have decided I will take you back."

The shuddering ceased, and Rimas refrained from adding the words, 'but not to Mack.'

He had someone else in mind.

TWENTY-TWO

Mack handed Mara the packet of documents he had taken from the apartment and accompanied it with a fast, insistent series of instructions in German. Skosh heard the ominous name, Justin, and tensed. Mara took the packet apart and fed page after page into the fax machine.

As Skosh fell asleep on his folded arms at the kitchen table, the voices on the other side of the rug melted into disjointed dreams. There were discussions, between Mack and Charlie, Charlie and everybody, Mara and Sergei, and then more order barking by Mack. Then Candace had her say, grey eyes flashing vengeance, while his boss's boss, Henry, reinforced the new directive about information security breaches.

Henry growled. No, that was Mack, Skosh decided through the haze of a half-doze. Maybe roaring would be a better word. There was a name, a contact he had never heard of. An in-country contact, who duly received a call from Mack on the telephone in Skosh's kitchen with instructions about the street Antanas lived on. The team's phone was tied up with the faxing of those documents.

Skosh sank into a deeper sleep. There must have been a quiet period for the team as well, he thought, as he woke late in the afternoon with a sore neck and an extreme caffeine-withdrawal headache. He went through the rug in search of coffee and filled a cup at the team's machine.

Nearby, next to Mara's computer, sat the console of blinking, many-colored lights from Sergei's myriad perimeter sensors. Mack stood before it, wearing an earbud. Its wire led to a small receiver on his belt.

The room, the entire two houses, felt dark and cold as everybody sat wearing earbuds, sipping coffee, and saying nothing, with only Mack and Skosh standing. The phone next to the computer rang. Mack moved like a cat to answer it. Skosh congratulated himself on what he thought was a pretty good job of not letting on that the sudden jangle had stabbed his brain. The coffee would cure it in time.

Mack hung up the phone, turned on his transmitter, and began a long series of statements or instructions in the microphone on his wire. He grabbed his coat and pushed Skosh through the rug, handed him his jacket, and led him out onto the street.

Skosh assumed the one-sided conversation Mack was holding via the wire was directed toward the team. The man communicated with him only by means of glares and impatient gestures.

Hurry up. Put your coat on. Stand here. Don't talk.

He said all of this without speaking. Skosh watched him inspect his rental car with a small flashlight. It must be Sergei on the other end of the conversation, he thought, telling Mack what to look for in the way of Skosh's private alarms. It was the exponential creep factor of knowing the light-eyed Russian held that kind of information that bothered him most. Eventually satisfied it was free of booby traps, Mack unlocked the driver's door and indicated he should get in.

The talking in Mack's ear did not allow conversation until they were almost on the ferry.

As Skosh had expected, they secured the car several blocks away from Antanas's flat and made their way to it carefully. Mack took a signal from a watcher across the street, and they entered the building.

They made no noise, but Skosh doubted they would have been heard anyway over the din coming from the upstairs apartment. Mack gently tried the door. It was locked. He pulled out a lock-picking tool and opened it.

They walked into an interrogation. Rimas stood against the wall on Skosh's right with his head back, holding a bloody rag to his nose. A drum set had been scattered around the room. Most of the pieces were bent or broken.

Kestutis interrupted an angry monologue directed at Rimas to emphasize his point by slapping Jade, who sat on the floor with her back against a badly damaged bass drum.

Skosh could see this was not the first slap she had received. Her cheekbones were bruised, and one eye was rimmed in purple. Her upper lip had a cut on one side and the lower was swollen. The sight pushed him closer to crossing the line between babysitter and specialist. He wanted to kill Kestutis at that moment and knew he would have if Mack had not given him a warning glance when he raised his hand toward his holster.

The entire edifice of Skosh's previously stoic character was falling like a house of cards.

TWENTY-THREE

When the man hit her a third time, Jade reconsidered her early desire for a little bit of danger. This had now, officially, crossed the line from little bit to some and was well on the way to too much. She was sure a front tooth had loosened. Her nose did not bleed all over her clothes like Rimas's, but it was only a matter of time and the location of the next blow.

The man who wanted to know about Mack was about the same age, blond with a hint of grey like Mack's, and violent like him, too. When the man met them at Antanas's flat, Rimas had initially treated him as a trusted friend and called him Kestutis.

That bonhomie ended when the man broke Rimas's nose demanding answers to such questions as where was Antanas and where were the documents that had been discovered under the drums. Besides punching each question into Rimas's body, Kestutis illustrated his intent by destroying most of the drum set and strewing the pieces across the room.

Jade's interrogation resumed, but by then Rimas had provided an example of total silence that she followed. If he found his friend untrustworthy—and she supposed a broken nose could sour any friendship—then Jade was not about to divulge anything she knew, which was precious little anyway. Thus, the repeated bruising slaps across her face.

What with clanging cymbals thrown against walls and drums being kicked in, not to mention shouting and scuffling, she wondered what Antanas's neighbors must be thinking and why they did nothing. She had fallen with her back against what had once been the large bass drum when she saw the door open. She hoped it meant police. It did not.

It was Mack.

His presence did not comfort her, but that Skosh stood to his right made her heart leap.

Kestutis turned to the intruders and dropped the hand he had raised to hit her again.

"Who in hell are you now?" he said to Mack, using English.

"Most still call me Mack. We have come to retrieve the girl." His voice had that low, even growl she had come to know and fear.

"Are you her lover? Is that why you are here? More likely you are her father." Kestutis spat the words, heavy with sarcasm.

"That is not your question, my friend. What you need to know is whether I am willing to die for her." Mack paused in his still, slow way. "I am not." He pointed to Skosh. "But he is."

"Pfft! He is an office boy."

Mack's next pause lasted half a beat longer before he answered, in an unconcerned, almost bored, soft voice.

"I know that he is at least as capable as your man there." He pointed to Rimas still holding a rag to his nose.

"What were the papers you took from here?" Kestutis demanded. Then, without waiting for an answer, he took a step forward and pointing his chin at Skosh, said, "If he can fight as you say, we are evenly matched. I want those papers."

Mack held up a hand to halt him.

"I think not unless one of you is also willing to die for the girl. Our sole purpose here is to retrieve her."

Mack stepped to one side of the door and breathed normally, but she sensed his tension. He never took his eyes off his opponent.

"You cannot recover the papers," he said. "I have secured them. You may leave." He indicated the door with a minimal lift of his chin.

After a brief mutual glare, Kestutis made up his mind. "We will meet soon."

"I look forward to it."

The man moved almost as silently down the stairs as Mack had done coming up, leaving a sense of unfinished business behind him.

Having stopped the bleeding from his nose, Rimas stood awkwardly shuffling his feet.

Jade wished fervently that Kestutis and Mack had beat each other to a pulp for what they had done to her but knew better than to expect it. She held no more than a nanosecond of their consideration. She also seriously doubted Skosh would be willing to die for her.

Mack held Rimas in his characteristic scary-as-hell blue-eyed glare. It surprised her, then, when Rimas broke the silence not with belligerence, perhaps, but at least irritation.

"Why did you let me take her?"

"That is my affair."

"Who are you and why is she with you?"

"I have given you and Kestutis a name. Is he your mentor? Did he train you to fight?"

Rimas paused, considering, as the purple bruising spread beneath and around his eyes, highlighted by the surrounding fair skin.

"He has been good to me," he said finally. "I owe him everything."

Mack raised one eyebrow. "But not your brother's life?"

Rimas had no answer. Silence reigned again until he seemed to come to a decision.

"I wanted Jade to tell me who you are," he said, looking Mack in the eye. "But she had hysterics, a fit I have never seen before. I did not know what to do. I brought her back and called Kestutis to help me."

Jade allowed herself a small self-satisfied smile until she saw that both Mack and Skosh had noticed it. She would not be able to use that ploy with either of them. But then, she imagined both had enough experience to be proof against it anyway.

Skosh gave Rimas a scornful smile.

"And he fucking hit you when you tried to defend her? Some mentor."

Jade remembered the bruises on Skosh after one of his interviews with Mack but considered that theirs was no mentor/protégé relationship.

Rimas answered quickly. "No, I asked for help with an interrogation, and he was giving it, but I had to tell him about this man, Mack, that I had met at your house because that was the intelligence I wanted from her."

Skosh winced, and Rimas continued.

"He wanted to know more, but I could not tell him about my brother's problem. Kestutis has no use for Antanas."

Rimas looked at Mack. "He asked about you and how you found the documents. He said the words 'your brother's documents'. Did you tell him about the papers you found?"

"You know I did not."

Rimas sighed. "I would not tell him, and he became furious. He broke my nose and then went back to Jade to try for the information he wanted. She said nothing and I was debating what to do when you came in. I was sure she was about to suffer more than a broken nose."

Jade picked herself up off the floor, shaking not a little, but whole and intact and grateful that her nose remained centered on her face.

Rimas held up his hands in a pleading gesture.

"Kestutis is a good man, a patriot, and a hero, but he is not himself. He is convinced Prion is doing something good for Lithuania."

Mack let the silence build for a moment before he broke it.

"But you are not."

Rimas nudged a cymbal on the floor with the toe of his boot. "How does killing a gentle Lithuanian help my country?"

"Did he come to kill Antanas or to find the papers?"

"Both, I think. He was angry that I had moved my brother and wanted me to tell him where. Thank you for advising it. He is safe."

"And Prion? Is he doing something good for Lithuania?"

"Tommy told my brother that his father hated Lithuania after his wife left him and Tommy admitted he was gay. I tried to explain this to Kestutis, but he would not listen."

Rimas turned to Skosh with a pleading look. "He is a good man, Skosh. Give him time; give me time to get him away from Prion."

Jade marveled that Rimas had grasped so much of the truth but mistook Skosh for the boss here. It was the man standing next to him who was calling the shots. Skosh threw a significant glance to his left.

Rimas nodded his understanding and offered Mack information in return for his friend's life. A move Jade hoped she would never have to make.

"Something has happened to Prion's money," he told Mack. "He will try to act earlier than planned."

TWENTY-FOUR

They stamped their feet and swung their arms to keep circulation going. Misha did not wear a scarf. Michael's was failing in its mission to keep his face warm. The briefing his father gave him about the late afternoon's events caused clouds of breath in the air and of doom in Michael's mind.

"You may want to consider this man Rimas," said Misha.

Michael raised an eyebrow and he continued.

"Twice now he has declined to fight."

"Is he shy?"

"No. He is disciplined. He took an undeserved beating from his teacher without replying. That is not shyness. Like you, he knows sometimes not entering a contest is wiser than winning it." Misha paused and said, "I should not have taken this commission. I am sorry."

A compliment and an apology on the same day, Michael thought. But he could not let the apology stand.

"We made the decision together, Papa. Access to their information was too important to turn it down."

"That bank is east of Berlin. I heard you asking Sergei who he thinks may still be assigned in that area. Are you thinking the SVR is involved?"

"I am. I sense another mind behind Prion, not just money. This man Rimas, what makes you think he would be willing to join us?"

Misha turned to look at him. "He was born to fight."

"How can you know?"

"I know his teacher."

"Kestutis? He is deceived by Prion."

"His judgment has deserted him, not his skill."

They walked further along the shore of the lagoon in silence, while Michael considered his next question. Most of the changes he had seen in his father lately seemed positive, but any change at all felt threatening until he forced himself to view the man through adult eyes.

"Papa, if Kestutis has lost his judgment, he may be mistaken about Rimas."

"He has been deceived, Michael, but not by Rimas. You should embrace this deception as additional weight for your suspicion that there is another player. Prion does not have the capacity for a deep game. Regardless of his present deception, Kestutis could always spot talent. He would not have taken on this young man without it."

"Has he killed?"

"Rimas?"

"Yes."

"I doubt it."

"Then what can we offer him? I don't want anyone motivated solely by money. Protection from our enemies binds us more securely. He is too young to have serious enemies, especially if he has not killed. Why would he volunteer for such a life?"

Misha stopped and turned to him with a sardonic smile.

"You can offer protection for those who are important to him."

"Who?"

"His brother. Also, he will want to see that Kestutis is undeceived and alive. And there is the woman."

"Which woman?"

Misha's brow furrowed, forcing Michael to think along an unfamiliar path.

"Jade? But Skosh wants...."

Misha sighed audibly, a sound meant to remind him of the odds against them. Michael could be more ruthless than his father—if that were possible—but occasionally he caught himself wishing for another world in which there were no losses.

"I will need to test him," he said.

"Of course."

"And she may not...."

"Leave that to me."

TWENTY-FIVE

Jade gave herself a much-needed sponge bath, remaining vigilant behind the supposedly locked bathroom door and thankfully, she was uninterrupted. They had met pandemonium when they returned from Klaipeda, with free-flowing f-words from Skosh as he helped the team prepare—for what, she didn't know and didn't care. The bruises on her face occupied most of her attention. Surely they would fade in time, wouldn't they?

Rimas's nose was still crooked. Skosh had fitted him with an earbud and transmitter because he was to accompany Charlie that night. Unarmed. He would be the only unarmed person in the group.

His introduction to the team had been entertaining. Steve was less than friendly, but nowhere near as unfriendly as Sergei when Rimas's eyes latched onto Mara. Rimas understood every Russian threat Sergei threw at him and responded in kind. Jade could see him wondering if he had joined the wrong side.

Charlie cooled the situation as only his ice-cold manner could.

"Rimas will stay by me on the Baltic side of the compound to translate anything we may hear. He will never go near Mara, Sergei, and now he knows better than to even look at her."

He issued more orders and instructions, and Jade heard a few dark jokes at Rimas's expense, spoken in English so that he fully understood before the team had finally slunk out of the house. Their absence made Jade feel safe enough to use the bathroom.

She unpacked a worn pair of corduroys and a flannel shirt sporting old paint splotches from past decorating projects. She had brought them just in case she would be required to march in the rain or dig a ditch. They were the last clean clothes in her suitcase and the occasion qualified as ditch digging.

While she detangled and tied up her hair in a tight ponytail, she laughed into the mirror at the Jade of yesterday, who thought of make-up as a necessity. The smile hurt but made the bruises less ugly.

Cautiously opening the door and listening carefully, she crept the few steps into the empty little kitchen. A single bare lightbulb hanging from a wire over the table gave her enough light to see that she was alone. At first, she sighed with relief, but the silence had a creepy quality after all the noise and threats and incomprehensible language, even words supposedly spoken in English. If this were a movie, she thought, the eerie music would be playing, and the stupid heroine would proceed to investigate those dark corners against all common sense.

Leaving the dark corners and hanging rug alone, she sat down at her laptop like a good girl, found Charlie's new list of questions, lengthy because of the hours she had been gone, and got to work.

She called Dennis to give him a heads-up before she tied up the phone line by hitting send. He was still pretty grumpy about his tires and not all that gracious about her pledge to make it up to him. A fresh pot of hot coffee cheered her up until she turned from pouring a mug and sloshed a sizable splotch on the floor, because Mack was sitting at the table, across from her chair. He had an earbud in his ear and held a portable radio.

She could not have had her back turned for more than a few seconds. A pin dropping to the floor would have made a noise like a gong in that silent, close space. Her voice came through for her after a few stammers.

"Would you like a cup of coffee?"

He nodded with a half-smile.

She sat across from him, holding her cup with both hands, wondering what he would say or do next and dreading it. He had let Rimas take her to Vilnius, she was sure, to force Skosh into giving up access to the vault's computer. Without Jade, there would be no Dennis to make her system work. Skosh could never convince the assistant to carry on without her.

Knowing why he sent her away, though, did not explain why Mack then arranged her rescue. She was sure it was a rescue. It had all the earmarks of danger and pain and bruising followed by intervention by a scary guy telling the other scary guy to let her go. And the quiet, minimal way in which he did it, without any actual violence, though she had sensed his readiness to fight, was an engineering job of the most subtle kind.

Her internal question remained, why had he done it? His insistence that he would not die for her held more truth in her mind than the fact that he risked a fight to retrieve her.

She looked up from her coffee to find him regarding her silently. The alien blue eyes again reminded her that she would never understand this man. He broke the silence.

"Sometimes, the most unlikely events bring forth the best intelligence."

Jade did not hide her bewilderment.

"Kestutis has become Prion's man. Your brief captivity gave us enough intelligence to solve half the puzzle."

He took a sip from his mug and continued, answering her unspoken question.

"You required rescue when I needed information. It was convenient. Also, I cannot allow Skosh to have more reasons to reproach himself. Please do not make the mistake of thinking I will make a habit of protecting you."

If he was in the mood to answer unvoiced questions, maybe a direct one, out loud, would succeed.

"Are you going to kill me?" she asked.

He answered with a sardonic smile. "No."

"Are you going to kill Skosh?"

She shivered and gulped air when he did not answer.

"What can I give you that will stop that? I mean, aside from my password, but anything else. Anything. Name it."

Jade had reserved the password for purposes of future negotiation, but she meant that she was offering anything in the way of information, of course, so she could not hide her alarm when the man smiled at her in that way. The smile widened further when her wide eyes betrayed shock.

"You must be more careful what you put on the table, Jade. In all of our contracts, it is my interpretation of the terms that controls."

The following two-hour grilling by Mack covered every unimportant detail of her job and left Jade feeling safe again after her unthinking offer. He wasn't taking her up on it, so she began to relax.

Then he stood over her, offering his hand to help her up. She automatically took it, feeling the power with which he boosted her to her feet.

"Come," he said and began leading her back toward the bedroom.

She tried to pull away.

"I... I didn't mean... I was referring to information."

He gave a soft, amused chuckle, but held her arm as he led, or pulled, her through the bedroom door.

"By now, Kestutis has told Prion about you. I cannot leave you alone and you need sleep, proper sleep, on a bed. I have set the perimeter sensors to give the alarm on the radio." He held up the portable in his other hand. "Now, lie down."

Jade had no idea how she would be able to sleep with this man in the same room, let alone sitting next to her on the bed, propped up by several pillows. She lay flat out, her shoulders raised slightly on just two pillows, her body stiff with fright and her eyes wide open. Mack quietly put an arm around her shoulders, barely touching her flannel shirt. She felt relaxed by this, almost against her will, and turned on her side automatically so that she curled up facing him. Her last thought before exhaustion overtook all thought was that no man, including the father who had shown up on rare occasions when she was a girl, ever made her feel so protected as this man did, this man who had insisted he would not die for her.

TWENTY-SIX

"Do you prefer Rimantas or Rimas?" asked Charlie from the back seat.

"Really, Charlie?" said Skosh as he turned the car toward Nida. "Are you trying to tell him he has a choice about what you guys call him?"

Rimas looked over his shoulder at Charlie. They were barely acquainted and came from different countries, but they shared a fighting culture. He suspected Skosh might fight as well. He had the muscle development and the usual, mildly belligerent attitude of latent violence, but he acted like he played only a side role. This much, Rimas understood. He also sensed that in the next few hours, Charlie would become either a valuable ally or an enemy.

Everything else about these people remained a mystery. And one was Russian.

"Call me Rimas," he said

Skosh cut the headlights and coasted to a stop under an evergreen canopy tucked into a dark stand of trees hidden from the road. "The compound is straight ahead. We're facing south." He switched on the transmitter attached to his belt. "I'll monitor you guys from here."

"Like hell you will," said Charlie. "You'll come with us."

"It's not good for me to get too close."

"Spare me your babysitter rules. You'll come with us and protect Rimas. He's not armed."

Both Skosh and Rimas turned around in their seats. "I can't …"

Charlie interrupted. "Don't make the mistake of thinking I'm as patient as my father, Skosh."

"He should not come inside with me, Charlie," said Rimas. "He looks too exotic. It will raise questions. I will ask them if they have seen Kestutis and a few other questions, casually, while I place your listening device."

Inside the long wooden building that housed Prion's Lithuanian volunteers, Rimas recognized a former childhood classmate and three others he had trained with as a teenager. It felt good to enjoy a bottle of beer amidst Lithuanian voices. He followed Charlie's advice and avoided showing too much curiosity about Prion.

"I'm looking for Kestutis," he said. "I thought I might find him here."

"No, he's not sure about Prion yet," said Vytautas scornfully. "He went to Šiauliai to look for something, probably information."

"Something or somebody," interrupted Feliksas.

Rimas sipped his beer and wondered if he looked as dangerous as these two. Feliksas had added muscle mass since they were teenagers but seemed more confident and sober. Vytautas had the same wild-eyed look, though, the same jumpiness, and Rimas remembered he could never be trusted in a fight.

"You should join us," said Vytautas as he opened another beer.

"I don't know...."

"It's a chance to kill some Russians."

Feliksas hissed at Vytautas. "Don't talk about it. Leave that to Kestutis."

"I'll talk all I want. Rimas is all right."

Another man Rimas did not know sat down on a footlocker next to Vytautas and took away his beer. Feliksas introduced him as being one of those in charge. The man's scrutiny was enough to make Rimas ask no more questions. He finished the beer in his hand and took his leave.

As he slipped through a break in the fence, he expected to meet Charlie at the side of the pathway they had made on their way in. Instead, Sergei whispered to him in Russian from behind a particularly stout pine. Even in mottled moonlight, he recognized the pale grey eyes behind Sergei's balaclava.

"Wear this," he said, handing Rimas an earbud and transmitter. Charlie's voice came over the wire.

"Change of plan. You'll help Sergei place the rest of the touches in Prion's office. Did you find Kestutis?"

Surrounded by forest, instinct made him tilt his head in a minimal, silent negative.

"You have a microphone, Rimas. Just whisper."

"He is in Šiauliai."

"Good. We'll debrief later. Follow Sergei's direction."

Sergei handed him a stick of camo paint and a black balaclava and turned his back to him to lead the way.

The two hesitations came simultaneously, each man noticing the other's momentary pause before they made their silent way back to the hole in the fence.

...

Jade sat up, alarmed, but still next to Mack as the overhead light flooded the bedroom. His arm remained protectively around her shoulders, and he wore a self-satisfied smile. Three men had burst into the room, their hair disheveled, their eyes and hands blackened by night camo paint.

She recognized Skosh and Rimas immediately by their height and belligerence, one by his black hair, the other by his blue eyes. The third, the blond, had to be Charlie.

Skosh opened his mouth to say something. Rimas stepped forward. Mack gathered her into his arms and kissed her every bit as seriously as Skosh had done, but he had the decency to keep his eyes closed like he meant it. She checked.

He let go when the sounds of a brief scuffle had quieted. Jade saw Rimas sitting on the floor against the dresser, once again holding his nose, and Skosh doubled over against a wall. Charlie stood over them looking disgusted.

"All right, Papa. You made your point."

"Which point is that, Michael?" Mack still held Jade with one arm.

"That you are not past it," said Charlie or was his name Michael? Jade suspected she had landed in some family tiff.

"What else?" said Mack in that soft purr.

"That Alex has not entirely succeeded in taming you."

"And?"

Charlie sighed and rolled his eyes.

"That you are correct. They both want the woman. I now agree with your plan. Are you done?"

"Yes."

Mack stood, pushed Skosh up against the wall, and said, "You have three hours to debrief your assistant and sleep. I will instruct Sergei to turn off his devices."

Returning Rimas's glare as he walked to the door, he said, "He will not touch her. This is no time for such nonsense."

What Mack did not do was look at her again. Not even a glance. She felt a little miffed. It had been an excellent kiss.

TWENTY-SEVEN

Skosh locked the door behind them when Rimas, Charlie, and Mack left the room—a symbolic gesture really—and kicked off his shoes. He lay down beside Jade on the bed.

That was as sexy as they were ever going to get, Skosh mused with a sense of loss. They had been told to sleep in order, he knew, to keep them out of the team's meeting. That Rimas would be in that meeting rankled. He had not been armed when he went out with Charlie, but the uneasy combination of suspicion and respect with which the team treated him told Skosh the younger guy was no babysitter. Hell, he might even be under consideration for a job. A deadly one, no doubt.

Once again, he and Jade lay side by side fully dressed on top of the duvet. He quizzed her over every word said during her night with Mack. When she told him of Mack's silence after her question about his own danger, he said nothing for a long enough time that she nudged him, probably thinking he had fallen asleep. He turned his head to look at her, still thinking.

Then she told him about her offer and Mack's smile.

"I don't think I've ever seen him smile," said Skosh. He was sinking into a comfortable lassitude he did not want to leave. Death seemed not so bad in this state.

"He looked younger then, even younger than Charlie," said Jade.

"He's right, you know. All agreements we have with them contain a clause that gives him the right to construe the intention of the parties. He might not need to kill me; he could probably win his point in court and make us print out every word stored in your system."

"Which court would he sue in?" She sounded genuinely curious.

Skosh turned his head and looked at her. "I was being facetious."

"Oh." She paused. "Skosh?"

He raised his eyebrows and waited.

"Who is Alex?"

"His wife."

"He has a wife?"

"He told you they're all married now. Not that they all view being married in the same way as most people. I would have thought Mack did, though."

"I don't think he meant it, Skosh. It's hard to explain. He meant the kiss, but not as a prelude to anything else. He had some other purpose."

"Mack always has multiple agendas."

As far as Skosh was concerned, that kiss was a prelude to something, the son of a bitch. He ground his teeth, comfort gone, and changed the subject.

"He didn't demand your password?"

"No. He just asked questions."

"What questions?"

"He asked about people in the building and especially in the leadership, but none of them operatives, only support staff like me."

"What did he want to know?"

"Nothing secret or even confidential. He didn't even ask for addresses or phone numbers. Mostly, he wanted me to talk about their personalities and any gossip about them or stories they put out about others, no matter how absurd."

After a long silence, she nudged him again. His eyes were still open.

"The bastard," he whispered. Then after a deep breath, "Listen, Jade. When we went out again tonight, I was sure Mack would stay back to protect the safehouse now that it's blown, and I was right. He's been letting Charlie make more and more decisions anyway. In a few hours, he'll talk to you again. I want you to tell him something from me. It's important.

"Tell him not to let his natural inclination to eliminate a supposed threat cloud his judgment. Tell him that. He's wrong. It's not what he thinks. It is not a betrayal, just pressure, purely personal, not operational. Candace is not a threat to anybody but me."

Before he let himself sleep, he made an effort to warn her about the larger threat.

"Whatever you do, talk to me before you agree to anything Mack says. Promise me that, Jade. He's a master at manipulation besides being just fucking dangerous."

Skosh fell asleep before she could answer but woke in what seemed no more than a minute when he felt the presence of Charlie in the open doorway.

"Is there any fucking lock that can stop one of you?" he demanded, springing to a stand.

Charlie's answer was the very image of Mack's smile after that kiss. Skosh was having difficulty forgetting it.

"Get moving," said Charlie. "Now that we have a touch on that hovel where Prion is hosting his banker, I want more information on him. That reminds me...."

He half turned to Jade, who had been trying to sneak past him.

"Your information is slow and incomplete."

Poking her sternum with a forefinger, he continued, "Stop playing games, Jade. You can skip the encryption if that is what's taking so long. We've known the key for some time, and you confirmed it this morning. Don't look so surprised. Your assistant had it bookmarked on his bedside table. Sidney Reilly he is not. I've left a list of questions on the table by your notebook. Get to work."

"That's ludicrous, Charlie," said Jade with a defiant glare. "The material is still classified. Just because you're cleared to see it does not mean I can broadcast it to the world by sending it unprotected across seven time zones."

He answered her with a head-to-toe examination, stopping at important points. "You have fifteen minutes to make yourself ..." Another smiling pause, then, "Presentable."

Skosh spoke through his teeth. "That's enough, Charlie."

"Unclench your fists, Skosh. Her ultimate fate is your responsibility, but you know you won't affect it that way."

TWENTY-EIGHT

It was a working breakfast with food that, though made by Lithuanians, tasted foreign to Rimas. These were all foreigners, and one was even a filthy Russian—the worst kind of Russian. He might as well have had 'checkist' tattooed to his forehead, he was so obviously KGB.

Rimas worried again that he had it all wrong, that Kestutis was right and he deserved his broken nose. Then he remembered Antanas. Mack had been correct about the danger. Kestutis had been sent to kill his brother, and the filthy Russian had fixed and bandaged his nose. It hurt like hell, but it was straight again, though the Russian's nose remained crooked.

Sergei was a typical fucking dictatorial know-it-all Russian, though.

Rimas spotted Jade as she came through the rug with Skosh. He gazed at her bruised face. A new resentment rose in his mind concerning that kiss. What did Mack think he was doing? Kestutis was right. He was old enough to be her father. Was there something going on there? She was younger than Charlie for fuck's sake.

Rimas's English vocabulary had expanded in just a few hours under Steve's tutelage.

Steve wore headphones, listening to the tap—called a touch by these people—in Prion's office. They had placed several devices throughout his quarters and in the rest of the compound outside Nida. The system was capable of taping three conversations at once. It was an awesome setup, arranged and controlled by the blonde woman. How in hell had that crooked-nosed Russian ever attracted her? The bastard better not look at Jade.

The live conversation Steve was hearing interested him because he raised his hand. The room became quiet.

"The banker speaketh," said Steve, flicking a switch.

Speaketh? Rimas wondered again about Steve's Texas dialect.

"I don't understand!" came a whiny voice over the main speaker. "You can't pull my funding just like that. I'm good for it. You know I'm good for it. I'm just waiting for the court to close probate. I'm the only heir."

"That's Prion," said Steve. "He's talking to the banker."

"The Michigan court has delayed the case," said the banker, also in English. "Someone intervened and produced a will. If the will is found to be genuine you will not inherit your son's estate. You are not in the will."

The voice recited these points as if he were repeating a well-rehearsed list. A list he expected Prion to know by now.

Prion expanded Rimas's education in American idiomatic expressions further with a long series of oaths—at volume.

"We're only halfway to the recruitment goal. How the fuck am I gonna pay these guys? I got six more waiting for flights out of New York, but I'll lose them if I don't pay their goddamned airfares. You said yourself it has to be a big enough force to make it credible."

"Numbers can be adjusted by propaganda. You have enough for the plan already. A few bodies, a few pictures are all we need."

"But will the Russians respond like you said? That Lithuanian bitch I was married to loved her village, Juodkrantė. Will they level it like you promised if it's only a small attack?"

"All we require is the provocation. But your son's will…"

They were interrupted by somebody bringing coffee and spoke little while they drank. The listeners in the safehouse likewise filled their cups.

Charlie took advantage of the pause to give a pointed look toward Jade, eyebrows raised in a question.

Skosh answered for her. "The banker flew in from Germany an hour ago. Our in-country resident loaned me some watchers, now that Kestutis is considered to have turned."

"He is a loan officer at Felixsee Bank southeast of Berlin," said Jade, reading from the screen of her notebook computer. "There is not much information about him at all, only as much as you might get from a telephone book, just phone number and street. His name is Karl Weltung."

"No, it is not," said Sergei. "I know that voice. Very scratchy and he mispronounces the 'th' sound. He is SVR. We took the same initial language course in the KGB."

Sergei paused for universal appreciation of his mastery of the 'th' sound, then continued.

"His name is Ignat Gurin. He was posted to Berlin after training."

Ahah! thought Rimas. He was right about Sergei's background, and unfortunately correct also that Kestutis was being deceived by Prion.

"Silence!" hissed Mack, pointing to the turning tape machine.

Why did they call him Misha? He was certainly not Russian.

Weltung-Gurin spoke with exaggerated patience. "From Moscow. It should have told you about the will."

"Yes, yes," said Prion. "I got the message. My damaged son left the whole jackpot to the pervert who damaged him, and killed him for all I know, though he's still alive in his filth while my son is dead. I sent Kestutis to take care of it. He couldn't find him or the will and came back with some weird story about a guy named Mack…"

"Mack?" interrupted the banker. "Was he Austrian?"

"I don't know what he was, but Kestutis is convinced he's some kind of fighter. An older guy like him, though, so he can't be that good."

"If it is who I think it is, he is better than good. Did Kestutis mention any Americans?"

"Just an American government guy he was appointed to work with on a secret project. He said the guy looks like he's Asian. What? Why do you look like that? What's wrong?"

After a pause, Gurin said in a low voice, almost a mutter, "Charlemagne's babysitter."

As the listeners and their equipment fell silent during a long pause, Rimas enjoyed watching Sergei squirm a bit under the questioning stares of both Mack and Charlie. The Russian shrugged, then nodded.

"Skosh has been our babysitter only four years," he said. "If Gurin knows who he is, it means that he is still active. This must be an SVR operation."

TWENTY-NINE

All eyes turned to Charlemagne's babysitter, even before Steve returned to the headphones and turned off the speaker at Mack's signal. At first, Skosh thought they might be blaming his noticeable presence for a material disadvantage he couldn't see. So what if some fucking SVR toad knew who he was? At least they were the acknowledged enemy, not so-called allies who might kill him at any moment. Besides, Mack and Charlie had worse security concerns to worry about now, like how they were going to face some forty fighters within what Skosh estimated to be the next twenty hours.

He had begun a review of possible scenarios when he noticed the continued silence and felt the blue eyes burning through his consciousness like lasers. He returned the gaze with a slight questioning head tilt but found the answer as if by telepathy.

"You don't need my password," he told Mack.

"Do you prefer I get it from Jade? Which of you would better weather the storm caused by a breach, should it be discovered?"

"You're forcing me into a moral dilemma. That's unfair since you engineered it."

"Fair? Do you think facing forty men when we are six, with one of us untried, is fair odds? Yet, we agreed only because the provision in the agreement that you say I 'engineered' makes it barely possible. When I looked into your government's proposal, I requested that provision and was as surprised as you were when it was agreed to. The money is nothing compared with the information. We had no choice but to take the commission. Then you, Skosh, 'engineered' a way to deny me the access we need to succeed, to stay alive."

Skosh closed his eyes, sighed, and nodded slightly.

"Jade can ..."

Jade was staring at him wide-eyed.

"Jade cannot," said Mack immediately. "Her assistant does not have access. It may not be in her system, and its classification will be too high for her little encryption device. Did you think I do not understand how you are organized? How your office operates?"

Skosh had often seen him hot with anger. He had felt the power in his fists when Mack thought it was the only way to gain his attention. He had been lectured and insulted too many times to count, but he realized he was not the only person in the room holding his breath. The entire team, even Charlie, had become cautious before the smoking volcano that was Mack.

"What, exactly, do you need?" He managed to keep from squeaking it, but only barely.

"I need the message to Gurin from Moscow, the one he forwarded to Prion, both the original in Russian and the English translation Prion received."

Skosh had seen others in this position. He knew Mack had compromised his predecessor in some way. Was this how he'd done it? He had also saved the man's life and the lives of his family. Skosh loved this job, with all its difficulty, and had nothing else apart from martial arts to go to. Maybe he could open a dojo, teach kids....

Fuck.

But then he would be free of Candace, free to date Jade if she were willing. He looked at her. She was as breathless as the others. She better not faint. Would she date a washed-up babysitter? What if they prosecuted him? They wouldn't. They would not want the agreement brought into evidence.

They might have a different solution.

Fuck.

There was no vertical way out, only horizontal, with or without his blood supply. He understood bleeding out could be relatively painless. Bullets were faster, though.

"I will spare Candace Seston," said Mack, still quiet, still seething, "though I owe you nothing in return for abiding by the agreement she arranged to punish you. She is a worthless exchange for what you imagine to be your honor, Skosh, and will not survive you otherwise. I am not fond of anyone who costs me a good babysitter."

Skosh dug deep. He had reconciled himself to his ending and felt free to go at any time. But as selfish and venal as Candace was, her stupidity did not warrant a death sentence.

Mack snorted. He was becoming impatient and, with a show of reluctance, put one more thing on the table.

"I will not ask more from you in future."

"You won't ask because I don't have a future."

"You need not die painlessly or quickly, you know. We will do what we can. That is all I can give you." He turned to Mara. "Allow Jade to use your machine."

Fucking mind reader.

Jade turned to stare at him, eyes bulging, asking for permission to do what Mack had ordered and no doubt trying to tell him to say yes. Hadn't she already made a deal with Mack? But it didn't include her password. If he couldn't let Candace die of stupidity, he couldn't let Jade suffer unemployment because of his failure. He nodded to her, and she took the seat Mara was offering.

He stood next to her as she brought up the sign-in screen and looked up at him, then vacated the seat when he touched her shoulder. He sat; he typed his log-in and password, and he left the seat to Mara.

Seven minutes later, the printer came to life.

THIRTY

She wanted only to curl up all alone under that duvet with a working lock on the door. Exhaustion born of extreme tension made Jade's legs weak, and the words alone and working were mere myths in this new universe of deception and necessity. Maybe she could downgrade the adjective meant for the lock to functional, but with this crew, that would be equally inaccurate. She doubted a bank vault could keep them out. She had just watched them penetrate her vault, almost silently and with superb efficiency, in seven minutes.

Mack disappeared upstairs and came into the main room carrying a heavy overcoat. He put it on as he crossed the room toward her but spared one cold glance at Skosh, making Jade wonder if this was it, though she still could not believe completely in the reality of lethal danger. He had done what Mack wanted, hadn't he? It was all too much like a movie, except everything was grubbier and more complicated and less explained.

Instead of sitting in a comfortable chair eating popcorn, she stood in the midst of chaos, purposeful but incomprehensible, because it was conducted in multiple languages, none of which she spoke. She regretted the emptiness in her coffee mug and the beginning fullness in her bladder but forgot about both when she saw Skosh blanch under Mack's glance. It confirmed to her imagination that this might be the big 'it' for her boss, even though he had caved.

But Mack passed him by, still buttoning his coat. He grasped her upper arm. Skosh sent out a stream of vehement German as Mack swept the rug aside and pushed her through. She caught a glimpse and heard a scuffle when Steve intercepted Skosh.

"Put on your coat." Mack took her jacket off the door and threw it at her.

Jade still held her mug, and anyway, her hands shook too much for the buttons. Mack took the cup from her, placed it on the table, picked up and opened the coat while she put each arm into a sleeve.

"Do you have a scarf? Gloves?"

She nodded and looked at the cardboard box in the corner that provided a form of organization in the tiny room. He pointed toward it with an open palm indicating she should put them on, but she remained paralyzed. Mack rolled his eyes upward and sighed. He grabbed her pink mittens and Skosh's black scarf out of the box and put them in her hands. Then he buttoned her coat.

She considered, surely, it would not be important to dress warmly for the big 'it,' would it? And what kind of assassin buttons the coat of the quivering victim before doing the deed? The absurdity of her situation clashed with the very real danger all around her and gave her the strength to don her pink mittens on her own.

As Mack pulled her outside, cold air struck her face while disordered reality crowded her mind. This was no neat movie plot with a foreordained ending. Back in that pair of safehouses, any of them, all of them, each of them could die very soon, she realized. Odds favored that at least one of them would.

She watched the toes of her boots as they shuffled over familiar paving stones near the dry dock. Mack halted at Skosh's favorite stopping point but remained silent. Forcing herself to look up, she stared into those blue eyes.

"Skosh is no longer in danger from me," said Mack. "It is time to discuss how you will fulfill your part of our bargain."

The nerve of the man! Anger became a great aid in overcoming fear. It gave Jade's reply all the bite she could wish for in her words.

"He's out of danger because you won. You trapped and defeated him. I had nothing to do with it, nor did our so-called agreement, which ends right here and now."

She stamped her foot.

The bastard laughed out loud, took her arm, and began moving further down the walkway before he spoke again, still chuckling here and there.

"The gossip you shared with me helped me convince him to behave rationally. I commend you, but now that I have arranged for him, and possibly the rest of us, to continue living, I am calling in your debt to me. You said, as I recall, 'anything' and also 'name it.' I am naming it."

Anger gave way again to fear, but maybe it was adrenaline that was speeding up her thinking.

"Surely, you wouldn't want to cheat on Alex."

"Cheat on? I am unfamiliar with the expression. You are not suggesting I should forego a pleasure merely because Alex is not here to provide it, are you?"

He gave her that wicked, boyish smile again. She decided it would be tactless to mention his age explicitly, so she reworded her next argument.

"I'm younger than Charlie."

Realizing too late that this was worse, she tried and failed to stammer a retraction.

He laughed again, then became suddenly serious.

"You always divert me, Jade, but I am not here to be entertained. I will hold you to the agreement, but not for myself."

This made her blanch, unless he meant Skosh, which seemed unlikely. She held her breath.

"Breathe, Jade. I have no desire to see you faint. Now listen to me."

She looked up and saw no hint of a smile; the eyes had hardened as well. She made a show of taking a deep breath.

"Good. I transfer your generous offer to Rimas. In a little while he will need incentive, and then if he lives, in a few hours he will require your understanding. You will give him both. Whatever he wishes, you will say yes. He is young and fit and reasonably good-looking. It should not be difficult for you."

How very like a man, thought Jade. Sex need not mean anything beyond the appearance of the parties. She was arrested by the words, 'if he lives' and began to worry about Rimas. She liked him enough to be concerned but not enough to bargain with a devil as she had for Skosh. At first, she swallowed this instruction as being not so bad if it got her off the hook but then found herself wondering about her own sexual attitudes. Rimas was rather delightful.

Mack had watched her face, no doubt reading each thought as it traveled across her brain, and as if satisfied with her conclusion, began a lecture about how to behave in the next few hours. Most of it

Quiet Move

swept by her, but three things stuck in her mind along with his low purring voice as he said them.

"Do not become emotional."

"Follow Charlie's orders exactly."

And finally, "Keep your hands where they can be seen at all times, unless they are tied behind you, of course."

"Then this is end game?" she asked.

She had surprised him into another wicked smile.

"You must know you will not succeed with Skosh," he said.

She tried not to show her disappointment but knew she failed. "He is married then?"

"No. Worse. He is honorable. But to answer your first question, we have entered the middle game. There are still too many pieces on the board."

As Jade tilted her head, puzzled, he answered the unspoken question.

"Our opening succeeded. I shall call it Mack's Gambit. We are now in a position to win the advantage through a series of exchanges. The next move will involve our knight, Rimas. Give him an enthusiastic yes."

She felt bruised, unwashed, exhausted, and ugly. Enthusiasm seemed a pipe dream. Mack stopped and turned her to face him. He was not smiling.

"The end game, when it comes, may require a sacrifice of one or more of our pieces."

THIRTY-ONE

"If you are Austrian, why do you speak American English?" Rimas asked Charlie.

They walked slowly down a path in a small park by the shore. Rimas noticed Mack leading Jade toward the dry dock.

"My stepmother is American," said Charlie. "But what you want to know is why Sergei is on the team. He is married to my sister. The family is like a mini-United Nations, though without the peace-keeping. Any more questions?"

"You are a wizard."

"No, I just watch people carefully. You will pick it up soon enough. If you live."

Rimas raised his brows in alarm and Charlie continued. "It is a superstition of ours to never assume we will live through the next op. Kestutis gave you the physical skills you will need, and maybe mental strength, but we also have our own ways that you must learn if you are to join us and …"

"And if I live," interrupted Rimas.

Charlie smiled. Then he told Rimas what it was he might not live through.

"Be sure to go to the Lithuanians first, then the Americans. Who knows, you might be able to walk out again. If that's the case, disappear quickly, before they can think. I know Kestutis taught you how to move through the forest. We will do what we can for you if you're taken, but it will take time."

Rimas nodded. "I am prepared. If Kestutis…."

"Don't count on Kestutis. He may not be there. We think he is still in Šiauliai."

"He will be there—eventually. I know him. He will not stay away. The others will...."

"Stop dreaming, Rimas. It is not a good habit. Look, there's Jade." Charlie pointed to her as she walked with Mack. "Rest your mind with her. She is very real and if you just think about her, it won't deflect your path; it won't make you add or subtract from the plan. You have memorized it?"

Rimas nodded as he watched Jade walk back to the house. He doubted she was safe with this team, but the thing called safety was relative after all, and Charlie was right. He had no control over what Kestutis might do. He also had no intention of passing up Charlie's implied promise of better luck with Jade.

...

"Lunch is due in five fucking minutes," Skosh hissed at Jade as she came in the door. He glowered at Mack behind her. He knew how to lose a sparring match with grace but surrendering his password had not gone smoothly down his ethical gullet. He would need copious antacids to keep the resentment down.

He added an insolent glare to his glower.

Mack answered with a silent, cold challenge.

Skosh did not feel that crazy. He looked away.

That the son of a bitch had something up his sleeve regarding Jade had not escaped him. Preserving his skin was suddenly not enough. He needed to preserve hers as well, or he knew, as surely as he knew his name, that he could never live with what he had done to her.

Mack's low voice reached his ears despite the chaos in the room.

"She is in no more danger than you are, Skosh."

"If that's the case, then use me instead."

"There are some things only she can do." Mack's chuckle as he said this told Skosh everything he never wanted to know.

"So Rimas is joining Charlemagne," he said through clenched teeth. "Or are you just using him?"

"Yes, if he lives, he will join us."

"So both."

"He is a fighter, Skosh, trained by Kestutis, one of the best in this part of the world. His eyes are open. You need not fear for him. He will find plenty of that on his own."

"Mack, you know it's part of my job to minimize the impact on the surrounding population. That young man is a Lithuanian citizen. If you're sending him on some suicide mission, I need to make him aware of it."

"Charlie has fully briefed him. Rimas will play an important role. As I told Jade, Rimas is our knight. There are some moves only he can make."

Why, thought Skosh, has Jade been made privy to information he had to pry from Mack? Because she plays chess? And how did they find another language, though expressed with English words, that allows them to communicate with so much nuance?

He resolved to take up the game.

If he lived.

...

"What? Are you my pimp now?"

Jade risked the acid in her voice because she knew she had the higher moral ground. Minimally higher, like maybe a millimeter.

Charlie pulled the last hairpin from her coiled braid and laid the pins on the dresser.

"I want him to think about only you and his task. You are competing with Kestutis for space in his mind. Your hair is an advantage. Use it."

He picked up her brush and began arranging her hair about her shoulders.

"I tried putting makeup on the bruises," said Jade. "It made them worse."

"He won't be thinking about your bruises."

She felt his icy cold stare as he held her shoulders, boring his words into her with such solemnity it made her shudder.

"This op is his first and it is difficult. He needs a reason to survive. You will have five minutes to provide it."

As he turned to leave the bedroom, she couldn't help herself. The way they all took her obedience for granted grated on her.

"That's it? That's all I get from you? Not even a 'thank you for your service?'"

He turned at the door, eyebrows raised. "I will be happy to give you much more than that."

"A sim ... simple thank you will suffice."

The bastard smiled and left the room without saying anything.

...

Skosh saw the minimal lift of Charlie's chin as he came through the rug into the team's larger room. Rimas stood by the computer, dressed now in winter forest camouflage and armed with a semi-auto pistol and an earbud. Sergei was dressed like his twin. The two were about to leave, but Rimas went through the rug alone.

Skosh followed him, stood in the kitchen, and waited. It took no more than two minutes for the bedroom door to open. Rimas had the same grim set to his face as he left that Skosh had worn when he prepared himself for death only a few hours ago. He sincerely hoped the young man would live and fleetingly wondered what kind of specialist he would become. Wired and crazy? Silent and sinister? Analytical and cold? Or some new combination not yet present on the team?

He stepped into the bedroom.

For a moment, he could only gaze at her. Who ties her flannel shirt tails at the waist during an op? Jade does. He had never known a woman so completely out of her depth yet who could remain herself, from kitten heels to a flannel fashion statement.

Why was her hair down? Stupid question. Another confirmation of his suspicions. She had just been kissed, judging by the redness around her lips and the way she licked them. Kissed hard.

She smiled at him.

"Jade," he said after a deep breath, "I know what they're up to. I suspect it's their idea of psychological support, specialist style. You've been pressured, threatened, and tricked. I want you to know you do not have to do this. I will take you out of here right now, bring you to Vilnius, and put you on a flight home."

The smile disappeared.

"At what cost, Skosh? Mack told Kestutis you would die for me. I won't let you do that. As costs are counted, mine is very light. It is not optimal, but certainly not unpleasant. Relax. We will get through this."

He kissed her then. Properly. Stealing an illicit moment from Rimas, from the team, from grim reality.

THIRTY-TWO

Rimas had more trouble with the Americans than he expected. To be sure, the Lithuanian fighters read with a critical air the printout of the message from Moscow that he brought, but it held too many genuine marks and Russian abbreviations to be dismissed outright as a forgery.

Kestutis was not there, but thanks to Feliksas, the group recognized Rimas as his protégé, giving his words added credibility.

"Who are you working for then?" asked a suspicious younger man. "The Americans?"

"They are not Americans, but they are here with an American government agent."

"Are they Russian?"

"No."

Rimas considered it wiser to leave off explaining Sergei.

"Have you seen Kestutis?" asked another man.

"Not since yesterday."

Again, details seemed inadvisable. There had been no curiosity about his bruised face.

"What does this mean about Prion's funding?" asked a more seasoned fighter. "We carry our own equipment. He does not supply it."

"The Americans are paid," explained Rimas.

"Those thieves in that other building? They are being paid while we are not?"

"No," said a tall man at the back. "That is the point of the message, Jonas. They are not being paid. It means they are not likely to stay. We will be left on our own, to be slaughtered. Or, I should say, you will be on your own because I am leaving."

Eleven more Lithuanians joined him, shouldering knapsacks and AK-47s as they made their way into the night. Rimas told them about a convenient hole in the fence behind their barrack and they melted into the forest. Two more followed them, deputed by the others to find Kestutis in Šiauliai and show him the message from Moscow. Three remained to wait for him before making a decision.

Rimas was not entirely sure of one of them and was careful to check his back while making his silent way to the American barrack.

There, he had more difficulty being believed, but there was a phone in this building. When one of the men reached his bank just before close of business in a place called Birmingham, he hung up the phone, turned to the others, and announced, "I didn't get the dough."

Rimas worked out how many English words for money he now knew while another three men called their banks to confirm the first man's result. They began packing. The exodus was both less orderly and less complete, with only ten gone and eight waiting for the phone when a large man came through the door.

"What the fuck?"

"We ain't been paid, Lowell."

"So what? It's only temporary. Who the fuck is this?"

All eyes turned to Rimas. He would have drawn the gun Charlie had given him, but Lowell had already swung the muzzle of his rifle in his direction. Rimas was getting sick of surrender but swallowed his self-disgust as the first blows reminded him that he was still alive.

THIRTY-THREE

Dinner arrived in four rectangular tubs covered with foil. Jade thought it odd that just when they had plenty of table space, the food took up almost none at all. All the gear, the computer, radio equipment, and most of the sensor apparatus had been transferred that afternoon to an old rust bucket of a van that she heard Skosh assure Charlie would run like a top. Charlie gave his trademark belligerent stare in reply and Skosh laughed. His mood had lightened.

Jade gathered four of her large wooden spoons and placed one in each bin. These contained nothing but the delicious meat pies in pastry called *kibinai*, a specialty of Lithuanian Tatars, Muslims who had come to the country as early as the fourteenth century. The caterers provided one tub each of chicken, beef, pork, and lamb. Jade's spoons were surplus to the team's needs. They grabbed the pies by hand and ate them standing at the table before grabbing more. Well, Mara used a spoon to fish out a whole meat pie from the remnants caused by all the hand-grabbing but then ate it the same way as her teammates.

They seemed different somehow, Steve and Charlie especially, but also Mara. Her blonde hair had been pulled back tightly, accentuating the fine bones of her face and exceptional brightness in her green eyes. It was the brightness that caught Jade's attention. They all had it, even Mack, though he had not dressed like the others, in forest camouflage.

The portable radio Mack held squawked. He caught Charlie's eye, who then pointed at Skosh and Jade.

"You two. I'll see you in the bedroom, now."

"Which bedroom would that be?" asked Skosh, with the merest hint of insolence.

"Jade's bedroom, the one that does not smell like a pig sty. Now."

They stood by the dresser as Charlie closed the door.

"Rimas is taken. You two will bargain for him."

Jade gasped. Skosh raised a fist.

"You mother fucking son of a bitch! You assured me Jade would not be used as a dangle."

"You are confusing me with my father. I gave no assurances whatsoever."

Motionless and menacing, Charlie's voice held all the venom required by the occasion. He continued softly, making Jade suppress shudders after every other word.

"Here's what you're going to do. Start by cleaning yourselves up. Skosh, go shave and put on your best suit. Jade, wear makeup. I don't care that it won't cover the bruises, make it look like you tried. Put your hair up and put on something stylish. Those little boots with the funny heels will do nicely. Did you bring a skirt by any chance?"

And so on. Jade dressed, hearing brief snatches of the conversation in the bathroom next door as Charlie explained the plan to Skosh while he shaved. Skosh interrupted him frequently and with vehemence, but Charlie replied with quiet force. She could not understand the words.

"I would never …" insisted Skosh.

"You will this time," said Charlie.

In the car, Jade smoothed a wrinkle in the vintage designer stirrup slacks she found at a flea market and had worn on the airplane. They tucked neatly into her favorite half-boots. The makeup made her feel like a painted clown because it was excessive, but Charlie insisted.

"You know," said Skosh, turning onto the road into Nida, "I don't know what the real plan is. No doubt there will be double-dealing and this is only a conjecture. Treachery is likely to be what the targets want, but Mack is probably in on it, so Charlie's right. Save your emotion for Rimas and play it up when the time comes."

"Why do you think Mack is in on it?"

"Because I'm pretty sure Charlie would never betray his dad and that's what it feels like. Mack told you not to be emotional. He didn't mean don't feel something for Rimas. They want you to do that. So he probably meant don't let your emotions about him cloud your obedience to Charlie."

Jade thought it more likely that Mack had been referring to how she felt about Skosh.

"If I know you're sweet on the old guy," he continued, "he knows it, too."

It was time to change the subject.

"Charlie noticed my designer boots."

"Charlie notices everything. Don't be so pleased with yourself."

"I'm not. I'm pleased with the price I paid for them. They were next to nothing when you count the T-shirts they came with. Those were useless, so I cut them up for rags."

She prattled to pass the time, to squeeze the situation into a dark corner of her mind. He listened the way all men listen to such things: not at all.

Skosh showed his passport to a camera at the gate of Prion's compound. It swung open.

Thugs was the word Jade would have used to describe their escorts into what appeared to be the main building. It was the largest wooden structure surrounded by a number of smaller sheds, all of them dotted among tall pines with straight, bare trunks. The hoodlums frisked them both for weapons. Skosh lost his H&K semi-auto pistol, and Jade thought the man with his hands on her lingered too long in some places. He was ugly as sin with a bald head and ink all over his face, but it was the leer that made him especially loathsome.

There weren't too many people around as they crossed a small, paved area in front of the building. Inside, a long, narrow hallway ran through the center, with four doors opening onto it, staggered, two on each side, and a grander (had it been painted) wooden double door at the end. It opened and they were ushered into the presence of Earl Prion, father of the late rock star, Tommy Taurus.

The desk was too grandiose for him. It made him look like a janitor, here to clean the furniture on behalf of an executive. The tall, well-built man standing to one side fit that role better. He wore a well-cut suit and wire-rimmed glasses and held a briefcase in one hand.

"What do you want?" Prion's voice sounded peevish.

"First, I'd like my sidearm back," said Skosh with some heat. "It cost a packet and I've been authorized to carry it by the Lithuanian Defense Ministry. I'm here on official United States government business and don't expect to be treated like a criminal by a fellow American."

Prion pursed his lips and looked to the guy in the suit for guidance.

"Tell us why you are here," said the man smoothly. He had an accent that faintly reminded Jade of Sergei.

"Who are you?" Skosh remained belligerent.

"My name is Karl Weltung. And you are?"

"John Nakamura."

Jade wondered if Skosh saw Weltung's reaction the way she did. She understood he was a major player in this secret game, but he betrayed himself like an amateur. She would have done a better job not reacting to Skosh's name. He opened his eyes wide and blinked slowly to give himself time to think before he spoke.

"What do you want?"

Skosh played the bluff, harried government bureaucrat to a tee, explaining how he was responsible for this chit of a secretary who'd fallen in love with some Lithuanian who was here in the compound, and could she see him?

Thus began negotiations.

THIRTY-FOUR

They produced a beaten and trussed Rimas. Skosh could see a few more bruises on his face, and he limped a bit, but he was alive. Jade made a show of sobbing loudly and trying to run to him. He joined the drama and held her back. He was not about to let her go anywhere near the brutes standing to either side of Rimas.

"She is the only person who thinks he's important," insisted Skosh. "Just let him go so she can patch him up. He has no power to threaten you."

"Then how did he know I lost my funding?" screamed Prion.

Gurin raised a hand in warning, and Prion corrected himself, speaking quickly and shuffling a pile of papers on the desk to mask his nervousness.

"I mean that's what he told my men, showing them a forged message about a purely routine holdup in the final funds. Right guys?" He looked to the two men holding Rimas, who nodded.

"Overzealous in your interests maybe," said Skosh, "mistakenly trying to help you, but essentially harmless. Let him go home to lick his wounds. We are in-country on other business and pose no threat to you."

Gurin's shoulders twitched. So did one eyebrow. His dark eyes caught the American in a steady glare as he spoke quickly.

"I believe the popular English expression is 'bullshit,' Nakamura. I know who you are, what you are. This man may be unimportant, as you say, but if he is connected to you, I must know how. He will tell us—eventually."

"He knows nothing. He's just an interpreter for Miss Wilburton, who is my administrative assistant."

Skosh had also dropped the pretended bluffness. He tensed his muscles while loosening the fingers at his sides. He was ready to fight.

Prion stood with the tip of his tongue showing through his teeth, moving only his eyes from Gurin to Skosh as they negotiated.

"I presume he has eyes and ears," said Gurin. "He will remember what he has seen and heard. We will help his memory."

"But he has no real information. You can let him go and keep me instead."

Gurin's eyes opened wide again. He took his time with his next careful suggestion.

"I know you can offer a bigger prize. Kestutis has described him to Mr. Prion."

Prion tilted his head and wrinkled his brow, trying to remember everything Kestutis had told them.

"What prize, Weltung? What the hell are you talking about?"

The banker held up one hand to silence him.

"Let me handle this, Earl."

"I want to know what you're talking about. This is my operation, damn it."

"It's mine now. This is beyond you. It will be the highlight of my career, even if the other fails."

Gurin instructed the guards to leave the room with their prisoner, bypassing Prion entirely in his haste to secure the bigger prize.

Prion nodded at the guards, pretending he still held authority as they turned away. When they had gone, he gave his banker an ingratiating smile.

"Very wise, Karl," he said. "It's better they not know anything Kestutis said. I don't entirely trust him."

Jade had stopped crying, leaving her mouth open in surprise at Gurin's suggestion.

"You see," Gurin told Skosh with a satisfied smile, "even your assistant knows. She was there when he and Kestutis met. Perhaps I should keep her."

Skosh frowned in dismay. Charlie had foreseen every move.

"What do you propose?"

THIRTY-FIVE

Rimas thought he must be dreaming as they shoved him toward the van.

"Oh my darling, what have they done to you?" said Jade, running alongside him.

Darling?

The van's back door swung open with four men already inside. Jade kept talking.

"You look terrible, but I will nurse you. I'm taking you out of here."

Terrible? He had an extra bruise or two from the futile fight he put up when the Americans seized him—for the sake of self-respect—but nothing more since she saw him in Prion's office. The real interrogation had not yet begun. He gave her his best question-mark look, hoping she could read it. He had been held in another room during what seemed an eon squeezed into half an hour, while Skosh and Gurin bargained.

"I've arranged your release," Jade said. "We just have to make some arrangements at my house. These men are going to assist us, and once that's done, they'll let you go. There. At the house."

He read her look as meaning 'play along; this is mandatory.' He played along.

They were both bundled into the back of the van with the four heavily muscled men. His hands remained tied behind him, but hers were free. She kept them in front of her, visible. Two more men sat up front. Rimas ventured a question, focusing on Jade because if he looked at the leering gargoyle next to her, he knew he would explode.

"Will Mr. Nakamura meet us at your house?"

"No, my dear, he elected to remain with Mr. Prion to finalize the arrangements for your release."

Six men. Skosh held hostage. It was all wrong, but Jade's plastic smile demanded cooperation. He returned an equally fake grimace.

The van parked under the trees, twenty meters behind the house. Their six-man escort stood hesitating, arguing and asking the same questions repeatedly. Six men, one woman, and Rimas with his hands tied behind him stood freezing in clouds of breathy argument.

"Look," Jade said with some heat. "I told you Mr. Nakamura dismantled the sensors. See? I have the part that controls the alarm system."

She pulled a metal computer part from the back pocket of her slim corduroy pants. A ribbon connector dangled from it. Rimas recognized the used part she had bought during their early shopping trip in Klaipeda. Why, he wondered, were six fighters worried about the sensors? Who were they after? He became uneasy and uncertain. So far, he found nobody around him to be trustworthy—not the Americans, not Kestutis, not the girl he had kissed and wanted to kiss again. He could handle violence; conjecture would kill him.

After ten minutes of noisy education in American words, they left Rimas standing in the snow, still tied, with one man as a guard. The other five accompanied Jade through the back door of the team's safehouse.

His concern for her lasted no more than a moment after the door closed. He heard a soft pop-zip and watched his guard fall with a thud, a neat hole in his temple. Sergei stepped out of the brush holding a knife. He cut Rimas's bonds and shoved a suppressed MP5 submachine gun into his hands.

"I thought they would never make a decision," he said in Russian. "Come. Help me hide him."

"Jade …"

"Jade will be okay. She will see a good fight. We cannot stay for it."

THIRTY-SIX

Jade had a front-row seat, or rather, stand. They left Rimas outside, guarded by one man, then pushed her ahead of them, storming single file through the team's narrow kitchen, past the massive brick stove, and into the main room.

Mack jumped from his chair and whirled to face them, gun in hand. He shot the man behind her as Jade stepped to her left in order not to be in the way. The next man also moved left and stayed behind her.

The third man ran at Mack, leaping as high as the ceiling allowed and swinging one leg in a wide arc. Mack blocked the kick before it could reach his head, held the foot, and shoved the man into the table that once held Mara's computer. He slid along the top, scattering empty tubs of kibinai remnants, but was on his feet again beginning another leap when Mack shoved his knuckles into the man's throat, throwing him back a second time. This time he fell, stunned and struggling for breath until Mack's bullet found him and ended the struggle.

Numbers four and five wasted no time. They dashed around the bodies and came at him from both sides. By now, Mack had his back to a wall as the man on his right grabbed his arm, beating it against the wall until the SIG Sauer fell to the floor. The one on the left kicked the gun out of reach. Mack pulled out a knife with his left hand, swung into the man holding his right arm, and kneed him in the groin. As the man doubled over, Mack pointed his knife upward and shoved it into his chest. He fell face up, the knife implanted to its hilt.

"Fuck," said the man to the left, pulling his gun out of a hip holster.

"Don't!" shouted the thug behind Jade. He grabbed her arm. "Weltung wants him alive. We can't shoot him, but he didn't say nothin' about her."

He pressed the muzzle of his weapon against Jade's temple.

She refused to die with her eyes closed and so had them open to watch Mack surrender to two American hoodlums. She gasped, suddenly understanding what Skosh had been trying to tell her in the car. He must have known about this and thought Mack also knew about the attack, but now he had lost the fight, and it was because of her. She reviewed all the instructions. Each word Charlie said came back to her with perfect clarity. She followed all of them. She had not moved. Her hands were visible. She had controlled her emotions, and still, Mack lost.

He said he would not die for her, but she was alive, and he was captured.

And now, so was she. The two goons had plans of their own. After a disgusting conversation, they decided to tell Prion it was a trap and explain they kept both her and Rimas for that reason. Then, they would await their opportunity.

They took some revenge on Mack, inflicting severe bruising as payback for their dead comrades. While they occupied themselves with this, she slipped through the rug, out the front door, and ran as fast as her boots would let her along the side of the house, behind the wood pile, and into the forest, where she tripped over a body and fell flat on her face in the snow.

The sound of voices kept her down and still, raising her head just enough to watch the clearing beyond the trees that sheltered her and the grisly thing that had brought her down. She saw them frog march Mack, his hands tightly zip-tied behind him, out the back door.

"Where the fuck is Gansen?"

They called the name, followed a few footsteps they could see in the deeper parts of the snow leading into the dark brush under the trees, but did not dare go further lest they lose the prize they had come for. With a shrug, the two men decided Gansen had legged it.

If this was Gansen, wondered Jade, where was Rimas? She was terrified they would kill Mack in front of her because she had done something wrong, though she didn't know what, not that she ever knew anything, but she knew now she didn't want him to die. Not him, not Rimas, not any of them. And above all, not Skosh. She wanted to apologize as a way to erase the past and make everything better, but Mack was captured, Skosh held hostage, and the team nowhere to be seen.

...

"Location?" Michael used English for Rimas's sake. By now, Sergei should have given him another earbud. Also by now the two should have been at the team's van. A surge of foreboding intruded on his thoughts. He quashed it.

Sergei answered the call.

"There was a shot, but now nothing. They have not come out. What should we do?"

It had been Michael's idea to use his father as bait. His idea and his plan, a plan without much flexibility in the timing. Michael closed his eyes. Silence took hold of everyone in the van. Mara avoided eye contact. Misha was her father, too, but the operation must come first.

"Get back here," he said.

"On our way."

Michael wanted to scream loud, elemental, belligerent fury at the malevolence of a destiny that would make his father the earliest victim of his solo leadership.

Sergei's panting voice again came to his ear. "Another shot …"

"Get here."

The order came automatically, without hesitation. A supreme test of ruthless leadership, and he had passed it. Michael marked the moment for thought later, not letting it delay the calculations he needed to make now.

"Drive," he told Steve in the seat next to him as Sergei and Rimas fell inside and slammed shut the back door. Mara came forward and lifted one earphone.

"The watcher at the ferry says Kestutis has boarded the boat."

Michael turned in this seat, calculations finished, necessary rearrangements decided.

He looked at Rimas. "You will wait for Kestutis beside the road. You know his car?"

Rimas nodded.

"Stay with him. Do what you can."

The young man nodded again.

"Pull over three kilometers before the compound to let Rimas out," Michael told Steve. "Then bring us to the departure point. You'll run to the front gate and watch for the van Sergei said the tangos are driving."

"Me?"

"Yes, you. I want to know if and when it gets there. If it's not there after half an hour, take your position by the American barrack."

Michael turned to Mara, who stood holding the back of his seat.

"You and I will go to the Lithuanian barrack. Three of them are still there."

Steve interrupted. "I thought I …"

"Change of plan," Michael said with gritted teeth. He made a mental note to address this creeping democratic tendency in the team. "Mara is more likely to persuade them to leave before the shooting starts."

Not that Steve deserved an explanation.

"I don't know any Lithuanian," said Mara.

"Use Russian. They all speak at least some of it."

Michael looked Steve in the eye as he spoke his next order.

"I need you to clear the American barrack. When we're done with the Lithuanians, I'll send Mara to back you up before I quietly take out as many as I can in the main building prior to the start of gunfire. It's a long hallway with too many doors and may take time. You will begin the op. Wait for her to get in position."

Steve's answering smile confirmed Michael's dispositions. The man loved a firefight and Michael was happy to oblige. Unless the rank-and-file tangos were at least half as good as Steve, which was unlikely, they had no chance. He turned to Sergei last.

"I am guessing you did not retrieve my father's weapons."

"We did not go in."

Michael nodded. "Assuming he is a prisoner and that Skosh will do as he's been told, both will need weapons. Take one of the spare semi-autos and a knife out of the weapons locker and an extra MP5. You'll meet Skosh and then back me up as I come out of that building."

"Yes." Sergei hesitated. "I am sorry…."

"For what?" Michael hoped the glare he gave would stop them all from dwelling on it. They had no time for distraction. Sergei nodded slightly, swallowed, and looked away.

THIRTY-SEVEN

Rimas stepped out from under the trees and onto the road leading to Nida just as Kestutis's car approached.

"Where are the others who went to get you?" he asked as he settled into the passenger seat of his mentor's car.

"They came to inform me, not to get me. I let them go on their way."

"Then why are you headed for Nida?"

"To confront Prion. The message you brought appears genuine, but it could be a forgery."

"If it is," said Rimas, "this is too complicated to be Russian."

"How so?" countered Kestutis.

"A Russian rescued me from Prion."

"There you are. The Russians want us to abandon Prion's attack on Kaliningrad. They are using you as a pawn."

"No, Kestutis, they want Prion to attack. They intend to use his attack as an excuse to invade us. Sergei—that is the man who rescued me—allowed me to hear a tape of Weltung explaining it to Prion. I learned their voices very well when they held me. I am not mistaken."

Kestutis scowled. "But Prion loves Lithuania. Why would he work for an invasion?"

"He hates Lithuania." Rimas followed this statement with the history of Tommy Prion and his brother Antanas.

"Why do you trust such people?" demanded Kestutis. "They are unnatural."

"Because I know my brother. He does not lie."

"But the Russian...."

"Is on the team that will kill Prion. I have been invited to join them."

Kestutis pulled off the road and into heavy brush growing under young trees.

"Team? Then he is the man I remember. They have always been anti-Soviet. But I must confront Prion to see for myself if you are correct. Why does this team want you?"

He climbed out and set off into the forest. Rimas followed like the puppy he knew he was.

"Because you trained me."

"Thank you for the flattery, but you will learn how little I have taught you in comparison with what will be expected of you. You have never killed. They are experts."

Kestutis halted, listening. Rimas heard it, too, sounds of movement through the undergrowth, then voices. As the noises grew louder, he recognized his own language. Kestutis pulled out a handgun and stepped out into the path of two men. Rimas recognized them as two of the stalwarts who had refused to believe the message he brought them.

"What the hell are you doing, blundering through the forest like a bloody herd of elephants?" said Kestutis.

"We are leaving," said one of the men. "Something is about to happen, and we have no protection. Vytautas is dead. A woman shot him. A girl. Just like that! In the chest. I'm sure he meant only to frighten her, but he got no further than taking his rifle off the locker. He was always a hothead. But this woman and the blond man with her were cold as winter. They told us to leave, and we left. The Americans in the compound are not friends."

As the two moved on and became invisible within meters into the forest, Kestutis hung his head.

"I knew Vytautas's father," he said in a low voice. "He worried about the boy. I should not have allowed him to join Prion."

He moved southward toward the compound.

"I will go with you to confront Prion," insisted Rimas. "What is your plan?"

To his dismay, Kestutis had only skill, courage, and guilt. It would be up to Charlemagne to produce enough of a plan for a successful outcome.

If they lived.

THIRTY-EIGHT

The others were already running when Steve used his luxurious extra three minutes to tighten the Velcro on his Kevlar vest and add more magazines to his belt. The van was well hidden on the side of the road past the turnoff to Nida, less than two kilometers from Prion's compound. The short run would keep him warm. But then he would freeze as he waited for that other damned van full of tangos. Maybe it would come fast. He hoped it would come fast and that it would have Misha, alive, inside.

As if the hope had made it happen, he heard a vehicle approaching. He stepped to the edge of the forest, then out onto the road when he recognized the team's rental car, not the tango van. He saw a lone driver illuminated by the late afternoon sun and pointed his MP5 at the car.

"What the fuck are you doing?" he asked as Jade rolled down the window.

"He's been captured," she said, tears streaming down her cheeks. "It's my fault. I don't know how, but it has to be my fault."

Steve hauled her out of the car and under cover of the trees. She carried a pillowcase with something in it.

"They were ahead of you?" he asked, turning his transmitter back on, then said into the mic, "We missed them." Again looking at Jade as she shivered, he asked the main question, the one everybody wanted the answer to, "He's alive?"

Back to the microphone. "She's nodding, Michael."

She tried to hand him the pillowcase. He already had enough to carry, and one hand had hold of her arm to stop her from going anywhere. What the fuck was he going to do with a pillowcase.

"They're his." She was blubbering now. "He'll want them."

They began walking toward the compound. Steve didn't know what else to do with this extra baggage of a female. It wasn't like he could just leave her in a frozen forest with no shortage of unknown tangos lurking about, and he'd be damned if he let her anywhere near the comm equipment operating in the van at a time when they most depended on it. Michael would fry him with those blue eyes of his.

He stopped, took the pillowcase from her, and looked inside. His mind spun as it sought a way to explain this over the air. There was a long pause from Michael, then instructions for a meeting with Sergei to hand it over.

"The knife's bloody," Steve said to Jade.

"I had to pull it out of the man's chest."

"The man?"

"The one he killed. One of the ones he killed. Before they took him."

He stared at her and nearly tripped over a tree root. She had stopped crying but melted makeup made streaks down her face. Almost like camo paint. She limped because the heel of one of her too-dainty boots had broken off. If he had a nestlike snarl of hair like that, he'd probably just shave it all off. She was just fluff, wasn't she? Out of her depth, not meant to be anywhere near the likes of them, even more unsuited to an op than Claire had been.

Claire had survived. Barely.

Jade had pulled Misha's knife out of a dead man.

Women. Scary creatures. That reminded him. "What do I do with the, uh, assistant?" he said into the mic.

"Hand her over to her, um, boss—with the items to be returned. Let Skosh deal with it.

Sergei and Steve both copied.

...

"It was a trap, but we got 'im," said a heavily tattooed bruiser.

Skosh hung his head, praying this was the plan, playing it for all he was worth.

Prion narrowed his eyes, twirling a pencil in his fingers. Gurin raised his eyebrows and fairly danced where he stood, chin up and triumphant. He tilted back his head, flaring his nostrils as if sniffing an imminent kill.

"How many did you lose?" asked a more morose Prion. The twirling pencil had calmed him. He scowled.

The bruiser winced. "Four. Three dead and one missing."

"How many are left, Lowell? Altogether?"

"Nine, including me. All the Lithuanians are gone. One of them is dead, too. Jones told me on my way in."

"Dead? How?"

"Shot. Accurate, too. Right through the heart. We can't find any of the others, but Jones heard that some of 'em went to Šiauliai to talk to Kestutis. Two of 'em expected him back any minute, but now they're gone, too."

Prion turned to his banker, insistent, sweat forming on his brow. "We can rebuild. We'll just need to postpone. And, of course, we need the funds."

Gurin grimaced, brought back from euphoria only long enough to register the worsening situation, then returned to his triumph.

"But you got the man?" he asked Lowell, who nodded.

"What man?" demanded Prion, dropping the pencil. "You need me Weltung, or your plan is toast, but I can't do anything without my son's estate. Help me out here."

"The plan is nothing compared to this capture." Gurin snorted and looked again at Lowell. "Where is he? I will go as soon as we are done here."

Lowell nodded. "He's alive like you ordered. He's in the locked shed, tied tight. I set a guard. The girl and her lover are gone, though. You want I should go rough the guy up a bit?"

Skosh threw him a malevolent glance. It was his cue to act.

"I demand to see the prisoner," he said to Gurin, dropping all pretense that Prion had any authority in this situation. It gratified him to see Prion's scowl.

"The man is an American ally," Skosh continued. "I voluntarily allowed you to detain me while you sought your prize, but now you have him, I must speak to him and explain his rights so I can assure my government of his continued welfare. Have your man bring him here or escort me to a suitable place for an interview."

He hoped he sounded like he knew what he was doing. Charlie said he would find the necessary weapons when he needed them. How that was supposed to happen remained a mystery. Skosh marveled that he had been reduced to relying on that cutthroat son of Satan as he followed this goon down the long hallway.

Then, as Lowell passed a door on the right, it opened and Skosh caught a glimpse of Charlie, still and silent as a specter, waiting for him to pass before going on to the next room. Lowell led the way out of the building and across a paved assembly area toward a shed in the darkening forest at the edge of the compound.

Dusk dampened all sounds. Even the wind had stilled. Their boots crunched through thin ice atop a cinder path as they walked. Skosh saw Lowell beckon to an invisible man in a shadow with a jerk of his head and realized they had other orders concerning him that no amount of American officialdom would countermand. Gurin knew damn well Uncle Sam would deny any knowledge of his existence, just as Moscow would never have heard of Ignat.

Skosh prepared accordingly, casually turning his head in a narrow arc as he scanned the open area before the shed.

Lowell struck too early. The other man was still three yards away and could do nothing. Skosh broke his attacker's windpipe and used an upward thrusting elbow to snap his head back, then planted a front kick to the solar plexus, pushing him into his would-be assistant. They both fell, one of them dying, the other pinned beneath the body.

Skosh retrieved his H&K pistol from the dying thief's holster and considered. He had no suppressor on it and did not want to raise an alarm, but the other man was rolling out from under the body. It was time to make a decision. He ran behind the man before he could stand fully upright and broke his neck.

Sergei sauntered out of the forest at that moment, silent, with eyebrows raised. He must have seen it, thought Skosh. Of course, he saw it.

Of all the people he never wanted to see in that moment, Jade stood behind Sergei's right shoulder.

Sergei kept his voice low as he handed over the SIG Sauer and Mack's knife. And Jade.

"She is rightfully your problem."

She looked like hell, but there was no time to wonder why.

Skosh had killed two men. And now he was being given access to a specialist's weapons, not just any specialist, either. Misha was more like specialist royalty. Mack, he reminded himself. You don't have the right to call him Misha. You don't want that right. But it was the irritable, adrenaline-filled specialist attitude in himself that irked the most. He was taking orders from Sergei as though they were equals.

THIRTY-NINE

Skosh knew Mack could read what had just happened on his face as he handed him the knife. There was a speculative look, a question mark in those blue eyes. He responded with his first-ever successful blank stare. This might be the end of his career as a babysitter, but he refused to be propelled into the shitty world of the specialist.

Mack glanced briefly at Jade and gave a silent signal that directed them both to disappear. Skosh concurred. He never wanted to be near their work. But as they stepped out of the shed, the entire compound became brightly lit, as though by the flip of a single switch.

Deep shadows cast by corners of various wooden buildings no doubt contained enough firepower to save Prion, but because of his experience with Charlemagne, Skosh knew better than to place any bets on the man's survival. He heard the occasional scrape of footsteps on gravel in the still night air, then the muted sounds of two suppressors on the far side of the compound, or was that three?

He plastered himself and Jade against a wall in a narrow shadow at one side of the prison hut, feeling exposed. He still had not seen Mack since cutting him free. A body fell out of a corner shadow of the next building, a lessening fountain of blood sparkling under the bright light at the center.

That would be Mack's work, thought Skosh.

Jade vomited. Luckily, she hadn't eaten much and was soon able to move with him. He was deciding where it might be safer when an unsuppressed burst of rifle fire ended the relative stillness.

Skosh had seen the muzzle flash of that burst. It was forward and to their left. He pulled Jade to the right, briefly considering slipping back into the prison hut when another gunman ran from one shadow to the next on a course that threatened to put them uncomfortably close to the action.

At the first sound of a suppressed zip from what must be more firing by the team, he hit the ground, bearing Jade with him and covering her with his body.

...

Misha let the body drop and ran crouching toward the sound of the MP5s, then veered in the direction of the first burst from an AK. He found the shooter forming a sight picture on another shadow. The SIG had been returned to him without its suppressor, but once the gun battle began, stealth was no longer necessary. He fired and the shooter dropped. The other shadow ran toward him, diving into the shade on his side of the shed.

"Thanks," said Steve. He took a moment to catch his breath. "I'm counting the hired tangos to make sure we got 'em all. Michael took a bullet in his back. Not deep. Vest worked. Kind of. Said to tell you to see to the two principals. He can't. They're hiding in the big building. Kestutis and Rimas are here. They helped clear the American barrack. Mara is injured. Sergei's been ordered to back you up."

Both of his children. Both. Misha stamped it down; could feel the anger growing. Wanted to spray automatic fire into the already dead. Wanted to obliterate the still-living.

Steve spoke again. "I got the guy who shot Michael."

Misha looked at him and noticed he held his MP5 in the wrong hand. He looked at the other. It hung uselessly. Even in shadow, he caught a glint of wetness dripping from the fingers. He nodded.

He stepped sideways to peer at the main building from around the corner of this shed.

As he stepped the other way, Steve added, "Michael said to tell you he'll live. So will Mara."

It was going to be a joy to kill Prion, not an act of despair.

Misha sauntered into the tableau of aftermath in the center of the compound, where Kestutis stood swaying in the light calling Prion a fucking coward at top volume, in English.

He waited, instinctively understanding what the team needed, what the Lithuanians wanted, and what he required. As Prion and Gurin stepped out of the door and stood under the floodlights, he held his fire.

Quiet Move

...

Jade wondered why it was so loud. Then she remembered being required to wear ear protection on the Army range. All those gun battles in the movies never show the hearing shift. The suppressed weapons did not hurt as much as the AKs, which made her ears ring even after the gunfire stopped.

Skosh helped her up, and they stood together quietly in the shadow cast by Misha's former jail.

She counted the people standing. Prion and Gurin stood before the doors of the main building, both of them holding pistols. Mack, absolutely still, faced them to their right, the muzzle of his SIG smoking in the cold air. The dissipating heat from other muzzles helped her pinpoint two members of the team still in shadow.

Kestutis faced Prion from a distance of ten yards. Rimas stood next to him. They did not have their guns raised, but Jade could see the weapons in their hands at their sides.

Kestutis began proceedings.

"Who are you working for?" he asked Prion.

"I work for myself. I told you."

"Why are you here?"

"To help Lithuania. Again, I told you that."

"But I heard you hate my country."

"Of course not. I only want what's best for it. You know Lithuania is only weakened by people like that pervert who is trying to steal my son's money."

"Are you saying we are too naive to know what is best for us?"

Prion paused and reddened under the bright lights, then blurted "Sometimes, like my ex-wife, you are too stupid to know what's right!"

Gurin held up a hand in a calming gesture.

Jade watched as Kestutis mastered his anger. The lines relaxed with his jaw. He looked younger. It was then that she saw him sway. Rimas held his left arm to steady him. As he raised the gun in his hand, she saw that the side of his jacket had stuck to him like it was wet.

"I see that it is you who are not right," said Kestutis. "You hate too much, for too little reason, and you infected me with it, and for what?"

"For patriotism, for your country, for decency!"

Jade wanted badly to complete it with '...and the American way' to highlight the hypocrisy.

Kestutis muttered 'decency' as he eyed Gurin.

The banker spoke up.

"Please understand, we mean no harm to Lithuania. Only good. Such impulses must not prevail in a strong nation. They are unpatriotic."

It was the kind of argument that appealed to Kestutis. Jade could see him mentally tasting it, but before he could speak, Sergei stepped out of a shadow to their left, dressed as the fighter he was, festooned with weapons, ammunition, and radios, face painted in camo colors, twigs in his unruly hair. With one arm he supported his wife, similarly dressed, as she limped by his side, leaving a patch of blood behind each step of her right foot. Both carried MP5s in their free hands.

"Hello, Ignat. It has been a long time," Sergei said quietly.

He said it in English, but Gurin responded to him in a long stream of Russian, emphasizing every other word. He did everything but spit deliberately, though there was plenty of the involuntary kind. He also raised his gun, pointing the muzzle toward Sergei.

Jade did not understand the words, though the sentiments were clear. Kestutis understood both. At first, she wondered who shot Gurin, there were so many candidates. In the next moment, she realized the suppressed MP5s would not have been that loud. As the man fell, so did the man who shot him, Kestutis. The lights above them picked out the spreading red stain on his jacket. Rimas knelt beside him.

Prion let go a stream of English swear words as he swung the muzzle of his gun toward the dying man.

Charlemagne's newest member fulfilled its deadly commission. Unready and in a crouch, Rimas placed a single bullet in Prion's forehead.

FORTY

Rimas heard the Challenger's wheels go up but resisted the urge to sleep while he contemplated the ring. It had been a gift from Kestutis as he lay dying and was too small for any finger but his pinkie, so he wore it there. Fighters of the past were smaller, he surmised, because nutritious food could be scarce in a forest bunker.

Kestutis apologized for trying to find and kill Antanas.

"You hid him well," he had said, as Rimas knelt beside him. "He was not in Šiauliai."

"No."

"Where?" The word caused a wince.

"Vilnius. Užupis."

The dying man nodded, then raised his hand. The ring had been on his pinkie as well.

"Take it," he said. "My father gave it to me. It is the ring of the Kestutis partisan regiment, after the second Soviet invasion. Žemaitis himself gave it to him. My father followed his example during the war and did not participate in the killings. He had judgment. He tried to pass it on to me with the ring."

Kestutis paused in an effort to breathe. Rimas sought a way to comfort him, but the dying man continued in a broken voice.

"He failed."

After another pause for tortured breath, "I was a fool … should have known better. Learn from me. If you like or do not like … do not follow … or kill."

Rimas slid the ring from his teacher's finger but kept hold of the hand.

"Your father did not fail with you, Kestutis. Your judgment prevailed in the end. My brother is alive. The false American did not succeed."

Kestutis murmured with his last breath, "Because of you."

...

"What did the doctor say? How soon must you have surgery? Are you in pain? I can give you something. The op is over. You can have something for pain."

"Sergei, stop," said Mara. "I will be fine. There is no need to break the rule. I can wait until we are at altitude."

She heard the whine of the engines starting and thumps beneath them as the rest of the team stowed their gear. The pain was incredible, but she could not show Sergei. He would pitch a fit about her ever coming out on an op again. She could not bear that.

"It should have been me," he said. He fussed with her seatbelt, put a fresh bottle of water in the cup holder next to her, and patted her hand.

Five words, she thought. With five words everything she thought she knew about herself, about what she wanted, about what was wise, changed. What if it had been him?

She gasped and he looked at her with alarm. Eight words.

What if it had been both of them?

"Sergei, I think we must make a difficult decision."

His grey eyes opened wide, but he had the sense to wait for the rest before replying.

"Yelena will be four years old next month," said Mara. "When I was growing up, I always had my mother even when my father was away."

"You wish to stay home?"

"Of course not," she said with some heat. "I cannot be a housewife or whatever the term is."

"You want me to stay home with Yelena?"

She looked at him. He was prepared to do that for her. She could see it on his face, and she knew it would kill a part of him, a part that made him so dear to her. She loved every scar on his body, every joke he told, funny or not, and the way he touched her, cradled her, loved her. She could not do that to him.

"No, Sergei. What is that phrase Misha always uses when he wants someone to put up with something unpleasant?"

"Operational necessity."

"That's it. I will not like to stay home, and neither will you, but Yelena should not lose both of us at once. She is old enough now to feel it. I think one of us must stay to keep her from being orphaned during just one op."

He bowed his head over her hand, lifted it, and kissed her bloody fingers. As the airplane taxied and the others took their seats, he gazed at her. They understood each other perfectly.

"It will not be the same to be out without you to watch my back," he said. "And as you say, I will hate staying home when it is my turn. But you are correct. It is an operational necessity."

...

"What did you tell Jade about your plan, Michael?"

Misha sipped a fine whiskey and waited for his son's reply.

"I told her we would offer her in exchange for Rimas."

"And she agreed?"

"I assured her we would rescue her eventually."

Misha raised an eyebrow. "I saw her reaction when I surrendered to them. I thought she would faint again. It took the idiot hiding behind her too long to think of putting a gun to her head."

"She has grown to like you. I am amazed." Michael wondered if age would soften him enough to become likable to normal people. He shifted sideways in his reclining seat to ease the pain in his back and to look at his father.

"Only as a father figure, I am sure," said Misha.

"That kiss was not fatherly."

Michael was reminded by his father's answering grin that the man had been smiling a lot lately. More than he could ever remember while growing up. He had once been able to manage a wide grin and could still smile gently—within the family. Would joyful grins ever return? How old would he have to be? Would he live long enough?

"Tell me again why I was required to surrender so ignominiously," said Misha.

"It was hardly ignominious, Papa. You took out three within minutes."

"And surrendered to only two, both of them barely competent in a fight. Why?"

"To unbalance Gurin so he would betray himself to Kestutis."

They both sipped thoughtfully. Misha splashed a bit more into his glass, raising the bottle with a questioning look. Michael shook his head.

"It did unbalance him," he insisted. "Gurin could not resist such a chance. He was beside himself with glee. We have it on tape."

"But it did not save Kestutis."

"No. That is true. Kestutis took out the sniper who hit Mara."

"Your plan worked. It also made a specialist of Rimas."

"How did you know, Papa, that he would fit us so well?"

"Because I knew Kestutis. He had judgment when he was younger."

"It must have deserted him."

Misha grimaced into his glass. "There was a time when he better resisted his prejudices. It is difficult to know friends from enemies and to separate patriotism from fanaticism. In the end, he remembered verification is not optional."

Michael considered asking for more in his glass but knew he was losing the battle against sleep, the sleep that would help ease the pain, though he would dream about it as he always did when injured. His father's next words propped his eyes open, all thoughts of sleep banished.

"I will not come out with you next time, Michael."

"You will retire? Can you bear it?"

Misha shrugged. "I mean to try."

"Alex will be happy."

"She will be very happy. So will the ghosts of my youth. Kestutis is the last whose fate I ever wish to know about. I prefer to allow the others to live on in my memory as they were when I knew them." He finished his whiskey. "I think I will help Tobias move the cattle up to the summer pastures this year."

Michael searched his father's face, peered into those impossibly prescient blue eyes, and saw the same man he had always known. There was no sign of sickness or softening. He signaled for a splash more whiskey in both their glasses. Misha obliged.

"We have taken more damage than usual, Papa. I hope I will fill the gap you leave, but I think it is a good thing," he said, smiling wryly, "to make such a decision when you know you are not past it."

Misha smiled. "Oh, you may always call upon me when you need a dangle. I have discovered I have a particular talent for playing the bait."

FORTY-ONE

They sat in embarrassed silence. Skosh reminded himself he was only surmising Jade's mood. He knew why he was mortified and reviewed why he thought she shared the feeling. During takeoff, he had twice caught her glancing at him, then hurriedly looking away. Of course, he was doing the same, avoiding eye contact, glancing surreptitiously, trying not to be caught at it.

The conclusion that she was embarrassed was also supported by her blushes each time he caught her turning away.

But the definitive proof had come from Mack.

Uwe, not Claire, was flying them back to the U.S. in the Lear Jet. Claire would fly the Challenger, Mack said, to be home with her injured husband, Steve.

Skosh had argued.

"Look, we can fly commercial. I don't know how you intend to bill Uncle Sam for these flights, but our money people will not be thrilled that we got to ride in style—both ways, even. They'll take it out of my fucking hide, or rather, my paycheck."

Mack gave him the blue glare Skosh had learned usually meant more than 'you are an imbecile cheapskate,' but he wasn't sure about the rest. It took a few extra moments before Mack coughed up a minimal assurance and a devastating counter-argument to taking an airline flight. Devastating because it demolished his protest and informed him about the last thing he had ever wanted to know.

"We will not charge for it," said Mack. "Jade should not fly on a commercial airline."

That was it. A complete explanation in the most minimalist expression the bastard could give it. Each successive thought brought Skosh lower.

They were flying courtesy of the team because of Jade.

'Jade should not' did not mean she was somehow special, but that the issue involved her security.

Her security was at issue because she could be connected with a member of Charlemagne. The newest member.

The bastards. When had they arranged it? While they were ransacking the place for documents and other intelligence. While he had been busy on the phone—to the resident, to Kestutis's ministry, to police, to the doctor on standby. There were too many sleeping quarters in the compound, with plenty of beds.

"He's too new," Skosh had said, trying to mask the desperation he felt. "Nobody even knows about him; no one will connect them yet."

Mack answered with a glare.

"At least …" Skosh faltered, then resumed. "At least keep the surveillance light so she doesn't notice."

He was not sure whether Mack's slight head tilt meant yes or no.

…

The last person Jade knew anything about at this moment was herself. Oh, she knew her history and her favorite color, her best outfit and most comfortable shoes. But aside from a steadfast love for her cat, Sekmet, her feelings gurgled and bounced in random patterns between mind and heart.

She could not look at Skosh, no matter how much she wanted to. He would see her blush. He would know with that mysterious male sixth sense about the sex she'd had but not with him.

Rimas had been hasty and vehement, pouring all his emotions into the act, emotions that he must have stuffed down a black hole until they erupted into and around and through her body. She had seen his cool, unemotional gaze when he shot Prion. That the two could be the same man unsettled her. She decided she preferred the emotional Rimas to his killing alter-ego.

And what about Mack? Had he meant that kiss? Surely not. He was making a point that had nothing to do with her. But did his surrender at the safehouse mean he was willing to die for her after all? She remembered how safe she had felt with him, despite the threats. Then she watched him kill three men.

So what did she feel? Respect, certainly, and a kind of affection that she had never before experienced for such a strange being. She caught herself on the last thought. She did know this feeling. It resembled her attachment to her own carnivorous hunter, Sekmet.

Her heart sank beneath her feet as she contemplated Skosh. A heart this low must be in love, she thought, but how is that possible? Infatuated, definitely, but love? He would not look at her. He must be angry. Mack said there was no hope. Why? Because he is honorable. What the hell did that mean?

At least she knew her mind regarding Skosh. She wanted him with every molecule of her being but strongly suspected Mack was right. Maybe on another planet he could be wrong, or in a fourth dimension, a parallel universe where Rimas had not happened and where being honorable didn't mean it had to be impossible.

What the hell did Mack mean?

Skosh sat across the little table from her. Two hours into the flight, after days of complete exhaustion, neither of them had even tried to sleep. She caught his eye.

"You meant that last kiss, Skosh."

He raised his eyebrows, dumbfounded.

"Yes, I did."

At least he admitted it.

"So did I," she said.

He paused, then said, "I know."

"So what did Mack mean when he told me it would be impossible because you are honorable?"

She had to know both what it meant and whether it was true. No matter how much it might hurt.

He sighed, frowning. "It's complicated."

"Try me."

"I have power in the organization. I can't form a ... a relationship with anybody I could conceivably hurt. I can't because it's vicious and because it was done to me. That's what Mack meant. But hey, chances are pretty good I'll be unemployed shortly and then I can have a relationship with anybody who'll have me. Anybody free, that is, which you are not."

"I am free, Skosh, and surely that won't happen. Mack said he would do what he could. He's omnipotent. And you can't affect my job. You're not in my chain of command."

He snorted. "There you go with that military shit again. I will always be in your chain, as you call it, every time I—we—go out on an op because you will go with me. You'll be requested to assist me, or to assist my replacement, from now on."

It was her turn to snort. "Rimas will move on as the memory fades. I'll just say no when the personnel people call. You can get somebody else to go with you. That's all. Find another assistant."

Preferably male, she thought.

Skosh leaned forward, locking eyes with her as he said in a low growl, "Jade, you saw almost every member of the team come out of this op injured or at least badly bruised. It was a light outcome for them, given the odds. There has been a time in their history when the only reason one of them wasn't considered badly injured after an op was because he was dead."

His words made her shiver, but she stiffened herself.

"I'm sorry for that, but I am hardly qualified to change it. I'd be more of a liability than an assistant. It was my fault Mack was captured."

Skosh froze with his mouth open, shook himself, and replied with some heat.

"Jade, that was part of Charlie's plan."

"It was?"

"Yes."

He watched her face turn pale as she took in this revelation.

"His father?"

"Can I ask what you thought you were going to do with his weapons in that pillowcase? Just curious. I think everybody is curious."

"I was going to find where they took him, sneak in and rescue him, then give him his gun so he could defend himself. I figured I owed him. He rescued me from Kestutis."

"And the knife? The one you pulled out of a dead guy?"

"I would need something to cut the zip ties he was tied with."

Skosh could not fully comprehend how such a woman had come into his orbit. He wanted her to never change. He wanted the universe to stand still. But his duty required that he enlighten her, just a little.

"You need to understand a lot of things, Jade, but let's start with what's immediate. Anything you thought you knew about relationships and obligations doesn't work here. You and I are in a kind of triangle now, and the third member is a working specialist."

He took a deep breath to support the next thing he had to say.

"I know you like Rimas."

She opened her mouth to protest but closed it again because it was true. She wanted to say, 'Not more than I like you,' but what good would that do?

Skosh continued softly, "You can't tell me you'll say no when he could be dead the next day. You're not that cold-blooded, or I am much mistaken about you. It is part of what attracts us both to you."

The effort it had taken him to admit this to her and to himself made him sit back and shake his head before finishing the thought with a sad smile.

"Neither of us—none of us—is free anymore."

EPILOGUE

This is when they'll fire me, thought Skosh. He sat at a table before a raised dais. On the dais, behind another table, sat three men: his boss's boss, Henry, his boss, Bill (not his real name), and a colleague from another office. He tried to remember Seeker's real name.

Bill began proceedings.

"We are here, Skosh, to give you the results of our investigation into the data breach of your section's library computer system last month while you were out of the office conducting an operation in …" He looked down at the document before him, turned the page, turned it back, found the name and said, "Lith-oo-ain-ee-a."

It surprised Skosh that even after five years in his position, Bill was still unfamiliar with the geography his subordinates experienced daily. Bill had been a first-rate field officer and Middle East expert. Skosh could see he longed to go back there.

He could identify. It had broken his heart to leave Asian operations to someone else and learn two more languages, recently adding French as required by edict of Mack. But he had done it and also learned enough about his subordinates' work to hold an occasional intelligent conversation with them.

Bill's boss, Henry, piped in with, "I see that you took seriously my admonition about information security, Skosh. I commend you for that." He looked to Bill to continue.

"We interviewed Penelope Prendergast, the chief librarian," said Bill, "who accompanied you on the op, her assistant Dennis Watson, and Candace Seston, who ran administration quality control."

Skosh hoped he did not betray how startled he was to hear Candace named. He found the past tense verb 'ran' also concerning.

Bill chewed his pen a moment before continuing. "We also conducted extensive forensic examinations by qualified computer experts to try to pinpoint the source of the intrusion."

Henry interrupted again at this point.

"Watson and Prendergast explained the system you devised to both fulfill the terms of that unfortunate agreement with the operatives who had the commission and maintain info security. Again, I commend you."

Was Seeker looking just a little sour? Both sour and superior, Skosh decided as the man leaned back in his chair and threw his eyes toward Bill.

"Yes, well," said his boss, "aside from that, we do have an issue to resolve regarding your conduct in this."

"My conduct?"

"Yes. But first, let me give you the findings of the forensic computer examiner. It seems the breach came through Ms. Seston's computer. She denies it entirely and denies knowing your password, but she did have a program installed on her machine that could run through various combinations and eventually break in. We believe this is what happened."

Seeker leaned over and whispered something.

"I'm getting to that," Bill said irritably. He looked back at Skosh. "In the course of this extended investigation, we discovered that you had been having an affair with Ms. Seston …"

"Once," interrupted Skosh. "We had sex, not an affair. Once."

"Let me finish. It was highly unprofessional of you …"

"Me?"

"Yes, you. We believe that she was motivated to break into the system as an act of revenge for her broken heart. She inserted an unfortunate clause in the agreement with your operatives and then caused a breach in security in an effort to blame you. Thus, you are not free of all culpability in this incident."

"I am junior to her."

Seeker gave him a pitying look. "Come, come, Skosh. You're the man in the relationship. The man is always the pursuer. The poor woman had no choice but to fall in with your proposition."

"There was no relationship. The poor woman made the proposition. She was the senior party to a not even one-hour stand."

Skosh uttered this defense through clenched teeth.

"Nonetheless," said Bill, "you are to be verbally counseled. It will not be part of your record unless you are found to be involved in any more incidents of the same nature. You are directed to have no further contact with Ms. Seston. She has been similarly directed. I expect you to respect her situation and cease all communication."

"Her situation?"

"Her security clearance has been downgraded and as a result, she was relocated to a less sensitive division in another state. Any more questions?"

"No."

"Do you understand the conclusions and instructions of this tribunal?"

"Yes."

"Will you initiate an appeal against any or all of our findings?"

Skosh's first instinct was to say, 'fuck yeah,' but he remembered that twenty minutes before, he had assumed he'd be dismissed and sanctioned—the final kind of sanction.

"No. I will not appeal."

Bill smiled. "Then you are hereby verbally counseled not to conduct sexual relationships with any coworkers who may perceive a power imbalance between you."

Seeker smirked.

Skosh could not help his next words. "How about Seeker here? He's my equal and he's male, or so he says. Can I have sex with him?"

Seeker's glare suggested he should eat shit and die.

Bill scowled, rolled his eyes, gathered his papers, then filed out with the other two.

Skosh sat contemplating the shaky nature of his status quo. To all appearances, he'd had a serendipitous escape. He had prepared himself for ultimate disaster and was ready to die when Mack pulled his hand away as it held the knife point at his belly.

Serendipity in the person of Mack now owned his very life.

The End

GOAT ROPE
1999

Author's Note

By design, the racist language used by Charlemagne's targets in this book jars modern sensibilities. The author hopes the truthful depiction of an ugly worldview in a story otherwise meant to divert and entertain will alert those who do not hold such views to think again before forming alliances with those who do.

PROLOGUE

Montreal, October 1970

So kill him, Rusty Tobrin wanted to say. He paused to rearrange his words, to make them more palatable to ensure compliance.

"If the Canadian minister were to die under your care, shall we say, the authorities would be more willing to negotiate for the life of the British diplomat, would they not?"

He observed the young Mountie carefully, tracing the thought he had implanted as it developed behind his eyes. Their friendship—or what this agent thought was a friendship—was too new to risk by giving a direct order. Use suggestions only, Rusty's revered teacher and mentor, Ignaty, had stressed, though he would never be so impertinent as to call him Ignaty out loud. The man was now more powerful than ever in the First Directorate.

Give his thoughts a path to follow without posting arrows on the trees, Ignaty had advised.

"There might be other ways to convince them the FLQ is serious, but..." Rusty left the rest of the sentence to be completed by Antoine's own thoughts, shook his head slightly to indicate hopelessness, watched for the dawn of understanding in his eyes, and pulled an envelope out of his pocket at just the right time, taking care to activate the tiny camera in his tie pin by pressing the switch behind it as the young man gratefully accepted the payment he had come to depend upon.

It may have been this conversation or similar conversations by officers senior to him who controlled another agent among the more extreme inner members of the FLQ, or perhaps it was a natural progression in the logic of violent political action—no matter which—the minister died. The government reacted with predictable extremist measures, further demonstrating the decadent impotence of liberal democracy. Rusty liked to think he had a hand in it. Damage done: the Canadian military diverted to internal affairs, and NATO weakened. There couldn't be a better outcome. He and his colleagues celebrated with quiet jubilation—and vodka.

After a few weeks, Antoine brought him more intelligence, setting the ambitious young Rusty on the path of what he hoped would be a brilliant career. He indulged in fantasies of sitting behind Ignaty Slavin's desk in Moscow while still young enough to enjoy the perks that came with the job.

A turncoat among the FLQ was cooperating with the fascist authorities, Antoine told him. The authorities had custody of the traitor, having suspended habeas corpus, but that was no matter.

What to do? He surveyed the man—young, fit, greedy, ideologically ambiguous. Antoine had inside information, an accurate eye, and access to a police rifle.

And Rusty had Antoine.

ONE

Montreal 1999

Brother,
You know I'm yer most committed and valuable agent of our angry God. I know yer his anointed. You said don't be noticeable, stand down till you can give us our assignments. I'm the best fighter of all of us in this here cleansing work for the cause and a helluva lot more obedient than all the others, now that Sal's dead. Nothing stops me doing what you say. You said we gotta help our Canadian brethren in their struggles for the white race, and you know I'm fully on board with that. I stand on my record.

That said, I'm reporting an incident. Minor, of course, but yer probably gonna hear about it. I aim to tell you the facts involved so's to alert you about a small possible problem that'll probably never come up, but you never know. Right?. You like us to report the truth, and you always take it into account before you react to a problem, even when nobody's at fault. I get the need for order and discipline in the ranks. I always agree with your decisions, even when I'm the one that needs correcting, and even when a criminal from a degenerate race is the real cause of that there difficulty.

I was just walking, that's all, heading for St. Catherine Street through a small park, maybe five hundred by three hundred yards a couple blocks west of it. There was some woods on one side and a big street on the other. Some benches was there, and some bushes. Nobody was around, but then I saw this guy, a coon so black he were almost blue, lollygagging on this here bench. He took up the whole seat so's nobody else could sit there, and I knew, I just knew, no decent white person would want ever to sit there again after this. It enraged me.

I kicked him in the shin, told him to move his black ass. He didn't have no business being there, I said. I pointed at a dumpster behind the bushes. Go hang out where you belong, I says.

Can you believe it? He starts jabbering away at me in that French lingo they use so much around here. It could've been Swahili or some such shit for all I know, except he has enough respect for a white man that I hear him say the word mon-sewer that the shopkeepers on Guy Street use all the time.

I kick him again cuz he ain't moving. I scream pretty loud, trying to make him see he's got no business there, when he stands up and starts hollering, too. He's a big boy, and he raises a fist like in an uppercut and holds it under my nose, and then he's got the nerve to look me in the eye, spouting his gibberish.

It were automatic, really, the fruit of all the great training the brotherhood give me. Anyway, I drew my weapon cuz I didn't have no choice.

So I fire, and he falls down dead with his head in a flower bed and a hole in his chest spouting blood and making a mess of the flowers. I don't know what kind. They was purple with white bits on the edges, but now the ones that ain't crushed has red spatters all over them.

Our mission is way too important to let things like this mess it up, so I think for a minute, then scan around me. People is running up but still a block away. I wheel round to disappear the other way and run into this bitch out of nowhere. I could have taken care of her, too, but a couple guys was running down the sidewalk to the right, no more than fifty yards, and the ones behind me was gaining, so I dodged left, jumped the bushes, and lost myself in a patch of woods long enough to come out on a busy pathway at the other side, pretending like nothing happened.

I got a little notebook and a pen at a newsstand on the street and will drop this in the dead drop you told me to use in emergencies. I remember the signal, so I hope you get it. I ain't got time to do any coding shit, but who's gonna know, right? I'll keep low for a day or two and watch the news before I try making contact again.

The bitch is about five-five, slim, not old, but not young, either. Her hair's brown and tied back in a ponytail. Eyes are brown, too. I don't think she's entirely white. Probably some kind of mulatto with high cheekbones and funny eyes, like a chink. She were wearing a dark blue or maybe black tank top with a design around the bottom, pink and green and blue, and khaki shorts and maybe sandals. She'll be easy to find, though, because of this here little dog she had on a leash. It were real small, but not like one of them tea-cup dogs. About ten pounds, maybe. Easy to spot, though. It's brown and white with big, stand-up ears. One of them rat dogs. Barked like crazy.

I'm sure the other guy you got coming can find her and eliminate the problem. She ain't young, maybe, but her face and body don't agree with the coupla grey streaks in her hair, so there's extra incentive in case they need it.

Sincerely,
Smitty

TWO

"I never liked the girl," Misha said as he sat in the seat facing Rimas. "I suspected she was dirty."

Rimas tore his dark blue eyes from the clouds below to look at his mentor as their jet turned downwind on its approach to Montreal. Soon, he would see Jade. He drew in his long legs to keep from hogging the space and brushed back the dark hair on his forehead. What was Misha talking about? Was he hinting Jade might be dirty? Impossible. They knew everything about her, even the double date her friends dragged her into last week. That guy was lucky he had no chance to kiss her. Rimas did not trust himself to let him live if he had.

He thought he had learned enough German in school, but after two years of living and working with Misha, the man's Austrian accent and occasional archaic word choices still mystified him. He needed clarification. It took only a puzzled look to get it.

Misha sighed as he re-fastened his seat belt and leaned back. His handsome face showed a light network of wrinkles competing with a few faded scars. "Not Jade, Rimas. Why must you think every mention of a woman refers to her? I told you the girl's name was Gloria, and Vasily did not believe me. Were you listening? It was 1971."

"Vasily? Do you mean the man who bought the pretty carpet in the corridor at home?"

"Yes. Gloria was one of the first American girls he spoke to. He had difficulty talking with women, but she had an easy manner, and he was able to speak in sentences. They met in a café on the street where we had set up surveillance of our target. It was the Rue de Montagne."

"In America?"

Misha's patient stillness reminded Rimas to try a little thinking. Funny how the man had the same manner when dealing with both lethal threats and ordinary stupidity.

Rimas nodded to show he understood. "In Montreal," he said. "But the girl was American?"

"She was. Vasily took every opportunity to meet American women even before that operation. It had become a new hobby of his. He wanted to collect them like figurines on a mantlepiece. They were always chipped or damaged or flawed in some way. Sometimes, the artist had been sloppy, making one too tall, another too slim."

Rimas remembered snippets of conversation heard here and there—no, not here, not operationally—at home, at Vasily's Carpet, where he could mind his own business with benevolent disinterest. He turned his head and narrowed one eye at Misha.

"Vasily married an American, didn't he? Just like you did."

Misha rolled his eyes, exasperated. "Yes. Just like me. The same American."

"Gloria?" Rimas never paid much attention to the relationships or personalities in Misha's gigantic house, but he knew he had never heard that name mentioned before. Was she an ex? Would Misha have an ex? Alive? He knew there had been an earlier wife who had been killed by enemies—Michael's mother. He was certain she was not called Gloria.

Misha covered his eyes with one hand and looked at him through the fingers.

"No. Alex," he hissed.

Rimas was still confused, though he recognized the name and could picture her presiding over the dining table, with soft brown curls and a dimpled smile—the only person with license to argue with Misha regularly. But further explanation would have to wait. His son, Michael, moved up the aisle, barking orders at the team as the jet began its final descent into Montreal.

"Rimas, haul that footlocker with the rifles up here now. I want everything ready to unload when we come to a stop on the ramp. Steve, wake up and give Sergei a hand."

The familiar chaos that always attended the beginning of an operation drove all questions about strange women in the past from Rimas's mind. He stacked one locker atop another while Michael took the seat he vacated. Shouldering his heavy duffel bag, he held a grab bar next to the door and anticipated the coming reunion with his beloved Jade. It had been months. Through a window to the left, he watched the ground swell to meet them, amazed at the patchwork of colors, a geometry in shades of green.

Father and son faced each other across a cloud-filled window on the other side of the cabin. Rimas turned to look at them as the clouds interfered with his view. Michael's hair was without grey and lighter than his father's, and he wore it shorter. Misha's royal blue eyes were striking, but his son's gaze contained more ice.

"Papa, do you think we will need the Škorpions?" said Michael, referring to the machine pistols in another locker.

Misha turned from his examination of the yellow and green quilt below them as the view cleared. "You have done very well these two years. Your judgment is flawless. Trust it. I do."

"I cannot believe you quit the game, Papa. I worry. Vasily…"

"I have not quit. I am operationally retired. Vasily only pretended he was normal until normality killed him. I am enjoying retirement too much to let that happen. I assure you I am armed; I will defend myself and the team if necessary, but please, do not assign me a specific task in your operation. It is bad enough your stepmother has required me to do her bidding. I will not take orders from you as well."

Rimas pretended not to listen, gluing himself to the window and the swelling size of the trees below him.

Michael shifted forward in his seat and lowered his voice. The engine noise would keep ordinary conversation private, but Rimas stood at the door, not quite far enough away.

"What reason did Alex give you, Papa?"

"She insists I created the problem and am morally bound to solve it. But what you want to ask me is how she induced me to bother with this. I had no choice. She threatened to come with us. After what happened in Florida, I cannot allow it. I will not have her injured like that again."

Michael raised the brows above his blue eyes with an ironic half-smile. "Just forbid her."

Misha grimaced, perhaps searching for a way to explain the hold they all knew the woman had on his heart. He never confessed any weakness, least of all one that revealed an emotional attachment, and Rimas was sure he would not divulge it now. At least not without torture. Maybe not even then.

Glancing again at the looming earth beyond the window next to him, Misha formed an answer. "Do you trust your wife's medical judgment?"

"You know I do. I must. I know very little…"

Misha gave a slow nod. "Alex is not a surgeon, but she knows human character—better than I do. She insists it must be done and I must do it."

Michael's eyes widened. "Your judgment of people is flawless, Papa. How can Alex be better? And how will you separate the two of them?"

Separate who? Rimas risked looking at them as treetops sped by beyond the cement runway.

"How will you find the tangos the Americans hired you to eliminate?" Misha asked his son.

The aircraft touched down as father and son locked their eyes in silent consternation. They would figure it out, no doubt, and Rimas would do as he was told. And Jade…?

And Jade.

Rimas searched the tarmac for her as they taxied in.

THREE

Skosh pulled the Mercedes M-Class SUV forward onto the ramp and parked alongside the jet's cargo bay. Jade pulled up to the stairs in front of him. She drove the S-Class sedan requested by Charlemagne, the team of deadly operatives they were there to meet.

He shuddered. He knew the sedan meant something he wasn't going to like. The team had never requested two specific cars before. Even after Mack retired, his son, who used the game name Charlie, maintained the one-Mercedes tradition, though he opted for the more practical SUV. Skosh suspected one too many people were about to get off that airplane. He had an uncomfortable feeling Charlie's father, Mack, would be that one. The man was a legend among babysitters like Skosh, earning his game name because of his facility with a knife.

Skosh hated being proved right as he watched the man climb down the steps. Mack still held a cane but didn't use it on the stairs. He didn't even hold the handrail. Skosh remembered the sight of that bloody hip as he had helped hoist him onto the gurney. He remembered the screaming fight with Charlie. He remembered losing it. It was a miracle of modern medicine and Charlie's wife, the surgeon, that Mack could even stand on that leg, let alone take the stairs without holding on. Grudgingly, Skosh added the impossible standards of physical conditioning these guys maintained to his private 'miracle of' list.

At the bottom of the stairs, Mack handled the cane like a gentleman's affectation rather than a mobility tool for a man with a dodgy hip.

"He's coming to my passenger door." Jade's voice on the radio sparked a fresh set of misgivings about this op. "What should I do?"

"Unlock the door."

Skosh wanted to add 'you silly girl.' He wanted to tease her and jest with her and call her names, little sweet names just between them, names only he would be allowed to say to her. He set aside the fleeting thought, ruthlessly tamped it down before it could become the usual lead weight in the depths of his psyche.

I can't have her, he reminded himself as he unlocked the SUV doors and climbed out to open the tailgate for the team to stow their weapons in the back.

Steve Donovan had a few strands of early grey mixed at the temples. He wore his thick brown hair a bit too long, a belligerent reaction to his military past, a personal statement that he was entirely civilian now, despite a vocabulary rich in the use of acronyms and f-words. He shared these generously in conversation—if you could call it that—with his fellow delinquent, Sergei, whose sandy hair showed no signs of grey. Skosh felt a ping of jealousy. His temples had more little white strands against the black than he liked. He blamed the team and the nature of their work. Skosh and the delinquents (his pet name for them) were all of an age, clustered just under forty. Not old enough to be completely serious, but too old to be forgiven their screw-ups. Especially when those mistakes got somebody killed.

The younger Charlie, now the boss, never screwed up, particularly when his decisions meant death. That was why he was in charge.

Weapons lockers stacked in the back, car stuffed with specialists on a mission to save the world—well, maybe a corner of it—Skosh drove toward the highway with Charlie next to him and three more killers sitting behind. The dark blue eyes of the youngest, Rimas, had aged a century in the two years since he had entered the world of black operations.

Jade led the way, meaning her passenger, Mack, led the way. Skosh tried not to let it bother him when she made every turn to the safehouses without a flaw, including a couple of double-right turns to dry-clean their route.

Mack is instructing her—because he knows where the house is, knows the route to it. Skosh's jaw tightened. The team knew every detail of his arrangements before he briefed them. Of course, they did. It was their superb grasp of detailed intelligence that allowed them to command big bucks when a government needed help with a delicate situation involving death. Besides money, their fees included information from everyone who hired them. They were a walking, seldom talking, often shooting team of operatives known as specialists.

And they had sent Skosh's predecessor, Frank, ahead—to assist him, they said. As a trusted retainer on the team's payroll, Frank would have told them all about the arrangements. The perfect situation: two houses in a worn-out residential neighborhood of short-term rentals that housed itinerant strangers intent upon their own business. Dream accommodation in an intelligence operation. And they were cheap.

Skosh worked for Uncle Sam, though the government would never admit it. His unofficial job title was babysitter, responsible for providing the support the team, known as Charlemagne, would need to accomplish what they had been hired to do. He technically didn't need the assistance of Jade, his section's librarian, but the team always requested her because, well, because Rimas. He ground his teeth at the thought.

FOUR

"We weren't expecting you," said Jade. She negotiated the airfield and turned left by order of Mack, who pointed the way using his whole hand, not just a finger. A long-ago childhood stricture against finger-pointing came to mind. "It's rude," her mother once told her. Of course, Mack would never do anything rude. The Austrian specialist might cut your throat but with faultless etiquette.

She glanced sideways, wondering if he would speak. So far, not. She tried another greeting.

"How have you been?"

More silence.

"How is Alex?"

She wondered how she managed to remember the name of the man's wife after seeing only a bare mention in a highly classified report encrypted on a caveated disk in a secure safe within her library vault. A woman she had never met and most likely never would meet. She found it difficult to imagine this guy in any domestic setting. Did he wear his gun to bed, she wondered? Did he use that knife to cut the tags off new clothes? Did he clean the blood off in the sink beforehand?

He spoke with a heavy accent. "Turn right. Do it now."

The tires squealed a bit despite the car's superb handling. This was an anti-surveillance maneuver, Jade knew. She had been studying tradecraft at Skosh's insistence. Skosh turned behind them. His move was less dramatic but every bit as hasty.

After a few more precautions, they reached a straight street and Mack relaxed.

"You have cut your hair," he said.

"Yes." A simple enough acknowledgment of the obvious, but Jade could not help a minor whine to go with it. "I got tired of trying to take care of it when Charlie made Skosh bring me along every time he hired you guys. The last place was a hell hole. There wasn't even a toilet—just a bucket behind a shed. I fail to see why you need a librarian in such places. I deal in electronic information. I cannot produce it where there is no electricity."

She tried glaring at him, taking in the expensive suit and silk tie, the blond and grey hair and very blue eyes staring back frankly with an amused half-smile.

"A remarkable progression from two years ago, Jade. Are you telling me you no longer believe it necessary to take a bath during an operation without a lock on the door?"

"There is no lock you guys can't defeat."

"What does Rimas think of your haircut?"

He had kept her in the car when Rimas came down the steps. The sedan's window tint would not reveal who was driving, let alone show her hairstyle. Rimas rode in the car behind, probably wondering where she was.

She answered Mack's question with silence, glanced right, and saw him smile again.

As Jade turned into the street leading to their two safehouses, she said, "Why are you even here? I thought you retired for good." Silently, she added *riddance*.

"I am here on an ancillary matter. It will have no bearing on Charlie's operation."

There was a note of uncertainty in that last bit and then a meaningful pause, so Jade filled it with what she knew was the team's mantra: "I know, I know, if you live."

"No, Jade, if *we* live. I include you."

She suppressed a shiver and signaled to turn at the next street to deposit Mack at the team's safehouse, but he waved her forward, indicating the narrow driveway at the side of a duplex Skosh and his old boss Frank had rented for themselves.

"That one's our house," she said. "For the babysitters."

Explanation unnecessary, she knew. The team made a point of both requiring and then cooperating on having their quarters separate from their handlers ever since she and Rimas had become an item two years ago. Awkward in the extreme, but better than occupying close quarters with that lot.

Jade stared ahead as the car came to a stop, remembering how this guy used language. "Why we? Are you saying I'm also in danger this time? I mean, more than usual?"

She expected his customary half-smiling silence, but as he opened his door, he said, "No. You must know your peril by now." The man knew how to make her shiver.

The two back-to-back safehouses shared a chainlink fence running through roughly mown scrub grass to a high brick wall along a street on one side and a lower wooden fence at the mid-point of the babysitters' building. They would stay in one half of a duplex, sharing a wall with an older man in the process of moving out. Skosh had arranged to pick up that lease as soon as the house was officially vacant. He would leave it empty as a buffer for additional security. The team's house faced a parallel street. Larger and more private, it included a garage with access directly into the house, handy for obscuring the comings and goings of a team of men in peak condition. Not that anyone in this hardscrabble environment would have time to notice. Invisibility was universally prized.

Rimas skirted the garage along the brick wall and smiled at Jade over the chain link as she locked the sedan. A hopeful smile, she thought with a sigh. He was sweet, kind, an excellent lover, and a journeyman assassin. She was stuck in a situation but, sadly, not stuck on him.

Skosh came around the same side of that house and told Rimas Charlie wanted him before climbing the fence to meet her at the back door. She stood, hand on the knob, leaning her forehead into the paneled wood. *Why* did Mack say *we*?

Mack stepped up and joined Skosh in looming over her. She was aware of the patience they practiced as they waited for her to gather her wits about her. She dealt with the jumble of emotions she held for each of them. Mingled fear, awe, and appreciation for Mack, the team's founder. Total, hopeless longing for Skosh, their babysitter. Why was Mack here? Because there weren't enough fucking complications in this situation. She caught herself thinking like Skosh. If she wasn't careful, she would soon be using the f-word out loud and just as creatively. The word already inhabited her interior thoughts, at least whenever they came out on an op with Charlemagne. She led the way into the kitchen.

"What the fuck are you doing, Frank?" Skosh stood red-faced inside the kitchen door, staring at a woman's tank top draped over a kitchen chair. It was not Jade's—she avoided pink, even in a narrow stripe around the hem. Frank sat at the table, his naturally tonsured head ruffled at the edges of the white hair circling a bald dome. Round, bulging eyes looked to the ceiling with exaggerated patience.

"Language, my boy, language. I told you about her. She's our link to them. They're looking for her. I'll explain it to Charlie if you don't want to."

"She?" Mack draped a suit bag over another chair next to the kitchen table.

Frank nodded. "A woman. A witness. Don't worry, there's room. This is a three-bedroom house. She and Jade can share, and so can Skosh and I. We'll show you where you'll bunk after Skosh detach… diseng… removes himself from off the ceiling."

"I can't let the team use a Canadian dangle, Frank," said Skosh. "You fucking know that."

"She's American."

Mack interrupted. "Nationality is immaterial. She cannot stay here. *I* am staying here."

"She has to."

Skosh loosened his tie and unbuttoned the top button of his white shirt, glancing sideways at Mack. "You know Charlie will find a way to put her in jeopardy if she's here, Frank."

Frank pushed back his chair and looked up at Mack, then Skosh. His voice became soft, the words precisely chosen and rehearsed. "Either way, she's dead. Who knows? Charlie might be the only one who can keep her alive. Besides, that little dog is devoted to her. You wouldn't want him orphaned now, would you?"

Skosh held up a hand. "One thing at a time before we start talking about dogs." He turned to Mack. "What the fuck are you here for?"

"That is my business," came the usual still, even reply.

After two years, the man had not lost the ability to send a chill down Jade's spine. It was the stillness of his manner that called up the indelible memory of watching him kill three men with all due speed. Watching him move was worse. Sure it was. But every time he got that still, she remembered how quickly things could change.

Skosh leaned over the sink, elbows on the counter, one hand on his forehead. "You're a fucking piece of work, Frank. You know that? So why is she supposedly a dead woman walking, and, by the way, when were you going to tell me about Mack joining this shit show? The team's house is crammed already."

"It's not like your worrying could change it, Skosh. And Mack's staying with us, not in the team's house. Anyway, she's dead because she can identify Chatham. He killed a guy right in front of her in a park. Broad daylight."

"So?"

"So he knows. He can find her."

"How's that?"

"She described it on local TV news. The camera even lingered on the dog."

"A dog. Fuck." Skosh ran a hand through his mop of straight black hair.

Jade loved everything about the man, even his language, but especially the way his body moved as he stretched again to touch the low kitchen ceiling. The slow military flight to Vermont had been cramped; the beat-up rental car they used to cross the border seemed designed without shocks. He needed the stretch, she knew, and she enjoyed the watching.

But he lowered his arms abruptly when the dog barked.

FIVE

Christine Barton forgot to hush the dog as she walked into the kitchen because the older man's strange blue eyes held her fast. She had encountered enough criminals to recognize that dangerous stare. He watched; he assessed. She held firm, careful to hide her sinking stomach. In her long career, she had never before met this level of professionalism. Had the funny, round-eyed older man—what was his name—Frank? Had he brought her into a trap by promising protection?

Fool—I better leave.

Fluffy stopped barking, cowed by tension he could smell. She picked him up.

"Ah, Ms Barton," Frank said with a smile she was beginning to mistrust. She had found his concern for her safety touching, thought she might learn something here because she suspected he was a Fed, and agreed to his plan for her own reasons.

"Let me introduce John Nakamura and Jade Wilmerton." Turning to them, he said, "Miss Christine Barton and...?" He raised his brow in a question mark as he gestured at her smooth-haired brown and white rat terrier.

"Fluffy." Every eyebrow in the room rose, except, of course, for the criminal who wouldn't care. She added, "Because he's not."

The criminal required no introduction, but she needed an ID. She directed her words toward him.

"And you are?"

Judging by the shocked looks from, again, everybody but him, she knew they knew what he was.

Must be trap.

His smile was all the confirmation she needed.

"Um... call him Mack," said Frank.

She hugged Fluffy closer to her, remembered her responsibility for his protection, and decided to play innocent. He licked her chin.

"Very nice to meet you," she said to the criminal without smiling. He turned up a lip at one corner but said nothing. Turning to Frank, she said, "I appreciate your concern for me, Mr. Cardova, but I'm sure there is no more danger. If I can call my friend again, I'll find my way home to Vermont."

Mack, the criminal, spoke for the first time. "I am afraid you cannot, Miss Barton." He was foreign, with a heavy, probably German, accent.

Great. A Nazi criminal.

Had she told Frank her Abenaki middle name? She couldn't remember. Despite her training and experience, the events of the early morning sped by like a blurry movie on fast forward. The fractionally-white DNA in her ancestry provided background only. She could be mistaken for many mixtures but never white. Not a good thing, then, to be in the presence of a Nazi killer. She had seen one of those shoot a black man not two hours ago. Frank was looking increasingly untrustworthy for a Fed.

Before she could argue, Mack spoke again. "I assure you, you are in no danger from us. But if you fall into the hands of our—let us call them adversaries—you will become a danger to us."

Does he read minds?

"Let me guess, then *you'll* become a danger to *me*," she said, hugging her dog again. She kicked herself for abandoning the innocent ploy.

Big mouth. No cunning.

"Very good," said Mack. Despite the compliment, if he was impressed, he hid it well. He took a walking stick from the woman they called Jade standing behind him and leaned heavily on it.

Left hip. Wonderful. A wounded, foreign, probably Nazi, mind-reading criminal. Adversaries?

She contemplated running, but the door was locked behind that tall Asian man, the one named Nakamura. Even Jade looked like she could run way faster than Christine, especially considering her need to protect Fluffy. She would never abandon him. Before she could formulate a plan, running or not, a younger man came through the locked door, slipped what she knew to be a lock-picking tool into a pocket, and dropped a heavy, clanking duffel bag onto silver-flecked linoleum in front of a small—by American standards—refrigerator.

He spoke to the criminal in what she supposed was German.

Another Nazi. Great. Why so beautifully packaged? Nazis should be ugly, like their souls.

This one had hair almost as dark as hers and eyes a darker blue than the criminal's, with a thick white scar snaking from one of them toward his left temple. He stood tall and lanky like a gazelle, built for speed. Between him and Nakamura, there would be no hope of outrunning them if they gave chase. She abandoned the idea and caught herself wondering what it might be like to be caught by this one.

But then, if he's a Nazi, nothing good could come of it. And anyway, he's too young.

He smiled at Jade.

Ah, I see.

SIX

"Charlie wants to know if you will attend the meeting," Rimas said to Misha as he quickly scanned the room. "In five minutes."

Jade did not return his smile. Why? A strange woman with dark hair stood holding something that moved. Why, again? The babysitters must have fucked up, Rimas decided. They have allowed a Canadian woman into their safehouse. Surely, they knew Misha was coming. Frank was present during the planning. Rimas settled his eyes on the woman's face. Not young, but hard to tell the age, with high cheekbones, full lips, concerned eyes, and... a dog?

Skosh and Frank have really fucked up.

Misha answered him, but he was too busy making conjectures to hear it. Before he could find a way to hide the lapse, the older man snapped. "Tell him to expect me."

Rimas took another look at the Canadian woman and turned to leave, wondering how Misha would eliminate this new threat.

Pity. She is rather pretty.

...

When Misha joined him outside, Rimas held the cane as he hopped the fence adroitly, the only clue to the injury passing in a momentary wince as he landed. He didn't think Rimas had seen it.

"She may be dirty," said Misha as he took back his cane.

"Who? The woman you told me about? The one Vasily liked here in Montreal so many years ago?"

"No." Misha used his stick to point backward to the babysitters' house. "That one. With the dog."

"How do you know?"

"I do not know. I only suspect. She recognized me and sees me as an enemy."

"She knows who you are?"

Misha sighed. Patience was not his predominant quality at the best of times, but he forced himself to seek it. Rimas had more than just skill. He had talent. With the right guidance, Rimas would someday become a formidable operative. If he listened to Misha. And if he lived.

"She does not know who I am. She knows what I am," he explained.

"Was it like that with Vasily's girl, Gloria?"

"Not entirely the same, but close."

Rimas paused a few feet short of the door to the team's safehouse, raising his brow in a question mark that gratified Misha. He was listening, developing a searching insistence on complete information, taking care to understand and trace connections behind everything he learned. It made Rimas a good fit in the field of intelligence despite his perilous habit of discounting the unpredictability of emotion.

So Misha took a moment to stop and explain more thoroughly than usual. "When Gloria met me, I saw a glimpse, a shadow of caution in her eyes. She was careful to limit eye contact, to keep her hands empty and always visible to me."

"And Vasily?"

"That was more important. He was more dangerous than me. I thought this should be plain to most people because of his solemn, closed and wary manner. He had very light grey eyes that saw all people as threats. He issued a challenge with every stare." Misha moved into the shadow under the wall to his right and watched Rimas clear the fence with effortless grace. "Gloria's behavior around Vasily was too playful, too fond," he continued. "Someone who could react to me, quickly hide it, and then pretend not to know about him must be dirty. I warned Vasily."

"Did he listen?"

"Of course not. He considered all American women exotic. This was a blonde who wore a mini-skirt. He became infatuated, entranced. Much like you are with Jade."

Rimas narrowed his eyes and blurted, "Jade has dark hair. Nothing similar."

"She is American."

"But not dirty. You said so."

"No. Not dirty," agreed Misha."

Rimas blew a sigh of relief, glanced back at the safehouse where Jade was staying, and said more slowly, "But this other woman, the Canadian?"

"Also American, not Canadian. She not only recognized me, she challenged me with her stare. She has had training and is not afraid."

"Jade was not afraid when she met you."

"Not sufficiently, that is true. She did not understand. This one does, like Gloria."

"Then how is she different from Gloria?"

"She does not pretend. And I wonder what is the purpose of the dog?" He paused. "I can see more questions in your eyes. Ask."

Rimas inhaled sharply, breathed out, and said, "I wondered how Vasily could be more dangerous than you, but then there is also Michael, after all."

Misha gave an almost smile to the young fighter who was blithely unaware of his own lethality. He held open the door to the garage. Rimas followed him in, still wondering about that dog.

SEVEN

Michael stood to preside over the meeting, feeling both his authority and its burden of responsibility. His team assembled with coffee in the living room, a long, narrow space with an open kitchen at one end, where the all-important coffee maker dominated a short counter along the back wall. A kitchen island created an aisle before it. The lumpy sofa of an indeterminate color closely resembling dirt provided a place to sit along a staircase wall, but nobody chose it. Stiff-backed wooden dining chairs filled that need and were preferred by everyone except him.

The others no doubt wondered, but Michael knew why his father had joined them on this op. What he didn't fathom was how he felt about it. He was smug in the knowledge his wife, Theresa, would never dictate his movements. *Only because she's too busy* came the immediate mental correction to the thought. She trusted him absolutely to do his job, never interfering in team matters like this. She had learned that lesson the hard way several years ago. Why was Alex so insistent with his father?

He opened the meeting, saying, "Chatham arrived in Montreal fifteen hours ago and evaded most of our watchers within an hour. We'll get Skosh in here in a few minutes so he can tell us what he learned from the Canadians. In the meantime, let's go over the bare bones of what we know. Steve?"

Steve tore his eyes from an unframed daguerreotype hanging askew on the wall beside him, showing Sherlock Holmes falling from a cliff, the evil Moriarty chortling at the top. He took a slow sip of his coffee and cleared his throat. "Chatham's a good old Southern boy, a proud patriot, saved Christian, and fucking effective killer. His favorite targets are blacks and liberals. We don't know who he works for, but we've suspected, and now we know for sure he's not freelance because he's too emotional. He goes off the rails sometimes, and somebody else has to come along and clean it up."

"How do we know this for sure?" Sergei walked to the machine for a refill, savored a sip, and waited for the reply. His worried, almost colorless eyes gazed at the liquid in his cup until he drained it and poured again. Michael noticed the distracted behavior. The man's mind was elsewhere.

"Before they lost him today," said Steve, "one of our watchers, not Skosh's, heard a shot and saw him run out of the park through a narrow screen of trees on one side. He stopped in a cafe on another street."

Sergei handed him the half-empty mug in his hand, turned to the coffee machine again, and poured into a clean cup. Steve stared at the two cups he now held, put them down on the counter, and pulled a crumpled sheet of notebook paper out of a pocket.

"Chatham's on the lam after a killing," he said, "and he stops for coffee and to write a fucking letter. He's pissed off and careless. Not even using code. The watcher followed him to the drop he used but lost him in an alley. So he went for the letter and brought it to Skosh."

"They put it back after I copied it," said Michael. "I don't think Chatham's people are alerted. It took less than half an hour, but the empty drop had only one watcher on it for that length of time."

"Is that the paper Skosh gave you at the airplane? Why have I not seen it?" Sergei gulped more coffee while standing at the machine, still not sitting down.

Michael could see he wasn't handling stress well and would be pinging with coffee jitters for hours. "You were on the satellite phone with Mara. I couldn't get your attention."

"She had two contractions," said Sergei, his Russian accent more pronounced than usual, eyes on the phone. "Far apart, she said."

"My sister can handle contractions, Sergei. Your daughter is proof of that."

"But this is a son! I worry."

Michael was about to tell his brother-in-law that baby boys are no more dangerous than girls, but he looked at Steve and Rimas and the twitch in Sergei's eye and wished Mara were on this op, not facing death during the ordinary practice of giving life. He wanted it because she was the most sane member of the team. Apart from himself. Maybe.

Steve continued. "The language Chatham used in his letter before going to ground was like you'd say to your boss, 'I fucked up, please don't punish me for it.' We doubled the watchers on both the drop and its approaches. They're deep and round the clock, waiting for whoever services it. We might get a line on who that boss is if we can hold on to the trail of a courier."

Michael ignored the deferential glance Steve sent his way when describing mistakes confessed to a boss. He liked to think he did not make a habit of painful corrections. The consequences of anybody's errors were usually punishment enough—for all of them. What worried him more was the absence of a similar glance from Sergei, who was the one most likely to fuck things up this time around.

Rimas set his empty mug next to the computer by his chair under another waterfall picture—one of several in this room, but this one did not feature Holmes. He stood and said, "Shall I go get Skosh now?"

Michael briefly wondered if having just one Watson when an obedient bit of muscle might come in handy would be easier than this. He loved these guys and depended on them, but had to resist the urge to bury his face in his hands when their minds were so scattered. Instead, he looked pointedly at the secure radio beside him and shifted the stare to Rimas, willing him to read his eyes.

You will not, I repeat not, spend your time looking for Jade.

Rimas blanched. At least he caught on quickly.

Michael's father cleared his throat and waited for a nod before speaking as if he meant to stay out of this op.

"There is another more recent development. Perhaps you should inform us." Misha addressed Rimas, who wrinkled his brow.

"Do you mean the woman?"

Steve groaned softly, "Not another one."

"Go on," said Michael.

"She is Canadian—no, American—pretty, with very dark hair like Jade, and she is staying in Jade's room. Also, she has a dog, and Misha thinks she is dirty."

"She saw Chatham kill the man in the park," said Misha, "and told police, the press, the world. Frank has rescued her." He explained the behaviors that made him suspicious, sparking a five-minute team argument about why an older woman evidently trained to recognize a fighter would have the confidence to challenge him.

Steve once again made himself indispensable by coming up with the solution in his slow Texas drawl, brown eyes languid under long lashes.

"She's a cop."

EIGHT

Skosh suppressed a momentary annoyance at the summons from Charlie. It wasn't the fact of the call or the nature of the meeting he was told to attend. These were routine. It was the respectful treatment he was getting from these fucking killers. Okay, he had to admit it. He had killed during that op on the Curonian Spit two years before. He had no choice. He didn't tell any of his government colleagues in The Section and didn't put it in the report because, well, that would have been the end of his career working for Uncle Sam. Babysitters don't kill. Period. But Sergei had seen it, and the team kept no secrets from each other.

He dragged his feet as he crossed the shaded pair of yards and jumped the fence to the other house, the one with different occupants, damn it. Different. He was not one of them. He would never be one of them.

At least the team had been decent enough to keep quiet about it.

"Took you long enough." Sergei held the door to the garage open for him. Again, the respectful gesture mixed with disdainful words.

Skosh received the jibe with the coldly impassive glance he had been practicing. To his mind, anybody who thought Asians came naturally to inscrutability must be racist. Typically, his emotions wrote themselves all over his face and trumpeted f-words from his mouth. Sergei had seen him break a guy's neck. The memory helped Skosh maintain the muscles of his face. Distance, maintain distance, he reminded himself. *Breathe.*

This house was different, more open, with no kitchen, per se, only a continuation of the living room. The coffee machine was the same, of course, and the old prints on the walls. Circa way back, all of them pictures of waterfalls, and every one crooked.

"Skosh," said Charlie as he entered from the side door under the stairs, "my father tells us you have a house guest. I must meet her."

With any luck, only the coffee machine witnessed his grimace; he was headed straight toward it. He controlled the tension in his back, poured, and turned, mug in hand. He gave a minimal nod.

"But only me," added Charlie. "She has already seen my father. I don't want her to see the rest of the team."

"She has seen Rimas," said Mack, holding out his mug to Skosh.

"And Rimas," agreed Skosh. He brought the pot and poured flawlessly into the suspended cup. No splashes. Meditation was beginning to work. He rooted himself to the earth beneath the house and felt every muscle become simultaneously relaxed and ready. Even the steady stare he exchanged with Mack's quelling blue eyes did not shake it.

Mack smiled.

Is that how these guys do it?

Skosh was pleased with his progress but not interested in becoming any more like them. He took a deep pull at his mug before changing the subject.

"We're trying to find out who is in town and who might be the guy Chatham wrote that letter to. Frank has a few older contacts among the Canadians. Retired colleagues. He's getting background on the more violent right-wing groups in Quebec and specifically asked for names of old members of the FLQ who are still around. They were Marxists, but he says that doesn't matter."

Mack nodded. "Frank was with us here in 1971 after the October Crisis. Do not expect ideological consistency from zealots. They are easily manipulated into violence. The KGB was always very good at that. Racist propaganda is as effective a tool as class division in keeping the West busy with internal threats."

"FLQ?" asked Rimas, eyebrows high with surprise. "Was that when Vasily met Gloria? What crisis?"

Mack nodded. "The FLQ were French nationalists, mostly bombers and bank robbers, but in October 1970, they took hostages, a British diplomat and a Canadian minister. The diplomat lived. The minister did not. We arrived in January to take care of the American involvement. Frank was our babysitter."

Skosh stepped away from the coffee machine and headed for an uncomfortable chair under a torn poster of a black cat, the only non-waterfall in the room. The caption was in French. He remembered a time when he didn't speak any European languages and longed for sushi on the Ginza. Steve hit him in the stomach with an empty mug as he passed. It was an overly familiar way to ask for a refill. He would have preferred the usual sneering demand.

I'm not one of you.

He wanted to shout it, but he refilled both cups instead.

"I've read your file all the way back to the '60s," he said to Mack as he handed Steve his cup. "There is no mention of an op in Montreal."

Silence and deleted official information. The team had infiltrated the system, as usual. It must have been done decades before when his latest safeguards were not in place. Rimas's question meant the old Montreal op involved the late Sobieski, explosives expert and martial artist on the original team, who was killed in the early '80s. Had Mack suddenly become the grizzled old uncle telling the younger generation fun stories of youthful exploits? Skosh looked at him sitting there, still as a stone, not a greyish-blond hair out of place, in a pricey suit and Italian shoes. Nothing grizzled about him, he decided. Mack caught his eye and smiled.

Yep. Still reading minds.

"At least, it would be nice to know what the American involvement was," he said between sips. He stood next to the machine, now reluctant to sit down anywhere. Unwilling to get comfortable. Determined to maintain his newfound control.

Mack glanced toward Charlie before answering with a shrug. "There was cooperation between the FLQ and a nationalist group in the US. The American group sent a specialist to exact revenge upon two targets. One was a Canadian press official the FLQ blamed for their almost immediate loss of public support. The other provided information that put most of them in prison or exile within the next ten years. They succeeded against the press official before we got here."

"Are there parallels?" asked Charlie.

"Yes."

"Metaphorical or direct?"

"Both, I suppose, but mostly direct."

Now Mack had everybody's attention. He looked to the ceiling, into the past, before answering. "First, the cooperation between foreign nationalist groups has not changed. Second, for us, it was a simple commission to stop an American specialist and his network from assassinating a Canadian official. That is all. The moment we landed, it became more complex. The official was already dead, and we learned our target had an accomplice. Then, the danger to the informant came to Frank's attention. Almost too late."

Skosh had become involved in the conversation, realizing Mack would not waste words on any immaterial part of the story. He could not keep from tilting his head as he asked, "I get the nationalism, and now that our guy has written a love letter to his boss, it can only mean he's got an accomplice here. I get that, too, but what else? It was twenty-eight years ago. Things are different."

"They are not."

The smile was either approving or condescending. Vintage Mack.

The secure phone next to the computer rang, and Sergei answered it as Steve said, "How so?"

Again, Mack took his time. At that moment, lightning struck and Skosh knew the answer. "Because of the woman Frank has picked up," he said.

Mack smiled his approval. "It remains to be seen whether she is the endangered informant or a deadly accomplice." He looked at his son. "I recommend you use her until she makes a mistake."

NINE

Christine studied the young man sitting across from her at the small kitchen table in what she had heard Frank call a safehouse. She did not feel safe. Did the man even blink? Not so as to be noticed. He was that motionless. Blond, impeccably and expensively dressed, like the older Nazi with a cane, but this one had no accent. Still, he felt foreign.

Frank sat to her right and made introductions.

"This is Charlie," he said, indicating the blond glacier. "And you met Rimas earlier."

Christine glanced to her left. "I saw him; I didn't meet him." She made a habit of correcting the record.

She returned Charlie's cold belligerence, knowing she was outclassed here and, more importantly, outnumbered. Frank had seemed okay. A government type, oozing bureaucratic authority. These two, Charlie and Rimas, would be best described as perps.

At long last, Charlie broke the subject, though not the stare.

"Ms. Barton, your description of the man you saw was remarkably thorough. We wonder who taught you to be so observant."

Definitely foreign.

He tilted his head and raised one eyebrow when she did not answer for several beats.

"I'm a State Trooper over the border in Vermont. I know how to describe a suspect. I also know when I'm looking at a criminal."

On her left, Rimas guffawed. Charlie threw him a warning glance and smiled. "And what is it that makes you *know* I am a criminal, Ms. Barton, or should I say, Officer Barton?"

"Lieutenant will do."

She reminded herself this was supposed to look like a holiday she gave herself as a reward for the long scramble and boatload of work it took to get the promotion.

So act like it.

She maintained steady contact with those ice-blue eyes as she answered.

"You move like a fighter. You're packing. You didn't introduce yourself as a government official. You're wary and alert. This is common to three of you: Rimas here and the guy with the cane. You, particularly, remind me of a large cat. That Asian guy…" She looked up at the man leaning against the counter behind Frank, sipping coffee from an enormous mug.

"Call me Skosh," he said. "You're not exactly white, either, so don't let me hear you call me 'Asian guy' again."

"I'm native. Abenaki on most of both sides. Sorry if I offended."

Touchy. He's got something going on.

She looked back at Charlie. "Skosh could also be government, but Frank here is not the kindly uncle-type I mistook him for."

"I'm only looking out for your safety, my dear," said Frank.

"So you bring me to a den of thieves?"

"They're not thieves," said Skosh. "They give good value for their work. They're killers, assassins, expensive ones. Get your criminal categories straight, Lieutenant."

Frank sighed. "The proper term is specialist. They are intelligence operatives who specialize. And you are correct, Lieutenant, Skosh works for the federal government."

"Call me Christine. Can I see an ID?"

"No," said Skosh. "I don't carry one."

Charlie finally broke his impersonation of a statue and spoke. "Do you have a weapon with you?"

"Hell, no." Christine laid her hands flat on the table for emphasis. "I'm not going to try crossing a border with a firearm, am I? This is supposed to be a pleasure trip with a couple of friends. They're going to be worried."

Nicely skirted.

Frank hurried to assure her, "I left word for you at your hotel when I couldn't find them."

What a chum, but awkward. She decided against pressing it.

"Where is the dog?" asked Charlie.

Here was her Achilles heel, and he put his finger right on it. Fluffy was non-negotiable. He had been with her five years now, ever since she pulled duty at the holding facility and had to take the dogs on death row to the vet for imposition of sentence. Crime: being homeless, unloved, and a public health hazard. She identified, especially with the small, brown and white one. He looked at her and she knew. He wasn't all that young, like her. He'd had some bad breaks like her. One of those breaks left his right front leg inoperable. She took him home. Her vet removed the leg.

She took a deep breath. "He's curled up next to Jade on the bed. They're both asleep."

Will he threaten Fluffy?

"The dog is in no more danger than you are," said Charlie, "but he is distinctive and known to the man we are looking for. We will use it to find him."

"I'm not letting you take him. He only listens to me. Sorry, no can do."

Charlie leaned back and pointed to the coffee machine behind Skosh. Like an expensive coffee boy, Skosh poured another mug and handed it to him. She was not offered any.

Bastards.

"I will not take him," said Charlie. "You will. You will walk him in the same park several times a day. Your boyfriend here, Rimas, will walk with you and hold your hand. Maybe you'll kiss a little. You won't stay long, and you will leave in the same direction each time you walk your dog—at the same times each day."

"You think anybody will buy that? They'll think I'm his mother."

"No. They won't. They won't get that close."

"And if I say no?"

Charlie calmly sipped his coffee, saying nothing, never taking his eyes from her face.

"At least tell me if I'm aiding and abetting a bunch of Nazis," she said.

"You're not," answered Frank. "You're helping us hunt them."

TEN

"We've been down this street twice already," said Christine. "Why? Are we on patrol or something?"

Rimas grimaced. This woman was in the way. Not in the way of the op. Michael would take care of that. Her presence interfered with something more substantial—his ability to be alone with Jade. Steve's expression would be 'pain in the ass.'

"We're dry-cleaning our route," said Skosh from the front passenger seat.

Misha explained it more graciously as he turned the wheel for another right turn. "I am making it difficult for someone to follow us."

How could he be gracious to somebody he thought might be dirty, wondered Rimas.

Typical Misha understatement. He made it not difficult but impossible to tail the sedan. Without any sign of hurry, without squealing on the turns, Misha made it look easy. Michael could do that, to be sure, every bit as effectively, but you always knew he was concentrating. Misha acted like it was a summer outing to the park. Which it was, so to speak.

"Misha, if this woman is dirty, who will dispose of her?" Rimas used German. He doubted she knew the language, and if she did, the knowledge would not help her, only provide additional evidence of guilt. She blushed easily. If she understood, they would read it on her face.

Misha answered in English. "It is impolite to speak a language unknown to a person in the party."

"Nonetheless," continued Rimas in German, "who had to kill the one in 1971? You never finished the story."

"You try my patience," came Misha's reply in German. Switching to English, he said, "You should explain to Christine how she is to follow you out of the car when we stop. It may be difficult for her with the dog."

Explain? Rimas looked at the woman. The dog panted in her lap, his large ears pointing up, alert. "Quickly," he said, then thought for a moment and added, "Very quickly."

Skosh turned in his seat to look at them both. "Let me expand that for you just a little, Christine. Rimas will pull you out of the car when we're slow but not quite stopped. Just keep Fluffy in your arms and go with the flow. He'll have an arm around you so you don't fall over. Right, Rimas?"

"When…?" She could not finish the question. The car slowed, and Rimas opened the door. He grabbed her arm none too gently. The dog growled at him, but she held Fluffy securely as they melted into the crowded sidewalk, Rimas's hand tight around her waist.

"All right, all right!" she said. "Let go so I can walk."

She stepped on his instep, and he glared at her.

"Not my fault," she insisted. "Let me walk."

He loosened his grip enough to stop interfering with each step but not enough to give her the impression she could make a run for it. "Why did it have to be you?" she asked. "Why is Charlie making me do this at all, let alone with an arrogant son-of-a-bitch like you?"

"Be quiet!" He used a harsh whisper, leaning into her ear as if to kiss her neck. "Too many people."

"An arrogant man of many words, I see."

He furrowed his brow.

"Sarcasm," she said.

Steve used a phrase with that word. What was it? Rimas remembered and decided it would not betray anything if overheard.

"It does not become you." He tossed the words at her.

Her unsuppressed laugh made him smile, not because it helped their cover as a pair of lovers out for a stroll, though it did. The sound of it sent a shiver of delight. Her low, dusky, rolling laughter made her even prettier, he decided.

"Now what?" she asked as they entered the park. Their feet crunched over a gravel path, staying clear of bushes and open to view on all four sides of the little green rectangular space. Rimas felt exposed. He reminded himself the team had his back and forced the muscles in his neck to relax.

"Now we walk slowly," he said, "and we talk."

"About what?"

He shrugged. "Anything. Just make it look good. What are you doing?" He looked down at her, appalled.

She had pulled a small plastic bag from her pocket and stooped over the grass where the dog had done its business. She put the bag over it and picked it up!

"Don't look at me like that," she said. "It's only polite to pick up after your dog before somebody steps in it."

"Misha tries to make me polite, but he never mentioned picking up shit."

"Misha?"

"Mack. You must call him Mack. Nothing else."

"I mentally called him the criminal Nazi until the government guy told me he's not. A Nazi, I mean. Not sure about the criminal part. So are you one of them or another fed?"

"Fed?" He stopped and looked down at her. Traffic drove by them a few yards to his left. With any luck, word would get to the target soon, and he could spend a little time with Jade.

"Federal officer. Do you work for Uncle Sam or Mack, the possible criminal?"

He struggled with 'work for.' Michael was the boss, certainly, but that was by unanimous consent because Michael's judgment never failed. How to explain? Must he explain? If she was dirty, she deserved no explanation. He looked down at her full lips bent in a half smile, her good humor sparkling from brown eyes. There were worse assignments. He tilted her chin and bent to kiss her. It was part of the job, after all.

"Well?" Her voice came quieter as they continued their slow walk, with Fluffy sniffing every blade of grass along the way. She still wanted an answer.

"I am a member of the team. It is not employment. It is membership."

"What team?"

"Charlemagne. The team is called Charlemagne."

"You're one of them? The guys Skosh told me about? You're an assassin?"

Was it the question or the kiss that made this conversation uncomfortable? He did not want to answer it. At the same time, he knew the quality of his next kiss depended on truth.

"Yes."

ELEVEN

Jade drew the short straw on this op. Nothing was as usual. Nobody behaved normally. Then again, they never did, did they? But this was abnormally abnormal. Well, maybe Rimas still threw her a few longing looks, but why was Mack acting like a babysitter? They had swapped cars, and he was driving.

"I should drive," she insisted. "I know how to evade surveillance now."

Mack glanced at her, then at the mirror, and made a sharp left across Montreal traffic so smoothly nobody even honked.

"I know," he said. "You study tradecraft. Are you dissatisfied with your library?"

"No."

"Your job, then? Is that why you practice what you are learning? Are you trying to become a babysitter?"

"No, are you? I thought you retired."

"I did. I am retired. I do not mind an occasional support role. Are you disappointed in Skosh?"

He pressed again when she did not answer.

"In Rimas?"

Jade contemplated her answer. She wanted finesse, truth, and tact sufficient not to irritate the man next to her. She could not tell what he was thinking and knew his mind-reading fame was no exaggeration. Neither was his reputation as a killer. She had seen both —multiple times.

For that matter, she had also seen Rimas kill. And Skosh, though that was never mentioned. Killing was not in the babysitter job description. Though he had not been at fault, Jade sensed his deep dismay when it happened two years ago. But each time she saw Rimas, he became more like the man next to her—much too much used to it. Were their nightmares like hers, or worse? Worse, she decided.

"Um." She cleared her throat. "I enjoy his company." She turned her head to watch the side mirror on her right, hoping he would not see the blush.

"You enjoy the sex. Do you love him?"

"You don't beat around the bush, do you? Do you like asking questions you already know the answer to?"

Was that a smile or a grimace? She hoped for a smile. Not good to irritate this man, retired or not.

The radio squawked. Charlie told everybody to begin leading their possible tails in different directions. Christine and Rimas had been picked up by Skosh and Frank near the park and were on their way north.

Mack turned right, then right again before saying, "I require you to speak it so that the sound remains in your ears. Do you love him?"

She sighed and closed her eyes. "No. I like him. But love? No." Her words rang in her heart. Would Mack try to convince her she was wrong? Hadn't she already tried to persuade herself a million times?

"Then you must tell him."

She choked at the impossibility. "How?"

This time, there was a smile. "I believe there are many popular songs with advice on this topic. Pick one."

"But I.... he's so emotional, infatuated..." She swallowed the next word, *deadly*.

Mack supplied it, "A fighter. But he is not a madman. One does not have to be a specialist to react badly to such news. The reverse is also true. Many people suffer similar disappointments without resorting to violence, even specialists." Mack took a deep breath and let it out in a huff. "Words I have heard repeatedly from my wife."

"Alex?"

He nodded.

"She's breaking up with you?"

He snorted and took one hand off the wheel to point with his whole hand forward into an imaginary list of arguments he had been required to memorize.

"No. She cannot. She assures me she has no desire to, but also reminds me that once you move to Vasily's Carpet, there is no safe exit. Our enemies…"

"Vasily's Carpet?"

"Where. We. Live."

She got the impression this would be the only explanation but could not help goading him just a little.

"You live in a carpet? Like fleas?"

He clenched his jaw and took a deep breath.

"My point is, if you do not love him, you cannot successfully live at Vasily's Carpet."

"Define successful."

He glared at her, checked his mirrors, and took another turn.

"I don't have the heart to hurt him," she said softly. "He is easily hurt, you know."

"I do. He is much like Vasily in that respect, though not as damaged."

"Vasily?"

"My friend from childhood. A founder of the team. He was killed many years ago." He paused as he sped through an amber light, eyes on the rearview. "It was Vasily who first called me Misha. He was very solemn, even as a child. He grew up in my house because his parents were killed when he was four years old. His mother died at the hands of the KGB, but we believe it was she who shot his father. He never spoke much and had little that could be called conversation in any language, but was a mathematical genius. Also, he was a deadly fighter."

"Charming. Is that the damage you mentioned, the loss of his parents?"

"Partly. It is where Rimas and he differ because Rimas had conscientious parents. He grew up more normally. Vasily's difficulty with talking was a problem, especially with women. It was not helped when the woman who made love to him for the first time tried to kill him. He killed her instead."

Appalling. She suppressed it. He was continuing, and it felt unwise to interrupt. Mack was not exactly a chatterbox. This conversation had a purpose that involved her. Alex must be a powerful woman.

Mack continued. "He was very young when he became active. Vasily's uncles in Poland encouraged him, and he took up the fight against the communists before age fifteen. His first kill occurred shortly after. He was captured often and tortured equally often. When he was eighteen, Louis and I helped him escape. Once he was free, he shot the woman who betrayed him. That was our first op—when we became Charlemagne."

Jade maintained as matter-of-fact a tone as she could manage. "You're saying Vasily killed before he had sex? And if I may ask, who is Louis?"

"Louis was also our friend and grew up in my house because his uncle Bertrand was training him to fight. Bertrand trained all of us. Louis was killed early in this decade in a place called San Antonio."

"I've heard of it." Jade reeled under the concept of children being trained to fight but kept her eyes on the street ahead.

"When your enemies are implacable," Mack said—just like him to read her mind—"you learn to fight or you die. This is why Alex insists if you do not love Rimas, you should not acquire our enemies. He was much older than Vasily was when he first killed a man, but in only two years, he has become noticeable to those who want us dead."

Time for another quick self-exam. *Do I love him? No. Care about him? Yes, a lot. But that's not a substitute. And who am I to think I am the only person he needs? Maybe if I free him, it will free me. Skosh ...*

As if the thought conjured it, Skosh's voice came over the radio. "Not pulling in with the package. Somebody is walking into the other half of the babysitter duplex. Doesn't look like the older man on the lease. Dry-cleaning our way to the team's quarters around the block."

Jade could not tell if the shiver running up her spine was the result of the bad news from the radio or the ultra-controlled anger in the voice next to her.

"What old man?" demanded Mack.

TWELVE

They were dancing a caffeine boogaloo. Christine saw Skosh bring a mug of the stuff to Charlie, where he sat in a corner easy chair, surveying the room, his eyes sometimes pausing on her with a scowl. She watched him from a straight-backed dining chair with her back to the window, across the room from the almighty coffee machine on the kitchen counter. They had all been out on this walk-the-dog adventure. If they learned anything, she sure didn't know it, nor have any idea what they were up to besides no good.

She abandoned all efforts at comprehending and concentrated instead on observing and mentally recording what she saw. It helped against the nagging worry, the overarching need for a telephone. The house was similar to the one they left, though larger, with a dark brick exterior and sash windows. The interior of this one had suffered a bad remodeling job in the recent past. The wall between the kitchen and living room had been removed, making one large room downstairs. Appliances were clustered at one end. A dirty, grey industrial carpet covered the floor throughout. To her left was a bolted front door, and behind her, a heavily curtained window.

Jade took a chair near the front door, next to a stack of footlockers barricading the door, partly blocking the landing of the staircase leading to the bedrooms upstairs. The big SUV had been squeezed into the narrow attached garage, and the Mercedes sedan was backed in on the drive in front of the garage door. The only door anybody used to enter the house was the one from the garage that opened under the staircase. To the right of the entrance, tucked in under the stairs, a doorway led down to a basement. Mack lay stretched out, coatless, on a shabby sofa shoved against the wall, feet toward the front door and the landing, left arm covering his eyes. A fully inhabited black leather shoulder holster gleamed against his white shirt.

At the other end of the long, narrow room, Skosh made more coffee. Charlie scanned a thick stack of connected tractor-feed paper fresh off a busy printer on a wobbly dining table against the long wall to Christine's right. A jumbled assortment of computer parts filled the rest of the table, with two monitors running stock screen savers in never-ending patterns of scrolls and swirls.

Frank dozed in another easy chair next to the table, his eyes bulging even behind closed lids. Funny old man, she thought. More like a bureaucrat than one of the criminals. Retired or not, still a Fed, like Skosh. She contemplated the words he had used when he pulled her from her hotel room.

"You're way too public a witness."

"I couldn't help it. The reporter met me coming out of the police station. He already had the camera running."

"It was not a simple murder. You need to come with me."

"Looked pretty simple to me. The guy shot a man right in front of me."

"You're in more danger than you know."

He won the argument, and here she was, feeling even more jeopardy, wishing she could use the telephone again. There was one on the wall by the computer.

Rimas sat in a third stiff chair against the long wall with a low coffee table before him under a crooked picture of a waterfall. There were several of these decorating the room, randomly breaking up otherwise blank white walls. He reassembled and reholstered his handgun, then pulled a rifle from the open footlocker next to him. Maybe that, too, was a semi-auto masquerading as something more to look cool, but she doubted it. There was nothing cool here—all strictly business.

How is this safer?

As if in response to her thought, two strange men walked in through the door under the stairs. The bulges under their arms, the bulges of their arms, the way they moved, the way they scanned the room, the way their eyes stopped for a long time on her face, her hands, and the dog in her lap, gave her the answer.

It's not.

...

Skosh had been standing next to Charlie under old Sherlock in free fall on the wall when he noticed him eyeing Christine. He could see the calculations speeding by behind those still, blue eyes. Charlie reached a decision a nano-second later, picked up his radio, and called the delinquents in from the car.

"Then you must not think she's dirty, Charlie," said Skosh, using German.

"I'm reserving judgment."

"Your father thinks she is."

"My father is living in the past. Steve and Sergei need sleep right now. They'll have to risk being seen. If she turns out dirty, they know what to do."

As if being mentioned in quiet conversation was enough to wake him, Mack pushed himself upright from his nap on the couch and limped toward them just as the delinquents came through the door. He studied the lieutenant sitting against the far wall before turning to scowl at Skosh.

"What old man has moved into your house?" he demanded.

Charlie raised an eyebrow to second the demand for a too-long delayed explanation.

Skosh sighed. He had been hoping for a chance at the coffee pot. "I couldn't get a lease for all three houses until next week, but I took the two empty ones and investigated the old man who still held that third lease. Very old. He checked out clear. My Canadian counterpart, Yannick, did the background check, and we have pictures. He's getting ready to move. We have surveillance. He's buying boxes. I saw the receipts. I put the babysitters' safehouse next to him in the duplex. It should have been okay—until this younger guy showed up."

"A relative?" suggested Steve as he and Sergei joined them.

Skosh shrugged.

Sergei scowled at him. "You said we would be able to secure our perimeters for both houses. We cannot monitor your house with a wall shared by an unknown. This is unsecure. They can put touches inside that wall. If this man finds the sensors I have installed...."

Frank interrupted, handing out mugs of coffee to Steve and Sergei. "I verified the man's bona fides through our sources. There shouldn't be an unknown in that house. His closest kin lives in Vancouver. This new guy has New York plates."

"It's worse than just New York plates," said Skosh, wishing fervently for coffee. "He's in the game. He moved wrong. Too aware. And he's packing. His coat flapped open when he slung a backpack on one shoulder. I saw a strap. It could only be a holster. He crossed the Canadian border with a firearm. He might not be a player in our game, but he's on somebody's team."

During the pause, all eyes on him, Skosh noticed Frank slip—more like slink—back to the coffee machine. Four killers stared at Skosh with respect. Only coffee would alleviate this discomfort. But when even Frank, his old boss and fellow babysitter, gave him the same respectful look while serving him a steaming mug of the stuff, discomfort became despair.

"We must remove our sensors near that house," insisted Sergei, the team's gadget man. Skosh noticed he already needed a shave.

Steve took a long sip and nodded. His face was displaying a healthy crop of dark brown stubble. Skosh unconsciously felt his chin. Not as bad, he decided.

"And why not put touches in that wall?" suggested Steve.

Mack tapped the floor beneath his stick. "Another coincidence makes me uneasy. When we came here in 1971, there were also too many connections. We had only a narrow escape from disaster."

Charlie answered with a slight nod. "But sometimes coincidence can help us, Papa. You have always used what fate throws our way. I will do the same. The policewoman and her dog are in play for our purposes, and I think it's time to employ Skosh's unexpected talent."

Sputtering on his hot coffee, Skosh turned red. "Hold on. I'm a babysitter. I'm not ..."

"Nobody said you were anything else. But you'll help tonight as usual."

"Not as usual. There is somebody in that house. If he's dirty and if there is a problem, it will require a specialist. This is more delicate."

"And you are more capable. Steve will lead. Sergei will stay back. Rimas can place touches. Skosh, you clear the sensors. Any questions?

"I shouldn't get that close to this," said Skosh. He looked down into the brown liquid cooling in his cup."

Charlie's answer came smoothly modulated.

"I said questions, not wishes."

THIRTEEN

"Can I help here?," said Christine. "I'm bored to tears. Did you have a good nap?"

Rimas looked up at her, puzzled. She was talking to Misha as if everyday pleasantries were expected in a place like this with a man like Misha. Rimas watched and listened, curious.

Misha sat in a dining chair across from him at the low table with a hot mug of coffee and a cleaning kit before him. He released the magazine of his SIG Sauer pistol, pulled back the slide, and emptied the chambered round into his hand before answering her question in his usual still manner, blue eyes locking on without a blink. He spoke English.

"My rest was sufficient, thank you. No."

She interrupted, "I know how to clean a pistol."

"I am aware you do, but you may not touch one of ours. I hope that is clear. You may bring a chair and join us if it will help relieve your boredom, though my storytelling will likely make the condition worse."

Was the older man becoming—what was the English expression—mellow? Rimas watched him remove the slide and lay out the barrel and recoil spring.

What story?

"Welche Geschichte?" he asked out loud.

"Use English," said Misha. "Christine does not speak German. I was telling you about the girl Vasily met here in Montreal." He soaked a patch in solvent and pushed it through the barrel.

Christine dragged over a chair and sat. Rimas wished Jade would do the same and wondered why she did not. He watched her face as she cleared notebooks, coffee cans, and mugs from the island counter that separated the living room from the kitchen. She was paying too much attention to Skosh as she worked. Rimas scowled. What were they talking about?

"Who is Vasily?" Christine asked as if she had a right to a reply. To Rimas's surprise, after taking his time to consider his words, Misha answered.

"He was an original member of the team and also my friend since childhood."

"Team?"

Rimas was sure she knew about the team. She had called him an assassin in the park. He still found the word uncomfortable, or rather, the knowledge that it was accurate did not sit well with his ego. He liked to think he was a good man. How can a good man bring death to anyone, even an evil man, without sharing the evil?

Misha sent a bore brush down the SIG's barrel as he told her about Vasily, his Polish roots, his mathematical prowess, and his skill as a killer. Misha used the word fighter instead, but Rimas remembered talk of Vasily during his earliest training as a boy in Lithuania. Vasily Sobieski's name was whispered with awe in anti-Soviet circles. He was to be revered—and feared.

Rimas pulled a cloth out of the footlocker at his feet and polished the rifle he had just finished. Now, the name was becoming the basis of a lesson he did not yet understand. Why these stories from almost three decades back?

"I heard them call you Misha," said Christine. "Are you Russian?"

Misha's silent stare, just inside the safer edge of belligerence, meant he found her question impertinent. No, not impertinent.

She is interrogating him. She must be dirty.

Rimas became less bored.

"I am Austrian." Misha's tone was unfriendly.

"You were talking about Vasily's girlfriend." She prompted, pretending not to notice the chill, almost demanding an answer.

Definitely dirty. Also brave, or maybe just foolish.

Rimas raised an eyebrow as she tried to match the belligerence in Misha's stare. She failed and dropped her gaze first.

"Vasily had no skill in speaking to others, especially women," Misha continued. "He saw the world as a collection of numbers, geometrical figures, progressions made by factors and exponents in elegant sentences called formulae. A sentence of words held no depth in his mind, could never be a thing of beauty."

Rimas paused in his polishing. Was this why Misha kept telling him about Vasily—because he shared this trait? He rejected the idea. He would never be as good with numbers as he wanted to be, though he continued to try. He simply had no skill at stringing words, not in any of his four languages.

Misha continued. "Women sensed he was dangerous and often stayed away. If one came close, Vasily soon learned she wanted something from him. All he had for them was pain and death because it was all he knew, both giving and receiving. But he came to my house very young, and my family civilized him as well as they were able. He had his own moral code and adhered to the team's rules. Such rules can be important for those with the authority to use deadly force, wouldn't you agree, Lieutenant?"

"You have rules?"

The woman looked Misha in the eye.

Brave. Foolish. Dirty.

The two paused in mutual animosity.

"Don't you?"

Another pause. She looked down. "Of course."

Another victory for Misha, who ran a dry patch through the SIG's barrel. It looked clean to Rimas, but Misha pushed another before inspecting the frame.

Misha broke the silence. "Rules may protect an innocent against injury, but they do nothing to shield the guilty from damage."

Christine tilted her head and squinted. "I don't understand. Why would we want to protect the guilty?"

"Spoken like a policewoman who does not understand she is among the guilty. Every exercise of raw power, even without violence, changes you. You are not the same woman you were twenty-three years ago when you joined the police.

"Twenty-three years? How did you…?"

"We have a computer." Misha pointed to it with the slide in his hand.

Rimas watched Christine gain control of her surprise and force her face into the worldwide official expression of stern wariness adopted by all with the power to hurt you. He had been learning the same.

"I am allowed to use force in defense of myself and others," she said with a convinced tone. "I follow the rules. Are you saying I'm damaged anyway?"

"No. I say you are changed. Rules cannot stop change. Damage comes when you feel altered but do not like or understand it. Some become arrogant and cruel, others fearful and jumpy. Some shun all contact with people, others crave it. Vasily created a fantasy world where he had never been orphaned or tortured or taught to fight and, most of all, had never killed."

Rimas laid the rifle in its case and conducted an internal inventory. He was not jumpy or fearful and indeed not cruel. Arrogant? He had to admit that. Christine had noticed it. Fantasy? Surely not. What would he fantasize about?

The noise in the room increased. The babysitters brought in lunch from the caterers' truck. Jade, as usual, had large spoons ready to dish the food, paper plates and plastic utensils to receive it. She was perfect in every way, Rimas mused as he plotted to make sure she sat next to him as they ate.

"I have never killed and hope I never have to," said Christine.

Misha slipped the barrel and spring into the slide. "Not everyone who enters your job considers the possibility. They glory in power and noble purpose but never consider the smell of sweat or the desperate strain of failing muscles clinging to life without hope. Defeated foes bring no glory to their vanquishers, only the threat of vengeance. Look into the eyes of a soldier returning from combat, or better, a soldier dying on the battlefield."

Rimas pushed aside a memory of the mentor of his youth, Kestutis, dying in his arms.

The noise increased as Sergei turned from the computer and began joking with Steve. Christine looked down at her hands on her lap, then up at Misha. "You are quite the philosopher."

"No, just a killer." He said it quietly, throwing a glance in Rimas's direction. "My wife is the philosopher. Vasily was her first husband. He discovered that he wanted most to be with a woman who would support the fantasy of not being what he was. Shortly before he met her, he thought he had found his dream here in Montreal."

"What happened?"

He gave her a half smile. "He was wrong."

FOURTEEN

Christine didn't buy it. Not any of it. They all had the look in their eyes, men with guns and extreme biceps who spoke too many languages. Even when they used English, it came out in indecipherable jargon. She should walk out. She should put them all under arrest and then walk out. *Where to?* She did not know where in Montreal Frank had brought her. A residential street of two-story rectangular brick boxes.

Skip the arrest; no jurisdiction. Where is my brain? Maybe walk out quietly when they aren't looking. At least, get to a phone.

She could find her way to the local Mountie station.

She surveyed the room. They made no sign of being impressed by her existence. Answers to her occasional questions came with minimal information, volunteering nothing. No facts advanced. Even Steve came downstairs and walked by her without his previous speculative *how-about-it?* glance. She felt more menace than flattery in his regard, but being a ghost was no fun at all, either. Even though no one looked at her, she knew they were all perfectly aware of her exact location. When she moved a hand to tighten her ponytail, Charlie and the Russian guy, Sergei, standing across the room at the coffee machine, paused their quiet conversation.

So Christine experimented. She moved cautiously toward the side door, concentrating on being as quiet as that guy, Charlie, though not expecting to reach his level of perfection. The so-called babysitters, the Feds as she called them, immediately looked her way. Frank's eyes bulged under raised brows. She calculated her chances in a sprint to the door—*nil*—and opted instead for more coffee. Charlie and Sergei moved away, still talking, not English.

I am a prisoner with coffee privileges.

Their discussion over, Charlie reappeared at her elbow like a specter, a malignant presence unseen but fully felt. She concentrated on pouring but contemplated throwing the pot at him.

"I wouldn't if I were you."

What the hell?

She hadn't even looked at him. She put the pot down and turned to face him. He spoke again.

"You don't know our capabilities, Christine. Best to go with the flow, as you Americans say."

The Russian guy, Sergei, approached again with a worried face.

"I need to call...."

He used English because, well, courtesy. These criminals had manners but no Algonquian languages. Not that Christine could boast about her fluency.

Charlie barked at him, "I asked you at lunch to look up the license number Skosh gave us. Have you?"

Sergei shuffled, needing movement to calm himself. "Please, Charlie. Very quick. She is having contractions. I worry."

"I do, too, about Mara, of course, but right now, about all of us. Go, do the search. First."

"She should not have kept this baby even though it is a son. It will kill her."

"I agree," Charlie said, visibly straining at tolerance. "My sister flirts with death at every opportunity. She has good doctors. Now, do as I say. No more discussion."

Christine cataloged the tension in their exchange, the family references, and the exchange of glances between Charlie and Mack. She knew she was again the topic of that silent communication. Mack holstered his re-assembled SIG, telegraphing with a glance in her direction an almost palpable distrust. Christine embraced invisibility again, reminding herself how good it was to be a ghost.

Steve walked up and handed her an empty mug. She looked down at the pot still in her hand, still tempting her to convert it into a weapon.

"I'd like a cup, too, if you don't mind," said Charlie. "While you're at it."

She put her mug on the counter. It would grow cold while she served them, but she took advantage of the chance to listen and learn.

"Sergei's losing it, Charlie. Any word from Theresa?"

Who the hell is Theresa?

Charlie closed his eyes momentarily. "Only with her usual, guarded medical-ese. Wait and see sort of thing. She won't say so, but it's not looking good." He took a deep sip of coffee.

Do these guys—should these guys—reproduce?

Charlie scowled at her as if he'd read her mind.

"He's a quivering bowl of pudding over this baby," said Steve. "He hasn't cleaned his Makarov since before we left. Rimas studies all that electronic shit. I'm glad you're letting me bring him with us tonight instead of Sergei. Don't give him any more pressure, Charlie. Not yet."

Charlie nodded. "We'll have a meeting as soon as he has a line on that neighbor. I will find a way to couch it without making it a slight to him."

Christine handed them their mugs robotically, wrapped in the cloak of invisibility afforded by simple service, barely breathing, and wondering when they would stop talking so freely in the presence of somebody they did not trust.

Steve's slow Texas drawl accompanied a half-smile. "I don't think he'll even notice, to tell you the truth. I don't get it. I've seen them in action together dozens of times. Never a glitch, even when she's beside him in a firefight. What is unhinging him?"

"A threat from an unknown direction?" Charlie looked up from a study of the liquid in his mug. "Casualties in action are one thing, but childbirth? I never considered it a factor until Theresa explained the danger back when Mara made the decision. I'm not used to the idea of losing her. She never lets me keep her out of the action on an op and made it clear this decision was only hers to make. She's right. The team can't share it any more than we can carry the baby. But I wish she didn't."

Steve drained his cup and glanced at the too-observant woman holding a coffee pot, a small dog at her feet. "Any sign of interest in the pooch?"

"Yes. We'll discuss it after you get back. That reminds me, we need you to bring back Jade's computer from the babysitters' house, too. We'll put it on the table next to Sergei's. Skosh will squawk. He won't be able to stop Sergei from watching her log in."

Charlie dropped a momentary delighted grin as he held out his cup for another refill, eyes suspicious and hooded.

As she drained the pot and made another, it occurred to Christine they spoke freely in front of her because the creature they wanted here was the dog, not her. They were making use of him. Fluffy couldn't repeat anything he heard, and they were confident in their ability to silence Christine—at will and for good.

FIFTEEN

"The dog was a pain in the ass. Just like she said he would be," Frank told Skosh as he handed him a damp cloth. "How did Christine do?"

Skosh could smell coconut oil and soap on the cloth as he buried his face in it, removing the camo paint after their nighttime excursion to retrieve the sensors. He shrugged. "She took the monitor from me and was gone before I jumped the fence. She's pretty fast." He turned the rag and gave his ears and neck the same treatment while watching the woman in question. Well, he had to admit he was watching Jade, who was helping Christine clean her face.

"How'd you do?" murmured Frank.

Skosh answered the same way. "I didn't kill anybody if that's what you're asking. Nobody did. For a change. I think the guy was out or asleep; the place was dark. Car was there, though. I don't know why I had to go. Too many cooks, in my mind. Could have been a disaster trying to get that many people to behave like they're not there."

"I think that's why Charlie sent you. To find out if you can handle it. Did you pass?"

"God, I hope not. This job is shitty—thanks a lot for promoting me to it—but theirs is worse, and the last thing I want is a job offer from Charlie. Where do we sleep, by the way? Not on rotation with the team, I hope."

Frank ran fat fingers through the thin hair fringing his head. He gave a half-shrug, one shoulder only, before answering. "The good news is there's an attic, and Jade was able to move a couple of old dressers and rig a sheet across the middle, so we can split evenly, men on one end, women on the other, team on the floor below. Bad news is spiders. Even worse, Jade says she's allergic, as in screaming bloody terror allergic. So far, she's kept it together. Accommodation-wise, it could be worse."

Another thing we have in common. Skosh sighed as he watched Jade set up her keyboard and screen in the space Sergei had cleared for her on the table. She plugged them into the CPU tower on the floor. The machines stood back to back to shield their hands from each other's sight as they typed. Skosh approved. He had gone to a lot of trouble to scrub the team's fingers out of The Section's file system.

"What about Christine? How is she with spiders?"

"I guess they call state cops troopers for a reason. She's made of granite."

Skosh nodded. "That's why Charlie doesn't trust her."

"Which is why he sent Sergei with her. I'm sure there was a clear order in the event of a misstep."

"Yeah. No doubt."

She was sitting in a chair near the front door, face free of camo paint, hugging Fluffy. Skosh heard her tell Jade the dog had to go outside soon.

A dog needs to lift his leg and it takes a fucking strategic campaign to get him to a tree, in this case, a bush by the garage's back door, led by a none-too-happy Rimas. Skosh always smiled when Rimas scowled like that. He walked over to Charlie, who stood looking over Sergei's shoulder at the computer screen.

"Charlie, how about we make it clear to everybody that the attic is babysitter territory? Team members should steer clear. It'll make up for the loss of our safehouse."

He had tried to make his tone friendly, casual, without agenda. The ice-blue stare from Charlie told him he failed, and the answer confirmed it.

"The comfort and security of you babysitters have never been high on my list of concerns, Skosh. But if it makes you feel any better, Rimas will be too busy this trip."

He dragged out the word busy, squinting one eye as he tilted his chin into his trademark arrogant challenge, then instantly softened it. "Why don't you fix the situation with Jade?" he demanded.

Skosh couldn't hide his surprise. He sputtered, "I can't…"

"Yeah, yeah, I know all those English words like taking advantage and fraternization that you people complain about, but couldn't you just marry her? I know it's old-fashioned, but she's probably worth the risk."

Of course, she's worth the risk.

He glanced inadvertently at Rimas coming through the door with a relieved-looking rat terrier. And, of course, Charlie caught it.

"Don't worry about the Rimas equation, either, Skosh. My father will take care of that side of it. You just ask her. Soon. Then, concentrate on getting us all out of this op alive."

SIXTEEN

Christine rubbed at the residual night paint near her ear while she processed the situation as Frank explained it. The paint would never come off. She had been glad to help cart things from the other house. It relieved the boredom. But she didn't trust the jumpy Russian who took the CPU from her only to leave her hoisting the heavier monitor with a keyboard and mouse balancing on top of it. He'd kept one hand free, she noticed. The one closest to her. And not so as to be helpful.

Steve of the melting brown eyes droned on about names she never wanted to know. She sat on another uncomfortable chair in a roomful of criminals, wanting to casually walk over to that phone on the wall, wondering how she was going to share a room with three people, two of them men. Not a room, a sleeping space, they said. Four-hour shifts. Sleeping only. That had been emphasized, with glances to both her and Jade, like all hanky-panky is ultimately the responsibility of the female. A snort of disgust escaped her, but her continued invisibility covered it.

There had been a time when all these fit younger men would be tempting, especially Steve, closest to her age, with his invitational glances, but the need to survive without the benefit of information occupied her now. She was too busy trying to figure out what the hell was going on.

She heard the words 'white supremacy'. *Shit. They are Nazis.* Then, she heard 'target' and then 'civil rights activist' in close succession and let out another disgusted snort. None of this made sense.

Mack interrupted Steve's narrative. "I believe the police lieutenant has a comment."

All attention swiveled to her. "What? No, please go on."

"A question then?" His blue eyes fixed on her, compelling an answer.

"I just don't understand any of it, that's all." She held Fluffy a little more tightly in her lap, gathering from him the courage to go out telling the truth.

Frank didn't rescue me; he captured me.

"I'm not armed and I'm outnumbered," she said, "but if you think I will stand by while you murder a civil rights leader… I'm a cop and I'll find a way to take you down."

From the grave if I have to.

Fluffy whined. She loosened her grip. The room became silent. Even the computer's fan seemed muted. Steve rolled his eyes and tilted his head in the traditional gesture of male arrogance. She tried to think of a witty way to spit defiance.

"Don't think your Texas accent will make an ally out of me, cowboy," she said.

"I don't have an accent."

"You do, too."

He put on a patient look and narrowed his eyes. "I don't have an accent that would confuse anybody speaking English, even somebody from Vermont. I don't know what unknown region you're inhabiting right now, Loootenant, but here on earth, in this here room, we're talking about our target, not our target's target."

It took less than half a breath to process his words before the blood rushed into her face.

Charlie entered the exchange with a note of venom. "Now that we have established you were not listening, Christine, I will briefly repeat Steve's more important points. I trust you can understand *my* accent."

His accent was all American, even if he wasn't, and he waited for an answer. She nodded ever so slightly to keep the tears of embarrassment from spilling down her cheeks, feeling everybody watching, willing them to look elsewhere, away from her false accusation—in her family, it was the worst of all sins—wishing for a wormhole to crawl into.

"Shane Chatham is our target," Charlie said smoothly. "He is the American you saw shoot a Canadian black man this morning. Our information is that he is using the name Smitty and is here to take out Sidney Alcoa, an American indigenous rights activist. Alcoa will arrive in Montreal tomorrow to give a speech the next day and receive an award honoring him for his work with local tribes. We hope to stop Chatham. We also hope to learn a few things. The incident you witnessed in the park has complicated both goals." He paused and raised one eyebrow. "Questions?"

She risked more embarrassment, thinking it couldn't be worse, but held her breath, expecting it to be.

"Why can't I stay in the other house?"

Away from you.

"We are getting to that."

When his gaze shifted to Sergei, Christine felt unnoticed again. She breathed.

"Tell us about the license plate, Sergei."

Christine considered the man as he turned from his computer keyboard. She would not want to meet any of these guys in a dark alley, but this one especially. The compact, muscular build suggested speed, and his almost transparent eyes looked right through you.

He had stood very still next to her at the fence where Skosh handed them the computer parts. Even in the dark, she felt the attention he paid to her movements, watching her hands with an assessing eye. The memory made her shiver as he answered with a thick Russian accent. She looked away and noticed Rimas watching her. He had seen the shiver.

"The plate is from New York," said Sergei. "The car belongs to a man who calls himself Paul Smith. Officially, he has an import business. He is not related to anyone with the name registered to the house where he is staying. He lives in Plattsburgh, New York, and frequently comes to Montreal for business. The house is listed as his destination every time he enters the country."

"Fake name on the lease," drawled Steve. "Any other signs?"

"Yes. There are two million Americans of that name."

"So it's common. What else?"

"I have a small indication that it may be an alias. There are several Smiths in Interpol database, but one is suspected to operate out of New York."

"Operate what?" asked Charlie.

"I do not know. I could not access the individual file. I also do not know why Interpol lists him. We need better access."

All heads turned to Skosh standing by the coffee machine.

"Jade is still setting up her system," he said, pointing to her as she knelt under the table, running a cable.

"Have you heard from the Canadians?" Charlie asked him.

"I have. They have light surveillance on what looks like a safehouse near the park. That's where the two watchers Rimas noticed entered. They were careful to dry clean their route."

"But unsuccessful." Charlie smiled. "If they turn up at Smith's safehouse, we will have stumbled into the network we're looking for. A useful coincidence. There is no sign we're blown."

"There is yet another coincidence," said Mack. "Smith is an old name."

"I am sure it has a noble history," said Charlie, "but I agree with Sergei it is probably an alias in this case."

"That is what I am referring to—an alias that has been used in this area for a long time."

"But he is American," said Sergei, "not from Montreal."

"It's a very common name, Papa, easy to use as an alias."

The muscles of Misha's jaw tightened under forced patience. "If you will listen…" He glared them into respectful silence before continuing.

"When we were here soon after the October Crisis almost three decades ago, we encountered a babysitter from Colorado calling himself Gary Smith. We watched him meet a specialist from New Hampshire, also named Smith, who had already taken out a Canadian press agent instrumental in changing public sentiment against the FLQ.

"Darren Smith was after an FLQ informant who was due to receive a light sentence for his role in the incident. He had taken no part in the killing and was now trading information for a few years of freedom. We were too late to stop the revenge assassination of the press agent, but the informant had more information to give, so we were asked to stay."

"Who were you working for?" asked Skosh.

"Us," answered Frank. "They worked for us. We wanted to know who deployed Gary Smith's specialists. Charlemagne was the perfect choice to find out. The Canadians blessed our proposal, just like they have this time. They—and we—were more than curious to know who wanted these two dead, I mean, aside from friends of the other government official who died in the crisis two months before."

"I'm seeing a parallel," said Skosh as he took the chair under the cat poster near Jade. "We need to know who Chatham is reporting to. We know he's not solo. The common names suggest a pattern."

Misha nodded. "In the earlier op during the '70s, we began surveillance of Darren. Frank worried because, on paper, the two Smiths had come from different American states."

Frank dabbed ineffectually with a paper napkin at coffee that stained his white shirt."It suggested a nationwide link," he said. "Then, the watchers I hired found a woman also called Smith. It looked like Darren and Gloria were an item."

Rimas wrinkled his brow and tilted his head back at the mention of the name.

Skosh shrugged, walked to the sink, and brought Frank a damp rag for the coffee stain. "So maybe they were married?"

"No," said Mack. "Her passport gave her an address in Wisconsin."

Frank nodded. "Now we had three people named Smith from three states. Using the same name must be a conceit of the organization, a mark of membership. It concerned us, and rightly so, as it turned out."

"Today, we have two Smiths," said Mack, "our target and this unexpected neighbor in the duplex."

Christine leaned forward in her chair. "Wait, earlier, you said your target's name is Chatham."

...

Misha studied her face, surprised at her determined grasp of information amid the chaos that threatened her. Her expression was serious, slightly puzzled, and fully engaged in the conversation, unlike Gloria Smith, who had feigned ignorance. And Vasily had fallen for it. This one was taking an alternate tack—if she was dirty. She might not be. It was theoretically possible for a woman to be intelligent and free of guile. He had learned to appreciate these traits in the women at home, though at the same time, they could be irritating as hell.

"We intercepted a message from him to a superior. He signed it Smitty," said Michael.

"A message?" She tilted her head sideways.

It described the murder you witnessed." He paused, also studying her. "And included a description of you. And of the dog."

"Oh." She parted her lips slightly, dropped her gaze to stare inward, and said slowly, "But you intercepted it. So there's still only one guy—this Chatham character—that I need to worry about."

When nobody answered after a few beats, she added, "Right?"

"We put the message back, and this evening, two men near the park noticed you. They show signs they are in the game."

Misha watched her critically and was gratified to see her eyes open wide. It appeared sudden, automatic, a genuine reaction to bad news.

"Why?" she croaked, her face now pale.

Michael sat back in his easy chair and held his empty mug in Skosh's direction. Skosh got up to fill it. "Because, Lieutenant, we don't want just Chatham. We are after the entire organization."

"But if he sent a message about me, then the whole organization is after me." She emphasized the last word and pointed to herself. "You're using me to ferret out an entire gang?"

Steve answered her. "Pretty much. Yeah."

Color came back to her cheeks; her eyes narrowed with anger. "Can I at least be armed? I saw that footlocker over there. You guys have plenty of firepower to share."

Amazing. A dangle who knew her danger, consented to it, though grudgingly, and refused to be passive about it. The team and babysitters all turned to his son for his answer.

"No." Cold and still as ever.

The woman's face blanched again, and Michael broke precedent by giving her the unusual benefit of a more complete explanation.

"They would notice you're armed and be suspicious of a trick. As are we."

"Me? I'm the cop here. You guys are… I don't know what you are, but I don't kill people willy-nilly like…."

"But you make assumptions willy-nilly, don't you?"

"What? Oh." She took a deep breath and blushed red again. Misha approved. She had the decency to be embarrassed. It seemed another genuine trait. If she was dirty, then she was, at least, a better actress than Gloria.

...

They were still talking when Jade told Christine it was her turn in the sack. She and Fluffy made their way up the attic stairs and onto a narrow cot surrounded by broken furniture and hanging blankets. A single bulb hanging from a hook in the rafters lit the space but did not interfere with Christine's ability to sleep within seconds.

Two minutes later, it seemed, Jade poked her shoulder with a finger, and Fluffy growled from under the blanket.

"My turn, Christine. Go downstairs."

"Already? How long…"

"You had four hours. Now let me have mine. You get to hear what the targets are up to. The Smith guy is awake, and Sergei is putting him on speaker. Lucky you. Fill me in on it in four hours. Not a moment sooner."

SEVENTEEN

It began with a radio squawk, shrill, full of static. The receiver squelched. The audience, Charlemagne, with their babysitters and prisoner, as she insisted on calling herself, had arranged itself in uncomfortable chairs, forming a lopsided arc around the computers.

Sergei switched the audio to the main speakers and played the recorded file. The caller's initial cough may or may not have carried over the air. It depended on whether he had pressed talk. Their touch was in the inside wall of the duplex, giving them more information about his state than he gave over the radio.

> Listen, Gary, I gotta talk to him. Can you give him your brick? And leave the room. It's confidential.

He slurped a drink. Probably coffee.

> Smith here.

A squawk cut short, almost as short as the clipped words.
The man in the house cleared his throat.

> Boss, this is Paul.
> Authenticate.
> Liberty.

Not very original.

> Go ahead.

The correct answer, though. The man cleared his throat again. And coughed.

> Um… I'm not questioning the order, you understand. He's been out of control for some time. I just don't know how

> to find him. Also, there is another
> development.

Another slurp and seven steps on a wood floor. Pause. Seven more. Pacing?

> His tradecraft has always been good.
> You'll have to lure him. What develop-
> ment?

The static on Smith's radio was heavy, but the team's signal from the house was clear. Paul took a deep, audible breath, hissing air into his lungs, no doubt keeping his finger off the talk button to hide the hesitation. When it came at last, his voice sounded careful, reluctant.

> I think the landlord rented out the
> other side of the safehouse. It's a
> duplex, so a security risk. Maybe I
> should move. About Chatham. Last I
> heard [static] Last I heard, he was
> looking for a fucking dog. I heard
> we're looking, too. I've been told
> it's your order. You took four of my
> watchers who should be checking out
> these new tenants next door. I don't
> know if I'll have enough watchers to
> catch Alcoa's arrival. We should have
> rented both houses.

The boss spoke in extra decibels.

> The house has always been secure, and
> it was expensive enough on its own.
> Perfect location. Any tenants next
> door will be short-term. We made sure.
> And say target, not the name. Get some
> fucking discipline, Paul. You're as
> bad as Shane. We've seen the dog.
> We'll deliver his quarry to you as
> soon as it can be arranged. You take
> it from there. He thinks he has to
> eliminate her before he can work.

The pacing stopped momentarily.

> The dog's a female?

The radio exploded again.

> No, you fucking moron. Its owner is. Once you have her, we'll make sure he hears of it. He'll come to you. Then you do what's necessary. I'm done with him.
>
> What about her?
>
> She's a brown nobody. Do what you want after I come and see if she's worth my time. Control the goons. I'll want her fresh, if at all.
>
> And the target? If Shane's too dead, who...?"
>
> To be determined. Get some sleep. And don't let me hear your voice again until you've done your fucking job. Over.

Charlie put down the headphones while Sergei turned off the tape, both eyebrows raised expectantly.

"Go, wake up Rimas. Have him meet me in the car. No listeners."

EIGHTEEN

Maybe he was too fond of kissing her. Perhaps that was why Michael's order made Rimas uncomfortable. It seemed a sneaky thing to do, but then, being a sneak was his job. To her, it would seem like a betrayal, he knew, and he hoped rescuing Fluffy at the last minute would help her forgive it. If the plan worked, he wanted another kiss, a real one this time, not part of a legend. If she lived. Insufficient as a substitute for Jade, but the woman could kiss, and he craved the touch of her softness.

The plan was simple, his part in it, flawless. Rimas took the leash from her, letting Fluffy pull him, straining towards intriguing smells at the gutter, creating a gap of only a few inches between them. He pretended not to notice the two unknowns who stepped up behind her, then moved to either side. She yelled his name only briefly, no doubt silenced by whatever weapon they showed her quietly in the crowd.

Rimas stopped in the gutter and watched her dark ponytail disappear in the crowds moving away down the sidewalk. Fluffy lifted his leg at the curb.

"I've got them," said Steve's voice in his ear.

Rimas jumped onto the curb in time to avoid being hit as Skosh slowed a muddy dark green Peugeot beside him. He picked up Fluffy and folded his six-foot frame into the passenger seat.

"Turning right," Michael murmured through their earbuds minutes later. Skosh pulled into position, allowing the silver Ford that carried Christine to pass him in heavy traffic on René Levesque Boulevard. Misha turned the Mercedes sedan behind them from a side street. They followed two cars back, took a right turn after the Ford, but continued straight when it turned again. Misha turned after them and followed until they hit Rene Levesque again and turned right a third time to continue in the original direction. He turned left as Jade took up the slow chase in an old, red Mitsubishi Steve had stolen in Laval. Steve was her passenger, probably making her uncomfortable. Rimas grimaced at the thought.

"They're still dry cleaning," Steve announced to everybody's ear. "These guys are good. Looks like they're headed for the Victoria Bridge. Need somebody on the other side of it."

Misha used the Champlain bridge to meet them as they turned left off the Victoria on route 132, heading north along the river only long enough to turn back across again, this time using the Jacques Cartier bridge, where Michael picked up the Smith car on the other side. Satisfied they had shaken any surveillance, Christine's abductors took their time crossing the island and heading into the residential neighborhoods of Laval. Michael and his team took turns keeping a light surveillance behind.

Skosh and Rimas were turning toward the safehouse when Steve's voice came over the network.

"You were right, Charlie. They're pulling into the house next door to the babysitters' and there's no sign of another visitor."

"Not yet, but give them time," said Michael, his voice as cool as ever, as if Christine had endless time. Like success or failure, life or death were all equally unremarkable.

"I will hear when they come in," said Sergei, back in the safehouse manning the computer and listening equipment.

Computers, plural, Rimas corrected to himself. Nothing Jade could have done to protect her system would keep Sergei out now. He glanced at Skosh, saw the seething scowl, and looked away to hide his smile.

Sergei held his mic to the speaker coming from the taps he had on Paul Smith. They listened in on the initial beating Christine was getting, then the first shouted questions, some slaps, grunts, one or two screams—from her interrogator, not from her. But the worst part, for Rimas anyway, was the laughter as they called her names he did not understand. In between the blows.

"It seems another coincidence that they are using that safehouse," said Misha, "but at least she has not blown us."

NINETEEN

It wasn't the first blow that made her decide. It was the first words from the older specimen with a crew cut wearing a football jersey.

"You're not white, but you're not black, either. What are you?"

"Human."

The answering blow was substantial. It cut her lip on a tooth.

"Don't smart mouth me again, squaw, or I'll split the other lip."

She believed him. And now she credited Charlie, too. These were the Nazis, not Charlie and his team. They were just the bastards who had let this happen to her. There was no way Rimas didn't know they were taking her. He had to be obeying an order from Charlie.

"My boyfriend will be looking for me."

She hoped it was true, that it was part of the plan.

"Boyfriend! Who'd fuck a mutt like you?"

Loud laughter from the two goons who had brought her there, then racial epithets and comments about her skin, her face, and private body parts.

"I know, right Paul?" said the greasy-haired one. "He's kissed her a bunch of times. And he's a white guy. Go figure." He handed crew-cut Paul a picture."

We kinda got into the role…

He looked from the photo to her face, studying it. He glanced away quickly to break their brief eye contact like it burned his retina. "Isn't he a little young for you?"

If our ages were reversed, you wouldn't even think it, let alone say it, you son of a bitch.

But this was not the time, and these were not the guys to discuss gender inequalities. She sucked on her bloody lip.

"Somebody's looking for you, bitch," said Paul, "but it ain't your boyfriend."

"Who?" The question escaped her because of genuine curiosity. She did not expect a reply.

"Let's just say it's somebody you met in the park yesterday. He thinks he's gotta do damage control to stop you telling lies about what you think you saw."

"So you're a friend of his?" So much for Frank's concern for her safety. She should have said no.

"You might say that." The man kept engaging and avoiding her stare as if both fascinated and repelled by her eyes.

"I've already given his description to the cops," she said. "He should get as far away as possible, as soon as possible."

"That's not our plan."

"I thought you said you were his friends."

The man nodded, still avoiding eye contact. "As long as he does as he's told. He thinks solving the problem of you will fix the problem he's caused with us. He's wrong."

"Then you're not going to let him kill me?"

"I didn't say that."

How did that early morning walk in a park to let her dog take a piss turn her into a worm on so many different hooks, all of them criminal? She found herself choosing sides in this deadly game and wondered when Charlemagne would rescue her. How they would rescue her.

If they would rescue her.

TWENTY

"Do you plan to retrieve the policewoman?" Misha asked his son.

The two sat in the sedan inside the closed garage of their safehouse. Summer heat, magnified by closed windows, brought out a healthy sweat. Both men were unaffected by minor discomforts. Michael used the car as a private place for the team to meet, guaranteed out of earshot of the babysitters. He paused to consider an answer to Misha's question.

"Papa, you've anticipated the reason I asked you here. I could use your perspective. Rimas is struggling. Sergei is a mess. I can't have two of them unreliable. Ever since that op in the Congo last year, the servants at home tell me Rimas's nightmares are more frequent. To disappoint him about Jade now…"

"You agreed, Michael, before we left for this op. Better a disappointment on this trip than disaster within months. You know your stepmother is right. Jade cannot live with us. Rimas will adjust."

Michael sucked in air through clenched teeth. "I did not let Rimas listen to all of the woman's interrogation. It should not mean anything to him, but he took extra time on that last kiss before letting them take her. He keeps looking at me with moonstruck concern. How does he get attached so easily?"

Misha turned his head away to hide a smile, but Michael saw it in the wing mirror.

"I got over it, Papa."

"Which one? The one you married after nine years or the other?"

Michael ignored the uncomfortable reminder about the crush who had tried to kill him and kept the conversation on his excellent wife. "You often say Theresa is perfect. She has always been…."

"Theresa is Frank's daughter. She is accustomed to men with nightmares, who explode without warning. And you both had time to mature in those years. Rimas is a puppy, like Vasily was in 1971, happy to be petted by any woman—until he learned to fear treachery from the softest quarter. Jade will never understand the likes of us."

"She will have to if Skosh makes his move."

"Skosh has killed, but he is not committed to a specialist life."

"I admit I could use him. He and Steve would be highly effective together on the team."

Misha chuckled. "They speak the same language. Liberal use of the f-word with an occasional noun."

Michael returned the chuckle with a guffaw. "Imagine the two of them at the dinner table with Great Aunt Battle Axe."

They indulged in a laugh until Misha sobered long enough to say, "I have told you repeatedly, do not call her that out loud. You will let it slip at the worst moment."

But the image was too much for both of them, and they gave themselves up to a few seconds of full belly laughs until Michael sighed.

"I have to retrieve the woman, don't I, Papa?"

"You do." Misha laid his head back against the headrest and shifted in his seat to ease the injured hip.

"I'm not concerned about Chatham," said Michael. "He's a dead man the minute they lay eyes on him. They'll do that part of our job for us. But this guy Paul Smith is calling somebody 'boss.' I need that one. He's also using the name Smith. I can't ask Jade and Sergei for a simple computer search; there are too many with that name. Skosh says his government wants the whole network, or at least as much of it as we can find, and especially the money source."

Misha took a deep breath, eyes closed, chin up. Michael took advantage of the silence to solidify the decision that had formed in his mind. It was always easier to decide after speaking the problem aloud, even if no one was listening, and in this case, he had the best listener possible.

"The timing must be perfect. Who should I send, Papa?" He struggled to strip the whine out of his voice. This part of the decision always made him uncomfortable. To play with his own chance of survival was one thing. To weight the odds against others…

Misha's chin came down, and he turned his head to look at his son. "Rimas, of course."

Michael nodded. "But the Smiths must not die. I need them to lead us into the network. Rimas cannot manage it alone, and Steve is coordinating the search for the man they call boss."

"Smith's watchers need not live."

"True. But I cannot leave the management of Sergei to Steve. The word 'fuck' does not soothe him, though he uses plenty of it himself in Russian."

"Then send Rimas. I will run point for him."

Michael dropped his chin, surprised. "But your retirement…."

"Do not tell your stepmother. She gave me a task to do. It is no business of hers how I fulfill it. Rimas will retrieve the dangle. I will run point, and that is the end of it."

TWENTY-ONE

They drove past the Paul Smith safehouse in the babysitters' old beater of a Peugeot, parked it three houses down, and walked back casually. Misha deliberately emphasized his limp. An injured man does not look dangerous.

"You did not bring your cane," said Rimas. He remembered his transmitter was on, grimaced in shame at the mistake, and became silent as they approached the short walkway to the door.

...

Skosh felt used again. Okay, he'd been promised there wouldn't be any action. He appreciated that. What bothered him was the way they treated him. He preferred insults. Not only had the team become comfortable with him, but he also was getting used to it. His relationship with Steve was now a way too cozy camaraderie like it had been when they were both babysitters working for Frank. Back in the day.

Charlie's voice came through his earbud. "Move the signs."

Skosh stepped out with two orange plastic barrels. Moving slowly, he placed them evenly across the beginning of the street. He took his time attaching a cable to each barrel and unfurling a sign reading 'road closed.'

Sergei's voice: "I estimate one minute."

Skosh tried to look busy for that minute, making a meal of unfolding a sandwich board, placing it facing the wrong direction, correcting himself, letting it fall, picking it up, and holding up the detour arrow just as the car approached.

It wasn't the car they were looking for. It was full of young women talking and laughing.

Radio silence reigned. Another car approached. Skosh found something else wrong with the sandwich sign, picked it up, and put it down again. Memorized the license plate before the car turned on the detour. Spoke it quietly into the live mic at his throat. Sergei copied.

...

Paul Smith grimaced at the cold coffee in his cup. Bad enough to play hurry up and wait with the twits the boss had hired for this gig. He had worked with Canadians before and expected better. It didn't surprise him then when they admitted they were from Iowa. Damn. If you want us to act for you, the least you can do is supply the manpower, don't you think? Not a couple of hicks who lust after raping a half-breed and can't stop talking about it. Disgusting.

The boss was on his way and would, no doubt, take matters, and the woman, of course, into his own hands, then let Chatham come get her. Paul would complete the picture with a neat nine-millimeter hole in his head. The boss would be happy. The allies would worry about the objective, and he would wind up having to complete the mission. And not get paid for it.

Effective management was not a Smith strongpoint. Chatham had been a wrong choice from the get-go. Too damaged by action in Bosnia.

Paul sat on the sofa, musing into his cold mug.

These two trolls were Americans, but not Smiths. One watcher—was his name Talon?—sat in a corner on the floor. The other, the one who went by the name White came out of the kitchen where he had ostensibly checked the prisoner, and by God, that better be all he did. There was a sound at the front door, and White walked toward it to open it. Must be the boss. He was running late.

Blood went everywhere. It sprayed. The guy with the knife stepped aside like he knew how to avoid it. Of course he did. Paul had begun to connect dots in the silent chaos in front of him and recognized a pro. He heard the pop-zip and felt, rather than saw, the man in the corner slump over. He looked into the barrel of a suppressed pistol, no bigger than a competition .22. He raised his eyes to meet a pair of dark blues in a young face, implacably set, raising one brow in question.

Involuntarily, Paul glanced at the kitchen door. Knife-man moved toward it, limping.

Dark Blue motioned for him to lie face down on the floor, and he complied with alacrity. He heard movements around him, saw the nicely creased summer wool pant leg of knife guy, and enjoyed relief at having his wrists tied painfully behind his back. It beat a fast bullet to the head—hands down. Then he remembered the boss should be on his way.

Relief vanished.

TWENTY-TWO

Christine bent over the toilet as Jade kindly held her hair back. Only a few ounces of bile hit the water despite the mighty heaving that wracked her. She felt finished, empty, no longer sick, only tired. When she stood and turned to the door, she noticed the bloody footprints she had made, looked down to see blood on her bare feet in ruined sandals, and barfed again. Nothing came though, just a thin dribble down her chin. Jade handed her a towel.

"I'm a cop. I have seen worse," she told Jade. "I've seen car accidents you wouldn't believe. I've seen fights. I don't know why...."

"Because they accumulate," Jade said, filling a glass at the sink and handing it to her. "Just sip it. You need to watch for dehydration but don't push it. These things add up. The first time I saw it, I was so numb; I watched Mack use his knife and really didn't know what was happening, so I could shove it to one side of my brain and not look at it. But every time we're on an op and something happens that I can't avoid, it gives me more understanding and makes me sicker, even when it's not as bad as that first time. Hard to explain."

Christine took a sip and nodded as she swallowed. "When Mack cut the ropes on my wrists, I saw the knife in his hand as he helped me up. There was blood. Only a little, and some on his cuff. Then he took me out the front door, and there was this thing, this pale lump wearing blue jeans and this large pool of it, and I'm not even wearing socks. He made me keep walking. I'm so empty now. I wasn't then."

Jade took a clean washcloth from a stack on the vanity, wet it, and handed it to her. Christine wiped her face and sat down on the toilet seat to clean her feet while Jade washed her sandals in the sink. She told herself over and over again that now the squelching with each step was just water. It helped tame the threat of more dry heaves. When Rimas paused beside Frank at the coffee machine and looked at her, she felt an ounce of relief that this beautiful young man had not been the one with the knife, but it came with a pound of anger, and she headed toward him to share it.

"What the hell did you think you were doing? Why did you let them take me?"

He simply looked straight at her, no expression, a studied, practiced non-expression. It chilled her anger enough to make her find her answer.

"You were ordered," Christine said softly, with a defeated voice. She glanced over at Charlie. He stood next to Sergei, holding one of a set of headphones up against his right ear. Tape reels turned on a machine next to Sergei's computer. He met her glare and returned it with indifference. She shuddered and turned to Frank.

"What …?" She could hardly get it out; the thought was too painful. "What happened to Fluffy?"

Frank grimaced at the clear, sinking tone in her question despite the noise in the room. She wondered if he had been waiting for it and expected terrible news. Probably, they used this guy for things like that. He was too old and fat to be one of them. He'd be an arranger instead of an enforcer, all smooth talking at high speed, with adrenaline. She braced herself for devastation.

"He's in the attic," he said, bulging eyes bloodshot from lack of sleep like all the rest. "He didn't want anything to do with me or Sergei and acted pretty unmanageable about it." There was resentment in his voice.

"I don't hear him." She whispered it as if that would quiet the room enough to amplify any remaining whimpers.

Frank shook his head. "He's been quiet for a couple of hours now."

"What did… did you…?"

He shook his head again. "He bit Sergei, but not me."

Fluffy was never silent.

Paralyzed by the realization that her sanity depended on a ten-pound rat terrier, Christine took in her surroundings in three-dimensional high-contrast reality mode. She heard the noise of voices, heavy footsteps on an old wooden subfloor, the computers, a printer, and a radio squawking random static. The squalor of spilled food and oil-soaked gun patches next to every chair, wet coffee filters filling the sink, and the smell. Everybody stank now. She knew she did. Only Jade didn't. Though she was just as marooned without luggage as Christine, she had a perfume sample in her pocket.

Fluffy could blur a reality illuminated by the blood she had stepped in. He kept her whole every time she remembered her son. Fluffy was there when she opened a letter from the man who had promised before God to love and cherish her for all eternity, a letter full of threats, full of ways he would kill her. It was the need to protect that small furry body looking up at her with a face full of concern that gave her the courage to fight, to file the complaint and follow up, and show up in court to obtain a restraining order. Her ex quickly disobeyed it, of course, and now would never be eligible for parole. In the meantime, ordinary peace, quiet, and Fluffy had saved her life.

Fluffy and her in a one-bedroom, third-floor walk-up at the top of a Victorian farmhouse badly in need of paint. That was home. How could she go back there without him? How could she spend even five more minutes in this place without him?

"I will take you up there."

She heard the voice, its accented low pitch; what was his language again? Did he say Lithuanian? Where, exactly, was that? She looked up. He was so very tall. She had no power to move her feet. He put his hand on her shoulder.

"Come."

He stepped behind her and pushed gently. She turned to look up at him again. He tried again, and her feet began to obey her.

Two narrow flights of stairs ended at that rough plywood door; all around it a musty smell and still no sound, only the activity on the ground floor. Rimas reached the handle from behind her and opened it.

Fluffy launched himself into her arms, wiggled free, and fell to the floor, shrieking with joy, his entire back end wagging the skinny little half-tail at its end. She fell with him, not worried about the drops of happy pee he had sprinkled. He licked her face. She would have held him, but he could not be still or silent. He licked her face again, no doubt to taste the salt in her tears, then ran an obstacle course at top speed, leaping from cot to cot, jumping to catch the dividing curtain with his teeth and hang from it for an instant.

Rimas stood with his back to the door, watching. Christine stood up and faced him, cheeks wet, eyes still brimming. "I thought...."

His brow wrinkled into a vee at the bridge of his nose. "We are not monsters."

She kissed him. He kissed back. She accepted the depth of that kiss, sank into its intimacy, and returned it with every emotion inside her until he was inside her, where she needed him so badly to be. Hasty, maybe, a bit of a fumble here and there, always where the fumbling did the most good. Her nervous system kicked into overdrive. Every touch sent her to the mountain, and she stayed there a long, long time, savoring wave after wave at the pinnacle. A feast granted when she was starved for a simple touch.

...

At first, Fluffy wanted to protect her, but she wouldn't let him. He tried, but there was no room for him on the narrow cot. Then, he was jealous. She belonged to him, and this man was touching her, and she spoke sharply when he tried to make him stop. He found a shoe that smelled like another man, the one who had brought him up here to shut him away from her. It was brown and had laces.

He settled under the cot for a satisfying chew.

TWENTY-THREE

"Do you still think she may be dirty?" said Misha after a long sip of coffee.

Michael set down his headphones on the table next to Sergei and shook his head. "No, we heard all of it. She had opportunities to burn us and plenty of provocation. You saw the bruises. She held her own. For the most part, Lieutenant Barton is who she says she is. She may have a reason we don't yet know to do something stupid, but when Smith's boss rescues him, we can flip on the main speaker and let her hear it."

"I suspect she may be useful in more ways than as a dangle," said Misha. "She knows her way around a firearm, but I still would not give her a weapon. It is strange that Smith's boss has not returned after our detour."

Michael nodded. "But the flies are already in residence," he said, "and having a party."

Misha surveyed the room as it filled and became busier and louder. Frank put a large fan near the door to the garage, where a steep flight of steps descended into an unfinished basement. The door was open. If you stepped near it, you felt the cooler air from below that Frank was trying to circulate, but mostly, the fan just added a hot wind.

"When we were here in 1971, it was winter. We struggled to stay warm."

Michael smiled. "You're still not sure of her, are you?"

Misha answered slowly. "When you see too many coincidences among a great many unknowns, disaster is not far behind."

"You said you thought Gloria was dirty. Was she?"

Misha nodded.

"Then you took her out?"

"No." Misha gazed at his son, his firstborn, the hope of his youth who had turned out better than his father but at the wrong thing. "You know our psychology, how close we are to madness, especially in the moment of peril. Vasily was closer to it than most. He could easily have become like Chatham. He could blow the op. He nearly did. Chatham's team will delete him, but Vasily was my friend from the time I was five years old. I could not."

Michael's jaw gaped, surprised at his father's memory of the man he had loved as a child.

"What did you do, Papa?"

"I did not know what to do at first. It took me time to devise a plan. I needed Vasily to become rational again. I waited for his madness to move him to a place of reality. It was more difficult to control myself, to not interfere. It worked, but only barely."

Michael watched the staircase. Rimas had not yet come down.

Misha calculated the time it should take to retrieve a dog from the third floor and smiled. "I hope when we are home— if we come home," he said, "no one will let slip my role in Christine's rescue. I can explain my reasons to Alex, but would rather not. There was justification. She will say nothing, but her strange notions of fate and responsibility will make her regret she talked me into joining this trip. I do not want her to regret anything."

Especially not me.

"It is a perilous time to fix this problem, Papa, but I agree there seems no other way. And it must be done. At home, Rimas is too comfortable to listen. Theresa saved his eye after the last op, but the wound changed him."

Misha watched Michael pick up the headphones again, remembering the weight his son carried, though he gave no hint of it. Misha knew it well.

Christine came down the stairs carrying the dog. The tie that had bound her hair was gone. It would take extra effort to pass a comb through it, tangled as it was in asymmetrical tufts at the back and over one ear, smashed flat at the other. She didn't smile, but her light brown skin over prominent cheekbones glowed. Even the yellowing bruise beneath one sparkling eye seemed well on the way to healing. Any doubt Misha might have had was removed by Rimas's languid stride behind her as he approached the coffee machine.

Steve punched him lightly in the shoulder. Sergei looked up from the computer and grinned. Misha handed him an empty mug.

Rimas narrowed both eyes in confusion, bringing the edge of his scar into the vee formed on his brow. "How is this different from when I have been with Jade?"

"What do you mean?" Misha poured coffee into his mug, then into Rimas's.

"There is no such reaction by my friends when it is Jade."

"Perhaps because Jade does not smile so compellingly." Misha raised his cup toward Christine. She took a comb from Jade and headed for the bathroom, grinning. Fluffy followed her. "And also," continued Misha, "you are not usually as relaxed."

Rimas glowered. "You are hinting again that Jade is not for me."

"I am not hinting. I am saying it outright. This is proof. Pay attention."

"Christine is not for me, either."

He was implacable, defiant like Vasily.

"Perhaps not, but better a satisfying reality than a shadow fantasy. Vasily constructed a life he did not have, would never have, solely in his mind. As he came out of the hotel room where he bedded Gloria for the first time, we could see his intensity, his excitement. Not joy, not peace. It was more like how he approached placing charges to bring down a well-engineered bridge. I caught a glimpse of her standing behind him in the room, disheveled, troubled."

"That is not how I am with Jade, nor how she is."

"Not exactly, but two things are the same."

Rimas looked at his coffee; the furrow in his brow deepened, shielding his eyes, and waited.

"Like Vasily, you have constructed a lie and required yourself to believe it. Like Gloria, Jade complies. For Gloria, it was a duty. With Jade, a kindness. Neither is what you want."

"You are wrong. She loves me."

"Has she said it?"

After a deep breath, Rimas said with a hint of defiance, "Neither has Christine."

"I am not advising you to refuse what is offered. Only accept such boons without making up myths that will devastate you when shattered." Misha watched Rimas clear a look of momentary open rebellion from his face and continued. "Louis, Vasily, and I were waiting for the elevator when it opened. Darren Smith walked out of it and down the hall to Gloria's door. We knew who he was. His dossier was in Frank's file. It included a photo. He also knew us. Specifically, he knew Vasily."

"How?"

The return of curiosity was a good sign. Misha continued.

"Vasily was as well known in our world as his father had been. A rich target for any specialist wanting to be famous for bringing down a Sobieski. I saw Smith's reaction. It confirmed my suspicion about Gloria. Vasily did not see it—or did not wish to."

"Did she open her door to him?"

"No. Worse. He had a key."

"Then, Vasily must have believed you."

Misha shook his head. "He told himself a lie and saw only reasons to believe it."

"What about the op? Wasn't Smith your target? Wouldn't Vasily be glad to see him go?"

"Then, like now, we needed more. Our commission was for the entire network."

Misha poured more coffee into his cup. Rimas had let his go cold despite the heat of the room. The next question came in the form of an expectant silence, and Misha responded.

"Louis and I had difficulty getting Vasily into the elevator. He was the best fighter I have ever known, but we were more desperate. He was well bruised by the time we arrived on the ground floor."

"And his fantasy?"

"Lived on in his mind and nearly killed us all."

TWENTY-FOUR

Rimas wanted... he wanted... what the hell *did* he want? He watched Jade hit the print key, adding the printer's noise to the room as it surged into action, reams and reams of information they'd have to burn. No, they'd take it with them. If they lived. He wanted her, even with short hair. He would make her grow it long again. Christine was making coffee. What the fuck did she think she was doing wearing a ponytail in her line of work? So easy for criminals to grab her by the hair and....

He wanted Jade. But he wanted Christine again, too. Then again, mostly, he wanted to live.

The gun in his hand fit his long fingers precisely. He looked down at it and saw its history. Always history. From earliest childhood, his family impressed him with an appreciation of the past. The resistance against oppression. Mortal oppression. Deadly resistance. He rummaged in a footlocker for a cleaning kit and set it on the low table.

"I think I've earned the right to help."

Rimas looked up into Christine's dark eyes, the memory of her soft body still fresh. A response grew in his own body, whether responding to memory or anticipation, he could not tell. He glanced at Misha, who stood by the printer, reading from a thick stack of tractor-feed paper. Rimas made an executive decision.

"Sit down." He ejected the magazine and pointed it at an empty chair beside him. She sat. He turned the take-down lever and removed the slide. She unpacked the cleaning materials. They did not speak until he put the last piece on the table.

"I've never seen such a long spring," said Christine. "What is that? It looks like a competition .22 or maybe a .32."

"It's a Modele' 1935. French. It fires a 7.65 French Long."

"It looks old."

"It was made before the war."

"Which war?"

He glowered at her, trying to stop liking her, trying not to let her like him.

"Okay. It's pretty old then," she said. "Is this the weapon that put the hole between that guy's eyes?"

"Why do you ask?" *Nosy.* Jade never pried like that. But then, she didn't have to.

"I'm a cop. I like to know when I discover a murder weapon."

Rimas scowled, not needing the uncomfortable reminder. "You know nothing."

"I surmise. Sometimes I get it right."

"You saw nothing."

"I walked through the crime scene."

"Alive. You walked out alive, yet I hear no gratitude in your words."

She selected a bronze brush and screwed it into the end of a rod. She had picked the right caliber. Rimas could not help but be impressed.

"I would have thought my actions upstairs were a pretty big thank you."

"Your actions were to satisfy your own need. *You* should thank *me.*"

He had to admit, but only to himself, that she was helpful, handing him what he needed as he cleaned each piece.

"You are a special kind of arrogant bastard, aren't you?" She held onto the patch she had been about to hand him. He snatched it from her fingers, grinning.

"You flatter me," he said.

"So where'd you get the gun?"

"Misha—I mean Mack—gave it to me. It belonged to his friend, who was on the team."

"Is that the guy named Vasily he was talking about earlier?"

She handed him another patch. He shook his head as he took it.

"No. Louis. Mi... Mack says I am more taciturn than Louis, more like Vasily in manner, but he gave me Louis's gun. There are legends about him. He was very accurate."

"That's why Mack gave you his gun, then. You are also very accurate. I saw the hole in that forehead. Not even a double tap." She had become still and serious. Rimas was not sure why.

"One was enough," he said. "The weapon is very stable."

She spent a solemn minute watching his face as he worked.

"So why'd you leave the other guy alive?"

Rimas shrugged. What to tell her? "Charlie wants information."

"Funny way to get it, leaving him trussed like a turkey in a room with two dead guys. Skosh over there is having a conniption fit with Charlie. I suspect he disagrees."

"Skosh must arrange clean up with his local contact. He disagrees with the delay."

Christine leaned toward him. "Charlie's waiting for...?"

This time, Rimas knew precisely what to say. Nothing.

"I see. Or rather, I don't, but I know when I'm not supposed to. You guys do understand your trussed turkey's a helluva lot more dangerous than the fool I saw shoot a man in the park, don't you?"

Rimas found the silent treatment remarkably easy to do and repeated it. He figured she wasn't likely to hit him in the eye the way that filthy interrogator did.

She changed the subject. "Speaking of Skosh, I suspect there's some kind of triangle going on here, the way Jade looks at him."

He jerked his head up, chin forward, glanced toward the red-faced Skosh, sought Jade but did not find her, then glared down his nose at Christine.

"She does not look at him."

"You mean it's a surprise to you?" Christine squirted more solvent into the jar lid they were using for dipping patches. "I got the impression everybody was aware of it. Not healthy in a high-pressure environment. You know the old saying."

"What old saying?" Rimas did not move, could not move. He was reviewing a long list of smirks and glances, innuendos, elbows to the rib, quiet guffaws, a few winks, careful distancing, especially by Steve, in particular regarding Jade. Michael had made no effort this time, no arrangement for him and Jade. He was told it was impossible, yet he and Christine had not been impossible.

"What old saying?" he insisted.

Christine raised an eyebrow. "Don't shit where you eat. Of course, Skosh would have the same problem you have, wouldn't he?"

Rimas was silent again, but not by choice. The boiling in his gut showed itself on his face. The scar beside his eye ran a bright white warrior line down his flushed temple.

Christine screwed the lid on the solvent bottle tighter and glanced up at him. "I shouldn't have said anything. Don't tell me you're thinking about doing the whole fairytale fight over a girl thing. I can tell you there's no future in it. Some girls think it's romantic, but I'm here to tell you it's nuts. I speak from experience. My ex is doing life. He killed the love of my life in a fit of rage. Problem was, it wasn't just one life irretrievably damaged. Besides him, and me, and the guy he killed, we had a son."

Rimas noticed Misha watching him. Watching them. Reading the conversation. He breathed and dropped his chin. The woman next to him deftly threaded a patch into a slotted rod. She had remarkably graceful hands. And a heart-shaped face.

"But you are not for me either," he said to her.

"Never said I was. It doesn't mean I can't share what I have with you. A romp in the attic and a piece of advice."

"What advice?"

"A triangle will do more damage than one man with a Modele 1935. In a roomful of men with guns, it will be a catastrophe."

TWENTY-FIVE

"I didn't like the way Rimas stared at you at dinner, Skosh." Jade turned down the static on the radio attached to the center console of an old Ford that had spent too many winters in Quebec. Peeling best described its paint job. They had procured it from Rent-A-Jalopy. It smelled.

Skosh finished his dessert, a toffee chocolate bar, crumpled the wrapper, and threw it over his shoulder to the back seat. He didn't answer right away because he didn't know how to respond, how to tell her he knew a fight was coming on, and he intended to win it.

It occurred to him she might want some agency in this. It was almost the twenty-first century, after all.

"Yeah, I saw it, Jade. It was pretty belligerent. Did… um… did Christine mention…?"

"That she had sex with him upstairs? No. She didn't have to. Does anybody not know about it?"

Headlights in the dusk approached from behind their parked position. She read the plate as it passed. "Bingo," she said into the radio handset.

Skosh cleared his throat. Twice. "Does it…? Are you okay with it?" He held his breath.

"Okay? How? You mean jealous, heartbroken, insulted, devastated? I'm delighted. It's like finding a genuine Burberry trench coat in a thrift store for a buck—which I've done, by the way. I couldn't be happier for them."

They let silence take over for a few minutes. Skosh used the time to wonder if she was using sarcasm. He decided she wasn't. He had to ask it."

"Why?"

She turned to look at him, saying nothing, punctuating it with a sigh.

He plunged. The most foolhardy moment of his life was at hand, and he went with it. The radio would explode with noise very shortly; this was his last opportunity, his only opportunity.

"Marry me."

"Don't go overboard on the romance here, Skosh. Is this an order?"

"Do you need an order?"

"I need more than two words.

"Okay. Please, marry me."

"You think it will work?"

"Frank does."

"Frank is managing my love life now?"

"So is Mack."

"Really? Mack?" The darkness hid her face, but the voice screeched a bit. "You think Mack will stop Rimas from killing you?"

"I can handle Rimas."

And he knew he could. Rimas was good, but Skosh was better, with more weight in his kicks to counter Rimas's agility. He could shoot almost as straight, and now that she said yes by not saying no, he had incentive. He had no doubt he would respond in kind if Rimas cheated by pulling a weapon. The specialists were right. No amount of meditation could erase the change in him from two years ago.

But he would not become one of them. He knew that now, too. The choice was his alone. He was in charge of how he spent his body. He did not have the long list of enemies the team had. Aside from Jade, there was no one in his life a would-be enemy could threaten. And he was perfectly capable of protecting her. His extended family would not interfere. They had disowned him long ago when he refused the marriage they had arranged for him.

The radio squawked. Mack was in their safehouse managing the network. Sergei had gone out with the others. The mic was picking up more than buzzing flies. He switched the audio to network.

Back to work.

```
Where the fuck are you, Paul?
```

A pause. It came over the Smiths' network and into the bugged room where Paul Smith lay bound and gagged in a swarm of flies.

> Maybe we should stay away, boss. The house is dark from this side.
>
> Dark here, too. Over.

Another pause.

> I'm warning you, Paul. No games.

Then

> I hear sounds, boss. Should we go in?
>
> Wait til I get there.

"Yes, do," murmured Skosh.

"That's his license plate," Jade whispered as the car passed them, though their mic was off. They could monitor but not send.

Skosh picked up the car phone and spoke to it urgently. They settled to listen, with nothing more to do as the boss and two other men entered the unlit safehouse to rescue Paul Smith and slap him around for incompetence and bad luck. They heard him beg for water and waited in vain for the sound of a suppressor. The man was being allowed to live after he gave a complete account, including a pretty decent description of Rimas. He blanked on Mack and could only describe the crease in his summer wool trousers.

> I dunno, I dunno. Shit, give me some water. It's been hours. I heard you calling but couldn't reach the radio. Hours. Fuck these flies. Any sign of Chatham?

He's gone deep. No sign of him. I put
out signals, but he hasn't touched
them. So, you're saying it was the
boyfriend?

Yes. Had to be. Fucking shot the guy
in that corner.

Who cut the other guy?

I dunno. I didn't see it. It was so
fast. They were out of here too quick.

I know this mark.

    The last voice was new, male, with no accent, but a hint of the foreign nonetheless. Skosh heard the careful language training in it. Knew who it must be. Of course. Leopards never changed their spots. If the aim was to disrupt, dismember, and destroy a functioning community, that guy had his orders. He'd pass them around to people like the Smiths. Plus, the man said he knew Mack's mark. This was an old enemy.
    Frank called on the car phone. "Yeah, I know, Frank," said Skosh. "Keep the line clear. I need to call my Canadian friend as soon as they leave."

TWENTY-SIX

Chatham stumbled on a root, slammed his ribs against the trunk, a fir, and falling flat, lay still, listening. You never knew when one of them Serbs might be in the brush. He registered the smell of moldering needles and leaves. Last year's autumn feeding this year's green seedlings.

It was the comfort that warned him. Thirst was easy, brooks and puddles plentiful. Hunger came harder, but he recognized a few plants that hadn't killed him last time, and there were lots of slugs. He was careful about the fungi. Some of it was strange, but he avoided that and feasted on what he knew. But the comfort, the urge to close his eyes and settle into the dirt, to dream about home.... That was going to kill him.

He forced himself to stand. So they'd take him prisoner. So what? How bad could that be? Uncle Sam would ask for him back, right? Naw. There was no Uncle Sam for the white man anymore, Slava told him.

He swayed where he stood, left arm up high to hold a low branch for balance, squeezing his eyes tightly shut and then forcing them wide open. Where did that name come from? Slava. Rostislav. In the forest. Memory came in tiny parcels, like those little pepper packets they give you in an MRE to provide the illusion there would be flavor in your meal-ready-to-eat, and you were in control of how much.

He ripped open packet one. Slava was not in this forest.
Packet two. This forest was not in Bosnia.
Packet three. He again had to survive.
A low-frequency rumble caught his ear. He followed it and found transport, then drove it until he saw a sign pointing to a num-

bered road he knew would take him back to Montreal. He added power to the tractor, running it up and over an embankment, jumping out before it hit the water on the other side. He was sorry about that. Shooting the farmer hadn't been a problem, but the tractor was a good one. Even though he was white, the farmer talked that foreign stuff like the nigger in the park. Besides, he needed the guy's lunch pail, especially the sandwich.

Chatham climbed out of the drain and set out to cross a corner of the field. At the numbered road, he stuck out his thumb and trotted to the semi as it pulled over.

…

"Listen," said Yannick. "There's news."

Skosh regarded his counterpart as more than competent, a power-packed short man with quick manners and no time for nonsense, but his refusal to acknowledge Skosh's facility with the French language grated. "I heard your radio, Yannick. A dead farmer and a tractor. I got that much."

"And witnesses, including a truck driver."

"Yeah, I got that, too."

"What you didn't get was the gun he used was the same one that killed the man in the park."

Skosh scowled. They stood across from the blood on the living room floor of the other side of the duplex, watching the mop-up. Paul Smith and his boss had taken the radios. Yannick's clean-up crew had taken the bodies.

"So he's back in the city. Nice to know he's been away."

Yannick nodded, his smile sardonic. "The semi driver said he kept talking about a boss. He had to find this boss and tell him something. Stuff like that. The hitchhiker sounded scared and not too coherent, he said. The farmer was Quebecois. The driver is Anglophone. Maybe that's why he's alive. I told him not to pick up hitchhikers anymore for his safety."

…

Paul Smith ditched the pants he had peed himself in. The boss's safehouse in an economical hotel was not fancy unless, like Paul, you considered a working shower a luxury. His greying hair still damp and his clothes wrinkled but clean, he closed his suitcase and walked into the suite's living area to appear for sentencing.

The boss sat on a hard kitchen chair, facing the weird guy, who was comfortable in an upholstered armchair. Weird, Paul decided, because he was too calm, too quiet, and coming out of nowhere. Add the deference he received from the boss and the recipe called for caution. Paul was cautious.

"Paul, this is Rusty," said the boss.

He did not introduce Paul to the weird guy. That meant he had already briefed his life story to the man. Caution became more imperative.

"Hello." Paul kept his face under control and forced his muscles to relax.

"Rusty brings news." The boss's attempt at sounding optimistic produced the opposite effect. "Chatham is back in the city. He's looking for me. We believe if he thinks you're me and he finds you, then that'll kill two birds with one stone."

Which two birds?

"He's a lunatic, Boss, but way out of my league skill-wise. He'll shoot first. Somebody else will have to bag your second bird."

Both boss and stranger nodded slightly, impressed at Paul's grasp of how dispensable they saw him.

"Tell him Slava sent you," said Rusty. "He will pause to ask a question. Use it."

TWENTY-SEVEN

She would marry Skosh. Knowing it, just feeling the conviction, the understanding that Mack had ordained it, brought a different color to sunlight, a softness to shadow. It changed the nature of every task, every view, and all smells. Especially the smells.

Jade knew she had to give credit for better smells to the move back to their less crowded safehouse, but because it happened at nearly the same time as Skosh's proposal, it added to her new Elysium. She floated.

Then Mack walked into the kitchen.

They had a strange rapport, an uneasy way of relating to each other, like an uncle and niece in a fractured family. She was sure he considered her frivolous. She thought—no, she knew—him to be a violent man who filled the space around him with an almost palpable atmosphere of menace. She could not be easy around him but was somehow glad to see him. It had been two years.

"Coffee?" Jade surprised herself with her newfound ability to act normal in a situation that was anything but.

Only the barest lift of his chin indicated yes. She poured and placed the mug before him at the table as he took a seat.

Uncharacteristically, he spoke early. As she recalled, he usually waited until everyone around him was suitably uncomfortable.

"So you will marry Skosh," was his conversational opener.

"How did you know? Did you guys put a touch on that old beater of a car we were in?"

"You are calm and happy. There can be only one cause."

"It could be Rimas." She brought her mug to the table and sat across from him—like you could have a cozy domestic chat with this guy.

"Ah, yes. Rimas. You have yet to tell him. He may not take it well."

Jade swallowed coffee with a half choke. "How is the op going?" She wanted a change of subject.

He shrugged. "The target belongs to Charlie. My purpose here is not the same but is going well. Both plans, as always, may end in disaster, but we know much more now."

"So Christine's black eye was a big help?"

She tried an innocent tone, but he wasn't buying it. He raised his chin with a half smile and a glare.

"Yes. A huge help. We know who is using the Smiths, who leads them, and from what safehouse."

His use of the word 'using' meant they had traced at least one player to an intersection with another intelligence operation. Probably Russian, she thought offhand with a touch of pride in her newfound grasp of the game.

"How did you find the safehouse?"

"Paul Smith wears a scrap of tape on one shoe. I put it there when Rimas tied him. It will soon fall off and be discarded as trash, but the micro transponder it carries has already done its job. Sergei devised it. They unwisely chose a popular hotel of suites downtown."

"Why is it unwise?"

"It makes it simple to place a touch."

"But you don't like it. Why?" She wasn't sure why she knew. The man never seemed to change expression or tone. Maybe it was his easy acquiescence to her change of subject. He must want to talk about the op, she decided, even though it belonged to Charlie. *It bothers him.*

He did not exactly sigh. It was more of a puffy exhale but close enough. That and the extra time he took to speak again showed her the level of his concern.

"There are too many coincidences," he said slowly. "And too much is unknown. It increases pressure on the team."

"Surely the coincidence of Christine being here is a bit of serendipity, isn't it? It can work both ways."

"Yes." Another Mack-style sigh. "Her presence has been helpful. And it is always the case that no matter how carefully we plan, the situation will be fluid. In 1971, it felt the same. We barely survived it. Coincidence can be a trap contrived by an enemy. And now there is Yandarbin. Again."

"Who?"

"Anzor Yandarbin—an old enemy and capable of setting just such a trap. He will exploit any weakness. Back then, he worked mainly with the left. Our contract did not require us to gather intelligence on our quarry, only take them out. I had assumed the Smiths were also Marxists. It seems Yandarbin was not a slave to ideology even then."

"That's quite a shift. You know this guy?"

"In the killing game, there is very little space between left and right. Yes, I have met Yandarbin. He was KGB then."

Was that a wince? She caught herself worrying about him, told herself to stop it, and set aside the emotion to sort out later.

Frank came yawning through the kitchen door from the stairs yawning and headed for the coffee. "Did I hear you talking about old Rusty?" he asked as he grabbed a clean-ish mug and poured.

Mack nodded and explained to Jade, "Yandarbin uses Rostislav Tobrin as his game name; some call him Rusty or, sometimes, Slava."

Frank rubbed his prominent eyes under the yellow glare of a bare bulb hanging over the kitchen table and yawned again. "This is his op then," he said, "which means he knows we're here."

Jade studied Mack's face as the pieces fell into place for her. She liked Christine and hoped like hell she was not caught up with this new guy because if she was Yandarbin's tool, the solution would fall to Mack, and for the first time ever, Jade could read his expression. He didn't want to.

TWENTY-EIGHT

Paul Smith took a bite of the pastry before him, surveying the coffee shop, watching the door, and contemplating his next move. What move? He wondered. There were none left. The man he sought had killed in a public place on a busy street fully lit by the morning sun. Skulking in the corner of a dark coffee shop would not deter him. Paul waited for death to walk through the glass door at the front.

The coffee was gone, and still, death had not come. He would have to coax it.

A motel at the edge of town gave him a room at the back, away from the street, facing a wooded area. Chatham preferred wooded areas, shady approaches, and dark corners. Paul took the key from the counter and walked to his new, un-safehouse. He knew better than to think of it in any other way. Chatham would find him. He made sure of it by visiting the two nearest dead drops by day, never looking around, inviting a tail.

The mile walk from the drops to this dive helped Paul compose himself. He had long considered himself a dead man, accepting the ultimate consequence of his decision to serve the Lord in this way. The boss's offer of martyrdom should be grasped with glee, embraced as a boon, a guarantee of his membership in the elect. What was it then that niggled?

He pushed away the image of her face. He shouldn't even think of 'her,' only 'it.' It, then. A serpent's seedling with high cheekbones, dark hair, and a swollen lip. So inhuman, he reminded himself, that she did nothing when he hit her. It. Damn it.

It was that face, with those deep brown eyes, feigning intelligence, regarding him with understanding. That was it. A thing, a non-human, should not look through him. She never cried, spoke little, sounded intelligent. She regarded her enemy as being beneath her notice. He had seen it in her eyes.

For six hours, he had lain trussed like a steer at a rodeo, crying, shouting, suffering, and covered with flies. He peed himself. In all that time, the face peering at him from behind his lids each time he closed his eyes was not that of his blue-eyed savior on the wall calendar in his kitchen. No, not the Lord bringing vindication, but a calm, knowing gaze in a face that accused. It was the eyes—and the mind behind them. But she could not have a soul. *Could she?*

Morning rain dripped its last contribution to the day's summer heat, steaming the night's cooler air just enough to make it fresh. Sunlight broke through a hole in the clouds, pretty, hopeful, but the old motel before him allowed no touch of relief. He returned to despair and let himself into the secluded room at the back.

"Who the hell are you?" Paul discarded a brief notion of running. He recognized, of all things, the crease in those grey summer wool trousers and the Italian shoes, the last moving things before six hours in hell. The man sat in one of the stiff chairs on the other side of a small table—the one facing the door. Casually still, but ready to move.

"Call me Mack," he said.

"What the fuck do you want?"

"Information."

"Yeah, don't we all? What makes you think I'll give you any?"

Mack pointed to the other chair. "Sit down."

His back to the door, Paul accepted death a second time that day. This particular martyrdom was not going well. He understood nothing, trusted no one, and suspected it was all a bit pointless. He waited for the question before deciding whether to answer it, anticipating only the bullet that would follow, whether he answered or not.

Mack gave a minimal nod of approval as Paul placed his hands on the table. "Tell me about the woman," he said.

How did he know? Of all the plotting and danger and animosity Paul faced, how did this man know it was the woman that bothered him most? He tried to stop his face from betraying surprise—tried and failed.

Mack rewarded him with a half smile. "You once knew the woman who called herself Gloria Smith. She died in this city in 1971. Tell me about her."

Relief flooded through him. Paul did not bother to hide it, letting his memory spill out in words. "Her real name was Gloria Sessions. She had to keep the same first name when she went out to do God's work because she would always react to it. She was a little older than me, the daughter of a friend of my dad's. A real stunner. I was old enough to see that. Long blonde hair, grey eyes, a body any man would dream of. She wore hip-hugger bell-bottom jeans and no bra. I adored her. Most of us did."

"What happened to her?"

Paul shrugged. "She met a guy."

"In Montreal?"

"Yes, here in Montreal, too, but I'm talking about Stan back home in Colorado. He was a warrior for the Lord. We kids looked up to him. He was a great speaker, and we thought he was our champion. Gloria caught his eye. He took her under his wing, so to speak, and probably to his bed. She was maybe fifteen—sixteen? Nobody talked about that, but I don't see why he wouldn't have. He was quite a bit older than her, and I don't think her dad approved, but there was nothing he could do about it because she'd been tapped to do God's work."

"God's work?"

Paul nodded, warming to the subject, letting it strengthen his resolve. "To cleanse the planet of the serpent's seed, the descendants of Cain. Stan trained her to be a warrior."

"And he took her to Montreal?"

"Yeah. She'd do anything for him. The rest, I don't know. I was just a kid listening to the church elders talk while drinking brewskis out on the deck." Paul cradled his forehead in his hands, elbows on the table. He remembered those winter nights, all the men in their compound bundled against the cold, their breaths clouding the air. He hadn't understood it then, only caught part of the meaning now with the hindsight of adulthood. He picked up his head and met Mack's eyes.

"There was a name. And I heard it again recently. A funny name out of the history books. Charlemagne."

Mack only raised an eyebrow. Paul went on.

"And another name. It must have been her mission. Some guy named Vasily Sobieski. I'll never forget that. I heard it a lot that night. She was doing great and had him in the crosshairs, but something happened, and she came back to be buried. She was twenty years old." Paul let his glare convey a challenge, but he was careful to moderate it, trying to hold back martyrdom for a little while. "Did you kill her?"

Mack did not return glare for glare. "No." His expression softened with a momentary glance downward that returned to meet Paul's eyes. "Now, tell me about the other woman. What did you find in her pocket?"

Shit.

TWENTY-NINE

"You let him live?" Michael nearly choked on his sandwich, a bland concoction of lunchmeat and mayonnaise packed with protein and devoid of flavor. He made a mental note to tell Jade what he thought of the catering.

"You are surprised?" Misha curled a lip as he contemplated the stringy roast beef and stale bread he held in his hand. The dim light in the garage mercifully camouflaged the appearance of what they ate out of necessity.

"Of course, I am surprised. I have never known you to spare a cartridge on an enemy whose return round could doom the mission. Why, Papa?"

Michael took another bite of the sandwich, mashing it and not tasting it, concentrating instead on the other discomforts for a moment, the heat, fatigue, and worry, to get his mind off what his father had uncharacteristically done. Sweat poured into his right eye as he turned to glare at the man sitting in the car's passenger seat. This was the second time ever that he openly defied his father. The first had been his decision fifteen years before to join the team he now led.

Misha picked up the second half of his sandwich, looked at it in the dim garage light, and put it back in its wrapper. "Paul Smith may be more useful to you alive."

"How so?"

"Either he or Chatham will be eliminated, one by the other, without any agency on our part. If Chatham lives, he will be too disintegrated to be effective. If Paul survives, he may be turned."

"You think so?" Michael rested his chin on his knuckles, holding the top of the steering wheel. He saw his father nod out of the corner of his eye. "Why?"

"There is a tear in the fabric of his ideology."

"The ideology that killed my grandparents?"

Misha nodded. "I brought it into our discussion. He told me I was so obviously 'Aryan' I must be a race traitor and began explaining my eternal salvation and why the species must be cleansed of the contamination of Cain. It was all I could do to not shoot him immediately."

Michael looked at his father. There was no sign of emotion on his face or in his voice, but from long experience, he knew the words Misha had heard must have sparked a tempest of grief and anger. Michael envied his control. He waited, not needing to prompt.

Misha stared ahead through the windshield into the past. "I told him even I, an old assassin, do not believe the human species can be improved by wholesale murder. I asked why my brother, who was equally Aryan, had to be cleansed from the planet at the age of six. It must have been a mistake, he said. Only the soulless seeds of the serpent, those who are not white Europeans, particular races, he emphasized, who are not human, will be eliminated." Misha paused and turned to look at his son. "I reminded him that he has been nominated for elimination by his leadership."

"How did he react?"

"He stuttered and then fell back on the honor of martyrdom. What if, I asked, once his so-called martyrdom is accomplished, it turns out he is wrong and he is only an executed murderer of the innocent? He will be as dead as his victims. Perhaps they will be the elect and he, the damned."

Michael reluctantly took the last bite of his sandwich. His body needed protein for what was coming. He would be discussing this with Jade. He swallowed and met Misha's eyes.

"Did you tell him about Rusty? He has now met the man. Does he understand what he is?"

"That his salvation ideology is being used by a foreign intelligence service to disrupt his country? No. I did not have the opportunity. He changed the subject, pouring out his thoughts as if I were a confessor priest. He wanted only to talk about the woman."

"Which woman? The policewoman?"

Misha nodded. "I asked what he found in her pocket, and it sparked a long, emotional diatribe. He was in no condition to notice that we could only know he found something if we had been listening. By the way, have you taken up this mistake with Frank?"

"I did."

"What was his excuse?"

"He apologized and said he checked thoroughly for weapons but did not realize the little card in her pocket could be significant. Technology has left him behind. Then he thanked me for shoving him against a wall. Said it was like old times."

Misha smiled and shook his head. Michael continued.

"We have checked everything now, all her pockets and her shoes, and Sergei has been monitoring for outgoing signals all along, so barring new technology we are unfamiliar with, there has been no breach. I think if there were, we would have picked up on it by listening to them with our touch on their safehouse, as we did this lapse. I only wished they had said what, exactly, they found. What did Paul Smith tell you?"

"It was a ticket to Alcoa's speech." Misha pulled it from a pocket and handed it to his son.

Michael studied it, taking a moment to organize his thoughts, saying only, "That is concerning."

"Indeed."

"But she is not one of theirs?"

"She is not. She may be working for someone else, but he confirmed she is not working for the Smiths."

"How did he confirm that?"

"In his long, jumbled diatribe, I understood she is at the heart of his ideological disintegration. He questions everything because he cannot stop thinking about her."

Michael pushed his chin forward and raised his brows, allowing surprise to show itself. "How? What did he say? What were his words?"

Misha repeated the English words Paul Smith had used, the words that saved his life, at least for the moment.

"She has a soul."

THIRTY

Rimas was late for lunch. Michael had let him sleep for five hours. Why? The tub of food on the counter held a half dozen sandwiches, skimpy beef or fatty ham, thin mayo or rancid butter, wilted lettuce, or old tomato. He curled his lip and selected one of each. He needed food. The bags of pretzels were the only saving grace of this meal. He needed salt as well.

He surveyed the room as he wrestled with gristle on stale bread. The babysitters had not yet come from the other house. The team would meet privately first. When Skosh and the others did arrive, Rimas would let Jade know what he thought of this lunch.

Misha, Michael, and Sergei stood together near the secure satellite phone. Steve sat in one of the uncomfortable chairs not far from them, a half-eaten portion of the sandwich in his hand. He was not chewing. He watched the three at the phone.

The room was too quiet. Only Sergei's face betrayed his emotion. Something was wrong, no doubt with Mara, and no doubt seriously—as in, deadly serious.

Rimas checked his watch. They had less than twenty-four hours to eliminate the targets, and they still did not know how many guns the Smiths planned to deploy at that speech. The wild card, Chatham, was still loose, outside the control even of the enemy. What a goat rope. He wondered about the expression, another of Steve's Texas idioms. He caught Steve's eye, raised one eyebrow as a question, and Steve left his chair to join him near the coffee machine.

"She's in labor," he said. "Seven weeks early."

Rimas wondered if any of the others felt the same combination of fear for what may become the loss of Mara and anger at her for choosing such an impossible course of action as to have a baby against medical advice. He moved one shoulder in an awkward half-shrug to hide his despair. "It is, as you say, a real goat rope."

Steve turned up one corner of his lips in a corresponding half-smile. "I'd say we've graduated to full-on cluster fuck, partner." He dropped the smile and continued before Rimas could pin down the definition. "You remember we heard Paul Smith find something in the cop's pocket but he didn't say what it was? We knew it wasn't a weapon; Frank is thorough."

Rimas nodded.

"Well, Misha asked the guy. It was a ticket. To the speech tomorrow."

Rimas inspected the ceiling then met Steve's gaze again. "She has been in the meetings. She knows our objective and said nothing."

"Precisely. Also, more news. Misha let Paul Smith live."

Rimas assured himself he hadn't formed a fantasy about Christine, but he liked her. Now, Paul Smith was an enemy still walking the planet after meeting with Misha. In ten minutes, small pieces of his world had tumbled around him, chunks of crumbling mortar raining down in warning that soon the bricks would follow. Jade's sudden failure at providing an edible lunch grew in consequence, not because it was important, but because it was another wrong thing.

Misha approached, limping and looking… old—a remarkable achievement for a specialist. Though his body retained most of its power, it was Misha's mind that mattered most to the team now, and, Rimas realized, especially to him. He needed strong mortar to shore up the bricks.

"Tell me more about Gloria," he said as he handed Misha a mug of hot coffee. He poured another for Steve.

"Gloria?" said Steve. "Who the hell is Gloria?"

"I have been telling Rimas about the operation here in winter 1971," said Misha.

"Oh, that. From the sound of it, that was also a real cluster fuck. I remember Louis talking about it. Everybody had a different agenda."

Misha nodded. "Rusty was here; Montreal remains his primary posting even today. His English is perfect, and he can pronounce the Canadian 'ou' sound, so he often passes as an Anglophone. He was then KGB, young but moving up. We discovered later that it was his idea to use the fascist Smiths to kill a Marxist nationalist who betrayed the FLQ extremists. At the time, only Frank suspected he was not a native English speaker. We could not hear it, but Frank insisted. It was the one element that helped us find the other threat besides Gloria and her lover."

"Lover?" Rimas arrested his mug before it reached his lips. "Darren was her lover?" He considered this. "Of course, the key to the hotel room."

"And the key to her behavior," said Misha. "On our second morning, the day after Vasily succeeded with her and we pulled him into the elevator, he went back to the coffee shop where they met. I made Frank go with him."

Misha set his empty mug on the counter and leaned more heavily on his cane. The move was subtle, the sole indicator of pain Rimas could see. "Frank never liked to be too close to Vasily. I don't know why. Without coercion, he did very little I required during the early days."

Rimas was acquainted with Misha's persuasive style. It explained Frank's persistent nervousness in his presence.

Misha continued. "Frank and Vasily entered the shop and found her there with two men. She introduced her lover as her brother, Darren, and the other man as his Canadian friend, Rusty.

"They had coffee and a pastry, and Frank heard the false note in Rusty's accent. He became more nervous than usual, Vasily told me later, which I thought must be something to see. Frank was jumpy most of the time back then, but perhaps it was an impression made by his prominent eyes. He pulled Vasily from the shop by his sleeve. One cannot say Frank lacks courage.

"Louis and I waited not far away, and Frank gave his opinion of this new man, Rusty, while still walking up to us. He is probably Francophone, argued Vasily. No, said Frank. He misused English articles twice. The French are all about articles, *le, la, les*; these are second nature to them. Rusty's first language doesn't use articles. It could be a Slavic language."

Misha looked significantly at his mug. Rimas took the hint, filled the cup, and waited. He shifted his weight again and went on with a sigh. Another dislodging brick in Rimas's world. Misha was definitely in pain.

"For a second time, we wrestled Vasily to stop him from strangling Frank." Misha smiled at the memory. "When our surveillance followed Rusty into the Soviet consulate, Vasily had to admit his precious Gloria was compromised, but he insisted she could not know it, was innocent, misled by her brother. The discovery put us on guard against our customary enemy but did not yet destroy Vasily's illusion about Gloria."

"Sergei says Rusty typically employs two back-ups," said Steve. "He's one of the few colleagues Sergei never cuckolded, probably because he was older and always in Canada. He heard about him in training."

Rimas recognized a significant puzzle piece falling into its place. "Then, do we have three against us?" That would be easy. Steve alone could take on three.

"Yes, said Misha, "but we know only two."

"But there is Chatham and Paul Smith and the man they call boss."

"Skosh and Jade are trying to identify this boss, but he is not the third specialist. He represents the American money behind the Smiths." Misha leaned lightly against the counter. Before Rimas could ask the obvious question, he answered it. "Skosh wants the funder; we want the killer."

"Similar to the time of Gloria and Vasily?"

Misha nodded minimally. "There are too many goals in too many factions, all of them armed."

Steve raised his mug to Rimas in a mock toast. "The very definition of a cluster fuck."

THIRTY-ONE

Fluffy made a racket, so Christine picked him up to quiet him. He always knew when change was imminent. Change made him nervous. Frank grumbled as he tried to tie a brown shoe with half a lace and a chewed eyelet. Skosh checked his H&K nine-millimeter before putting it in its holster. He picked up a handheld radio. Jade took a stack of papers from the printer and stowed them in a zippered pouch.

Christine edged backward toward the hall door of their safehouse, regretting the significant glance from Skosh that Fluffy's hysteria had called up. She had hoped to be forgotten. No such luck.

"You can let him do his business on our way over there," said Skosh.

"I will be okay here. It's secure enough and I don't mind the risk. I will keep an eye on things for you." *And use the phone, even though it's likely to be monitored.*

"No, my dear," said Frank. "You'll be wanted at this meeting."

"But I don't have any business attending your meetings, and I'd rather not know too much." *And I have people to contact.*

Frank gave up the struggle to make a bow and resorted to a knot to close his left shoe. "I agree it can be unhealthy, but Charlie particularly asked for you. He's not a man whose wishes we can ignore. Especially now. The speech is tomorrow. Even Yannick will be present via Skosh's radio."

There it was. Charlie knew. Of course, he did. Christine reviewed the past two days, searching for the threads he must have followed. No doubt Jade or Sergei or both had found every computer file in existence with her name in it. They must know about her ex, about his sentence. Not many knew the rest, but Charlie was capable of too much thinking.

He stood by the computer with Sergei as she came through the back door of the team's house. Christine felt his attention, one hundred percent of it on her, and tried to veer toward the coffee machine on the counter. Maybe he would forget, decide it wasn't necessary, ignore her.

The first thing she thought of, strangely enough, when he flipped the thin piece of cardboard between long fingers as he walked up to her, was how his hands resembled her son's.

"Do you play piano?" she blurted.

It arrested him. Why? Definitely a minimal hesitation in that still, controlled countenance of animosity.

"Let's talk about you," he said. "I'd like to go over your itinerary in Montreal. In detail."

"You mean my incarceration by you since day one? Or the beating I got when you abandoned me to the other set of criminals? What itinerary? I got here. I took the dog for a walk and witnessed a murder. Frank met me, said I was in danger, and took me to what I thought was his house. The rest, you know."

Shit. Belligerence? Really? I have to try it on with this guy? Where did that come from?

Now, everyone's attention focused on her. She heard a sudden quiet and felt the general tension in the air around her, especially those behind her, the babysitters and Jade. In front of her, she saw Steve Donovan's sardonic smile, Sergei's lip curled in a snarl. Rimas and Mack stood strategically positioned, with separation and sight lines preserved. Everybody looked as seedy as she felt despite the welcome change of clothes her suitcase had provided. Charlie's sleeves were rolled up, shirt collar open, shoulder holster gleaming, and weapon—a Glock—looking fully operational.

His slow smile made her swallow hard. The smile broadened, and she felt the blush rising in her cheeks. He raised his hand, holding up the ticket in those long fingers, giving her eyes an unwelcome focus point while her mind scrambled for a toe-hold on plausibility.

"It says 'Elder' under seating. Are you an elder?"

Stall for time to think. Come on, think.

"Where...?" She swallowed again. "How did you get that?" Memory blurred. She was sure it had been in her pocket. She remembered hands reaching into her clothes before and during that beating."

Shit. They're all in league. I'm dead. Alcoa has no chance. What were we thinking? The warriors were right. We cannot depend on the word of the White man for our safety.

...

Michael watched her think. Her face betrayed everything, pathetically easy to read. Every glance told him she knew her danger, and the blushes proved she was conscious of her mistakes, which were many. Point one in her favor.

But if she's not in the game, how the hell does she know about my music?

Point one against her. Even odds, so far. Maybe not—the music question was worth a thousand points against. She must have access to detailed intelligence. Police files do not provide this level of precision, do they?

The ticket, the lying, the coincidences. Points two to four against.

The dog. *Is he a point for or against?*

Fluffy strained in her arms, baring his teeth, riveted on Michael.

He decided the dog was a weapon, his weapon, and he would use it.

...

Christine's brain was unhelpful in coming up with an answer, but it excelled in observing, recording, and interpreting the next moment, rejecting telepathy as an explanation for the sudden move, but it was pretty damn close.

All Charlie did was point his chin in Steve's direction and crook an index finger in hers. No, not hers. Fluffy's. The dog managed a strangled yelp as Steve took him from her, clamped his muzzle shut, and locked his straining body into immobility until only his eyes could express his terror.

"He is innocent! Please! Don't!" She got no further than half a step before her arms were pinned behind her. When had Sergei moved? He was by the computer at the time of the yelp; she could swear it.

"Now," said Charlie, the voice low and smooth, his creepy stillness reaching new levels of malice. He raised the ticket again in those long fingers and manipulated it between them. To prove dexterity? "*You* are not innocent, are you? We will determine what you are before Fluffy dies of—shall we say—fright. I will have the truth from you."

Suspicion, confusion, desperation, she recognized the smell in the air because she was fully engulfed in it. There was just no safe way to explain, she thought, until she remembered the Mexican Mafia guy. They had him cold, but he had the information they needed. The DA cut a deal. For a reduction in the charge, he'd answer any questions with the truth. Every answer was brief and, indeed, true. They stopped the vehicle, found the compartment, and hauled in a high street-value load. Later, they learned five more truckloads made it through that night. They had never asked the man one key question: how many? He did three years of what should have been a twenty-year sentence.

The memory took no longer than Fluffy's yelp. Worth a try, learning from criminals. "Ask," she said. "I will answer. Truthfully."

Just not fully.

"So, is it to be a game of twenty questions, Christine? I am not playing. We have only hours. I must know what you are and why you are here. In detail. Begin now." He signaled Sergei, who released her arms but stayed uncomfortably close beside her.

"I came to hear Sydney Alcoa. He is an inspiration to us."

"You are not cooperating." He gave a significant glance in the direction of Steve and made sure she saw it.

"I am on his security team. I need to contact my deputies."

"You have deputies? Then, you lead this team you mention?"

Charlie raised his chin to someone behind her. Skosh stepped forward and scowled at her. "What team? There is no American team involved here other than the tangos."

Skosh might have thought his stern voice of officialdom would shake her. It had the opposite effect. She pushed her shoulders back and picked her head up. "There is a Native American team to coordinate security, and I lead it. I tell you this only because you say we have parallel objectives, and," she spoke through her teeth, "you have my dog."

"An ad hoc committee of volunteers can't do anything the governments—ours and the Canadians'—aren't already providing," growled Skosh, "but at least you're not armed. Stay out of this for your own safety."

Concern for my safety? Really? She closed one eye with a lopsided grimace of scorn. He had the decency to react. He threw his hands up at the absurdity of what he had just said and stepped away from her.

"Besides having to legally cross the border," she said, "I'm well aware of how the government views an armed Indian. We also know how much 'protection' we can depend on from the White man."

She was holding her own, keeping it short but not conceding. She could breathe. They would get out of this, she and Fluffy. There was hope.

Then, it was Mack who said, "Is it your plan to become armed?"

Too close. Hope wobbled. "No," she said, mentally crossing her fingers.

Charlie picked up the thread. "And your associates?"

She had argued against it and been overruled. He was waiting for an answer. It was taking her too long to grasp at one. She chose deflection. "We know we need not pull a trigger to be locked up for life by the White man's justice system." This was the most compelling argument that had won the day, the one she agreed with but argued against, the one that prevailed over her objection.

After four beats of no answer from her, Charlie said, "How many?"

Deflection. Deflection.

"We knew about Chatham. I was tailing him." *Ask me about that.*

"With a conspicuous dog? Really? How many?"

Fluffy whimpered.

"Two." *On my team.*

"Out of how many total on your team?"

"Three."

Mack chimed in again. The man had a dangerous mind. "And how many teams are there, all together?"

Shit.

THIRTY-TWO

When Michael gave them ten minutes to prepare for the meeting, Rimas set a chair next to the sofa where Misha sat sideways, leg stretched forward. Christine was directed to a chair across from him, between Sergei and Steve, where she sat hugging Fluffy, asleep on her lap. Steve asked her if she wanted coffee and she nodded.

Rimas stepped up to the counter after Steve, cutting in front of Skosh, grabbed two cups and brought them, full, back to his chair, handing one to Misha, then took his seat and watched the throng at the counter as he drank.

Two pots were soon empty. Jade started two more. Rimas saw her turn to Skosh, handing him a cup drawn from the bottom of the last pot. There was a fond smile. Too fond. Rimas would call it meaningful. Intimate? He could not see Skosh's face but could read the mutual pause in their body language. This was the first fully dislodged brick, falling from a great height of hopes and fantasies. It hit him in the solar plexus. He took a deep breath and turned to Misha, who was also watching Skosh and Jade—and, at the same time, him.

"Was this what Vasily saw?" Rimas asked in Lithuanian because he knew Misha appreciated the practice.

"*Taip*," said Misha. "He saw it on her face. We all saw it. At the coffee shop."

"Did he believe you then?"

Misha tilted his head a quarter inch, the closest he came to a shrug. "Vasily brooded. We went back to our safehouse and he would not speak—a new level of silence, even for him. We discussed who could be our third target. We knew only Darrell and Gloria, and because Rusty was involved, Louis and I argued there must be another. Vasily insisted there were two we needed to find because Gloria was not one. He left us, angry, saying he needed air.

"We trailed behind him, and once outside, he turned toward Gloria's hotel. We protested. Louis told him he was crazy. I tried to convince him to come back with us to our safehouse. He ducked into an alley and began to run. We ran after, of course, and climbed a high gate into a courtyard behind him, but by the time I landed on the other side, he had disappeared. Louis entered before me and thought he saw Vasily move left into a shadow. There were doors on both sides of the courtyard. All were closed, and there was only the sound of cats fighting behind us.

"Vasily was going to confront Gloria, we were sure, so we returned to the street and were coming off the elevator in her hotel when we heard the shot. Vasily had not bothered to suppress his Makarov."

Rimas considered. "He killed Darren."

"*Taip*. How did you know it was not her?" Misha drained his cup and handed it to him. The pots were full again.

Getting the refill saved Rimas from having to admit out loud that he wanted to kill Skosh. No doubt, Misha would disapprove. Wasn't the point of this story, or one of the points of it, that Vasily almost destroyed the operation? Was this how he did it?

As he poured, his eye rested on Christine, still hugging her dog. How vulnerable can you get? It must be why Michael let her live. Unarmed and emotional over a pet, any game she was playing must be strictly amateur.

There was nothing amateur about her lovemaking. It made him smile. She looked up at that moment and returned it, loosening the grip she had on that poor dog. He forgot about killing Skosh—momentarily.

...

Michael spoke carefully, monitoring Christine's reactions. Point two in her favor: he could read her every thought with ease. He sat across from her and began.

"Christine will now explain to us all why she is in Montreal, who the other members of her security team are, and what new complications we can expect."

She visibly composed herself with three deep breaths, loosening her grip on the dog, holding up her head, and sitting straight in that uncomfortable chair. Christine had made decisions.

"I have decided to accept your help in a limited way but will tell you only what you need to know."

Michael scowled. She damn well better produce what she had promised. He stared pointedly at Fluffy to reimpose that leverage, though if she refused, he figured the dog would live, but she would not. He was fed up with her games.

"Proceed."

She relaxed at this acquiescence and began. "I am head of a team of three. You have been gracious enough to allow me to speak by phone to one of my deputies, John, to assure him again that I am okay after two days of imprisonment here, so you probably already know his full name anyway. The other is Eric.

"Sidney Alcoa is an inspiring speaker. He offers advice, hope, and leadership. Many people in the movement to secure our sovereignty and our rights will be present, primarily elders of the Eastern nations of Canada and the US, as well as a few who will travel from the West and Alaska.

"We know from history that we are not safe in our land. Some nations have begun to take a more organized approach to security, using training and techniques we have gained in the White world. As a police officer, I am naturally part of that movement, as are my deputies. John is a patrol officer in a small town. Eric works for Border Patrol. Both are from New England.

"What you want to know is how many are armed and how they will be deployed to protect this man. You also need to know something else, and I will get to that."

"Sometime soon would be advisable," said Michael. He saw her suppress a shudder. She would hold to the bargain, he decided, founded on mutual distrust the way any would-be alliance should begin.

"I am not armed," said Christine, "but my deputies are, and likewise, another team of three from a northwestern Canadian tribe out of the Yukon." She paused to suppress a smile. "They are all named Smith. An uncle with two nephews. Powerful fighters and armed."

"Smith," said Michael without expression, the irony apparent in the one word.

Christine nodded, her cheeks dimpling as she fought the smile. "The White man gave the family that name in the nineteenth century. It is not an alias for them. Or maybe it is a kind of alias because they have real names in their language, but most people can't pronounce them. So, they are genuine Smiths."

"Why are you the only person not armed?" asked Rimas.

Michael gave him an approving nod. The young fighter became more valuable by the hour. She took a moment to gather her words from where she thought they resided: on the floor, the ceiling, the coffee maker, the computer, and all points in between. Michael's patience, always tenuous, stretched to near breaking while her gaze bounced around the room.

"You know," she said, "or you should know the line between freedom fighter and terrorist is a river of mercury, with all crossings determined by the other side of the argument. I disagree with terrorism, but I value the right to self-defense. My own decision is more practical than philosophical. I like my job. I want to keep it. It is valuable to my people that I have access to the information it gives me.

"I told you we knew about Chatham, though not Paul or the man they call boss. It was you who introduced me to them." She glared at Michael before continuing. "Through my sources, we know about another threat. Four members of a gang of American skinheads have crossed the border, or will cross shortly, with a supply of weapons for a similar gang in Canada. I don't know how many are in that gang or how many will attend the speech. They will be equipped with ten assault rifles and fifteen semi-auto handguns, with high capacity magazines and a large supply of cartridges for all of it."

"How are they crossing the border?" asked Skosh, holding the radio to his ear. The question must have come from Yannick.

"By boat. Up the Richelieu from Lake Champlain. They launched from the New York side. I should say, not by boat, but by yacht. It's very comfortable, well equipped, and flying a Canadian flag."

"Who provided that to a gaggle of skinheads?"

Christine nodded. "I would also very much like to know."

"An important question for the governments, no doubt," said Misha, "but more immediate for us is how do *you* know about this gang?"

As usual, his father had seen the essential point, and Christine's face lost all color, confirming it as Michael raised an eyebrow. She lost more color, accurately reading his imperative in the small gesture. He was impressed.

She sighed. "We have a source in the gang." Confronted with only expectant silence, she went on. "He is a member of the tribe but looks very white. From contacts on that side of his family, he has become connected to several white supremacist groups." She paused again, almost choking on her next words. "He is very valuable to us and is the fifth man on that boat." She looked at each member of Charlemagne in turn. "I ask you to do what you can to preserve him."

It was in the wobble of her lower lip. This was too important to her. The rest of her information, whatever she was withholding, might not be essential to his team, but she had no business deciding that. Michael wanted the whole story, this piece included. Yet, she had come across with most of what they needed, largely in good faith, and if she was bona fide, their separate interests could blend well enough in this instance. His glance flew to Rimas.

Another weapon for extracting information from this woman. This time, she would likely enjoy it.

THIRTY-THREE

Fluffy growled.

"What are you doing here?" Christine asked as she shook off the torpor of a deep, replenishing sleep. "Hush, Fluffy."

"What do you think I am doing?" Rimas slipped his hands into her shorts with unerring accuracy. Her body responded as he reached the zone, but her mind demanded explanation.

"Charlie let you? Skosh let you?"

"Skosh does not dictate my actions."

Irritation marked his voice, and she remembered the triangle. *Fair enough, but that means…*

"So Charlie *sent* you."

His fingers became busier while the other hand cupped her breast. He covered her lips with his own, his tongue meeting hers in mutual exploration. Every nerve along the path of his touch fired a salvo of pleasure. *Not a time for discussion, except…* She broke off the kiss reluctantly.

"Slow down, cowboy. Let's make the most of this."

…

They emerged into the kitchen of an empty safehouse, a rare event on an op, Rimas told her. The coffee was still hot, and as he poured two mugs, he assured her somebody, probably Frank, would be monitoring all the sensors from the other house. He conversed with her, telling her about his brother, a musician in Lithuania. *Where the hell IS that?* She made a mental note to look it up later. If she had a later.

He asked polite, get-acquainted questions, sweetly, like he was interested. She gave him Fluffy's history. He asked about hers. She recited the good parts. He probed gently for the not-so-good, and she couldn't help it. She spilled some.

"Your ex-husband is in prison? For what crime?"

She nodded, swallowing hard. This was too close. "Murder." She croaked it.

He said nothing, only waited. It was not a word she wanted to leave hanging in the air, so she added some more.

"We weren't married anymore. There was... He was abusive and jealous." She took a deep breath. "He killed somebody I cared about."

"Was he also Native American?"

"Who?"

"Your ex-husband."

"No." This line of questioning helped. An oblique detour from the worst pain.

"Do you have children?"

Back to the bullseye.

"I have a son."

She said it without knowing how to put the rest into words. Everybody said Cody was a credit to her, but if Rimas asked how she felt, how would she describe the burden of fear? Her son was, after all, also his father's son.

"Does he look like you?"

It was almost a relief, another detour. "Oh, no, he's almost as blond as Charlie."

It was easy returning to the team's house because somebody—Sergei, according to Rimas—had thoughtfully cut a gap into the chain link fence at the back. They walked into a hushed kind of noise, full of movement and purpose, men dressing in black clothing, with protective vests and unobtrusive communication systems, slides chambering rounds, large capacity magazines loaded, H&K MP5 submachine guns going into hold-alls, Rimas had a murmured tête à tête with Charlie. Nobody else spoke. It was like a frenetic ballet of mimes.

There were tubs of food on the counter—if you could call it that. Something grey and congealed, evidently untouched. Another low-voiced discussion by Charlie, this time with Jade, who nodded quickly, face pale, and ran to the phone.

Rimas changed into the regulation black, slipped his Modelé 1935 into a holster on a web belt, extra magazines in Velcro loops on a black mesh vest over light-weight Kevlar. Now, that was a misnomer, thought Christine. There is no lightweight armor. Only two sizes, heavy and heavier.

An hour later, as Rimas piled into the SUV in the garage with the rest of the team, Mack led her to the Mercedes sedan and held the passenger door for her. "Where are we going?" she asked as he took his seat behind the wheel and pulled away from the safehouse. He didn't answer. Skosh and Jade were in the rusted beater ahead of them. Frank stayed behind in the team's house.

She was glad this time they didn't paint her face, attach her to that strange Russian, and use her to schlep heavy equipment, but having this particular criminal as a silent companion was no better. He made a left turn across Montreal traffic with no hurry, no g-force, and without hitting a pedestrian. At least he was a good driver. But he still didn't answer her as he headed east across the river, out of Montreal.

The silence continued until he turned the car south onto Autoroute 35 when she asked again. This time, he simply pointed to a sign giving the distance to St. Jean sur Richelieu.

"Are you taking me back to Vermont? I need to stay here, you know. My deputies need me to be present at that speech tomorrow. It's essential."

She stopped when he held up one hand, finger pointing to his ear. She noticed for the first time the earbud and wire he wore and answered his glance with a wry smile, wondering what he was hearing. The team, of course. They were somewhere ahead, as were Skosh and Jade. They meant business, for sure, and everyone traveled on empty stomachs with way too much firepower. Only Fluffy had said yes to a plate of whatever the grey stuff was. She rolled her eyes in protest to being kept in the dark, and Mack sighed.

He reached for the mic on his tie and turned it off, then flipped a switch on the main radio on the console. More silence, but with static.

She supposed she should feel flattered that he was letting her listen in. Then she heard a brief sentence in a low voice. In German.

Christine sat in the growing dark, listening to a language she didn't know for another half hour. Mack pulled off the highway and wound through residential neighborhoods as the sun sank into the flat earth to their right. She recognized Skosh's voice, but still speaking German. Experience told her these guys were about to pull a caper. All she could think about was Rimas in danger. That thought connected to Cody and then to despair.

Mack killed the headlights as they left the neighborhood and entered a waste area of broken-down heavy equipment and brush. He pushed that beautiful car through thorn bushes and over ruts until it rested only a foot or two from the gentle bank of a river. She saw the other bank as a dark line under a stars-only sky, unlit by a new moon. She figured it must be the Richelieu River, at a narrow point, maybe 900 feet. She knew because of the information she had given them. *They have additional intelligence they're not sharing with me and our teams. And, oh God—Cody. They are going to hit that boat.*

Skosh droned on, much good it did her, but she heard names. Mack's attention to it was total, and strangely, she felt the others listening through their earbuds from wherever they were on this river. Armed.

A voice interrupted Skosh, probably Charlie. Even the static paused, and in that short silence, Christine felt rather than heard a diesel engine. It grew into sound. She heard Steve's voice. "Secure." Unenlightening, but at least she understood the language.

Mack reached behind her seat and brought something to the front. She recognized a Gen 3 night binocular as he slipped it out of its case. An Omni V, quite new. He adjusted and watched as the dull throb of that engine grew nearer, but never louder, as it idled to the other shore. She saw only a patch of deeper darkness approaching and heard the engine cut before it stopped moving.

Mack turned on his mic and spoke, still in German. It sounded like numbers. He was counting. Charlie's voice came again, was acknowledged, then said something that broke off Mack's concentration and made him turn to her.

"You told Rimas your son is blond. These," he gestured across the river, "have shaved their heads." He handed her the binoculars. "Which one is Cody?"

Her hands shook as he helped her point and focus. She brought herself under control, concentrated, studied. Five green figures carried heavy boxes onto a small jetty. They all looked the same! Christine could eliminate the shortest, and that one was too heavy, with no grace in his movements. She studied the three remaining, all of them about the same height and weight. Nothing, nothing distinguished them. Nothing reminded her of the small tow-headed boy or the fine young man, the light of her life, until one of them pointed to a crate on the boat. It was the way his hand moved, the length of those fingers, glowing green in her vision, and she knew her son.

"He's the one on the jetty, farthest from the boat." *Oh God, let me be right.*

Mack spoke to his mic. As she watched, she saw them fall, saw the heat from the muzzles around them, but heard very little. All was suppressed in a pantomime of death. The one on the jetty, farthest from the boat, remained standing for only a moment until another figure appeared from his right with astonishing speed and bore him down.

"Your name," said a heavily accented voice in English. She recognized Sergei.

"I'm not telling you nothing, mother fucker."

The sound of Cody's voice flooded her with relief—and tears. Mack pressed his mic and made a suggestion in German. She exhaled and lowered her head to clear her vision, then watched again as another figure approached the two on the boards of the jetty, and she heard that slow Texas drawl.

"So tell us, Cody, all about the animal your mother is willing to die for."

The figure pinned under Sergei became still, then replied, "Are you talking about Fluffy?"

THIRTY-FOUR

Euphoria had worn off. Jade still had to break up with Rimas and tell him about the engagement, and at the moment, all she wanted was sleep. And privacy. And Charlie was right, damn him, decent food. She sat at the wheel of the babysitters' car, parked a few feet from the aftermath of mayhem. At least she didn't have to watch somebody she loved being beaten and trussed. At each gasp, she glanced at Christine in the passenger seat.

"Did Mack explain before he dropped you here, Christine? This is just to make it look good in case anybody's watching. Yannick's people are beyond those trees with one of the guys who was taking delivery of all that hardware. The other one's dead. I assure you, Steve and Sergei are pulling their punches."

The darkness inside the car obscured Christine's face, but her breathing was readable. She exhaled. "Does Mack ever tell anybody anything? I wouldn't mind if Cody was blown enough to make those skinheads kick him out. I want him to quit this. It's a boulder sitting on my chest, and I can't shift it."

In the past two years, Jade had begun to understand a few things. First, her more trusted status with Mack. He told her more than he did most people. But besides that, repeated encounters with this team gave her a glimpse into the nature of having enemies. "Christine, Cody can't quit this if he leaves behind a bunch of reasons for people to want him dead. The team is trying to give him a way out. Do you think he'll take it?"

Christine took a full minute to answer. "He is his father's son as well as mine." After another pause, she said, "Except he's not heartless. We have disagreements."

Jade waited a beat or two, then prompted, "About?"

"About the best way to retrieve our rights, for one. And about his future, of course. He is just under half Abenaki—I had a white great-grandparent, and maybe one further back—but you wouldn't know it to look at him. There are so many things he didn't face as a kid. Teachers never discounted him. Nobody ever ignored or sidelined him or—It's hard to explain to somebody who isn't considered... less than."

Sergei hoisted Cody to his feet and frog-marched him to the SUV as it pulled closer to the jetty. Jade pulled the old car onto the road and headed for the bridge to Montreal. "I grew up 'less than' in my family," she said. "Nothing I did was ever good enough. I can't imagine what it would be like to face it everywhere. It would even be hard to just be anonymous."

"Exactly. Cody has an advantage, but he let his father introduce him to these men he met in prison. Political, violent gangsters who hate everybody. So, instead of working on his music, my son decides to use his whiteness to gain information and access to one of the gangs. He is twenty-two. He should be finishing his degree!" Christine stopped, sighed, and in a near whisper said, "And it's so fucking dangerous."

Jade heard the confused mix of emotions in Christine's words and the way she spoke them, sometimes breathless, occasionally choking. She was the mother of a child, after all, worried for but proud of the adult, scared to death of the fate he seemed to be choosing. Jade looked forward to children, Skosh's children. Her only concern until now had been to hurry up and get started.

This conversation brought new questions. She was pretty sure none of the team, whose lives were frankly shit, had a mother still living, but she thought of Sergei's wife, also a vital member of the team, instead risking her life to give birth to a son. She knew she would do the same. But all these guys were white, and presumably, if they wore the right clothes and behaved themselves in a certain way, they blended, became invisible, at least in most parts of the world they inhabited. Skosh's child might not. Were people really that narrow? She remembered hearing the Smiths on Sergei's tapes talking to and about Christine and the disgusting language they used.

"Of all the hazards a child faces growing up, I can't imagine that one, Christine. I'm sorry."

"I think every parent wants their children to do better than they did," said Christine. She brought her hands up before her face, fingers spread wide, shaking. "But Cody is so talented! He doesn't have all these barriers, and he chooses this?"

Layer after layer of realization struck Jade as she turned the wheel and accelerated onto the bridge. She had read all of The Section's files on Charlemagne, which weren't many because of their policy of breaking into her system to erase. Way back in the day, as a youth, Charlie had attended a prestigious European conservatory. How did they manage the security? She wondered. And after all that trouble so he could study, Charlie chose this? What did Mack think about that decision?

...

Mack turned the radio knob, changing it from Jade and Christine back to the network the team was using to dry-clean their way back. Skosh sat in the passenger seat of the sedan, staring ahead, still processing the fact that the bastards had bugged the babysitters' car. *Of course they would. Why not?* Then he turned his attention to the conversation he had heard, glancing at Mack behind the wheel, who stared straight ahead into the gloom, frowning. Skosh mirrored the frown, and they waited in silence for Yannick to come clean up the mess.

THIRTY-FIVE

They sat on the basement floor of the team's safehouse, enjoying its cool temperature. Skosh tried not to think of the eight-legged co-inhabitants lurking outside the glare of fluorescent shop lights hanging from the floor joists above them. He distracted himself from the thought by wondering if Jade would object to their children having Japanese middle names. It might be a sop to the extended family, an amendment to their perpetual disappointment in him.

He studied the face of the prisoner and decided the bruises were not all that bad, considering. The angry snarl was not justified. Mack had taken a high stool over by a work table under the stairs. Sergei stood at the last step down, MP5 casually pointed in the direction of Christine's angry son. He was steady as a rock. Considering the strain of no news since the bad news about Mara, Skosh was impressed. The man had righted himself somehow, or adrenaline had kicked in, and he was now himself, or at least, his operational self. Meaning focused and deadly.

Charlie held court, Steve on his right, Rimas to his left, at the top of a circle surrounding Cody, defined by Mack and Sergei at the bottom. Christine sat across from Skosh, to the left of Rimas, Fluffy in her lap. The cool, dusty floor underneath him made Skosh wish he could sleep down there. But then, there were the spiders. He shook off the image and marveled at Mack next to him. Even without the benefit of the cool floor, the man looked as comfortable as ever. He always did, no matter the ambient temperature or the state of his left hip, injured earlier in the decade. Skosh closed his eyes at that memory.

Charlie got on with it.

"Before we arrange for your escape, Cody, I need information, and you're going to provide it."

"I don't know who the fuck you are, man. You won't get nothing from me." It was a remarkably deep snarl from someone so young.

"Call me Charlie."

It was said with the usual cool, low voice that could still make Skosh miss a breath, only the lips moving with no other facial expression. It wasn't the cold basement that made him shiver. This was his job, Charlie included. He hoped the bald rookie in the center of the circle had the sense to step carefully.

Cody's Mama intervened. "Cody, this man is an ally. Please cooperate." There was an emphasis on please, complete with clenched jaw.

"He's a creep, Ma."

"I know, but there's more going on here."

"Those guys are dead, Ma. Fucking dropped where they stood. All around me. I mean, what the fuck? They were shit, but it's pitch dark, and suddenly, boom. I dunno what happened to the Quebec guys. There were two when we got there."

"Cody, listen to me." Finally, she turned on her mom voice, leaning over her folded legs toward her son. "There is no time to process all of it. You have to answer Charlie's questions. Now. The speech is tomorrow—later today. Everybody is dealing with developments. We are, and these guys are, and like I said, these guys are allies." She slowed to add emphasis. "Not very nice ones. Do you get my drift?"

"I get it that they've taken you in. Grow a spine, Ma."

Skosh wanted to slap the puppy but instead added his own few words with forced patience. "Your mom didn't have a choice, Cody. I'd say she did pretty fucking well in the circumstance, and you being alive is proof."

"I was about to meet a bunch of Canadian skinheads, asshole. Now I'm blown."

Charlie rolled his eyes up and over into a side glance, eyebrow raised, toward Skosh. It was a signal giving him charge of Cody's education. Again, he resisted the urge to use Charlie's usual methods, electing instead to continue with uncharacteristic patience.

"Get this through your thick skull, fuckhead. We've gone to great lengths to make sure you're both alive and not blown. Those two Canadians you're worried about, well, one is permanently not an issue. The other is being held by the Mounties. He'll have some legal troubles and be released to tell his friends that one of the Americans on that boat was beat up pretty bad and taken prisoner.

"For now, you're out of this op. You can't show your face anywhere until after the speech. That's when you'll escape, and if you're not a total pain in the ass, we'll help you cross the border and maybe give you a sandwich to tide you over till you reach civilization." Skosh ended with a grimace at the thought of one of those sandwiches. Justice comes in many guises.

But defiance and anger remained features on Cody's face, contorting his lips in a sneer. "I'll die before I…"

This called for more mother's wisdom, and Christine gratified Skosh, and probably the others, by jumping right in.

She tilted her head toward Sergei by the stairs with the MP5 pointed at her son. "Baby, when that guy had you on the ground, and somebody else asked you who I'm willing to die for, you said Fluffy, but really, the only one I'd die for is you, Cody. What I'm willing to do for Fluffy is go on living. He has no one else. Please accept reality and go on living. For me."

Fluffy lifted his big ears toward the prisoner, bared his teeth, and set up a low growl.

It was the only sound in that basement for almost a minute while Cody watched a tear escape down his mother's cheek. He turned to Charlie.

"What do you want to know?"

THIRTY-SIX

The heat hit them and then climbed higher. Michael wished they could have stayed in the cellar, but there was no telling how many tunnels of sound might be at work in this safehouse. He needed his father's advice and a secure way to get it. They sat in the sedan in the garage, boiling. An observer would think they did not show it, but Michael was sure they both felt it. He knew he did.

"This problem is not entirely the same as it was in 1971," said Misha. He sat on the passenger side with the seat reclined slightly, no doubt to ease his hip.

"How is it the same?" Michael considered this the first question.

"It is the same because we know Yandarbin. It is different because we did not know him then. We learned quickly. He has been consistent through the years, according to the intelligence. We did know at the time that he was using a third asset, but we did not know who."

"Then that is similar, Papa. How did you learn there was a third?"

"From the primary source of all intelligence. Pillow talk. Gloria let it slip the first time she was with Vasily. She said a name."

"I thought he resisted the idea she was in the game."

"He did. But he remembered the conversation when he briefly conceded she might be dirty after she introduced him to Rusty. She had mentioned a man named Antoine. He said she spoke the name with awe, and it bothered him. An important person, she told him. She could not wait to meet him."

"What was the context?"

"That she expected to see him in Montreal."

"Another Smith?"

Misha shook his head. "No. Not one of her group. Vasily was clear about that."

"Then all you had was a given name? Nothing else? We don't even have that. Is that the main difference?" Michael wanted to start the car to use the air conditioner, but carbon monoxide was as deadly as he was.

With another shake of his head, Misha continued. "The difference is that you know more than we did. We knew nothing yet about Rusty besides his employer and only recently had encountered the phenomenon of the sleeper agent. A few weeks before Montreal, we had met our first one. It was another disaster for Vasily. Because of his name, he was much sought after by our enemies at the time."

Michael held the wheel with both hands at the top and lowered his forehead onto his knuckles. It only increased the heat. He took his father's example, sat back, and reclined the seat a little more. It helped. "Are you saying we are looking for a sleeper?"

Misha dropped his chin minimally in a kind of nod. "You know there are no other specialists here. We are hours from the event; the Canadians have good watchers. We have access to all of Jade's files, though she does not know it, and Skosh assures us his counterpart Yannick reports no known operatives in the area. Besides us."

Michael stretched his neck, looking at the ceiling to take in air. "I am aware, Papa, that Cody's band of skinheads and their Quebec friends are beneath Yandarbin's notice. I get that. So now you are saying there is someone already in place, someone close, who has Rusty's remit."

"Precisely. It was the Smiths who deployed their skinhead fellow travelers. Rusty has more finesse. In the weeks before the 1971 op, we were in Florida. Vasily met a girl he liked. She died from a bullet meant for him. The shooter was a sleeper."

"Was the shooter the one you were after? What was the op itself?"

"Frank's people had information the KGB had turned a deep cover mole, not yet activated. His office devised a way to use us to bring him out of the cold. They lied to us about the op and hired us knowing Vasily's famous name would give the enemy an incentive to deploy their sleeper. There were still many in the KGB who remembered Vasily's father. We knew the Americans were lying but took the commission because we needed the intelligence it would get us."

"And the mole acted?"

Misha looked out the side window into the past. "Yes. Vasily's infatuation with American girls was becoming a habit. When this one moved into the line of fire meant for him, Vasily could not save her. He did not speak for days after."

"You would be a high-value target, Papa, and Rusty knows your mark. He knows you are here."

"But initially, he could not know Charlemagne would be engaged for this, nor that I would be here. Everyone is aware I have retired. It is an unheard-of thing and therefore, famous. And here I am, unexpectedly. Rusty does not control Alex. Nobody does, including me. Similarities and coincidences go only so far, remember, but you can make use of them when they occur. As he will."

They sat in sweating silence while Michael reviewed similarities and differences, especially differences. He began with, "The Americans have not set us up this time."

"Correct."

"The purpose of Rusty's second backup is to kill Alcoa if the Smiths fail."

"Which they will."

Misha nodded. "The purpose of Antoine was the same. Vasily's presence was serendipitous for Rusty. A similarity."

Misha again agreed.

"You were seeking two; one was dead thanks to Vasily, and the other was Gloria, and Antoine was only a name. We don't even have that."

"But you have a deep understanding of how sleepers are made, Michael, and where they are placed. Use that." Misha paused, turned his head to look at his son, and gave a quiet order. "Use everything you have."

Michael sat forward, dropping his forehead onto the wheel. Sweat poured down the back of his neck and under the shirt collar.

"If anything happens to you, Papa, Alex will kill me."

"I am ancient history in this business, Michael, far exceeding life expectancy already. And like Mara, I make my own choices. Alex knows it. She also knows every one of us, my new grandson included, if he lives, depends on the team for safety. Charlemagne must not fail. The predators will not hesitate to destroy us."

...

"Who solved it?" asked Michael as he came down the stairs well before dawn, fresh from a two-hour nap. He felt the temperature change on the sixth step.

"Skosh," said Steve, stifling a yawn.

Michael surveyed his domain, his command post, his GHQ. Sergei slept at the computer, head nestled in his arms. The screen played a new saver, black and red monsters with fangs. Sergei was feeling savage.

Better savage than suicidal.

Rimas leaned back under a waterfall picture, his chair propped against the wall on its two back legs. Michael's father had stretched out on the sofa, an arm over his eyes. The coffee machine steamed. Skosh sat near it in Michael's stuffed easy chair but left it fast as he stepped off the staircase.

An air conditioner stuck in the darkened front window provided the only noise—and copious amounts of cool air.

"It took you long enough, Skosh," Michael said as he headed for coffee.

"Wasn't me. Jade bought it. Sergei installed it."

Michael knew he should be gratified. The two unreliables, one in each camp, team and babysitters, had somehow righted themselves. Jade was doing her job again. Sergei had adopted a more grim version of his ultra-competent self.

If he could be sure they were not about to face an entire army of sleepers, or if he could have any idea what Rusty was up to at that moment, Michael would be more confident. The swirl of contradictions and volume of conflicting intelligence pushed him to a decision. He woke his father, briefed him on what he meant to do, and signaled to Steve to change into a suit. They left during this quiet time, everybody in the same room, stealing uncomfortable patches of sleep while technically on watch. His father would pick up the threads if this did not go well.

THIRTY-SEVEN

Paul Smith remembered a name. Strangely enough, it was his own. Damon. They called him Damon when he was a child. His father was Mr. Kowalski. Mack's visit brought it to mind. The young Damon Kowalski became a warrior, a martyr in waiting, as he dropped his handful of dirt onto Gloria's casket when her body came back to Colorado from Montreal, though he didn't even know her—at least not to speak to. From that day, he dedicated himself to destroying the soulless sons of Cain. He joined the Smiths the next year and took the name Paul. Fought the good fight, killing in the name of the Lord, learning to conspire in the catacombs.

It was fucking hot in this motel room. He left the door open to air it out. To speed the attack, he sat facing the door in the dark, propped against the bed pillows, his Luger in his hand under the covers, next to his thigh. *For God's sake, Chatham, you need a fucking engraved invitation?* The night sky over Montreal was light enough to show a silhouette. It was all he would need. He'd blast anything that moved.

At midnight, the heat drove him outside for air. Stumbling through the trees at the edge of the parking lot, he pushed away the intruding dark eyes peering into his mind, the profound humanness in her expression, the challenge of her contempt. Each slap he'd landed on that face raised a bruise on his conscience. Tree branches stung his face as he pushed his way through them in a fruitless circle, counting the bruises, his, hers, and others. All the others. Would they matter in the reckoning? Would they keep him out of the elect like Mack said? He decided he'd rather not die this way, in thrashing ignorance, and broke out of the little wood near his car. He drove it back to the boss's safehouse.

Off the elevator and to the left down a long hallway, he passed a stairwell, then a man heading into the stairwell. Suit and tie. *In this heat?* Biceps, blond hair, the look that made the skin on the back of his neck tingle.

Paul still had a card key to the suite door in his pocket. He approached slowly. The boss was good at giving orders but knew nothing about security. He let himself in without knocking, his Luger in his hand at his side, not sure if he would use it or on whom. The boss was a candidate. To turn the light on, you had to slip the key into a slot beside the door, but he didn't need to. He could see plenty from the street lights below the open window. And he could smell it. He knew that odor well, having spent six hours immobilized next to a large pool of it.

He touched nothing. Kept his shoes out of it. Only checked how many. Two—the boss and somebody he didn't know. One by the window, one in the bathroom. The room had been tossed. The boss's pockets emptied.

He tiptoed out and closed the door. He would park someplace busy and sleep in the car.

Chatham watched the motel from a sheltering shadow on the edge of the wood as the man who must be the boss crashed into the open like he was being chased by a ghost. He wanted to talk to him and ask forgiveness but thought better of it when he spotted the room with an open door. Sure enough, it was empty. There was half a pizza on the little table. Chatham barricaded the door with a moveable dresser, ate the pizza, stood under the shower for twenty minutes, and slept—with sheets and pillows—until dawn.

…

Eric and John finished their walk around the park where Alcoa was to speak the next day, or rather later today since it was after midnight.

"Do you think she'll be here tomorrow?" Eric asked, his right eye winking fast in a kind of twitch, as it always did when he was nervous. He played his flashlight across the top of a high retaining berm surrounding the seating area.

"I'm not sure," said John, hearing Eric's nervousness but not seeing the twitch in the dark. "She was pretty rushed. Something about another team, and she couldn't get away. She acted like she couldn't speak plainly. I wish you had taken the call. You might've been able to tease more out of her. She likes you. She said the dog is okay. I was worried about it after she disappeared. When I watched her interview on TV, I figured the dog being shown like that could lead the killer straight to her."

"Did she say anything about what happened?" said Eric. "She should be armed. You would think a cop would know that. You're a cop and you're armed. I mean, it's part of the uniform. I don't go anywhere without my Glock."

"That whole uniform thing might be why she doesn't want to be armed here. On the TV news, she looked ordinary, in shorts and a T-shirt. Didn't look bad either."

Eric turned off his flashlight. "Doesn't she have a kid? Somebody said she was married to a white guy."

"I don't know anything about that. She's pretty private. Except for the dog. Fierce little thing."

"I have no use for unarmed cops."

"She says she's only here to supervise, and she's going to be right up close to Alcoa. No mistakes, no Rambo disasters is her mantra. Don't know if I agree, but I respect it. And I like her." John hoped Eric would hear the irritation in his last sentence and stop trying to goad him.

"Rambo? You think she was talking about me?"

"Maybe."

They walked back to the hotel in silence. When they got to the room, John took a long shower to help himself relax and sleep the few hours left in the night. Eric had gone out by the time he finished. Probably taking a walk for the same reason, he figured, to calm down. The guy needed to. He climbed into his bed, turned out the bedside lamp, and fell immediately into an untroubled sleep, waking to find Eric's bed still made.

THIRTY-EIGHT

Skosh reclaimed the comfortable chair when Charlie and Steve left. No sense in letting it go to waste. He considered the watch rotation in the other safehouse. Who would be up now? Frank, he decided. He briefly contemplated a quick sneak back to the sleeping Jade until he noticed Mack's blue eyes on him. *The bastard's reading my mind again.* He practiced three emptying breaths and saw Mack's recognition of that, too.

Rimas leaned against the wall to his left, chair and all, chin up, mouth open, eyes closed. Mack poked his midsection with his cane. The young fighter reacted predictably, pulling the Modelé from under his arm, but Mack was ready, using the stick to force his hand and arm up and to the outside, a trajectory that would put a bullet into a stair tread, nothing more. But Rimas was just as quick, awake before the barrel left his holster, aware before his finger entered the trigger guard, recognizing Mack before the f-word left his throat.

Mack took the stiff-backed wooden chair Skosh had abandoned and raised an eyebrow at Rimas, who took the hint and went to the coffee machine. He came back with two mugs and handed one to his boss. Skosh had become comfortably invisible.

Except for the droning air conditioner, the room was quiet. Sergei slept soundly on his keyboard. The only light was near the back door, giving the corner where Skosh sat a private, confidential mood. He practiced the stillness he had been learning in the presence of a world master of that skill.

"What do you want to know, Rimas?" asked Mack, as usual, reading the young man's mind.

Rimas moved his dark blue eyes, black in this light, up and away in a minimal shrug, thought better of it, and said, "What happened, of course? I want to know what happened to Gloria. Did Vasily kill her?"

"Not yet." Mack dropped that two-word foreshadow of his story's end in the dim, silent room, where it sat on the bare floor between them, presaging near-future explanations of long-ago pain. Skosh and Rimas waited, Skosh without breath, Rimas without expression. Mack resumed. His voice seemed to come out of the gloom itself.

"We caught up to Vasily at Gloria's new hotel on Rue de Guy. He came out of her room as we reached the floor. We took the stairs this time, having no time to wait for an elevator. He greeted us smiling." Mack allowed himself a huff of exasperation. "She was innocent, he insisted. Grieving for her brother. It had all been a terrible mistake, and he should have waited for verification. He did not tell her he killed Darren."

"What did you do?"

Mack's answer was interrupted when the back door opened. Rimas reached into his holster until Christine stepped in. Fluffy followed.

"Frank does not make good coffee," she said.

"He never did," said Mack.

She took a cup from the countertop, checked it for reasonable cleanliness, and poured, then stood near Skosh, drawing, he thought, unwanted attention in his direction.

"Find a chair and bring it here," said Mack. "Do not stand over us. We are discussing the past. I now have more of it than I have of the future, so I like to share."

Skosh relaxed when Christine settled near Rimas, shifting the weight of Mack's audience away from him. Fluffy jumped onto her lap, and Mack gave her a summary in English before resuming.

"Louis wanted to argue with Vasily. I told him to stop pressing and gave a little shove when he persisted." Mack paused and smiled slightly at the memory. "Perhaps more than a little shove. We covered each other to the safehouse. Vasily's movements were animated, free, happy—rare in him. Louis stomped. I spent the time worried.

"Frank's assistant met us with dinner. I needed a rational discussion about Rusty's backup, Antoine, but though the assistant had the clearances required by Frank's office, I did not want more ears hearing our disagreements. Frank has always been careless about files."

Mack gazed pointedly at Skosh, holding it there long enough for Skosh's studied stillness to crack and betray discomfort by shifting his weight. Skosh got the message and Mack continued.

"We were already disrupting ourselves and did not need additional help from the enemy. The assistant felt my stare and correctly decided to leave. He was using the name Harry Sycamore as his game name on his trip."

So, they had already compromised our files way back then. Skosh presumed that as a cop, Christine understood the many uses of information. He watched her expression. She was as adept at controlling it as he was trying to be.

"When Harry was gone," continued Mack, "I signaled Louis to check for devices and suggested Vasily should get some sleep. He was reluctant, with the blank, obstinate expression I had known since our childhood. He stayed awake in an angry turmoil over Gloria."

Skosh wondered if the grimace came from the memory or the present-day pain in his hip. Mack continued.

"Louis found a device behind a wall clock. It could have been placed at any time, but it meant our safehouse was blown, so we moved to a hotel on Rene Levesque Boulevard. The street was called Dorchester then. Vasily's anger cooled with activity, and we were able to discuss a plan.

"The FLQ informant the Smiths were targeting was to see a magistrate at the courthouse the next morning. Smith would have an opportunity to attack as he moved between the police van and the back door of the building. We assumed his killer would want to remain alive and free to work again and did not have to factor in the appeal of religious martyrdom, which is a more recent and cynical tool of terror."

Mack leaned back, sliding forward on the hard seat to straighten the affected leg at the hip. There was no sign on his face that it bothered him.

"Louis suggested it would be feasible," he said, "to set up a rifle in a window or on the roof of a building overlooking the courthouse entrance. We committed to the idea; there was no time before the event to try anything else. If we were wrong, we would fail. We used the remaining light of dusk and climbed every building that gave a suitable line of sight. Just before sunset, we found it at the second to last possibility. The pigeons gave it away. Rusty's backup sniper did not relish lying prone in pigeon shit. He had prepared a clean spot on a roof with a perfect view of the entrance."

"So you got him!" Skosh did not realize he'd been so caught up in the story until he heard his own voice.

Mack had no time to answer. Charlie came through the door under the staircase, turned on the bright overhead lights, and headed straight for Skosh's no longer invisible corner.

In that instant, Skosh decided against all comfy chairs during an op. By the time he got out of this one, Charlie hit him in the chest with a bloody set of documents.

"Two wallets, two passports, and a US Senate staff ID card," said Charlie. "We'll expect full payment on the intelligence."

Steve stepped up behind him. "All the IDs are Russian-made, except maybe the Senate one. The guy was too proud of his day job and not all that smart. The names are fake, again, except for the Senate card, so I took fingerprints." He handed over two sheets of hotel stationery.

"This is blood." Skosh's cheek twitched involuntarily.

"Yeah. It was the only thing available to make a print with. It came from the man the Smiths were calling boss. The other one broke his neck slipping on the bathroom floor."

THIRTY-NINE

Christine needed to understand this evidence. She stepped up to the three men at the corner chair and pulled on Skosh's hand to see the fistful of documents he had taken from Steve.

"Which one's dead?" she asked. "Paul Smith? Or the one he was working for? Or the one I saw in the park?"

She had a full glimpse of the bloody prints before registering their silence. She looked up to see shock in Skosh's wide-open eyes, narrowed suspicion in Steve's, and bemusement in Charlie's half-smile.

"I can't help it," she said. "I'm a cop." *It's in my bones.*

A crime, or a gaggle of them, a conspiratorial theater of crimes among criminals, had flipped a switch. She was all in, and it didn't matter that she couldn't trust these guys. Hell, she never trusted the Feds, either, but had always effectively worked with them.

Mack stepped up with the same suppressed amusement as his son. He politely held out his hand, asking Skosh for the documents. The man was always polite, Christine noticed. So polite that after a glance, he offered them to her. Like she was now in partnership with a bunch of hoodlums.

She stared at the passport photos. No enlightenment there. Then there was the staffer ID, with a different name than either of the passports.

"Is one of these guys the Russian from the consulate you've been talking about?" she asked.

Charlie gave an answer, again as if she deserved one. "No." He pointed to the passport picture that did not match the ID. "This one is the boss referred to by the Smiths."

"And he's dead? And those are his prints?" She indicated the bloody papers still in Mack's hand.

"Yes. They're both dead."

"Is the other one the Russian guy?"

"No."

She stared at the ID card in her hand. "The Senate is pretty high up there, I mean, power-wise. Please tell me they're just pretending. It's got to be a deception."

With the barest imitation of a shrug, Charlie said, "Could be. Probably not."

"You're saying a foreign intelligence outfit has a hold on somebody extremely well-placed in our government?"

"Had. He's dead. And yes. Of course."

Mack and Charlie both smiled at her. It was almost warm.

"Why? How?" She sputtered the words.

"Because he was well placed," said Mack. "There is no sense in working to turn a restaurant dishwasher."

"Unless the restaurant is popular with the well-placed," said Steve. "How it's done is simple. Sex, money, or both until you've got enough for blackmail."

Skosh chimed in. "You might add a dose of ideology—delusional before the turn or for the sake of the conscience after—but it's not a requirement. I'd better get to the Consulate to check these prints. I'll be back before breakfast."

"I can probably get them faster through police channels," said Christine.

"But not as secure. He was well enough placed that a simple public disclosure would be a payoff for them. Destabilization is the *aim* of the game." Skosh waved the documents at her, smiling like he was proud of his wit. "Breakfast will be here soon. I'll send Jade over before I leave."

Charlie told Rimas to go upstairs and sleep. It was an order.

So they know about the triangle, thought Christine. And they disapprove.

...

The morning of, thought Jade. In two years, she had learned the rhythm of a Charlemagne operation. They operated mainly in the dark. This one would be in daylight, a bright, hot, sunny day in a major city. But the lead-up was the same, inaugurated by breakfast this time. The scrambled eggs were going fast. The poutine, full of its comfy carbs, sat congealing in its tub on the counter. To be fair, Frank did take two helpings. Skosh put a spoonful on his plate when he came back from the Consulate. *Only to please me.* She could eat the whole tubful but skipped it in favor of the new dress she would buy for the wedding. *Only to please him.*

Rimas came down the stairs, hair sticking up at the back, eyes red-rimmed, jaw set. *Tell him.* This ran through her brain like an endless loop, along with *How*?

Private exchanges of words in various languages came short and at a murmur. The team concentrated on taking in protein and clearing out thoughts of a tomorrow they might not have. One pair, though, rehashed yesterday, and Jade got to hear their conversation because it was at the coffee machine and, surprisingly, in English.

Mack was being polite to Jade. He and Rimas were in her territory, where she kept breakfast going and the all-important morning, noon, and night beverage. He stood on that bad leg without support from cane or counter when Rimas approached with a sullen face.

"What happened? I must know," said Rimas.

Mack shrugged, minimal to be sure, but unmistakable. "She died. But you knew that already."

"I want to know how. And was Harry the sleeper?"

Mack shook his head. "Harry was undisciplined and incompetent, but he lived. Frank's office dismissed him when we complained. But Rusty's people noticed him—sloppy tradecraft is worse than none at all—and that led them to us. Rusty recognized the opportunity of taking out Vasily Sobieski."

"But Antoine? Who was Antoine?"

Another shrug. "Rusty's recruit. A Canadian policeman, a rising star among the Mounties."

"You stopped him, didn't you?"

Mack gave a slight nod. "Only just."

There may have been more, and Jade wanted to know the whole story, but she was pulled away when a bald man came upstairs from the basement. Behind him, Sergei had a hand on his shoulder, directing him to where they stood. He handed the man a plate. Jade gave him the large spoon beside the tub of poutine, and to her intense gratification, he filled the plate.

Empties were returning to the counter, stiff-backed chairs scraped the floor, forming a semi-circle from the computer to the sofa, with Charlie's easy chair as the focus. Jade recognized the beginning of a meeting, probably the last one before Alcoa's speech. Mack took only coffee with him to the sofa.

Rimas picked up a plate and the spoon next to the eggs.

They had as much privacy as any other moment in time was likely to give them.

No time like the present. Keep it simple.

"Rimas, I'm going to marry Skosh."

FORTY

Rimas could not swallow anything, least of all this. How did he get her so wrong? Had he been delusional like Vasily? Was she playing false? Was it her fault? He wanted it to be her fault. Blame would staunch the wound. Skosh had placed a chair to the right of Michael. That was a good place for blame, only a couple of meters away, easily crossed. With speed.

How could he lose her to a fucking babysitter?

He had to admit, as he watched his thoughts and emotions speed by his mind like an old-fashioned newsreel, Skosh's skills were respectable.

He put the plate he had been holding down on the counter and assessed his chances. Height and reach were comparable, but Skosh had weight. He also had a lot of formal eastern training. It made him move differently in defense. Rimas had burning anger—always an effective fuel for attack. He felt Misha's attention from the sofa behind him. Maybe he imagined it, but the thought paused his anger, and he turned, glaring with defiance. This was all Misha's doing. He was sure of it.

Reluctantly, he sat chin up and scowling, the cords in his neck taut with simmering fury, in the space Misha indicated on the sofa next to him. "I must know how Gloria died." He murmured it sideways to the culprit next to him.

Michael was beginning the meeting. The last formal meeting for this op. For some, maybe, the last meeting ever.

"Vasily shot her." Misha's voice was also at a murmur, covered by the activity around them as people settled into their seats.

"I'm not going to shoot Jade. I love her. I'm going to shoot Skosh." He hazarded a surreptitious glance to the side. Was Misha smiling?

"You love your idea of her," said Misha, "not the woman herself, or you would see a life with us would crush her." Rimas turned to face him, trying to glare but too confused to focus. Misha continued, "And you will not shoot him, or you would have done so already. The crisis has passed, Rimas, and you have done well."

How could it have passed when he was still in such turmoil? He opened his mouth to let loose a torrent of questions, but the room became suddenly silent as Michael began speaking from his corner armchair.

"Let me formally introduce Cody Johansen." He nodded to the bald young man sitting next to Christine, holding a plate filled with a third helping of poutine. "He has given his parole, as they say, and is cooperating to keep his cover and for the sake of breakfast. Please respect that."

A bit light-hearted for Michael, thought Rimas. He must have a plan.

Cody smiled. "The food is first-rate. Thank you."

The remark sank into silence. His mother kicked his foot. Michael, deadpan and with a pointed look at him, said, "I repeat, Cody's cover is imperative."

There were preliminaries. Michael started with a plan for leaving, appointing those who would move lockers of equipment, baggage, and Sergei's computer.

Cody volunteered to help. His mother kicked him again, not for the last time.

The lad had much to learn, thought Rimas.

Steve reported that the team's Challenger jet had landed and was standing by at Mirabel. Another dagger of jealousy for Rimas to parry. Steve's wife, Claire, would be flying them home. Those that lived.

"Why is Michael so relaxed?" he asked Misha in a low voice. He was looking for good news, anything to fill the void of emptiness the last thought had left in him.

"He has let go. It is the only way to face chaos. Without fear, without illusion. He is open." Misha left the low sofa as he spoke, standing to command attention.

"If I may interrupt."

Michael gave a near nod.

...

Christine wondered, was it age that made Mack keep bringing up the past? Would it help? He began with his gaze locked on Frank, who returned the stare with a slow blink of acquiescence over his prominent old eyes. That's right, she remembered, they go back that far. He must remember it well.

She nodded when Mack turned to her. She was listening.

"I have been asked again what it is an intelligence professional uses to turn an asset or agent. How can a person be persuaded to betray his or her most cherished loyalties? The answers are as many as there are people on earth, but they can be described in generalities. As Steve has explained, sex and money are the most potent motivators. Once these have been established in a target's life, they become enforcers as well, in the form of blackmail.

"Then there are those who adopt a philosophical perspective. They ally themselves with the adversary, either ideologically to begin with or as a rationalization afterward.

"But the essential thing to remember is that an operative like Rusty would not waste time and effort to turn an agent without position. Such a target must have access to useful information and influence."

Misha was studying Christine's reaction. She could not help it that her face paled, but her gaze did not waver. She nodded again to acknowledge.

"As it was when we were here in 1971," he continued, "Rusty's backup specialist is a sleeper, an unknown among those tasked to protect the target."

"Which one?" She whispered it.

"My money's on Eric," said Cody. All eyes swiveled to him.

"Why?" Charlie asked it, but everybody wanted to know.

"Because the guys I came upriver with liked him. They thought he was badass because he's heavy into the border patrol identity, but they weren't afraid of him."

"What about John?" asked his mother with a fond smile at the blond fuzz now covering his head as he shook it.

"No. John's a small-town cop from New Hampshire. What's he gonna do for Rusty? Hand out speeding tickets to the target?"

"You have your sleeper," said Mack, addressing Charlie specifically. "A young federal officer with a budding career. In 1971 we had only telltale pigeon shit. But still, it should have been enough. We squandered it."

Now Mack made a pointed surveillance of each member of his audience, pausing longest to lock eyes with the triangle, Rimas especially, and then with Sergei.

"We meant to be and should have been several hours earlier concealed on that rooftop. Our watchers were in position, but we were late. The woman Gloria..."

He paused. Christine heard mortified annoyance in the way he spoke the word woman. Twice.

"The woman, Gloria, met us in a coffee shop next to our new hotel. I asked Vasily if he had told her where we were staying. He shook his head. I should have acted then because I knew and I was responsible. He should have been alert to the danger, but he smiled and approached to kiss her, only pausing momentarily as she reached into her handbag with a troubled scowl.

"She should have fired through the bag. She would have had a chance then, a chance to succeed. She had no chance to live either way. Both Louis and I were in motion, but Vasily was the fastest. Illusion finally deserted him, and he met the threat the way he had always done."

Mack looked at Frank, who closed his eyes and bowed his head. Pieces of this history began to fall into place for Christine.

Frank continued the story. "The gendarmes were everywhere. They wanted your hide, all of you, but especially Sobieski. My in-country contact was God knows where. I had no ID on me. All I had was Harry. He pulled your ass out of the fire, Mack, not me. But I fired him anyway because of the bug in the safehouse. Rusty had us in view all along."

Mack grimaced. "We reached the door onto the roof just as the van opened at the courthouse entrance below us. Rusty's backup, cover name Antoine, lost concentration when he heard our steps. He turned suddenly, rifle and all, finger in the guard, squeezing already but no longer against his target. The first round sliced a television antenna to my left. The second embedded itself in the door frame to my right."

Mack pointed to a faint scar on his cheek.

"A splinter split opened the skin and I bled. Vasily pushed ahead of me from behind. I saw his expression, full of remorse and failure. He thought I had been hit in the face. The first shot from his Makarov made the sniper spin toward the right, sending one more round our way. It hit the masonry of a chimney a few feet from the door, changed its trajectory, and entered Vasily's liver."

He closed his eyes in a long blink. "The Canadian doctors were more than competent. Vasily lost only a portion of his liver and was warned to avoid alcohol, which was no hardship for him. But it was a high cost for the closest we ever came to failure, and Rusty was not responsible for that near disaster; we were."

"I had a helluva time getting you out of here," said Frank. "The authorities tried to confiscate the weapons. The Frenchman was livid."

Christine sat back in her chair, looking up at Mack, wide-eyed. "Eric has become a friend of mine. He is talented and passionate about our rights. You're telling me he's lying, and if I don't believe it, you'll fail?"

Charlie answered, shaking his head. "We won't fail. You will. We are not bodyguards. Our commission is to discover the American funding behind this operation and take out any killers. We have the intel and will finish this afternoon. We will respect your request to stay outside the theater perimeter. The Smiths are still the main threat we were hired to eliminate. But you will have inside with you an armed double agent with a commission from his true supervisor. We think we know which one it is but cannot help you if we are not there. Of course, he will not escape us as he leaves, but you will have failed to protect Alcoa."

Christine appreciated the forthright effort to make her understand. She rubbed her temples. It was a tell, and it was becoming a bad habit.

"Then you will not help us." She could not keep a note of bitter accusation out of her voice. How had she fallen into the trap of thinking a criminal ally could be honorable?

Charlie responded with a slow blink and strained patience. "I understand your need for agency and control, Christine, given your history. But in this instance, it comes with risky decisions that only you can make. Under your arrangement, Eric will kill Alcoa, then die when we see him step outside the perimeter."

"But we're not sure it's him!" She said it with some heat.

"I'm sure, Ma," said Cody.

She kicked him again, but half-heartedly. After taking a moment to rub her temples again, she sighed and said to Charlie, "Isn't there another option?"

Charlie glanced at his father, and Misha said, "I am a more attractive target than Sydney Alcoa. If I am inside when whichever of your deputies decides to shoot, he will start with me, giving you time to protect Alcoa."

"You're willing to be a target?"

He dipped his head to one side in a near shrug. "I have always been a target. I make only one stipulation. Vasily died a decade after our Montreal operation, living out his favorite fantasy that he was not what he was. I have no such illusions. He went to a business meeting unarmed. I will not do that."

Christine studied him as she reviewed the situation before her. The offer was enormous. Sure, he was fit, except for the leg. He moved like a cat—when he moved at all, that is. Was he fit enough? What if this guy died just to salve her conscience with proof it was Eric? It was probably Eric. She looked at the stoney faces around her, waiting.

She remembered the blood she had walked through, the corpse at the door, his neck open. That was not done by Rimas. He shot the other guy. She looked at Mack. Was he skilled enough? *What a stupid question.* Christine turned to Charlie. "My screening plan is solid. I'll need a way that looks natural to get him in with whatever weapon he needs.

Charlie raised a half smile and gave a near nod, his eyes on Fluffy.

FORTY-ONE

Christine took her position stage right and waited for the audience to settle. Sydney Alcoa was still greeting people at the front of the crowd, bending low to shake hands as far as he could reach.

It was not a large park, but they had filled it to capacity and more. She estimated a hundred and fifty people lounging on blankets or folding chairs with only a nod given to the organizers' attempt to mark out rows for ease of movement. It didn't matter. Those who needed to move were accommodated by people in their path with good-natured bustle as they stepped over and around each other.

The space was a grassy bowl facing a flat area with an awning and a curved ten-foot wall behind, where they had set up a low portable stage and an adequate sound system. Alcoa had already been fitted with a mic to be activated when he began his remarks.

Christine scanned the upper edges of the twenty-foot high bowl before her, a 270-degree arc, gently sloping to the two entrances on either side of the stage where her deputies, Eric and John, wielded security wands, denying entrance to any weapons but their own and those of the other three grim-faced men out of the Yukon, well-armed and capable. These had ranged themselves along the back edge of the crowd, watching. Why, she had demanded of Charlie, why couldn't it be one of them? He reminded her Rusty would not waste energy recruiting somebody who earned his livelihood tracking caribou through the wilderness. Behind them, beyond the steep backside of the bowl, Charlemagne held vigil concealed, she surmised, in plain sight.

The last arrivals were late by design. A dark-haired young woman wearing a designer blouse and skirt carried Fluffy in her arms. Her ostensible father, an older man walking with a limp and a cane, escorted her.

Christine crossed the space in front of the stage and reached Eric before he finished checking Jade.

"It's okay, Eric. These are the friends I mentioned."

As Eric finished running the security wand over Jade, Fluffy growled at him from her arms. Mack stood behind her, very dapper in a dark suit, white shirt, and tie. He stood straight, the cane held loosely in his left hand. Wrong hand for the hip.

"You said no exceptions." Eric's tone accused. His eyes strayed continually to the man with the cane, the right one blinking rapidly, brought back only reluctantly to engage hers."

"I know," she said, "but we're running late and need to start."

Fluffy growled again, and it began.

...

Chatham woke well-rested that morning and not even hungry. The boss's pizza had quelled the memory of the slugs. He was forgiven, else why would the boss leave him this safehouse, complete with food?

He consulted his backpack. The Luger was dirty, and he was out of patches and solvent because the bottle leaked. It was inadequate for the task, anyhow. Slava had said to always make a splash. Needs to be big. Headlines and crisis. That was how he put it in his strange way of talking. A very great man was Slava.

Chatham was glad he never ditched the AK. Sure, it added weight, but it wasn't like he carried anything else. An AK-47 with a folded stock fit nicely in a mostly empty backpack.

He knew he was beginning to smell. Maybe. Well, it was all the same to him. So what if he had a beard? He checked his magazines, inserted one, and chambered a round. It was a little risky with it on his back like that, so he checked the safety. Taking it off would be quieter than chambering, so the risk was necessary. He needed to get going. He hadn't even settled on his approach yet.

...

John stood at the lesser-used entrance to the bowl, the one approached from the back of the park. He had a wand but barely used it. What was up with Eric? When he asked him where the hell he'd been all night, all the guy would say was he needed to walk around to quell the jitters. But he didn't have any jitters. Steady as a rock, over there on the other entrance, except, of course, for the twitch in his eye. John had managed to tell Christine about it but wasn't sure she took it in. There was only a nod and an order to watch outward, not in. The Yukon guys will take care of the inside, she said; you watch the approaches to that side.

What about somebody climbing that slope behind those guys? He stepped outside when he saw the bushes move, then turned his head to catch Christine's eye, but she was at the other entrance, out of his line of sight. It couldn't have been more than a nano-second, and he felt the presence before he fully turned back, but by then, the guy was upon him.

...

Paul Smith woke up in his car, blinking in the sunlight. He reviewed his life. The prospect of imminent death will do that to you. He held on to a few things, like love of his mother, respect for his father, childhood good times growing up in the Colorado compound, dawn over Lake Champlain, those kinds of things. But other things had become dust, and more began to crumble from underneath. *What if she isn't a spawn of Satan? What if I am? What if everything is a lie?*

He had always been proud of his warrior status. Special. Fierce. Now, faces paraded across his interior vision, first hers, then others, some brown, most white. Why? That one had to go, didn't he? A nasty guy, right? Sure, all of them. No question. The end times required it. But doubt suddenly engulfed him. He saw clearly what he was, an expendable fool, and what he had to do now. Ironically, he would obey one of his dead boss's orders, but for a different reason.

He started the car, left the box store parking lot where he had taken refuge, and headed toward the park.

...

Michael spotted Paul Smith entering the park, heading toward the back, behind the outdoor theater. He alerted Sergei with a signal to watch. Acknowledged. All thoughts of their loss, nephew and son and grandson, were subsumed under the present exigency, but fear for the stillborn child's mother niggled him and must be tearing at Sergei. *When will we know?* He shoved it aside and hoped Sergei would do the same. Damn the woman and her decision. He wanted to force her to live, realized where his mind was drifting, and forced it back instead, to the outside perimeter of an outdoor theater in a Montreal park.

Skosh's voice on the network: "Found the watcher, one of Yannick's, who made the initial sighting after dawn. He said the guy looked rough, like he's been living on the street. He carried a backpack. Disappeared into the park. The watcher didn't see him come out, but he could have left on the other side."

"What about the watchers on that side?" said Michael.

"They saw nothing."

"Steve?"

"Ours saw no movement until around nine o'clock," said Steve, "and accounted for all entrances and exits until the theater was set up."

So Chatham was inside. He would know Charlemagne was there. No matter how carefully they moved, this guy would be aware, and he wasn't moving. Concealed somewhere. In a patch of trees? Among those bushes? In the undergrowth behind that gazebo in the far corner? He would be noticeable among the bright, happy population, and he would have to move eventually.

With the thought came a word in his ear from Rimas. A very quiet "Maybe."

So he was headed for the other entrance.

Michael's hand signaled Sergei. Trade places. Michael studied his movement, looking for signs of emotion in those light eyes as they met his. None. The man was steady. It helped Michael maintain his own center.

He took his new position in time to see Paul Smith's careful approach from the gazebo in the back corner of the park. So Chatham wasn't hiding there, or he's already dead thanks to Paul, vindicating Misha's uncharacteristic act of mercy.

...

Paul Smith carried his training into the battleground with heightened awareness of his surroundings as usual and now also of himself, a killer and nothing more, with his knife concealed in his hand by his side, bent on silent murder. He was surrounded by others like him, all of them enemies. He sensed them in every good hiding place. He would die as a member of the elect. The question he could not answer was whose elect?

...

Last night's pizza deserted him, and hunger brought Chatham back to unreality, a state that had become more frequent. He knew where he was. In combat. What he didn't know was when.

All these open spaces meant a settlement. It meant the Serb army. There was a sentry. He needed food, but if he fired, the Serbs would hear it. He unfolded the stock of the AK but left the safety on and didn't like to use the knife. All that blood…. He ran to the objective, swinging the AK by the barrel.

...

Rimas put a quiet bullet into Chatham as he moved like a jaguar onto Christine's deputy at the back entrance. Disadvantages of a weak charge, he thought. The man was still attacking. The remedy was exact placement, especially when the target moved erratically. Louis would have done better, would have hit a lethal spot. Rimas adjusted.

"Wait," said Michael in his ear.

Obedience was automatic, and Rimas watched from less than ten feet as the two men, in a death roll in the dust of the entrance pathway, were joined by a third. He could see the glint of a blade in this one's hand, recognized the man they had trussed up in that duplex, and wondered if he should take him out. But the man was defending Christine's deputy. This was not the deputy they suspected, was he? Not the sleeper? Maybe Paul Smith was mistaken. Maybe they were.

"Hold," said Michael, out loud and in the clear, as he approached.

At the same moment, the struggle on the ground ended, blood spreading into the surrounding dust, two of three bodies panting in exhaustion.

Michael pulled up the topmost man and took the knife out of his hand. Rimas rolled the dead man off the deputy and helped him up. Then came the sound of a scuffle at the other entrance and Christine's voice. "John, call an ambulance."

FORTY-TWO

Misha took his place in the crosshairs. He exaggerated the limp as he approached the young man, watching his eyes register recognition, the right one twitching rapidly. *At least I am aware; Vasily was not. I will have the advantage.* He switched attention to the lad's hands. He had cheated death so many times in his long career that it did not increase his anxiety to be acting as the enemy's target. His sole concern was for his son.

If things went wrong and produced disaster, Michael would forever feel the weight of his choice to use his father as bait. It would color all future decisions, even as that missing piece of Vasily's liver had affected his. Maybe it made his judgment more effective; he didn't know. It did mean he would never let one live. Until now, when the narrowed responsibilities of retirement gave him the option.

He hoped Michael would be different.

And what if he was mistaken and Paul Smith's crumbling ideology stood firm? Funny how the most significant test of Misha's reputation for judgment rested on an instant of not killing.

He studied Eric's face, hoping to see another opportunity to decide for instead of against, but Fluffy's snarling crescendo confirmed what Misha saw. The dog stretched his neck, all teeth bared, aiming for the young man's face while straining to escape Jade's firm grasp.

Eric's right hand reached the holster on his belt. He was swift and had it out of the holster with practiced fluidity, but a momentary flinch at the threat from a small dog gave Misha more time than he needed. His hand was practiced, accurate, and silent.

Misha put his knife away while the two women gasped.

Fluffy stopped growling.

...

At least they hadn't executed an innocent man. Christine had seen it herself. She grieved but was at peace with the necessity.

She had been watching Eric's face, saw it settle into a determined snarl as he drew his S&W semi-auto out of the holster on his hip, eyes on Mack. The barrel barely cleared it. The gun fell by gravity, preceding his body to the cinder gravel of the entrance by only a fraction of a moment.

So fast. So silent. Except for Fluffy's noise. Her mouth hung open as she watched Mack pull out a handkerchief to wipe a smear of blood from his wrist. He had already stowed the knife… somewhere.

The beautiful young man she had enjoyed having on her team lay dead at her feet. He had been so confident, so careful to hide his underlying insecurity, always betrayed by his right eye. Maybe he would have overcome it eventually. Of course, he had made his own decisions, but who helped him make this one? With that thought, she reorganized her future. There was a mother somewhere who had just lost her son.

...

Paul reached for the door handle almost before he stopped running. Focused and out of breath, he did not see the tall Asian man until he spoke.

"I wouldn't if I were you."

Paul's hand stopped inches from freedom. His hope sank and the adrenaline drained. He turned to face this muscular new opponent and realized he was at a disadvantage. Again.

"Who the hell are you?" he said, needing the name of this executioner.

"I'm a Fed from the Deep State, and I advise you to get the fuck out of here ASAP. Don't use your car. Don't go home. They know you killed Chatham."

"I was under orders. They'll know that," said Paul, confident the man was lying. It had only been ten minutes. They couldn't know, and the boss would… He remembered the blood in the hotel room.

"How do they know?" he asked suspiciously. He tilted his head back to make eye contact. The man was too tall, too close, and too ready.

"Let's just say someone told them. You'll need this." The Asian held out a thick envelope. Curiosity made Paul take it from him against his better judgment. He opened it.

"Who do I owe now?" he asked, looking up from a fistful of hundreds, both Canadian and U.S.

No answer.

"Why am I alive?" *And how the hell did they disappear so fast?* It was now twelve minutes since the blond man took his knife from him and shoved him toward the park exit. When he had turned to look back, he saw only Chatham dead on the ground, heard the sound of a siren, and took the chance of survival on offer. He ran to his car.

The tall man shrugged and said with a note of urgency, "There's a card with a phone number in the envelope. The message is—these words exactly—if you live and when you think you're safe enough, call." He paused. "Think about it. Those are my words."

Paul crossed the border in a forest after dark, hungry but thoughtful, and headed east. Every step brought him more questions resurrected out of answers he had thought were settled. His former friends were now enemies, his most firmly established belief system in shreds because of a pair of brown eyes.

...

Frank pulled the old car into a bumpy clearing in an expansive forest of mostly maple and pine. He checked the satellite map Sergei had given him, pretty sure he was in the right place. Over there, on the right, it should slope down to a stream. It did.

"Okay, kid, we're here. You got everything?"

"What do you mean everything? A knife and a granola bar? Yeah. I got it." Cody held them up for Frank.

He noticed the blond fuzz on the lad's head was already long enough to suggest it might curl. His third son had been like that. None of the others were as blond. He sometimes wondered....

"I don't even get a map?" demanded Cody.

"You have a compass, and I showed you how to use it. You also know how to use your wits, or you wouldn't be alive after that boat ride."

"Those guys back there are why I'm alive. Them and my mom. My wits would have made me worm food otherwise. I get that I'm in debt to them. This is a helluva way to rub it in."

Frank sighed and switched to a little grandfather mode mixed with case officer. "Remember where you're going. You'll be contacted once you're in place to start your training. After you've been taught a little tradecraft, you'll have the skill to contact your mom. We'll tell her you're okay in the meantime."

Cody surveyed the dense woods before him, listened to the sound of a stream, and saw the underbrush move under an unknown animal. "You're not going to know I'm okay until I get through all this, cross the border, get through more of it, and find a phone, so anything you tell her now will be a lie."

The kid had a future, thought Frank, but one thing at a time. "We'll know, Cody. Don't forget, you've escaped. You have your legend memorized. Don't stray from it. The more this little jaunt takes out of you, the better the legend sounds, so don't clean up. We'll be in touch."

He watched Cody jump the creek and disappear under the canopy of trees. Cody didn't know it, but he was already in training.

The bottom of the jalopy scraped the tops of ruts in the soft ground as Frank shifted to first and headed toward the road to Mirabel. He wondered what he would meet at the team's jet. How many bodies, and in what shape?

FORTY-THREE

Skosh had not seen this before. Not even a scratch on any of them. All hale, but not so hearty. They schlepped equipment without energy. Going through the motions of going home. Going home to a tragedy.

Two of their own were casualties. Two who hadn't even been on the most spectacular untying of a true goat rope Skosh had ever seen the team accomplish. No shots fired in a summertime crowd of 150 people, all of them sorry the nice young man at the entrance had a medical emergency but glad to hear a speech by a great man, even if it was a little delayed.

At the airplane, no celebration was possible. One had died before his first breath; the other was still a question mark. Wait and see, their chief pilot, Claire, had murmured when he asked her about Mara as she unlocked the baggage compartment.

Frank pulled up next to him at the airplane and handed him the keys to the babysitters' car.

"Jade and I are taking the car back to the States, Frank. We could have taken Cody to his starting point on our way. The team's inside waiting for you. None too patiently, I imagine."

Frank gave him a crinkled smile. "I had team business, Skosh. Happy to do it. Charlie knows. You should take the Mercedes back. It's much more comfortable."

"And have you guys listening to everything we say? No thanks."

Another, broader smile this time, from an old man with a grey fringe around his shiny scalp, not as chubby as he used to be, but every bit as sharp. The look in those prominent eyes set Skosh's mind in motion, like a train with no brakes. He remembered the babysitters' car was equally bugged and had been since the beginning.

"So Frank," he said, meeting that smile with a scowl, "Charlie's got plans for those two—Cody and his mom—doesn't he? He's creating another network, isn't he?"

Frank patted his arm. "You always were a pro, Skosh." Take the Mercedes. Your fiancée deserves the treat.

...

Rimas stared through the window, contemplating the clouds below as evening light faded over the North Atlantic. Reason helped him deal with the anger. He had to admit Skosh was an excellent babysitter. The team needed him. For survival.

The memory of Christine became another aid, a curated memory stripped of any illusionary future. It opened a new compartment in the rubric of his life: valued occasional lover. There might be another opportunity with her, but the meantime still stretched empty before him.

"Hey, partner." Steve took the seat across from him when Sergei fell into a troubled sleep across the aisle. Rimas responded with a tired smile.

"Danny's going back to college in a few days," said Steve. "There's something I need to do for him before he goes, after the baby's funeral is over, and I'm wondering if you want to help."

Danny was Steve's son, a formidable teenage fighter but untried because his father insisted on education first. Rimas raised an eyebrow. Go on, it said.

"There's a place I know about," said Steve, "on the other side of a particular mountain. Louis and I and Louis's uncle Bertrand used to visit occasionally—make that frequently— before I was married. Nice place. Reasonably safe. Thought you might want to go. Maybe you can keep an eye on Danny for me in the future, too. The Spare is still too young to go with him.

Rimas had never been to a bordello. Christine had opened his eyes to the extent of his ignorance of women. He refused to call it innocence because he was almost thirty, for heaven's sake. "Education is a valuable thing," he said, matching Steve's broad smile.

...

Michael poured a generous dram of single malt into a glass and handed it to his father before sitting in the facing seat.
"Claire says Theresa has been sending updates every hour, Papa. We'll know more before we land." Misha closed his eyes as he swallowed the entire liquid fire at once, feeling its warmth descend to his core. When he opened his eyes again, Michael was watching him.

"I never mention these things to Alex," said Michael. His tone was reassuring.

"She does not control me." He clipped each word, not hiding his peevishness, and saw Michael fight a threatening smile. Why did no one take him seriously on this issue?

"You will need to be careful in your handling of Damon Kowalski, Michael. It is a major shift for him, and he will have more enemies now, especially among the Smiths."

Michael nodded. "Frank is aware of it. No better man to set up an American network for the coming struggle, I think. Provided his health allows it."

The word health fell heavily between them, and Michael refilled both glasses, not saying the name Mara, at the center of both their thoughts. It overshadowed for a moment the heavier, more personal concern nagging at Misha's mind.

He had let one live, and so had his son.

EPILOGUE

Skosh had been seated at this table two years before, facing the same three critics: his boss, his boss's boss, and the slimy ass-kisser from another section he knew only as Seeker. He suspected Seeker was responsible for the urgent summons that forced him to curtail his honeymoon. His displeasure showed itself only in the still gaze he learned from Mack. It took Seeker a few moments to catch on to the threat. He swallowed and looked away.

Skosh's boss, Bill, opened a file folder and began proceedings."It has been suggested…"

"By whom?" Skosh was feeling reckless.

"That is not material…."

"I'd say it is very material, at least to me. My wife and I were enjoying the fall color in Vermont. The condo we booked is non-refundable."

"I am concerned," put in the division head, Henry, "that you appear unconcerned about the reason you are here, Skosh."

"That would be because there is no reason."

"You were told…"

"No, I wasn't."

Henry took a deep breath and shuffled through the papers in another folder. "You received verbal counseling in this room two years ago…"

"If it was verbal, why is it in a file?" Skosh raised his eyebrows in question, his face as innocent as he could make it."

"It isn't. Only the fact of the counseling is here, not the subject." Henry's exasperated tone made it clear he was unhappy. Skosh had no problem with that. He liked to share.

"We remember the subject because we were all here," said Henry. "You were counseled not to engage in an intimate relationship where there was the possibility of a power imbalance between you within this organization.

Skosh gave a near nod. He waited, interested to see how they planned to make this into something it wasn't.

"You can't wriggle out of this just by marrying the girl," said Seeker.

Skosh made a plan to alter the smirk on Seeker's face. It began in a dark alley.

"Marriage does negate the problem of a power imbalance," said Bill. "Provided it was not forced...."

"She said 'I do' in accordance with the laws of the state of Virginia," said Skosh. "So did I. We both agreed in front of witnesses. She even bought a new dress for it. We went halfsies on the reception. There are pictures if you need evidence."

"As I was saying," continued Bill after a deep breath, "it negates the reason you were verbally counseled, but there is still the additional problem of nepotism posed by this allegation."

"She doesn't work for me."

"She runs your library."

"As an employee in a separate administrative division. And I didn't hire her or even recommend her."

"You have been taking her as an assistant on your operations."

"She was recommended by personnel two years ago. We had never met."

"Come off it, Skosh," said the slimeball, Seeker. "You don't expect us to believe you never took advantage of her on any of those ops?"

Skosh let his gaze linger an extra beat before deciding on his attack. First, the nepotism charge. He and Jade both wanted to keep their jobs. Next, the destruction of a known enemy. The best way would be a political, bureaucratic method, though Skosh had the power and plenty of inclination to make it physical.

He looked at Henry. "Just because we're employed by the same agency doesn't mean we don't have the right to choose who we marry. We were hired and are supervised by different divisions. I'd say as long as the organizational structure keeps me from having any role in my wife's career, and vice versa, there is no nepotism here."

"There's still the matter of your disobeying the counseling," said Seeker with an almost snarl. "You know damn well you didn't leave her alone every time you went out."

"I have to wonder about people who spend a lot of time speculating what goes on in other people's bedrooms. As a husband, I will be sure to remember your insult to my wife, Seeker." He left no doubt of his meaning, but Seeker opened his mouth again to argue, saved only by an interruption from Bill.

"The bottom line, Skosh, is that you are hereby verbally counseled to take no role in the advancement of your wife's career. Specifically, you will not be permitted to take her with you as your assistant during an operation."

Best news ever. Skosh debated pulling a sour face to make them happy that they had somehow hurt him, but the smug look of triumph on Seeker quashed the impulse.

The meeting broke up, and Skosh left the room thinking about dark alleys.

The End

If you enjoyed this volume of the last three books in The Charlemagne Files Collection, please consider leaving a short review at your favorite bookstore.

Join the Charlemagne Files newsletter for more stories and information about the series, its world of covert operations, and the lives of the characters on the team. Sign up at charlemagnefiles.com/contact.

CHARLEMAGNE AND THE SECTION

The fictional world of The Section follows a few conventions. It may help the first-time reader of The Charlemagne Files to know some of these.

Who/what/ where is The Section?

The Section is a department of an intelligence agency of the United States. Its employees are civil servants. It includes support staff members who provide identity documents, financial controls, and physical and document security. The offices are near the East Coast, maybe Virginia.

The operational agents are called babysitters. They arrange on-site logistical support for freelance specialists during operations. Most operations are not conducted within the United States, with some exceptions.

Babysitters themselves do not carry identity documents in their names during an operation and never carry any official identification from their organization. Their purpose is to allow the organization to deny any association with them or their mission.

Nicknames

Babysitters in The Section receive nicknames from their coworkers when they join the office. These names are often undesirable and used mercilessly among the members of the office. It is part of the team-building process in a stressful occupation.

Coins

Challenge coins are traditionally stamped with symbols or mottos that designate the intelligence unit of their owners. The tradition is that when members of the unit are present at the bar and one produces his coin, all must produce theirs. Anyone failing to show their coin is responsible for the bar tab. If all produce their coins, then the challenger who first produced his or her coin is responsible for the tab.

File designations

The highest classification of information is Top Secret. Beyond Top Secret, more sensitive information is strictly controlled in a number of ways including designation as Sensitive Compartmented Information (SCI). This requires an additional clearance and often a named clearance based on Need-To-Know.

In The Section, files on specialists or specialist teams receive a one-word code name, printed across the file and restricted to very few people. When a solo or specialist team is employed on an operation, another designator word will refer to the operation and will be used for funding, reports, etc.

The Section's file name for Charlemagne is WEDGE. Thus CETUS WEDGE (second book of the Charlemagne Files) means an operation dubbed CETUS using the team called WEDGE.

Specialist

A team or solo operative used by Western governments for black operations conducted without fingerprints in high-risk situations expected to involve death.

GLOSSARY OF USEFUL TERMS (GUT)

AC - Aircraft Commander. The pilot who flies from the left seat of the cockpit and is in command of the aircraft, its crew, and any passengers.

AGE - Aircraft Ground Equipment. Air Force term for what is sometimes called ground support equipment in civilian contexts. Includes things like ground power units, air start units, dollies, jacks, lights, tugs, and tractors.

AFSC - Air Force Specialty Code, also called a career field in casual conversation. Designated by an alpha-numeric code that identifies a person's specific job and skill level.

Babysitter - term devised by the author to indicate those who provide logistic cover and support to the more dangerous operatives.

Bear - NATO name for the Russian TU-95, a strategic bomber used by the Soviets for reconnaissance missions at or over the boundaries of US airspace. Fighters, especially those from Alaskan or coastal bases, intercepted these forays regularly, a mutual game played by US reconnaissance platforms and MIG fighters near Soviet airspace.

Bring-Up Investigation: An expansion of a security investigation to add information because of a time-lapse, usually five years, since the last investigation, or to require additional details for a higher level of clearance.

Class B's - (Air Force) Blue uniform with shirt and tie but not the more formal blue coat.

Class B bachelor - person on temporary duty away from his/her home unit who removes his or her wedding ring for reasons not having to do with safety around the aircraft.

Cockroaches in the car - Okinawa's climate is hot and quite humid. Americans stationed there often buy their cars very used, somewhat rusty, and if not already home to the local insect wildlife, eventually infested. It is advisable at night to shoo them off the seat before sitting down.

COMSEC - Communications Security.

HUMINT - Human Intelligence. Not a comment on the thinking power of Homo sapiens. This refers to the gathering of information and leverage through the use of human relations, manipulations, and interactions.

Kadena Air Base - Large U.S. Air Force base on Okinawa, Japan. Known as the Keystone of the Pacific, it is home to the 18th Wing. Twenty thousand military members and federal employees and their dependents live or work on the base.

Making regular - Only graduates of the Air Force Academy are commissioned as regular officers when they become second lieutenants. All others, such as ROTC and OTS graduates, are commissioned as reserve officers even though they are on full-time active duty. Approximately four years later, a promotion board decides whether such officers should be offered regular commissions, usually when they pin on captain. It is the first real mark of successful career progression for a non-academy grad, though nothing tangible goes with it. One's boss knows one made it, and that means everything.

MREs - meals, ready to eat. Modern successors to K-rations and other attempts at field rations.

O-6 - A full colonel, as opposed to a lieutenant colonel. Also popularly referred to as a full bird colonel, because of the eagle insignia of rank.

Okuma Military Resort, Okinawa - Beach resort on Okinawa for use by armed forces personnel, federal employees, and their dependents.

Q - colloquial term for the BOQ or VOQ, bachelor officer quarters (for permanent duty) or visiting officer quarters (for those on temporary duty).

Škorpion - Czech-made submachine pistol.

Skoshi KOOM - Iconic restaurant on Kadena Air Base, now called Jack's Place after the man who made it the favorite haunt of so many, including the author. Skoshi is Japanese for small and KOOM stands for Kadena Officers' Open Mess.

Squadron Officer School - a military education course for company-grade officers (lieutenants and captains) held at Maxwell AFB, Montgomery, AL. At the time of Captain Nolan's attendance, it would have been 12 weeks long. Selection for in-residence attendance was somewhat competitive.

Tanker - An aircraft that refuels other airplanes in flight. A tanker of the 909th Air Refueling Squadron is a Boeing 707 designated as the KC-135. At the time of this story, the crew of a 135 included the aircraft commander, co-pilot, navigator, and boom operator.

TDY - Temporary duty, usually requiring travel away from one's permanent duty station.

UCMJ - Uniform Code of Military Justice - legal foundation of military conduct. All military members are subject to its jurisdiction, regardless of their location.

Zoomie - Graduate of the United States Air Force Academy

GLOSSARY OF NAMES

Linda and David Bertram - widow and son of the late mole, Richard Bertram (*Brevet Wedge* and *Vory*); deceased.

Viktor Borodinov - alias John Earnest, alias Paul Crutchfield, CFO of Brighton Associates, SVR agent.

Frank Cardova - long-time babysitter of Charlemagne; later, head of The Section; retired by the time of *Vory*; real name is Leo Vilseck; Section nickname is Buddy.

Antanas Dockus (Dots-kūs) - brother of Rimantas.

Rimantas Dockus (Dots-kūs) - called Rimas, protégé of Kestutis.

Claire Donovan - deputy chief pilot employed by Charlemagne, married to Steve Donovan.

Steve Donovan - member of Charlemagne; martial artist; former fighter pilot; abandoned real name was Daniel Martin Kessler..

The Frenchman - deceased marksman and technical expert of Charlemagne; real name is Louis; last name is unknown.

Justin Goodwin - FBI special agent and IT specialist; no aliases.

Sally Kessler - ex-wife of Steve Donovan; deceased.

Danny Kessler - son of Steve Donovan.

Kestutis - last name unknown. Son and grandson of anti-Soviet Lithuanian forest-based partisans, now a counter-intelligence officer in the Lithuanian security service, appointed as liaison to Skosh.

Mack - so dubbed by Western babysitters because he uses a knife at times; leader and decision maker of Charlemagne; called Misha by other members of his team; probable real name is Michael; last name is unknown.

Michael - Misha's son. Game name Charlie.

Misha - long-time founder and leader of Charlemagne. Called Mack by non-team members.

John Nakamura - official game name. Usually called by his Section nickname, Skosh; successor to Frank Cardova.

Sergei Pavlenko - former KGB agent, now the gadget and explosives expert of Charlemagne. Married to Mara.

Mara Sobieski Pavlenko - computer expert and marksman of Charlemagne. Daughter of Vasily Sobieski, the team's deceased explosives expert. Biological daughter of Misha, half-sister of Michael, married to Sergei Pavlenko.

Earl Prion - an American millionaire whose ex-wife was a Lithuanian.

Skosh - The Section nickname for John Nakamura, a game name. Skosh's real name is undisclosed. Charlemagne's American babysitter.

Alexandra Sobieski - widow of Vasily Sobieski and daughter of former Charlemagne babysitter and head of The Section Fred Dolnikov; no aliases; now married to Mack.

Vasily Sobieski - deceased explosives expert and martial artist whose father was a noted solo specialist; no aliases.

Charlie Taylor - marksman; son of Mack; probable real name is Michael; last name unknown.

Jay Turner - FBI counterintelligence agent with a private agenda; no aliases.

Maryann Vilseck - wife of Leo Vilseck, aka Frank Cardova.

Theresa Vilseck - daughter of Leo Vilseck.

Karl Weltung - Prion's banker.

Jade Wilmerton - game name of Penelope Prendergast, Chief Administrator of The Section Vault.

Marcella Vlacek - wife of Vlacek, aka Tante Caniche

Theresa Vlacek - daughter of the Vlaceks

Karl Welding - Tante's brother

Jack Williams - Karl's nephew / Theresa's fiancé, August Glock's nephew (Irmtraut's)